Acclaim for *THE SILVER WATERFALL*

Kevin Miller's new Battle of Midway novel brings the reader an experience not previously seen in the scores of books, documentaries, and films that have come and gone thus far: it's the Midway story delivered with spot-on factual accuracy, but in first-person real time—you are there in the midst of the battle as it happens, literally alongside the combatants of both sides.

— *Ronald Russell, author of* No Right to Win

Miller's ability to put the reader in the cockpit is unparalleled, as is his attention to both detail and accuracy. He provides us insights into the fears, doubts, motivations, and actions of his characters and presents these insights from both the U.S. and Japanese perspectives, providing a greater understanding of not only what happened at the Battle of Midway, but why.

— *Mat Garretson, author of* Blue Angels Decades *and* Vought A-7 Corsair II

Miller's depiction of the discussions on the bridges of Japanese and American flagships makes this book worthy reading material for case studies on command decision making.

— *Naval Historical Foundation*

Through the eyes of a handful of characters, Miller shows the intensity of combat, the low odds the Americans had and the disdain the Japanese had for them, the pressures placed on the various commanders involved, and how a few chance events changed the tide of war. It's an excellent book about some of the finest men in the Greatest Generation.

— *GenZ Conservative*

The author brings alive actual participants, both American and Japanese, in a fast-paced, action-packed version where aircrewmen to admirals, from both sides, expose their personal feelings in this deadly battle between ships and airplanes.

— *Military Writers Society of America*

History comes alive! The pivotal battle of the Pacific in WWII told in personal narrative. You know the ending, but you can't stop reading! A wonderful tribute to that generation of Naval Aviators.

— *Lou Drendel, noted aviation author and artist*

The Silver Waterfall is much more than a book, it's an immersive experience. By providing insight into different levels of the military within the context of one major battle, the reader gets a richer experience through holistic storytelling that allows you to piece together the bigger picture. It takes a lot of talent to utilize real characters and a real battle, add in tons of research and flying acumen, then add fictionalized context on what each character feels and does. But Kevin Miller does it quite impressively.

— *Best Thriller Books*

Miller's writing merges the verifiable truths of Midway with a credible, fascinating, and often heartbreaking treatment of the human element of war. He provides an unvarnished look at how egos, service parochialism, and (more than anything else) individual acts of courage shaped the battle. Following in the steps of luminaries like Michael Shaara (*The Killer Angels*), and Stephen Crane (*The Red Badge of Courage*), Miller brilliantly adds depth, intimacy, and personal connection to a story where imperfect men proved the difference between success and catastrophic failure. I cannot recommend this book strongly enough.

— *J.E. Curtis*

Absolutely magnificent work. *The Silver Waterfall* surpasses *Gates of Fire* for my all-time favorite work of historic fiction.

— *Rear Admiral Samuel Cox, Director of Naval History*

THE SILVER WATERFALL

THE SILVER WATERFALL

CAPT KEVIN P. MILLER
USN (RET.)

Braveship
BOOKS

Aura Libertatis Spirat

THE SILVER WATERFALL

Braveship Books

www.braveshipbooks.com

Aura Libertatis Spirat

This book was edited by Linda Wasserman,
owner of Pelican Press Pensacola

Pelican Press Pensacola

9121 Carabella St.
Pensacola, FL 32514
850-206-4608
www.pelicanpresspensacola.com
Proofreading by Incantation Ink

Cover art by Wade Meyers
Cover design by Ivica Jandrijević
Back cover photo courtesy of *Rusty Buggy*
Midway Islands chart courtesy of Naval History and Heritage Command
Snapshot chart composition by Alexandru Diaconescu

Book layout by Alexandru Diaconescu
www.steadfast-typesetting.eu

ISBN-13: 978-1-64062-115-2
Printed in the United States of America

Dedicated to:
My fellow dive-bomber pilot George Walsh,
who sought the truth

FOREWORD

In early June 1942 the entire Asia-Pacific theater of war was reeling under the seeming invincibility of the Japanese military. The Japanese Navy had been almost completely successful in every operation planned and executed by Admiral Isoroku Yamamoto. One notable exception was the Battle of the Coral Sea in May 1942, considered by many to be a tactical draw but a strategic victory for the United States, even though the U.S. Navy lost the aircraft carrier USS *Lexington*, and the aircraft carrier, USS *Yorktown*, severely damaged. Fortunately for the Americans, the Japanese strike on Pearl Harbor six months earlier was only partially successful in that no aircraft carriers were in port at the time of the strike. Thus, after Coral Sea, the U.S. Navy had only three aircraft carriers in the Pacific, USS *Hornet*, USS *Enterprise,* and the damaged USS *Yorktown*. Admiral Yamamoto, however, clearly understood the tactical importance, strategic significance, and power of an aircraft carrier striking force and was determined to precipitate an offensive opportunity to draw out and engage those three remaining American aircraft carriers and destroy them.

Thus, a large scale and very complex Japanese Navy plan was developed which included strikes and amphibious assaults on Midway Atoll and three Aleutian Islands. The only problem, though, for the Japanese Navy and Admiral Yamamoto, was that U.S. Navy codebreakers had broken the Japanese Navy operational code. The U.S. Navy was reading their mail. With the intelligence thus gained, Admiral Chester Nimitz, Commander in Chief, Pacific Fleet, was able to position his three remaining aircraft carriers in an advantageous location to surprise, interdict, and engage the Japanese Navy main striking force, the "Kido Butai," heading for Midway with four aircraft carriers, *Akagi, Hiryū, Kaga,* and *Soryu*.

On the home front in June 1942 our nation found itself immersed in a global conflict facing two determined and deadly adversaries of differing cultures and motivations. Our political and military leadership needed to make monumental decisions as to the prioritization of one theater of operations as opposed to another. President Roosevelt and the British Prime Minister, Winston Churchill, jointly agreed that the European theater should be our priority whereas the general sentiment amongst Americans at home was that Japan had attacked America, had killed thousands of our countrymen, and thus most Americans believed that retribution should be brought against Japan first. It was in that political context that the Battle of Midway occurred.

In the Central Pacific the ensuing complex series of events of 4-6 June 1942 have been closely examined and recorded by numerous distinguished historians, so the details of strike and counterstrike from the American and Japanese perspectives are well known. But the emotions and interaction of the individual combatants, American and Japanese, the interrelationship between commander and subordinate, between admirals and their staffs, and between pilots and their crew can only be assumed. Yet we continue to wonder as to how the American warriors carried out their missions. In other words, what would it have been like to have been the pilot of a U.S. Navy SBD dive bomber in a near vertical dive with a Japanese aircraft carrier flight deck centered on the cross hairs of the bombsight? What would it have been like to have been the pilot of a U.S. Navy torpedo bomber at the very low speed of 90 knots at wave top level trying to line up on the target while being attacked by numerous Japanese fighters and facing a massive antiaircraft artillery barrage? Did the torpedo squadron pilots and their aircrew know and understand that their mission was hopeless and similar to Tennyson's epic poem?

Through the use of historical fiction, author Captain Kevin Miller answers those questions and more by employing the story-telling technique used so effectively by *The Killer Angels* author Michael Shaara. Captain Miller tells a gut-wrenching tale describing the physical and emotional effects of WWII combat at sea. In his narrative all the protagonists existed. There are no fictional characters used to enhance the story. Relationships such as those between Captain Marc Mitscher, CO, USS *Hornet* and his Air Wing Commander, Commander Stanhope Ring and between Vice Admiral Nagumo, Commander of the "Kido Butai," and his main planner, Commander Genda, are explored. We are given full measure of what it must have been like to find and then strike the Japanese carriers at the extreme range of U.S. Navy aircraft and then to watch the fuel gauge approach the empty marking as they struggled to return to their ship and avoid an open ocean ditching. Captain Miller brings the characters to life. They live again through his narrative.

The immediate result of the Battle of Midway was a crushing defeat of the Japanese Navy in that four Japanese aircraft carriers were sunk and hundreds of irreplaceable Japanese carrier pilots were lost. As a victory for the U.S. Navy, it was, in the words of Dr. Craig Symonds, Distinguished Professor of History at the U.S. Naval Academy, the *"most complete naval victory since Horatio Nelson's near annihilation of the Spanish and French fleets at Trafalgar in 1805, and, like that battle, it had momentous strategic consequences."* The "strategic consequences" for the United States after Midway included a political confidence that the nation could move forward with a "Europe First" policy, the Japanese offensive posture throughout the Pacific Ocean areas was terminated, and the Japanese were forced to adopt a perimeter defensive policy. The Battle of Midway was not only the turning point in the Pacific War, but it has also been said by some to have been the most important sea battle in the history of mankind.

In *The Silver Waterfall* Captain Miller takes the reader on a journey to a place and time far away and immerses us in circumstances that through the judgement and behavior of good men and perhaps the presence of Divine Providence a victory was achieved.

"They had no right to win, yet they did, and in doing so they changed the course of a war" Walter Lord, WWII Monument, Washington D.C.

RADM Frederick L. Lewis, USN (Ret.)
Virginia Beach
Winter 2022

To the Reader

This is the story of the Battle of Midway, told through the eyes of the men who fought it on both sides, as they experienced it. It depicts real men who lived and actual events of this remarkable battle. No facts were knowingly changed.

However, this is a work of fiction, historic fiction inspired by the classic novels of Shaara and Crane…the sincerest form of flattery, and the highest compliment that I as a writer can pay them.

Volumes of material concerning this battle are available from which to construct such a work and in the acknowledgements section I cite those to whom I and the reader owe so much. Over several decades, "facts," including eyewitness testimony, have been disproved, and long-standing myths refuted. That said, the text here is written from what the men experienced during those uncertain days in June 1942 amid the pressures of war – and with flawed human pride, institutional agendas, and bigoted perceptions on both sides. Knowledgeable readers know how history has treated certain events, yet my hope is that all readers come away with a sense of admiration for the men depicted here as they wrestled with their mortal fears and confusion as the battle and the year 1942 unfolded. Another hope is that readers are inspired to delve deeper into the narrative non-fiction about this battle, first to be entertained, and to better understand Midway's meaning in world history.

Historic charts are rare and can be confusing to those unfamiliar. "Snapshot" charts designed by the author of key moments are included to assist the reader and should not be considered source reference material.

The Midway narrative is full of amazing vignettes and heroic stories of courage and survival. Not all are included in this work. My deep interest in what happened on the waters and in the skies north and west of Midway Atoll aligns with my background in carrier aviation. As Shaara said, I hope I will be forgiven that.

The interpretation of character is my own.

CAPT Kevin Miller USN (Ret.)
Spring 2020

Glossary of Jargon and Acronyms

1MC — ship's public address system

AA — Antiaircraft; aka "flak" or "ack-ack"

CAP — Combat Air Patrol

CarDiv — Carrier Division

Chutai — 9-plane Japanese formation

CINCPAC — Commander in Chief, Pacific Fleet

CO — Commanding Officer

F4F — Fourth Fighter design, Grumman (aka *Wildcat*)

g — the force of gravity. "4 g's" is four times the force of gravity.

HIJMS — His Imperial Japanese Majesty's Ship

JO — Junior Officer – lieutenant commander (O-4) and below.

Kido Butai — Mobile Force

Knot — nautical mile per hour (One nautical mile is 2,000 yards)

LSO — Landing Signal Officer, aka "Paddles"

Nugget — first-cruise pilot, signified by gold bar collar device

PBY — Patrol Bomber design, Consolidated (flying boat)

SBD — Scout Bomber design, Douglas (aka *Dauntless)*

SB2U — Second Scout Bomber design, Vought (aka *Vindicator)*

Shotai — 3-plane Japanese formation

Trap — arrested landing

Type Zero — Mitsubishi A6M fighter, aka *Zero-sen* aka *Zero*

Type 97 — Nakajima B5N2 torpedo bomber, aka *kankō*

Type 99 — Aichi D3A dive-bomber aka, *kanbaku*

TBD — Torpedo Bomber design, Douglas (aka *Devastator)*

VB — Bombing Squadron

VF — Fighting Squadron

VS — Scouting Squadron (sometimes VSB – Scout Bombing)

VT — Torpedo Squadron

VMSB — Marine Corps Scout Bombing Squadron

XO — Executive Officer

My dear family,

What a day – the incredulousness of it all still gives each new announcement of the Pearl Harbor attack the unreality of a fairy tale. How can they have been so mad? Though I suppose we have known it would come sometime, there was always that inner small voice whispering – no, we are too big, too rich, too powerful, this war is for some other fools somewhere else. It will never touch us here. And then this noon that world fell apart.

...Tonight I put away all my civilian clothes. I fear the moths will find them good fare in the years to come. There is such a finality to wearing a uniform all the time. It is the one thing I fear – the loss of my individualism in a world of uniforms. But kings and puppets alike are being moved now by the master – destiny.

It is growing late and tomorrow will undoubtedly be a busy day. Once more the whole world is afire – in the period approaching Christmas it seems bitterly ironic to mouth again the timeworn phrases concerning peace on earth – goodwill to men, with so many millions hard at work figuring ways to reduce other millions to slavery or death. I find it hard to see the inherent difference between man and the rest of the animal kingdom. Faith lost – all is lost. Let us hope tonight that people, all people throughout this great country, have the faith to once again sacrifice for the things we hold essential to life and happiness. Let us defend these principles to the last ounce of blood – but then above all retain enough reason to have "charity for all and malice toward none." If the world ever goes through this again – mankind is doomed. This time it has to be a better world.

All my love,
Bill

Ensign Bill Evans, Torpedo Squadron Eight
December 7, 1941
Age 23

The Commanders

Frank Jack Fletcher

Commands Task Force 17 from USS *Yorktown*, as he did only one month earlier at Coral Sea, where he is unfairly held responsible by Navy Commander-in-Chief (known today as Chief of Naval Operations) Admiral Ernest J. King for the loss of King's proudest command, USS *Lexington*. A battleship man like most admirals of the day, Fletcher wears the Medal of Honor from actions at Veracruz in 1917, of which King is jealous. As the senior afloat and tactical commander, Fletcher is given specific orders from Nimitz on how to operate his task forces off Midway…and does not follow them.

Raymond Spruance

Halsey's 55-year-old cruiser division commander who jumps senior aviators to replace him as Commander, Task Force 16, when Halsey, drained by combat stress, develops dermatitis and is hospitalized. Taciturn and methodical, Spruance flies his flag in *Enterprise* and expects subordinates to do their jobs. As battle nears, Halsey's aviator staff members do not know what to make of their substitute commander.

Marc Mitscher

Plank-owner captain of the U.S. Navy's newest carrier, USS *Hornet*, commissioned the previous October. Pioneer aviator #33 who attempted the 1919 Atlantic crossing in the NC flying boats. Known to all as "Pete," a nickname from his Annapolis days, from which he graduates near the bottom of his class. Accepts appointment to Rear Admiral while at sea in *Hornet* on 31 May 1942. Torpedo Eight Commanding Officer John Waldron is his sounding board. On the morning of 4 June, Mitscher disappoints him.

Stanhope Cotton Ring

The forty-year-old Commander of the *Hornet* Air Group, he is Hollywood handsome despite the scars on his face from an aircraft fire. After service as Assistant Naval Attaché in London, he carries a swagger stick for which he is mocked.

Prior to *Hornet's* sortie from Pearl Harbor, he orders his fliers to remain on base, an order which breeds heated talk of mutiny. Leads a coordinated deck-load strike of 59 airplanes – the only such American attack of the battle.

WADE McCLUSKY

Also forty, he assumes command of the *Enterprise* Air Group in April 1942, having served previously as skipper of Fighting Six. Capable and confident, he is a quiet man who gets things done. Aboard *Enterprise* on 27 May, Nimitz awards him the Distinguished Flying Cross for his 1 February action off Wotje. Nimitz then murmurs to the awardee standing on McClusky's left, Lieutenant Roger Mehle, "I think you'll have a chance to win yourself another medal in the next several days."

CHŪICHI NAGUMO

A career battleship man, he commands the First Air Fleet as he has since Pearl Harbor, winning an unbroken string of victories from Hawaii to Rabaul to Australia to the Indian Ocean. His job is to attack Midway and be ready to counter any American force that may offer battle, a scenario that no one expects. When it presents itself, he has minutes to decide on three inadequate choices – and selects the worst.

MITSUO FUCHIDA

Akagi Air Unit Commander and leader of the Pearl Harbor strike who under-goes emergency surgery for appendicitis shortly after the Mobile Force departs Japan for Midway. On 4 June, unable to stay below and undeterred by his weak condition, he climbs to *Akagi's* bridge to watch Japan's glorious day unfold.

MINORU GENDA

The First Air Fleet Operations Officer and brilliant operational planner, who bathes in the success of his Pearl Harbor attack plan so much so that the Mobile Force is called "Genda's Fleet." The overconfidence of seniors appointed over him, notably Nagumo, troubles him as he divines the complex Midway attack. Without thorough critique from above, he confides in his friend Fuchida, "When I consider that a stroke of my pen might sway the destiny of the nation, it almost paralyzes me with fear."

JOICHI TOMONAGA

Hiryū's Air Unit Commander, at 31 the youngest in the First Air Fleet. Though an experienced Sino-Japanese War combat veteran and considered well-qualified, the sortie he flies piloting a Nakajima B5N while leading 108 airplanes to Midway on 4 June is his first of the Pacific War.

In the first six to twelve months of a war with the United States and Great Britain I will run wild and win victory upon victory. But then, if the war continues after that, I have no expectation of success.

— Admiral Isoroku Yamamoto

PROLOGUE

In the weeks and months after Pearl Harbor, Yamamoto did indeed run wild. In quick succession, the Philippines, the Dutch East Indies, and Singapore fell. Rabaul and Wake were captured. The Royal Navy battleships *Repulse* and *Prince of Wales* were sunk, and the U.S. Navy Asiatic Fleet was attacked with many ships lost, among them the Navy's first aircraft carrier *Langley*. Darwin was attacked and neutralized, and, in the Indian Ocean, Yamamoto's carriers under Vice Admiral Chūichi Nagumo's command sank the British carrier *Hermes* and attacked their base at Trincomalee. By April 1942, Imperial Japan had command of the territories and waters of the Western Pacific and Eastern Indian Ocean.

Still reeling, the United States Navy responded with what it had, mainly carrier forces, and, within months, attacked Japanese Central Pacific outposts in the Carolines and Marshalls. Militarily insignificant, the Japanese largely ignored these raids, considering them little more than a nuisance. American carriers, however, remained in the forefront of Yamamoto's mind.

The Doolittle Raid in April 1942 stunned the Japanese. While again militarily insignificant, this attack on the Japanese home islands was a severe blow to the Japanese psyche. That the Emperor was placed at risk was unacceptable, and resources were diverted to defend the main Japanese islands from future attacks.

One month later at Coral Sea, an American task force, under the command of Rear Admiral Frank Jack Fletcher, met and turned back a Japanese force that threatened the sea lines of communication to Australia. In the first naval battle in history where opposing ships did not see each other, each side lost a carrier and suffered severe damage to the surviving flattops. Despite heavy American losses, the Japanese advance was thwarted.

Yamamoto and the Imperial General Headquarters now agreed that the American carriers had to be destroyed – or otherwise neutralized – to allow Japan to solidify gains in the Central Pacific in order to repel future American thrusts. Yamamoto sought decisive battle by capturing territory the Americans would defend.

He settled on Midway, a tiny atoll over 1,000 miles from Hawaii that before the war was a fueling stop for Pan Am Clipper Trans-Pacific flying boat service.

Once captured, Hawaii faced imminent attack. Surely the Americans would come out of Pearl Harbor to defend it, and, off Midway, Yamamoto himself would wait. He would take the Americans under his big guns, as Togo had against the Russians at Tsushima in 1905, a battle young Yamamoto participated in as a midshipman, losing two fingers of his left hand.

While the Americans were busy elsewhere, Yamamoto directed a carrier striking force to attack Dutch Harbor – and capture the Aleutian islands of Attu and Kiska – in order to secure the empire's northern flank.

Nagumo's Mobile Force, the undefeated *Kido Butai* consisting of four of the six Pearl Harbor carriers, would spearhead the attack to neutralize Midway the day before an amphibious invasion force could secure the atoll. The Americans would then come out to give battle, and Yamamoto's Main Body of battleships and cruisers would meet and smash them.

To offer the Americans decisive battle, almost the entire Combined Fleet put to sea in late May 1942, led by eight carriers including *Akagi, Kaga, Hiryū* and *Sōryū*. Japan deployed eleven battleships, 24 cruisers, dozens of destroyers, submarines, transports, and auxiliaries, arguably the most powerful naval force the world had ever seen.

Pearl Harbor veterans *Shōkaku* and *Zuikaku*, damaged weeks earlier at the Battle of Coral Sea, did not participate in the Midway actions.

The American carrier *Yorktown*, damaged during the same battle, did.

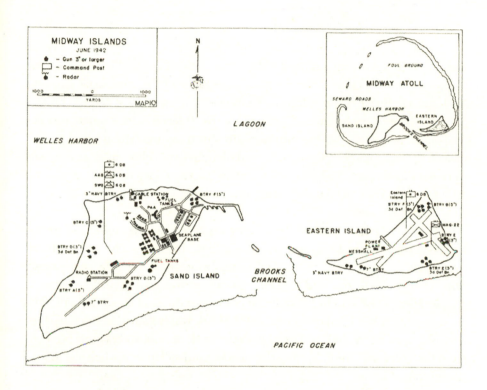

CHAPTER 1

HIJMS *Hiryū*, June 2, 1942

Moist North Pacific air buffeted Petty Officer 1/c Taisuke Maruyama as he squinted into the gloom from the port side gallery of the Imperial Japanese Navy carrier *Hiryū*. The morning sun, now halfway up the sky, had not broken through the mist as the carrier ploughed across the relentless swells. Another day of bad weather, and the dim horizon shrouded the Mobile Force, with unseen escorts encircling the carriers and big-gun combatants at close intervals to remain in contact. To his beam was sleek *Sōryū*, a wisp of spray exploding off her bow. Ahead, the flagship *Akagi* and fat *Kaga* rose and fell as they led the *Kidō Butai* southeast.

Had he been here before? These very waters? Last December the transit had been freezing, inside as well as outside the ship. Those who had ventured topside encountered low ceilings, high winds, morning sea smoke, and stinging rain. Inside, Maruyama and the others had kept warm in their flying togs as the steel decks and bulkheads radiated cold from the sea below and air above. He dropped his head and contemplated the dark water's surface, the sounds of it swishing along the hull and breaking over itself as bow waves emanated out from the great ship, audible amid the steady wind as *Hiryū* pushed ahead into the mist at 10 knots.

At 19 years old, Maruyama was a veteran observer in the Type 97 *kankō* torpedo bomber. Six months ago, after transiting the Central Pacific, he had tasted combat at Pearl Harbor. Since then he had helped torpedo ships at anchor in Darwin, and had bombed Ceylon. But nothing matched that first morning as he and his mates swooped down in a right-hand turn as geysers erupted on a battleship ahead. His pilot then lined up on the one to the left of it…

"*Konnichiwa.*"

Maruyama turned to see his squadron mate Miyauchi dog the hatch behind him as he joined Maruyama for some fresh air.

"*Ohayu*, Miyauchi-kun."

"*Ohayu,*" Miyauchi replied as he joined Maruyama at the rail. Away from the officers, the enlisted pilot pulled out a cigarette and lighter, cupping his hand to shield the flame from the gusts.

"Anything new?" Maruyama asked.

Miyauchi took a long drag and exhaled. "I saw the captain and Lieutenant Tomonaga climbing the ladder to the bridge. More conferences…involving us, no doubt."

"Tomonaga is eager to make his mark."

Maruyama studied the blinking light signal from *Akagi.* Course change.

"As am I. We must finish the job this time."

"I hope you get a carrier, Maruyama, instead of the sitting duck you sank at Pearl Harbor."

Miyauchi, upon his return that morning, had told Maruyama of the capsized battleship hull among all the flame and smoke of the second wave attack. The last time Maruyama had seen his target, it was listing to port. Then a flash, and a massive column of fire had shot from a battleship at the northern end of the line. The strong concussion swept them seconds later; it shook their *kankō* violently as they ran away to the west. All of Ford Island seemed to be on fire and was obscured by roiling black from the *Arizona,* hit by his mates in a level attack. After their triumphant homecoming, they saw the newsreel images of their work.

He learned his target also had a name; *Oklahoma.* Named after a province in the American interior known for cowboys and open plains. The ship was a sitting duck.

Maruyama watched *Akagi* flash the execute signal. Moments later *Hiryū* heeled slightly then steadied up, a change of only a few degrees.

Miyauchi extinguished the butt on the sole of his boot and placed it in his pocket. Flicking it overboard could cause it to be carried up on a draft to the flight deck. As a pilot he would probably avoid a beating, but why take the chance?

Maruyama continued to gaze northeast at the Mobile Force moving east. Since that morning, he had thought of Pearl Harbor every day.

Where are the carriers?

Maruyama peered through his binoculars at the western side of Ford Island. Empty! He scanned the docks, the long pier next to the submarine wharf. No carriers.

Lieutenant Matsumura was leading his formation of kankō *torpedo bombers toward ships moored along the west of Ford Island. The carriers they had hoped were there were gone, not one visible anywhere in the harbor. Looking south, Maruyama had seen a destroyer near the channel before he was startled by a black AA puff.*

More Type 97's from Akagi and Kaga swooped down in sharp descending turns as they picked out their targets on battleship row. To his left he watched a formation of Zeros dive on an American airfield, and flights of kanbakus dove on the Ford and Hickam runways.

Matsumura signaled to Maruyama's flight leader to skip the planned attack on the slim pickings on Ford Island's west side and circle north of the island and target battleship row with kankō from the other carriers. As the formation bore in on the lone battleship and cruisers along Ford's western moorings, Maruyama's veered north.

The harbor was full of vessels, crammed together in nests with fat battleships moored alongside each other. Fascinated, he noted the cage masts of some and tripod masts of others, seeing in reality what he had only seen in grainy images and drawings. Nothing moved on the calm water. They passed over a single battleship to the north, painted a darker gray than the others. On its decks he saw men – running.

His pilot banked right to stay with their lead over the submarine docks to set up on battleship row. It was just like their training in the Kurils, and Maruyama readied his aiming glass. Straining against the g-force, he again noted men running below him on the piers and harbor streets. The American battle wagons gleamed gray in the morning sunlight, and the first geyser appeared against the hull of one of them.

His pilot rolled upright to do a belly check. To the east the Aloha Tower stood out, with Diamond Head in the background, a postcard image printed indelibly on Maruyama's memory.

Over the wharf, they knifed down toward the water. To the south, some American ships were shooting – and missing – the kankōs ahead. More towering geysers, and Maruyama saw one battleship was not attracting as much attention as those on its left and right. His pilot saw it too, and lined up on a ship in the middle of the row as another geyser erupted from it.

"Stand by!" his pilot ordered. "Stand by...!"

Their kankō continued to slow and descend, and as it did a torpedo exploded against this new ship. Then another, with water climbing over 100 meters into the air! Maruyama was committed now, and through his aiming glass he saw the hulking battleship fill his viewfinder.

Release!

As Maruyama yanked on the handle, the weighty torpedo fell from the aircraft. Free of it, the kankō *jumped into the air as the pilot firewalled the engine. Behind him, the gunner shouted as he fired at something along the pier and Maruyama snapped his head left to see the threat. It was only the gunner taking a potshot at a moored cruiser. No enemy Grummans were visible.*

To his right, circular wakes fanned away from the struck battleships, and their targeted ship already listed to port. Three Zero-sens roared overhead then dove to strafe the airfield. The antiaircraft increased as tracers shot past.

"Hit! We got a hit!"

Both Maruyama and his pilot craned their necks right to see the result of their work, as spray hovered high above their target before settling back as a falling curtain. Ahead, fighters and dive-bombers worked over the Navy field at Ewa Beach, as Maruyama's formation of kankōs *veered clear as they clawed their way west to safety.*

Maruyama, looking south at the moment, sensed a flash behind and to his right. The gunner gave a whoop, and Maruyama turned in time to see a massive sheet of flame envelop the whole of Ford Island. As the flames turned to black smoke, they felt a shockwave and, a second later, heard the concussive BOOM from the massive blast. Maruyama noted that the antiaircraft fire had suddenly stopped as an enormous conflagration hundreds of meters high flared from one end of an American battlewagon. His Majesty's airplanes buzzed around it like insects near a flame.

Arizona. And *Oklahoma.* Hundreds had perished in the two ships, and Maruyama had played a part.

"Let's go below," Miyauchi said as he turned, and, with nothing better to do, Maruyama followed. They dogged the hatch and headed forward to a ladder under the bridge. Hearing commotion above, they stopped as Lieutenant Tomonaga raced down the ladder. Smiling at his *kankō* squadron mates, he continued down without saying a word.

Behind him, the Air Officer followed at a more leisurely pace. The two pilots waited at a respectful distance for him to continue.

"Ah, it is a good day for Carrier Division 2," the grinning Air Officer said as his eyes met theirs. He did not stop as he turned to descend the next ladder, but said over his shoulder as he disappeared below, "Tomonaga-san will lead the first strike."

Out of earshot, Miyauchi spoke. "What will we strike first?"

"We've been steaming east for days. Hawaii again? The American fleet? Midway?"

"Whatever it is, if there is a first strike there must be more strikes to follow."

Maruyama nodded. "And Tomonaga-san is given the lead of the First Air Fleet? Guess we'll know what it is before long."

"I hope we fly with him on the first strike," Miyauchi said. "Let's go below and spread the news."

"And take bets. I say Hawaii again."

"I say their fleet."

The two aviators trundled down the ladders to the mess decks, knowing that whatever tomorrow brought, Tomonaga would lead them to it.

CHAPTER 2

READY ROOM FOUR, USS *HORNET*, JUNE 2, 1942

Looking up from the Acey-Deucy table, Ensign Bill Evans noted the back of the skipper's head.

As the junior pilots next to him concentrated on yet another mindless game, Evans studied his CO. He *was* odd, and even after eight months with him, he had not figured him out. He was awake up there – he never dozed in the ready room – but he was motionless. Suddenly, his hand shot out and then curved back in. Evans caught the gaze of the duty officer, Whitey Moore, who, seated at a desk in front of their CO, suppressed a smile.

Evans had yet to figure Skipper Waldron. He was just a weird duck – that was the only way to explain it. *All* the ring-knockers were, from the pompous CHAG – Commander *Hornet* Air Group, aka "Sea Hag" – Ring to their bullying senior lieutenant, Swede Larsen. Captain Mitscher, the Navy's real-life ancient mariner, must have entered the academy a year after the Civil War ended. *What happened to men at Annapolis?* At least Swede wasn't aboard.

All the Torpedo Eight pilots were there, and all were on edge. They managed to keep it under the surface. Playing Acey-Deucy passed the time, as did reading the worn April 1942 copy of *Life* magazine. Grant Teats was writing a letter, and Abbie Abercrombie dozed in his chair with his baseball cap in front of his face. However, only yesterday the skipper had laid it on the line.

"They'll get here Wednesday or Thursday morning. I figure the odds to be about two and a half to one against us."

Evans and the others listened as Waldron then discussed how the morning and afternoon attacks would go, his dark prediction contrary to the upbeat assessment. The skipper predicted VT-8 would make two morning attacks, which gave Evans hope. But, in the next sentence, Waldron said he was trying to persuade CHAG to let them make a night attack "when they're punch-drunk and reeling." That comment left Evans punch-drunk and reeling. A night attack? After two daytime attacks against real ships defended by real *Zeros*? None of them, including the skipper, had combat experience. Nugget ensigns like Evans had never taken off from a carrier with a torpedo. They'd never even seen it done.

With a start, Waldron stood and turned.

"All right, listen up."

The players put down the dice and returned to their high-back seats. Abbie straightened up in his seat as he rubbed his eyes. XO Owens looked over his shoulder to ensure the room came to order. Waldron stood with arms crossed, waiting hawk-like for the junior pilots to take their places. Once satisfied, he began.

"The only way we're gonna get in is to maintain mutual support. Now, Sea Hag says that we are going to go out as a group, with us on the deck, VS and VB high above, and VF escorting all of us. Fine…but it's crackers to think that we're going to stay together all the way to the Japs, which will be probably 150 miles away once we depart. First, there's the airspeed difference, and surely there will be small heading changes on the way to spread us out. And once we find 'em, it's going to be a free-for-all. Trust me. When we get there, it's going to be us, alone."

Evans glanced over at Tex and Rusty, both riveted on the CO. In contrast, Abbie had his head down, but looked up as soon as Waldron stepped to the chalkboard.

"As we go in we're gonna keep our speed up; I'll set my RPM for 105 knots to give you guys behind me something to play with. The Japs will hightail it away at flank speed – they'd be dopey not to – but even with an 80-knot speed advantage it's going to take a while to catch the bastards. I figure in clear weather we'll spot silhouettes at 20 miles. Once I determine our target, which will be the closest carrier, we'll all – all – go in on it. So, 20 miles at 80 knots, that's fifteen minutes, and that doesn't count us overtaking them on their bow and reversing for launch. That's the math, so I give us twenty minutes."

Evans nodded. After months of the CO's drills, he could do this word problem standing on his head.

"Now, what else does that mean? That means we'll have to defend from their CAP fighters for most of that, maybe the whole twenty minutes, if they get lucky and see us early. XO, get with Chief Dobbs and tell the gunners; we've gotta conserve our .30 cal ammo and not spray it all over God's creation on edgy shots. I say this to let you pilots know, too. If your gunner back there fires everything scattershot in the first few minutes, it's gonna be a long day. Even changing an ammo belt will seem like forever when you're under attack. Make sure they wait till the Japs are in range, then give it to 'em."

Bill Evans was reminded of Waldron's words the day before. All of them knew some of them wouldn't return from the first attack, and, if one survived, it was only to return, rearm, wolf down a sandwich, and go back into another whirlwind of hot lead, with more culled from the herd. And then…return at *night*? Evans couldn't believe it, that he was even sitting in a ready room on a carrier in the middle of the Pacific. He glanced at the wings on his chest. *You asked for this.*

Waldron, energized, picked up a piece of chalk. "Now, we have our two tactical divisions. Once we run down a carrier…maybe the only one out there or one I choose, don't know what we'll find…we're going to split as we've been trained, as we've discussed. I'll take one side and XO's division the other. But before we split we need to stay together until the last minute. To give ourselves every advantage, we're gonna fly in close echelon."

Some shifted uncomfortably in their chairs. *What? Close echelon?* Waldron now began drawing on the board, speaking as he did.

"At some point our VF is going to be off engaged elsewhere. Enemy fighters will get through. My division will be leading in left and right echelon. Jimmie, your division will be stepped down, and about 100 yards aft, like this."

The pilots watched as Waldron drew on the board like a football coach diagramming a play. Evans looked at XO Owens. He appeared as dumbfounded as the others.

"We'll go in low and fast, together in echelon. Jimmie, your planes are going to keep lookout for all of us; the planes to the right look left and planes to left look right. When the *Zeros* attack, we'll mass defensive fire from fifteen guns. The near formation can only jam their tracking and maybe the gunners can get off some bursts, but the XO's division will have freedom of maneuver. With the Jap bellies exposed, you trailers can pull up and spray 'em with high deflection shots from yer fixed .30's that will either flame 'em or scare them off. Then re-dress the formation. I'll be watching, and if I need to will throttle back a bit so you can catch up. We'll stay close until the split point, probably inside three miles…they'll be running hard."

Evans was skeptical. Although his *Devastator* flew in Waldron's first division, he saw this as merely a way to buy time for it at the cost of XO's TBDs. But as Waldron explained the tactic through the blizzard of chalk dust, it made sense. Any way the Japs came at VT-8, they could counter. The Japs would likely swoop down from the high side and rake them; if Evans and his mates could just see them in time, their gunners could hold them off so they couldn't track.

Waldron loved these chalk talks, and he could tell his pilots caught on to the logic. He didn't tell them about his plan for fighter protection because it wasn't approved yet. He had to ask within the next 24 hours.

It was a long shot, but they needed hope. They needed something.

CHAPTER 3

FLAG BRIDGE, USS *YORKTOWN*, JUNE 2, 1942

From his chair on the flag bridge, Rear Admiral Frank Jack Fletcher watched as the oiler *Platte* fell off *Yorktown's* starboard quarter after two hours alongside. Even though he was no longer a ship captain like Elliott Buckmaster and therefore responsible, after each underway replenishment breakaway it was as if a weight were lifted from him. No fires and no injuries, and with full bunkers he felt secure. *Platte* was dispatched to the east as *Yorktown* steamed west with the rest of her escorts to find Ray Spruance and Task Force 16 already on station. Fletcher lingered as he scanned the horizon and assessed the positioning of his screen. Station keeping was an area in which he excelled; how he loved to eyeball a heading and ring up speed to get there with minimal corrections and no disruption to the formation. He liked passing his techniques down to junior officers of the deck, often taking the conn of his battleship *New Mexico* and maneuvering it like a destroyer. Frank Jack could handle ships. Carrier task force command? The jury was still out, at CINCPAC HQ in Makalapa Hill *and* in his own mind.

What more did they want? He'd stopped them at the Coral Sea. But for the loss of *Lexington*, he'd be lauded as a modern-day Nelson. A naval battle where he never saw a ship. Did King or Chester Nimitz ever experience *that*, or even imagine it? Hell, his ships rescued over 90 percent of *Lexington's* crew with the Japanese threatening from the north.... Did he receive any credit?

He took another look at *Platte*, and was reminded of *Neosho*, his vital tanker set on and sunk by Japanese carrier planes that knew their job. If he hadn't lost her and her fuel, things may have been different. *He* had to fight, *he* had to refuel, and *he* had to take risk, all while the courtiers at Pearl and Washington expected perfection. None of them had ever seen anything like this: *airplanes* doing all the fighting.

Lexington survivors said it was aviation fuel in the lines that doomed her, that fed fires her damage control parties could not extinguish. That lesson was passed, a lesson learned literally under fire. She burned that evening, horrible and magnificent, a towering column of black rising into the darkening blue. *Fire.* From enemy bombs and torpedoes. He had seen it. Main Navy had heard about it.

Here on his flag bridge he had stood that very morning, a helpless spectator as Elliott Buckmaster from the bridge wing shouted commands and twisted *Yorktown* like a snake to avoid the Jap dive-bombers overhead:

"Admiral, get down!" Lewis shouted.

Fletcher ignored his Chief of Staff, absorbed by the sight of enemy bombs separating from their aircraft. The cacophony generated by the antiaircraft guns was deafening and drowned out any aircraft noise, but through it he could hear Elliott shouting orders to the helm. Yorktown *heeled hard amid cordite smoke and the thunderous sounds of her guns, which together rose into a singular roar. It was as if the carrier were roaring like a lion in defiance of attacking insects. Fletcher was spellbound as he watched one bomb fall toward the starboard bow, visible through a sheet of his own flickering tracers, wobbling as it fell to the sea, harmless now, but with more black insects, more shouts, more thunder.*

Lewis yanked him down, and the admiral's World War I doughboy helmet turned cockeyed as the bomb exploded off their bow with a deep whump *within the firestorm of guns. They felt the impact aft as salt spray from the first bomb rained on them. They looked up in time to see another falling bomb as the deck tilted starboard as Elliott shifted his rudder to throw off his current assailant. It too missed to starboard. Seconds later, they were rocked by an impact aft which heaved the deck so high that for a moment they were weightless before falling back on their stinging hands and knees. Seawater slid down the sloping deck and was absorbed by their wash khakis.*

They heard a sudden whirr whirr whirr *and then were blown into the armored bulkhead by the concussive force of an explosion that pelted the island with fragments. The bomb must have hit the island, and for a moment Fletcher wondered if anything on the bridge and air plot was still alive. Shocked gun crews took a moment to recover before they – those who could – resumed their fire at the hovering insects. Fletcher and Lewis could only lay flat on the wet and heeling deck, the smells of burning flight deck mingling with cordite. How bad are we hurt? Though his ears rung, he heard more shouts from Elliott as he gave orders to the helm. Good.*

Fletcher returned his scan to the horizon. Sixty-six men were lost in that attack, most killed instantly from a bomb that tore through the flight deck. *The blood, limbs ripped from their torsos.* As he continued to reflect on the battle, it was clear *Yorktown* was wounded below the waterline, his task force was low on fuel, and aviator reports were suspect or wrong. Had been from the get-go, and the fires on *Lexington* increased. He had little choice to do much more than retire, but Washington blamed *him* for not attacking that afternoon. *What's the difference,* he thought. The two carriers he had defeated at Coral Sea were not involved in this operation off Midway.

So said the CINCPAC staff! Yes, the same intelligence staff that was in place on December 6, who were fuzzy about the enemy order of battle only last month. *Now they've pinned the enemy movements down to precise minutes and miles...and expect me to bank on that?*

Last month Nimitz's staff couldn't tell him the exact number of carriers arrayed against him. Now they identified specific ships.[1] And a specific admiral, Nagumo himself, like Fletcher a battleship man by trade, but also like Fletcher on a carrier bridge depending on boys flying powered kites to do the fighting for him far over the horizon.

Jutland? The battle they had spent their career studying and fighting on tabletops? When and where was he expected to form a battle line when the enemy could appear and strike from anyplace on the compass within minutes? Tsushima? Any lieutenant could "cross the T" when the enemy is visible from miles away, and cooperative. No, this new weapon – the airplane – was an order of magnitude different, and no one yet understood it. Naval warfare had been transformed inside Fletcher's career, before his eyes, and though they gave it lip service, most of his peer group was still in denial. The boys in the cockpits – many just babes in arms during the Great War – knew no different. They were *comfortable* flying over 100 miles and doing the fighting, talking on radios, and making decisions that Fletcher wished he could make. Once they disappeared, Fletcher, Fitch, Halsey, and now Ray Spruance could only wait for their return and *hope* for an accurate report.

Lewis stepped outside from flag plot and saw Fletcher gazing at the horizon. "Penny for your thoughts, sir."

Fletcher looked down at the sea. "Well Spence, here we are, on their flank if the intelligence can be believed. Tomorrow? Thursday? More waiting."

"Nimitz's staff was adamant about Thursday morning, and the dispatch sent three days ago confirms it."

---

[1] Through painstaking cryptoanalysis, Nimitz' radio intelligence staff led by CDR Joseph Rochefort correctly predicted the exact ships and time and place of the Japanese attack.

"So what am I to do, send everything we have to a latitude/longitude north-west of Midway at dawn and there they'll be? What if CINCPAC is wrong? What if they end-around us and go toward Hawaii? Am I to engage on a hunch from some commander drinking coffee in Makalapa Hill?"

An uneasy silence followed. After a moment, Fletcher continued.

"What choice do we have? We *must* launch our own planes to search the waters north of us. If we find them or Midway planes find them, Ray Spruance will be ready to strike after Nagumo is positively identified. We'll be ready to augment that and clean up what's left."

"How close, sir?"

"Inside 150 miles, but outside 100. The fliers are concerned about the range of the TBD plane. Between Ray's two carriers, he should have over 100 planes to attack four of theirs – if the intel proves correct."

"And if they have a fifth? The two 'Aleutian' carriers in the report could be a ruse."

"Or a diversion to get us to go up there. That's why I've gotta search and hold us in reserve. If we made it to this fight after last month, one or more of theirs may have, too." Fletcher then changed the subject.

"How *are* the brown shoes doing today?"

"Taking it all in stride, sir. Ready. Confident."

"Good, good. Just wish we had more fighters. We've gotta keep more back to defend us, and so does Ray."

"The aviators want to keep the carriers together in mutual support."

Fletcher concentrated on a far-off destroyer, blinking a light message to another.

"I know. What do you think?"

"That's one school of thought. The other is that the enemy will be better able to pounce on two. Once we rendezvous we'll stay in visual range, but operate as separate task forces. We'll probably become separated at some point anyway."

Fletcher nodded. The lessons of Coral Sea were seared into his mind. Lewis continued.

"Admiral, I'm worried about our torpeckers."

"That they won't get through or won't work?"

"Both, sir."

"Why? The VT and the planes on *Lexington* sank that light carrier[1] and almost sank their fleet carrier."

---

[1] HIJMS Shoho

"Sir, *Lexington's* air group was good – and we don't have them anymore. Our group is now cobbled together, but more than that, if we are scouting and flying CAP over the task forces, I'm not sure we'll have enough VSB and VF to help the TBDs when we send them in. They're slow, no getting around it, and, from what I hear, the pilots have little confidence in them. Halsey's staff has almost zero confidence...I met up with some of them at Pearl."

Fletcher gazed at the planes on the bow, parked on the port side. The TBDs were big – three seats – but the engine *seemed* small, perched way out in front, unlike the Grumman fighters with engines that took up the front half of the airplane. Some of the TBDs had their wings folded. One had only the right wing folded, as if to salute its readiness to follow orders.

"They won't go?"

"Sir, they'll go, and they want to go, but I'm afraid we are going to lose some this time, and the losses may be heavy. First, we have to get them close...and then we'll need some luck. We got lucky in the Coral Sea."

Fletcher nodded. Once again his boys would risk their lives. Eager to do it, and under his orders. What choice did he have, did Ray Spruance have, but to send them? They had to send everything. Over the damned horizon...and then wait, the agonizing wait. That was their best chance. Besides, practically every time they went out a flier was lost; it was almost a weekly occurrence *without* combat. None of them were under any illusions, and this time against Nagumo and *four* of his combat-proven carriers, *if* the CINCPAC staff was correct.

His orderly appeared with a cup of coffee. Fletcher, now sitting in his bridge wing chair, sipped it absentmindedly as he gazed out to sea, thinking of Nagumo, the TBD planes, and that curtain of racing fire. Above, he heard a shouted report to the bridge but could not discern the meaning. After a minute, Spence popped his head outside.

"Task Force Sixteen sighted off the port bow, sir."

Fletcher nodded. "Very well."

The American task forces were now rendezvoused at Point Luck, with Frank Jack Fletcher in command once again.

CHAPTER 4

HIJMS *AKAGI*, JUNE 2, 1942

Commander Mitsuo Fuchida favored his left side as he scuffled along the passageway. The emergency appendectomy the night they sortied required him to stay off his feet to heal, but after six days in sick bay he had had it. *Akagi* rode the gentle late afternoon swells with ease, and, as he passed an open hatch, he saw murky skies and the dim silhouette of a cruiser no more than 2,000 yards abeam.

Tomonaga would perform admirably as the strike commander, but that he, *Akagi's* Air Unit Commander, was missing this operation, the big one that would lead to decisive combat with the Americans, hurt more than the pain in his right side. They would probably not encounter the Americans until after June 6 at the earliest, almost a week away. The surgeon said he was down for several weeks...and no argument. Restless, he sought the familiar air control post forward of the island. Maybe his friend Genda would be there, or Captain Oishi, and he could get the latest.

Fuchida considered Commander Minoru Genda a worrier. *If only he had more faith in his own ability* he thought. The First Air Fleet Operations Officer was a brilliant planner, making it easy for units like Fuchida's to strike with success. Opening the metal door, he was greeted with the familiar image of his friend hunched over the chart table.

"Genda-kun, is the battle won?"

Genda turned to see Fuchida in a robe and slippers. "Looks like *you* are prepared to fight the Americans."

Fuchida smiled. "Yes, though I hope they don't come today." He closed the door behind him and unfolded a chair next to the chart table, wincing as he eased himself onto it.

"What are you working on now?" he asked.

Genda manipulated the chart dividers and measured the distance on the scale. "Our best launch position and time. We won't know till that morning what the winds are. I'm hopeful for southeast, but, if they're westerly, we'll need to move in closer."

"Like Pearl Harbor?"

"Yes, almost a copy, a smaller copy," Genda replied. "I want us to launch outside 200 miles when the horizon is just visible. All should be off in fifteen minutes."

"How many?"

"A total of 108; 9 *Zero-sens* from each carrier, 18 Type 97s each from *Hiryū* and *Sōryū* and 18 Type 99 *kanbakus* from us and *Kaga*. Three fighters from each ship as CAP."

"What will they carry?" Fuchida asked.

"Model 25s for the dive-bombers and 800 kilograms for the Type 97s. The facilities are of light construction and built on sandy coral; 250 kilograms will do the job and not run them out of fuel. Level-bombers from *Hiryū* will hit the fuel tanks and barracks facilities on Sand Island and *kankōs* from *Sōryū* have the crew facilities and power station on Eastern. Type 99s will dive on parked aircraft and the seaplane hangar." Genda motioned with his hand. "They'll swing around here to the east and dive with the sun at their back. *Zero-sens* will strafe parked aircraft and light targets of opportunity."

Fuchida nodded his understanding. Genda continued.

"As you can see, the attack will be a lot like Darwin. The *kanbakus* will have a long arc to the east to set up, but this time the enemy will probably see them."

"The Americans may have their own CAP."

"They may. Regardless, the level Type 97s will go in first and the dive-bombers second, per doctrine. We have plenty of fighters to escort them and to then tear up the islands. The objective is to eliminate their airplanes and their ability to fuel any reinforcements."

"Then what? Wait for the Americans? Where?"

"That's up to the Force Commander, but the landing force will attack a day after we do. That operation should take two days at most, and we can support them. I hope he positions us to the southwest as we wait for the Americans to come out of Hawaii, keeping us that much closer to Wake."

"Combined Fleet doesn't think they'll come."

"I know. They haven't been paying attention. The Americans have been 'coming' since February in the central islands. Hell, a playboy air racer attacked our capitol and put the emperor at risk! And they *still* think the Americans won't fight."

"Yes, and they thwarted us at Coral Sea."

"Because we sent the amateurs of CarDiv 5! Again, penny-wise and pound-foolish headquarters didn't send enough force. This time we have plenty, with carriers who know what they're doing – unlike *Shokaku* and *Zuikaku*."

Fuchida used his finger and thumb to measure the distance from Oahu to a position southwest of Midway. Genda nodded.

"That's well over 1,000 miles," he said. "I think they'll come out on the 5th, and it will take them two days to get here. We have a line of subs along the Midway-Hawaii chain to report and harass them. By then the *Hashirajima Fleet*[1] will be here to take any survivors under their *big guns*," he added. He coughed twice, his sarcasm hidden by the deep dry convulsions that wracked his body. Fuchida ignored it. Everyone caught something underway.

"Wish they would let us," Fuchida opined, more to himself than to Genda.

"They won't. They still don't get it."

Fuchida nodded. "Are you going to show this to Oishi-san or Admiral Kusaka?"

"They've seen it. They said it's fine and to carry on, like they always do. I'm just fiddling with time and distance."

Unable to bear being out of it, Fuchida still wanted more. "What's the search posture?"

Genda pulled a small chart lying at the top of the table. "Float planes, along this arc, let's see…031 to 181. That includes planes from us and *Kaga* on the two southern legs, southwest of Midway."

"Why?"

"If any Americans *are* nearby, that's where I think they'll be. It will also help us sanitize ahead for the landing force coming up from the southwest. Our Type 97s are faster and more survivable than the float planes, so they get the hottest sectors."

"You think of everything, Genda-kun."

"We did get this from Combined Fleet: have planes loaded with torpedoes and armor-piercing bombs in the hangar bay in case any Americans are nearby. We'll keep our best torpedo crews and crack dive-bomber pilots in reserve. We don't expect Midway will to be a moving target."

"You think of everything!"

"I wish I could think of a way you could fly on the strike!"

"Agreed. I am breaking rules now as it is."

"When will your stitches come out?"

"Tomorrow, with luck."

Fuchida pulled himself up to look through an open porthole. The cruiser to port had become even more difficult to discern in the thickening mist.

"Weather's coming down."

---

[1] Derisive comment in reference to the IJN battle line.

"Yes, at least we are safe from American patrols and probably submarines, unless we stumble upon them."

"Glad I'm not station-keeping on the bridge." Fuchida said.

"Yes, tempers are short…and it's still daylight. Go below, Fuchida-kun. Keep the doc off your back. I'll bring you a glass of sake later."

"Thank you, my friend. Your plan looks good."

"Would only be better with you in it."

Bill Evans shoveled a forkful of mashed potatoes into his mouth. Around him in *Hornet's* wardroom were his Torpedo Eight squadron mates, all nugget ensigns as he was, seated at a long table with white linen and china, eating the evening meal and trying not to think about anything else.

"Squire, could you pass the salt please?"

Evans picked up the salt and pepper shakers and passed them to Abbie.

"Thanks, shipmate. They don't prepare roast beef here like they do in Kansas City."

Whitey looked up from his plate. "*Kansas City. Kansas City.* That's all you talk about."

"When I ain't talkin' about the fine flying qualities of the Douglas TBD *Devastator*, yer right."

"What side, Kansas or Missouri?"

"*Kansas,* the only side. God's country."

"Well, we ain't in Kansas no more, are we?" Whitey said, with an edge that surprised those around him.

"That's right, Dorothy, we're in the middle of the blue Pacific, with Tojo comin' to meet us so we can flap our wings and give him the middle finger before he shoots it off. Sure wish *Toto* was comin' to meet us."

Evans knew where this was going. All were on edge, and Abbie wasn't going to help matters by goading Whitey.

"Knock it off, guys," Teats said. At six feet tall and muscular, he could stand up to Abbie.

"Yes, sir. Just enjoying the ambiance here aboard the Good Ship *Hornet*, our newest ship with the oldest airplanes."

"Yeah, and the TBD has been in the fleet only four years," Whitey said.

"Yep, and Orville and Wilbur had their first flight less than *forty* years ago," Evans said, fanning the flames without meaning to. Abbie threw another log on.

"That's right, good old American know-how. And thanks to the nice folks at the Douglas Aircraft Company, we get to fly the finest corrugated tin flivver money can buy."

None of the pilots at the table responded. Abbie raised his hand.

"Milford, coffee, please."

"Yes, sir," the steward nodded.

Around them sat other Air Group aviators at their tables, all in semi-wrinkled wash khaki uniforms, some wearing neckties. Here and there was laughter and spirited conversation. Stewards in white frocks served meals and cleared dishes.

"Think we have a chance?" Rusty asked of no one.

"Skipper gives us one, okay, half," Teats said, regretting his words as soon as they left his mouth.

"Half a chance is better'n none at all," Abbie said, reaching for an ashtray. The steward returned with black coffee in a white cup and saucer, trimmed in blue.

Evans pursed his lips. He didn't want to say it. Hal jumped in for him.

"The guys on *Lexington* all made it back. They went in coordinated and sank a Jap carrier. The Japs aren't ten feet tall."

"Did they do it with Sea Hag leading?" Abbie asked. By instinct, the pilots glanced about as Abbie, unconcerned, pulled a pack of Lucky Strikes from his pocket. Teats spoke next.

"The skipper is going to get us some fighters, and even if all of us lose sight of the bombers above us, we're all flying the same heading. We'll get there after them, and after they roll in their dives, I'm ready to put the yellow bastards on the bottom."

"Yeah, we've practiced this attack what, once or twice?" Whitey said.

Abbie nodded as he patted his ashes into the tray. "And never with a 'tin fish' under me. How about you, *Ulvert?* Tin fish or weenie under you? Or do you prefer pickle?"

Whitey gave Abbie a look. His sarcasm was wearing thin. The men ate in silence.

"Milford, what do we have for dessert tonight?" Teats asked.

The steward smiled. "Oh, we have a treat for the officers! Apple pie à la mode! That's with hard ice cream!"

The table perked up. Hard ice cream! A delicacy.

Teats smiled at Milford. "Hard ice cream, eh? Did you mess-cranks hand crank it?" The others laughed.

"No, sir! No, sir!" Milford beamed back. "We done kep' it in the ice box! Save it for special occasions!"

The pilots looked down at their plates. They could only force a smile, knowing what Milford didn't. A reminder that dawn was less than twelve hours away.

Teats raised his head and smiled back at the proud steward, still excited that *he* knew something the pilots did not. "Okay then, Milford. Mom's apple pie and a big scoop of ice cream for me, please."

"Yes, sir! Yes, sir!"

Teats pressed him. "A big one, now!"

"Yes, sir! Oh, yes, sir!" Milford basked in the attention.

All of the pilots ordered the same. Evans turned his coffee cup upright, something he didn't usually do after the evening meal. *Why not?* A steward quickly filled it, steam from the cup mixing with the table's cigarette smoke.

Across the room, a table of scout pilots shared a sudden laugh. Evans savored each bite of pie, for a moment remembering his childhood. Whitey broke the silence.

"Look, who would you rather fly into combat with? Skipper Waldron or the other COs?"

"Or Sea Hag?" Abbie deadpanned.

Evans had strong feelings about this. "You know, the skipper pushes us past the limit and the rest of the ship laughs at us, but Whitey's right. Ever since Pearl Harbor – before – he's been preparing us for this day. I'll admit I get sore sometimes, and he ridicules me about being a 'Yale' man, but we're out here now. We have to go. And because of him, we're ready for anything."

The pilots considered Evans's words. "Jus' wish we had the big Grumman TBFs aboard," Rusty said into his coffee.

"What? After all our experience in the flying coffin?"

"Knock it off, Abbie," Teats snarled.

Evans ignored them. "No, it's us guys. Just like Agincourt. We're the ones going tomorrow, and if the intel is right, we can end this war. Tomorrow."

Abbie took his cup in both hands. "Squire, I hope we do. And I hope you can add an addendum to Shakespeare."

Teats leaned in, ready for a fight.

Abbie noticed and raised his hand. "No, really. I'm glad Squire is in the CO's division and can record everything for posterity. Tell the folks back home that we slackers fought for them out here. Yeah, it's gonna be a big one, and we have ringside seats."

Slouching back in their chairs, the men silently considered their futures as they contemplated their empty china dishes and half-finished coffee. If they wanted more, fresh joe was available any time of the day or night.

"Let's go back to the ready room," Teats suggested.

Once they arrived, they noticed that the rest of the pilots were assembled. No meeting was scheduled, just a natural happenstance. The ready room was their home. There'd be word, the latest scuttlebutt. *Deliverance?*

"Boys, take yer seats," Waldron said as he stepped inside, making his way forward.

The pilots did so and talking stopped. *The CO has something...*

Waldron counted off a few mimeographed sheets he held in his hand and gave them to the pilots in the aisle seats to pass down their rows. Evans took one from Hal and read it, as did the others.

Just a word to let you know how I feel. We are ready. We have had a very short time to train, and we have worked under the most severe difficulties. But we have truly done the best humanly possible. I actually believe that under these conditions, we are the best in the world. My greatest hope is that we encounter a favorable tactical situation, but if we don't and worst comes to worst, I want each of us to do his utmost to destroy our enemies. If there is only one plane left to make a final run-in, I want that man to go in and get a hit. May God be with us all. Good luck, happy landings, and give 'em hell.

Stunned by the words, Evans looked up and met the eyes of Waldron, standing in front of the Teletype screen. Waldron held his gaze. *Serious.* Evans looked back at the paper and read it again. *If there is only one plane left...*

Fifteen men would be flying fifteen TBDs tomorrow. Could *fourteen* be lost? Who would make it? Hal? Grant? Would Abbie survive?

Will I?

Waldron, his face full of fierce intensity, was as determined as Evans had ever seen him. Their CO waited for all to finish, all of them wondering about who that one man could be. Was it even possible that only one...?

From the other side of the room, Abbie broke through the tension.

"Don't worry. We'll be back, Skipper. I'm leaving for Kansas City in the morning."

The room burst into laughter, a deep, devil-may-care release that only men living with death could know, gallows humor familiar to each aviator. The ship's crew picked up on it. The Army guys going to Tokyo knew it was a one-way mission and joked about it with everyone. Those guys had courage.

Waldron nodded with his clever smile, and the pilots waited in expectation. *He's got a quip.*

"Very well, Abbie, but only after you deliver your tin fish into the side of a Jap carrier. When they're all down, I'll join you!"

Amid the laughs and smiles, it suddenly hit Evans. Fate would choose. If he were chosen to live for another day or month, or into his eighties, fate would choose. Fate had brought him *here* of all places, from the middle of a continent to the middle of the biggest ocean in the world. Throughout his life, Evans had not known the day nor the hour, but now he and the others had a pretty good idea. He could face it now, prepared, ready. He might die...or he might live. Regardless, *he got to live life on earth.* Into adulthood. Better than some unfortunate kids he knew growing up. The boy down the street had polio and died. *Fate.*

And here, tomorrow, he could make a difference for his country on Skipper Waldron's wing. A real difference. At that moment, he considered himself fortunate to be here, a torpedo plane pilot on America's newest carrier.

Their moods uncertain, the pilots filed out. Whitey grabbed Evans's arm. "Hey Squire, wanna play poker in Rusty's room till lights out? Could be big money."

Evans smiled. "Yeah, I'll be there in a bit. Just going topside for a moment."

CHAPTER 5

AFT BERTHING, USS *YORKTOWN*, JUNE 3, 1942

Aviation Radioman 3/c Lloyd Childers threw down his cards in front of him.

"Two pair, kings and queens!"

Five other Torpedo Three radiomen and mechanics checked the cards, and, with disgusted groans, threw theirs down for the next deal.

"Shit," Childers's brother Wayne muttered. "How much you got there, birthday boy?"

Childers smiled and tried to cover his pile of two-dollar bills. "Doin' all right, and I'm still a 20-year-old kid till midnight. Your deal?

"No, dammit, it's yours. And shuffle 'em good this time."

Darce eyed both with suspicion. "*Both* you Childers boys'r doin' pretty good."

Lloyd shuffled the cards as the enlisted men sat around a table under the neon overhead light of the berthing compartment. Taps would sound soon.

The Cajun wanted an answer. "Watcha gonna do with all that, *Child-airs?*"

"Nunya business, *Dar-say.*"

"Just deal," Phillips growled, impatient.

Childers felt the eyes of the Cajun on him. Darce was from New Orleans. He was worldly in the ways of cards and juke joints. The street. Lloyd and Wayne had grown up with the red dirt of the Oklahoma dust bowl between their teeth. Most of their people went west when the topsoil blew away. Mother had stayed, and the pile of money in front of her son now could buy a new steer. Or a jalopy truck.

"Leave him be. He's havin' a good run," Barkley said in his thick Mississippi drawl.

"I'm allowed to ensure we all fair and square," Darce nodded as Childers shuffled.

"Today?" Wayne goaded his brother to deal.

"Bobby, you in this one?" Lloyd asked.

"Nah, you guys go ahead," Brazier answered.

25

"You just gonna sit there all night, *Bra-ssiere?*" Darce mocked.

"I'm okay watching."

Darce took a drag on his Chesterfield. "I'll *bet* you like to watch, 'specially being named after a woman's unmentionable."

Brazier ignored Darce, having heard it all before. On what could be the last night of his life, gambling didn't feel right. He was no good at it anyhow. Passing the time with his mates, even the disagreeable ones, seemed better than wandering around the ship thinking about tomorrow.

Childers dealt and, after tossing a bill on the pot, arranged his cards. Four diamonds and one club. He'd have a flush if he could exchange his worthless three of clubs and draw a diamond. He detected Darce watching him. The other three threw rejected cards on the pile and drew from the deck.

Of the group, Lloyd Childers was among the oldest. Tomorrow he would turn twenty-one. Legal. He wouldn't mind buying a legal drink. Hell, with this pot he'd buy drinks for all the gunners, even Darce, who was eyeing him now. But that wasn't going to happen aboard *Yorktown*. The officers were rumored to have bootleg bottles stowed away, and sometimes the Doc gave them "medicinal" brandy after a rough flight. Childers could be in the same airplane and would receive nothing. *Too young*. Damn officers got away with murder. The same officers who could lift up his rack while Childers stood at attention during a surprise health-and-comfort inspection and find a thimbleful of hooch in his folded skivvies would later be taking swigs from fifths of whiskey in their staterooms. If Childers did that, 21 or no, he'd be keel-hauled by Skipper Massey – if Captain Buckmaster didn't get to him first.

Childers drew a card. Four of diamonds. Expressionless, he tossed another two on the pile. Darce was first to react.

"What you got, Childers?"

"Just bettin.' You in?"

"*Whachoo got*, dammit?"

Barkley rebuked him. "He's bluffin,' Darce. Now call him; ain't nobody that damn lucky."

Childers held the gaze of the Louisianan, who had experience peering into men's souls. Darce threw in another two, as did Wayne and Barkley. Phillips was out, shaking his head with his arms folded, and Brazier watched, content. Darce showed his hand first, knowing it was between him and Childers.

"All right, Okie. King-high straight. Top that."

Childers smiled and laid down his cards down faceup.

"Diamond flush."

"Damn!" Darce exploded, glaring at Childers across the table.

"Don't you wanna see what these guys have?" Childers asked in mock indignation.

"They ain't got *shit!*" Darce shot back. Vindicated, Childers pulled the pile of bills toward him before he scraped up the cards and handed them to Barkley.

"Damn, Lloyd, I might just make it tomorrow, so I think I'm done for the night before I go broke," Barkley said.

Darce continued to shake his head at Childers and muttered. *"Luckiest sumbitch..."*

As the game broke up, Dodson walked in. The 1MC sounded at the same time: *Ding, ding...ding.* 2130.

"Where you been, *Ben?"* Phillips asked.

"Topside. Flight deck. Beautiful sunset."

"Have any money? If you do, you'll just lose it here," Darce said, still upset at his loss – and Childers's luck.

"Darn, I wanted to see the sun set," Brazier reflected.

"To see your last one?" Darce quipped. An uneasy silence followed before Dodson answered, ignoring his squadron mate.

"There's still some twilight left. Master at Arms coppers are about though, darken ship an' all. I saw it through an open hatch near the LSO platform."

"What's the deck spot look like?" Barkley asked him.

"Scouts parked aft and fighters forward of the 'midships elevator, three rows of each. What are *we* doing?"

"Chief Esders told me we're gonna be ready at dawn to hit whatever the scouts find. The ordies are breaking out torpedoes from the magazines." Brazier volunteered.

"Load'n 'em in the hangar bay?" Childers asked Dodson.

"They've got dollies at the ready. Ever carried one?"

"Nope," Darce answered, then added, "Just hope Mister Smith can figure it out."

"None of these ensigns have ever carried 'em. Glad I'm flyin' with Chief Haas," Phillips said.

Childers was glad to be flying with Warrant Harry Corl, one of the three noncom pilots in the squadron. The green naval reserve ensigns were only a year older than Childers. His brother Wayne spoke next.

"Bobby, you're lucky to be flying with Chief Esders. He'll get you back."

Before Brazier answered, Darce interrupted. "Maybe so, but, if you're flyin' next to the CO there's gonna be extra attention on ya. A lot of it."

"I'm ready for 'em," Brazier said.

The men sat around the table, backs against their chairs. Wayne had his chair facing backward, his chin resting on his hands as the 1MC sounded.

"Now darken ship. Set condition two."

Phillips secured the fluorescent overhead and flicked on the red darken-ship lighting. "Darken ship. Say your damn prayers…"

Childers was excited. They all were. Tomorrow was *combat*; the officers said it was a sure thing and that the gunners could get revenge for Pearl Harbor. You could bet money on it.

"Any of you guys visit the chaplain?" Brazier asked.

Another uneasy silence followed. Chaplain visits were a personal thing, and that the question was asked by a Mormon made it all the more uncomfortable. Services had been held in the hangar bay that afternoon, and the Catholics had their mass in the officers' wardroom, but individual meetings with the chaplains? It was so strange. The Catholics all wanted private time with the priest, to unburden themselves, to confess their sins. "Grace" they called it.

"No," Barkley said. "I'm a believer an' all, an' I know I'm saved. If that day is tomorrow, I'm as ready as I can be."

"The guys in VT-5 did good at Coral Sea," Dodson said.

"If they so good, why ain't they here now?" Darce asked him.

"Our turn, I guess," Phillips volunteered.

Childers didn't like this talk. That afternoon the skipper had said they'd be lucky to get three planes to a drop point. Seventy-five percent losses! Would he be shot down on his birthday? If so, he'd take a Jap or two with him. Harry was a solid pilot. He'd get them out of any jam. Still, the thought unnerved him. Death. It could happen on any flight, but tomorrow would be different.

"The TBD can take punishment," Brazier said absentmindedly, just staring ahead at the table. "Us gunners can take down most of a division of fighters, unless they attack us with a whole squadron."

"We know not the day, nor the…"

"Knock it off, Darce," Childers barked with an edge. *Enough!*

"You really that ready, Troy? Ready to go to your reward now?" Dodson asked.

Barkley considered the question, and after a moment could only shrug. "Well, it's God's will, ain't it? I mean, livin' a full life, marrying a girl, settlin' down. Sure, I hope for that, hope for that for all of us, and God may give all of us that. But the Bible says nothin' is promised. So, I'll just get in the back of Mister Suesens plane tomorrow an' do my best."

Childers shuddered to think of it. *I don't have courage like Troy.*

Phillips pulled out a pack of Lucky's from his shirt pocket and patted out a smoke. Darce flicked open his lighter and held it for his fellow gunner. The least he could do.

"Got an extra pack for tomorrow?" Barkley asked Phillips.

"Got a whole carton! Probably'll smoke half in the ready room before we man planes!"

"You got a whole carton? Well, share some with us, dammit," Darce said as he closed his lighter. "Least we can smoke 'em now before they get soaked after our ensigns' water landings."

Dodson ignored him. "How long would you guys like to live?" he asked no one in particular.

Childers thought eighty would be a good length of days. Eighty years. A damn long time. He couldn't imagine another *twenty* years. He was about to offer that when Barkley jumped in.

"Ya know, living to the year 2000 would be something. Two thousand years since Jesus's birth." Barkley shook his head in amazement. "Maybe that'll be the second comin' – nice even number."

The year 2000. Almost incomprehensible to Childers.

"How old will you be then?" Dodson asked.

"Lessee," Barkley thought, doing the math in his head. "Ah…eighty-one."

Eighty-one! Childers thought. *I'll be seventy-nine if I make it that long. If I make it through tomorrow.*

"Eighty-one is pretty damn old," Phillips said. "My uncle was almost ninety when he died five years ago. He fought in the War Between the States. Served with General Joshua Lawrence Chamberlain."

"Wow! Was he with him at Little Round Top?" an amazed Dodson asked.

"No, but he was with him at Appomattox. Said he stood at attention and saluted when General Lee passed on his white horse."

"*Traveller* was the name of that horse," Barkley said, with the authority of one steeped in his heritage.

"So, Phillips, your ancestors shot at Troy's ancestors?" Darce asked as smoke wafted around him.

"Don't know anything except he was at Appomattox. Wish I could have talked with him about it. I was fourteen when he died but to me he was just an old man who sat on a wicker chair in the kitchen, always lookin' at his pocket watch. He was a train engineer after the war."

"A regular Casey Jones!" Barkley exclaimed.

"Too bad you didn't talk to him about the war," Wayne said.

"I didn't know."

"Where you from, Troy?" Phillips asked.

"Faulkner, Mississippi," Barkley said, nodding with pride. When no one reacted, he added, "It's just south of the Tennessee line, near Corinth."

"Never heard of it," Phillips said.

"Tupelo is the next largest town."

"Heard of that."

The 1MC crackled and Childers checked his watch. Almost taps. Where did the time go? It's going too fast!

Now stand by for the evening prayer...

The men in the berthing compartment stopped to listen as the speaker crackled again. Soon the voice of the chaplain echoed throughout the ship.

Dear Lord, as we lay down to sleep, we ask you to allay our fears. We know that tomorrow may bring battle, but nothing more is assured. We thank you for the beautiful red skies we enjoyed this evening and ask you for clear skies and safe steaming tomorrow. However, if we engage our earthly foe, we also ask for strength to face the dangers, and peace in our hearts that we remain in your protection. Lord, tonight calm our troubled hearts, let us not be afraid, and grant that we may serve you and our blessed United States to our utmost with faith in you and faith in each other. Continue to hold us, Lord, in the palm of your hand. Amen.

The compartment remained silent, and Childers suddenly wished he had gone topside to see the sunset when he'd had the chance. *St. Michael the Archangel, be with us in our day of battle...*

Brazier got up from the table. "Taps in a few minutes, and the Chief is gonna be in here to put us to bed."

"Too keyed up to sleep," Lloyd said.

"Me, too," Darce added. "I know. Let's celebrate your birthday, *Child*-airs. I swiped two cookies from the mess decks."

"Today, or last week?" Wayne asked.

"Today, dammit. They fresh. Here."

Darce lifted up his bottom rack and retrieved a napkin. Inside were two oatmeal and raisin cookies. Darce broke them in pieces to share, offering a piece to Childers first.

"Happy Birthday, you cheatin' Okie. Cookies and a Chesterfield to celebrate you coming of age on a broken tub in the middle of nowhere. All we need is a pitcher of pink lemonade."

"Darce, I'll never know why a bum like you smokes them Chesta-fields. You'd think you're some kind of officer or somethin', puttin' on airs." Barkley chided.

Darce patted out some cigarettes from the pack he held. "Any Joe can smoke Lucky's, but the Crescent City has class when it comes to cigarettes. You only live once. Here, my good underage men, Chesterfields all around."

"The smoking lamp will be out in a few minutes…" Brazier said, wishing he hadn't. Darce didn't miss a beat.

"What they gonna do? Put me in the back of a TBD with Ensign Smith?"

The men took the cigarettes that Darce offered and lit them, mindful that taps would sound in mere minutes.

"Don't say I never gave ya nothin', Okie."

"Thanks, Cajun."

"Happy Birthday, Child-airs."

Though baked by other sailors deep inside the bowels of *Yorktown*, the men – reminded of the comforts of home, kitchens with familiar smells, devoted mothers in aprons tending to something on the stove – munched on their wedges of American goodness. They had to finish their cigarettes before lights out. Maybe the chiefs would cut them some slack at bed check. Nobody wanted to sleep just yet, and Childers was turning twenty-one. Childers hoped Chief Esders would be the one to check on them. He'd look the other way.

"Gotta say, Darce, these officer cigarettes ain't bad," Phillips said.

"Yeah, live a little, ya know."

The 1 MC sounded with four bells.

Ding, ding…Ding, ding…Taps, taps. Lights out. Maintain silence about the decks. The smoking lamp is out throughout the ship. Now taps.

"Okay, *Lloyd*, the party's over." his brother said.

"Birthday's not for two more hours!" Childers protested.

Darce gobbled the last piece of his cookie and swallowed it. "This is just like Fat Tuesday in the Quarter. At midnight it all shuts down. 'Cept here on *Yorky*, it shuts down at 2200."

"Here's to sinkin' those yellow Japs tomorrow," Barkley said before polishing off his cookie fragment.

"They're gonna wake us in about five hours," Brazier said, and Childers' birthday party broke up before it started. Some men hung their chambray shirts on pegs near their rack, and others grabbed their dopp kits and shuffled to the head to brush their teeth. Hundreds of men in adjacent compartments did the same under the red lighting – and the regimentation – of their nighttime shipboard routine.

Childers crawled into his rack and pulled up the sheet. Wayne was above, and Phillips below. He'd met Phillips only months before, and now he was as much of a brother to him as Wayne was. They had also been together aboard *Saratoga* when it was torpedoed. Felt like an earthquake.

In the darkened compartment, he heard Darce's voice from the bunk cluster at his head.

"VT-2 sank the Jap carrier, and VT-5 got in some good licks. Now it's our turn to join the fun. Aye, aye, sir."

"Go to sleep, dammit," someone growled. *Dodson?*

Childers had been as excited as the rest of them when they got the word they were coming to *Yorktown*. Big talk about sending Tojo to kingdom come. And on his *birthday,* of all days. They'd have fighter help tomorrow, and the *Dauntlesses* would soften the Japs up before they went in to finish them off. Harry wouldn't miss, and Childers would protect their six. He rolled over and pulled the sheet up over his head.

With his eyes open, he thought about tomorrow. June 4th. What would it be like to see a *Zero* pointing at him? He wanted one to point at him, to have a chance to bag one, but at the same time he was terrified of it. Harry could sink the carrier; Childers would be happy to shoot one Jap plane. Something to tell his grandchildren…

He had encountered the VT-5 guys about a week ago in Pearl Harbor when the ship was in dry dock. He knew one from before December 7th, but he was different now, offering just a quick wave before ignoring Childers and going back to the banter of his mates. Unspoken was that they were in a club Childers did not yet belong to. They'd already been in combat. Tested by fire. Childers hadn't. He wanted to face the test, yet now trembled in fear under the sheet of his bunk. Would they all make it? Would he measure up?

Please help us, God.

He said a prayer, asking for strength, asking for courage, asking for sleep. He thought of the open skies of Norman, and red dust. And red meatballs painted on the wings of a *Zero* fighter. How he missed that red dust.

Rocked by gentle North Pacific swells and in the company of his brother and brothers, Aviation Radioman 3rd Lloyd Childers drifted off to sleep, and turned twenty-one.

Chapter 6

HIJMS *Hiryū*, 0430 June 4, 1942

Maruyama looked along the left side of the nose as he sat in the observer seat of his Type 97, parked among a pack of others behind the center elevator on *Hiryū's* flight deck. At the head was Tomonaga's plane, and ahead of him was a 135-meter stretch of wooden flight deck that rose and fell in a gentle rhythm. On the bow, a steam vapor line indicated the winds were in takeoff alignment, and, high on the island, the windsock lay out at full extension. Next to it, at the truck, the red-and-white ensign above a column of signal flags snapped in the breeze, silhouetted against the brightening eastern sky.

The last escort *Zero-sen* had just cleared the bow, waved aloft by hundreds of men crammed along the bow catwalks and island perches, waving their caps in wild, joyous enthusiasm in the same manner they had that December morning, and for the Darwin strike and Trincomalee. He and the others could not hear their shouts of *banzai* above the roar of the fighter as it jumped into the air. Behind Tomonaga, Maruyama and 16 more *kankōs* waited with idling engines. Ahead was *Hiryū's* rubber-stained and grimy deck, telling evidence of the last six months of hard combat. Airborne, the fighters turned easy left so the wingmen could join on the leaders as they climbed overhead.

The torpedo bombers were loaded with 800-kilogram bombs to be dropped in level delivery. Lieutenant Tomonaga appeared confident. His first lead from a ship. Maruyama had heard he had plenty of combat under his belt, but out here things were different. They chose Tomonaga. Who was he to question? He watched his flight leader taxi his camouflaged green Type 97 to the takeoff stripe, showing no trepidation.

In their wake, *Sōryū* launched fighters, which, like her sister ship *Hiryū*, would contribute another 18 *kankōs* to hit Sand Island. Far to starboard, the flagship was now launching her dive-bombers, and soon the first *Zero-sen* departed from *Kaga*.

Maruyama spoke into the voice tube. "Ready for takeoff, Nakao-sen?" He saw the pilot nod his head.

"Checklist complete! Ready for takeoff!" Seaman 1/c Nakao answered.

"Very well. Hamada, you ready back there?"

"Ready!" the gunner answered.

Maruyama nodded his acknowledgment. He then watched Tomonaga's plane gain speed as the heavy Type 97 accelerated down the deck. If Tomonaga could get airborne from his spot on the center elevator, they all could. Before Tomonaga got to the bow, his tailwheel lifted off the deck, and the bomber became airborne without trouble. Dozens of men on the catwalks watched him fly away as they cheered in wild, delirious gyrations.

To the southwest, plump *kanbaku* dive-bombers from the two CarDiv 1 carriers lifted into the air and initiated their rendezvous turns as *shotais* of CAP fighters overhead transited to their assigned patrol sectors. Maruyama evaluated the clouds: *scattered to occasional broken.* Visibility clear. In the level-bomber next to him, Chief Tatsu smiled at Maruyama from his own observer position in the middle of the airplane's glass cage. The *kankō* crews waited their turns for takeoff with eager impatience.

One by one they roared down *Hiryū's* deck and floated off the bow as the main wheels of each slowly retracted into the wings. With his charges following in trail, Tomonaga led them left in a climbing rendezvous circle over the ship. Behind them, *Sōryū's* level-bombers did the same according to doctrine.

Nakao added a bit of throttle and taxied into position behind Chief Tatsu's plane, now positioned for takeoff. *Hurry,* Maruyama thought. *Too much interval!* Nakao inched ahead, waiting his turn as their airplane vibrated from the firing cylinders. Flames flickered from the cowl flaps as Tatsu's pilot firewalled his throttle, and, as soon as it vacated its spot, Nakao moved into it and aligned the Type 97 on centerline.

"Here we go!" he shouted, which Maruyama and Hamada easily heard through their leather flying helmets.

Sudden yet familiar force pushed them back in their seats as Nakao released the brakes. The engine thundered at full power, and, as they passed the island, Maruyama looked up and saluted. Admiral Yamaguchi was on the wing and looked down at them as they roared past. Picking up speed, Maruyama caught glimpses of the beaming faces of the crew, many of whom he recognized. They continued to wave madly, having not lost any of their enthusiasm since the first *Zero-sen* had taken off five minutes earlier.

On centerline and feeling their heavy load underneath, they rolled over the red flight deck *hinomaru* as the deck edge loomed up. Maruyama felt the tail lift, and, like the others, the *kankō* separated from the deck. Underneath them, the knifing ship's bow and the cobalt water came into view.

Maruyama counted the Type 97s in the semicircle ahead: nine, and Tomonaga's first *chutai* was almost formed, six sleek silhouettes on the red sky. Busy with his cockpit tasks, Nakao cleaned up and trimmed the plane as he banked to the inside of the circle to get on bearing line. Behind him, Maruyama heard Hamada ready the guns as the *kankō's* engine sustained its muscular purr.

As Nakao turned their *kankō* through east, the sun peeked above the horizon, a bright red line radiating streaks of crimson among the gray clouds. The striking symbol of their national emblem emblazoned in the dawn sky was not lost on Nakao, who let out a spirited *banzai* as the nose of the bomber passed above the low sun.

Now on bearing line, his pilot concentrated on the join up while Maruyama noted the time and heading to Midway. A magnetic heading of 150 was almost their takeoff heading, and the Mobile Force would be able to close the atoll and recover them without much maneuvering. Maruyama liked the fuel cushion this afforded them and watched content while Nakao slid underneath Chief Tatsu's bomber as small flames spit from its cowl. Once Nakao was stable on the right wing, Tatsu-san smiled his encouragement and clenched his fists in excitement. Above, a *chutai* of escort fighters glided over Tomonaga's flight as the last Type 97 cleared *Hiryū's* bow. Maruyama checked the time: 0441.

Below, a float plane suddenly shot from the side of *Haruna* and reversed course to the north. *Poor devils*, Maruyama thought, glad that he was in a frontline unit and not off alone in a sputtering biplane with floats. He spotted another scout below, heading into the spectacular sunrise on another lonely 150-mile search leg.

Around them, strike aircraft from the other carriers joined in recognizable formations, and Maruyama guessed Tomonaga-san would do one more circle before setting out to the southeast. Abeam *Sōryū*, some three miles aft, he spotted the *kankōs* that would be part of a simultaneous attack, with Tomonaga's group hitting Sand Island and *Sōryū's* targeting the airfield facilities on Eastern. The rendezvous geometry was working perfectly, even better than the Darwin attack, and, with ninety degrees to go, Tomonaga would have each *chutai* of strike aircraft converging on him. He would then lead a giant 108-plane formation to the southeast.

As Nakao held position in the climb, Maruyama scanned the airspace around them. Glancing behind him, he caught Hamada communicating in makeshift semaphore with the gunner in the *kankō* to their right. "Look for the enemy!" Maruyama scolded as a chagrined Hamada complied.

Holes in the clouds were easy to navigate through as they climbed to cruising altitude, and, once above them, Maruyama saw that the surface was obscured unless he looked almost straight down. *Good,* he thought. *The Mobile Force is protected.* With Midway over an hour distant, he could hope for clear weather to see their assigned target: the fuel tanks along Sand Island's southeastern shore.

Leveling at 15,000 feet, Tomonaga leaned his fuel and adjusted the RPM for cruise. The other *chutais* were aboard now, with the *Sōryū* Type 97s to his left and the dive-bombers stepped down and right. Above them the fighters weaved back and forth along their flanks. Maruyama rode among an airborne armada of black-nosed warplanes. Most were camouflaged green, while the fighters wore a buff color. Each carried a large oblong shape beneath them, bombs or fuel tanks, and all had a simple red ball affixed to their fuselages and wing tips. Battle-hardened sons of Nippon flew them for a determined purpose in the service of the Emperor. They had transited for almost an hour when Nakao sang out.

"What's that? To the right and low, about two o'clock!"

Maruyama snapped his head right and picked it up, an American *Catalina.* The big seaplane seemed to hover as it turned toward a cloud buildup in which to hide.[1] The fighters did not yet seem interested. Maruyama looked toward the strike leader to ensure that he saw it. They continued on course, and soon the American was obscured by the clouds.

He consulted his chart. "We should be able to sight Midway in twenty or thirty minutes," Maruyama said into the voice tube for the benefit of his crew. "Keep a sharp lookout for Grummans; we are inside one hundred miles."

The Japanese formation, designed as a jab punch to prod the Americans at Pearl Harbor into action, continued southeast. Unconcerned by the American plane, they flew above the scattered clouds in silence. Maruyama expected the Americans to come up but was not too worried. Maybe an American Grumman would get lucky, but antiaircraft was more of a concern. Some of his mates would not return to *Hiryū,* but he could not think of that.

"How is our fuel?" he asked Nakao.

"Plenty – on schedule," the pilot answered.

"Good, get ready. Hamada-kun, *get ready.*"

---

[1] LTJG W.E. Chase, VP-23

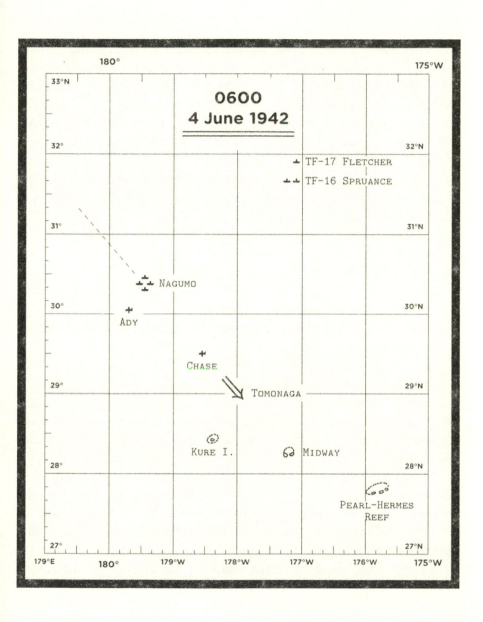

0600
4 June 1942

TF-17 Fletcher
TF-16 Spruance

Nagumo

Ady

Chase

Tomonaga

Kure I.

Midway

Pearl-Hermes
Reef

First Lieutenant Dan Iverson taxied his SBD *Dauntless* out of its spot on Eastern Island as the frantic lineman motioned him forward to catch up with the SBD ahead. Everyone on the flight line was going bananas, but to Iverson hurrying did no good when his flight lead was waiting for the major to take off anyway. The Japs were coming…as the colonel had said they would. The linesman taxied him forward with fear in his eyes, taking nervous glances at the sky, but neither Iverson nor the corporal directing him could do anything about it until the traffic ahead moved. *Keep yer shirt on, Mac.*

In the lead SBD, Major Henderson taxied to the runway as the new Navy torpedo bombers rolled for takeoff. Twin-engine Army bombers were next. Iverson squeezed this throat mic.

"Ready to go back there, Reid?"

No answer.

"Reid, can you hear me?"

Iverson turned in his seat and noticed Reid looking elsewhere. He shouted. "Reid! Can you hear me on the interphone?"

"No, sir!" Reid shouted back. Reid then tried his interphone; no response. "Didja hear that, sir?"

"No! Okay, we'll just have to shout. You ready?"

"Yes, sir! Green light from the tower!"

Iverson peered around the nose of his *Dauntless* to maintain proper taxi interval, the air raid sirens audible over the sound of his whirring engine mere feet ahead of him. He twisted in his seat to count the SBDs. Eighteen total, including him.

The sun had been up for over an hour, and skies were clear with only a few scattered clouds. The Army B-26s now rolled down the runway at double the normal takeoff interval. To the north, Iverson spotted the Navy Grummans[1] in a neatly spaced bearing-line rendezvous. The lead held a left-hand turn – going right at the Japs.

The major and his two wingmen rolled together and became airborne in section, their engine revs drowning out the wailing sirens. Along the runway, marines wearing old Brodie helmets test-fired their antiaircraft guns. To be sure, Iverson looked up into the blue – nothing.

---

[1] Six new TBF *Avengers* assigned to VT-8 that missed *Hornet*; LT Langdon Fieberling.

"Watch for Japs overhead, Reid!"

"Will do, sir!"

Another section of SBDs roared down Eastern's runway, and when it was Iverson's turn, he taxied onto the left half of the runway to allow "R" Bear, one of the green second looey's, to take position on his right wing. With his thumbs-up returned, they gunned their engines together and rolled down the runway as a formation.

Once airborne, Iverson followed Captain Glidden's section in a running rendezvous. Ahead, Major Henderson led them to the assembly area east of the atoll. Iverson's engine hummed as normal.

PowPowPowww

Iverson flinched in his seat at the sound of Reid test firing the twin .30s. He whipped his head back to see Reid checking the full firing arc of the barrels.

"'Preciate if you'd warn me next time!" Iverson shouted.

"Sorry, Lieutenant! Guns check good!"

"Good. Let me know if any of our guys don't make it!"

"Yes, sir!"

Iverson flew form and monitored his engine instruments. These new SBD-2s were nice; steady and fast, all metal fuselage and tough. He and most of the others had never dropped a bomb from one, and nobody in the squadron had combat experience.

In an easy turn on the inside, Iverson leaned his fuel. He'd need it later. The men in the SBDs next to him pointed back toward Midway. Iverson looked over his shoulder at Midway and saw large formations of green airplanes heading toward it. Above, wisps of contrails signified the presence of Major Parks and his fighters in their attack runs. Iverson hadn't heard anything on the radio.

"Reid, is the radio turned on and working?"

Reid fiddled with the set before shouting back his answer. "It's on, sir, but I can't hear nothin'. No DF either."

Iverson shook his head. *Fine.* No radio. He could see Major Henderson, and he could drop a bomb on whatever he was led to.

"Okay, skip it," Iverson shouted back. "Watch for Japs."

There it was.

Through the latticework of the cockpit canopy, Maruyama studied Midway through his binoculars. A faint circle of white on the sea, characteristic of so many Pacific atolls he had seen during the past six months. Resting on the far end of the circle were two small islands. Their target was on Sand Island, on the right some thirty miles distant.

Tomonaga banked left as the strike group followed. *Kankōs* from CarDiv 2 would attack in level delivery from northeast to southwest, minimizing ranging error on the fixed facilities. Once the Type 97s were in their run, Type 99 dive-bombers from *Akagi* and *Kaga* would float their turn and roll in from the southeast, out of the sun. With Midway now on the leading edge of their right wing, Maruyama had a clearer view, and specks of airplanes climbed from the runway on Eastern Island. In the lagoon he saw the wake of a small boat – no real warships. Surely the American flying boat had sent a warning. He scanned the skies around the atoll.

"Look for Grummans!" he barked as Tomonaga reversed them in an easy right-hand turn for the attack. Through his binoculars Maruyama focused on Eastern Island and saw a plane lift off. He studied it. Fighter? Dive-bomber?

Anticipating their run-in, Tomonaga's obedient wingmen tightened up. Behind him Maruyama noted the sun glint off the whirring propellers of *Hiryū's* black-nosed bombers.

Rolling out, he checked the switches and was about to move to the bombardier station when Nakao jerked the aircraft right.

"Grummans!" the pilot cried.

Maruyama looked up in time to see two of the American fighters dive past Tomonaga, fat barrels with big wings roaring through the formation in steep power dives.[1] The coloring of the Grumman fighters matched the sky, but as tracers rocketed past, his eyes were drawn to the black engine cylinders and blinking yellow lights on the wings. Maruyama saw one red-faced pilot clearly in his khaki helmet and flying suit. On the tubby fuselage was a huge white star.

The group leader's wing flamed up – *Tomonaga-san!* – and, from above, *Zero-sens* knifed down after the assailants to give chase. Black smoke from a burning *kankō* in the distant *Sōryū* formation produced a graceful curve down, and the formation became unsettled as the pilots nervously looked for more threat fighters.

"They're on fire!" Hamada shouted.

Flames from the *kankō* on their right wing billowed from the wing root as Maruyama and his mates watched their fellows struggle in the cockpit to put them out.

---

[1] Capt. J.F. Carey, 2Lt. C.M. Canfield, VMF-221

"It's Miyauchi!" Nakao cried in horror as the flames grew along the fuselage, watching as the frantic crewmen screamed in fear behind their pilot, Miyauchi, who held position with grim focus. The burning bomber drifted closer, and Maruyama could see their arms flailing amid the flames, burned hands working to throw the canopy back in wild panic. They were almost touching now, and were it not for the loud slipstream, Maruyama could have shouted encouragement to them. The fire grew, and the observer could no longer be seen in the cockpit as the Type 97 nosed down. In back, the gunner stood as he swatted at the relentless flames that funneled toward him inside the canopy, and, before it disappeared below the wing, a sickened Maruyama saw the gunner, his legs on fire, jump overboard in desperation.

Miyauchi!

His fire somehow extinguished, Tomonaga's plane trailed white mist from the wing as he continued in toward Sand with the surviving *kankōs*. To the south was a swirling dogfight of nimble *Zero-sens* and stubby American fighters. He caught a glimpse of one rectangular-winged Yankee burning as it corkscrewed down.

The seaplane hangar dominated Sand Island, and beyond it were the fuel tanks, their target. Forcing himself, Maruyama took his bombardier station, lying prone under the pilot, who continued to fly a loose formation on the *chutai* lead and Tomonaga. Maruyama found the hangar in the bombsight and waited until the fuel tanks drifted into view.

"Target in sight...*weapon armed*...two degrees left, fly heading two zero six!" Above, Nakao complied with his observer's instructions.

"Look for Grummans!" Maruyama shouted again, his eye glued to the bombsight.

"Hai!" Hamada shouted back.

The Type 97s continued in at 11,000 feet, and Nakao yelled, "Antiaircraft fire!" over the muffled cracks of detonations nearby. Maruyama held his concentration, fighting to anticipate drift that would require last-second corrections to Nakao. He would release the bomb once the sight crossed the edge of the big tank; a short hit would at least damage the smaller one.

Here and there, muzzle flashes dotted the sand and scrub. Lying prone, Maruyama could only ignore the hot American steel that was clawing its way skyward to meet him. Guns were all about the island, flashing yellow flames, silent reminders of an enraged enemy. He sensed Nakao drifting.

"Steady..."

The tanks came into view, and they were headed for the edge of the big one. *Still time for a quick correction.*

"Left one degree. *Left!*"

He assessed the wind from the gun smoke, a strong crosswind from seaward. *Blast!* Was there time to offset?

"Left one!" he snapped and felt the airplane respond under Nakao's hand. Bombs from the first *chutai* floated through the viewfinder as the crosshairs moved along the surface and touched the big tank.

"Release!" he cried as he pulled the bomb-release lever. The airplane shuddered with a welcome jump as the huge bomb fell free. Hamada couldn't contain himself.

"Banzai!"

Maruyama stayed on the sight, flinching as a shell detonated. The bomb time of fall was calculated for almost 20 seconds. While Nakao was free to maneuver as necessary, he maintained position on their lead and Tomonaga's *chutai* ahead. He wanted to sit up and see, to leave his vulnerable and cramped position, separated from hot lead by only thin aluminum. No protection. And no warning. The shells from flashes he saw seconds ago could be outside now.

Sharp cracks from antiaircraft sounded nearby, and Nakao cried in shock. *Sakamoto!* Maruyama forced himself to stay on the sight.

He then saw a flash on the main fuel tank with a huge secondary that generated an expanding shockwave from it. *Direct hit!*

"Direct hit!" Maruyama yelped, scrambling to extricate himself from the bombsight and sit up under the canopy. As he pulled himself up over the rail, he saw Sakamoto's plane trail black smoke and nose down. No movement in the cockpit was visible. Behind him, Hamada cried for his fellow gunner.

Ugly black puffs appeared among the formation as Tomonaga led them down the length of Sand Island. His *kankō* pilots could only hold position as they flew past at 150 knots of airspeed. The fire was heavy; sparks appeared on the tail of a bomber ahead that was sprayed with fragments. The American shells were leading them, and Maruyama checked that all the Type 97s were clean of their weapons. Sanctuary was to the west, and Tomonaga entered an easy turn over the breaking waves on the southern shoreline. Looking down, Maruyama saw numerous gun emplacements fire as if they were individual barrels in a rotating Gatling gun.

With the island falling back, heavy smoke rose over their target in a dense column and covered the seaplane base, all of it blown northwest. On Eastern it was the same, and Maruyama could see the *kanbakus* in their dives, flashes from their bomb hits on the parking aprons and runway. The skies over each island were filled with black smudges, and their perimeters belched a steady flame of antiaircraft, many of the guns heavy caliber. Tomonaga passed the lead and left the formation with his wingmen, circling northwest to get a better look and assess damage as the others continued west to the assembly area.

"See any Grummans?" Nakao asked over the voice tube.

Hamada answered. "None nearby. *Zero-sens* are dealing with them to the east. Our mates are scoring too!"

Around Maruyama, the *kankōs* formed up, some seeping fluid, others with canvas flapping from damaged control surfaces. One of the bombers had a gunner, his shoulder and arm bloody, slumped over the edge of his cockpit, jagged holes in the aluminum skin underneath him as evidence. Maruyama studied the ghastly image. *Who was he? What mate did I just lose?*

They were clear now, black puffs receding as they left the flaming islands behind. On them, the Americans continued to fire as flashes from high and low caliber guns sprinkled about the sandy scrub. Lucky for the Americans that their seaplane spotted them and sent a warning. The enemy was caught flat-footed at Pearl Harbor and Darwin, but Maruyama had never seen resistance like this.

"There goes Kikuchi-san with Araya. We are leading now!" Nakao cried.

The leader of the second *chutai* nosed his smoking *kankō* toward Kure Atoll to the west as his wingman Araya followed in escort. With Tomonaga and his wingmen in what was left of the first *chutai* gone back for reconnaissance, Maruyama now led the *Hiryū* level-bombers to the assembly area.

"Continue west. Once clear we'll begin a rendezvous turn."

"*Hai.*"

About him, only eight Type 97s remained as they closed up the formation. Observers and gunners took gulps from canteens and caught their breath from the tension of battle.

"Hamada, keep your eyes open. Let me know when you see the group leader come back," Maruyama ordered his gunner over the voice tube.

"*Hai.*"

Iverson – and every other head in 18 *Dauntless* cockpits – stole glances west as black smoke rose near the Sand Island seaplane hangars. Growing palls of smoke also bloomed on Eastern.

"Looks like the Navy guys are getting it," Reid shouted.

"Yes," Iverson shouted back, unable to intervene. He resumed his stationing, keeping on Major Henderson's wing line, who rolled out of the turn and steadied them up on a course of 320.

"We're on our way, Reid. Figurin' an hour, hour an' fifteen!"

"Yes, sir. Everyone's here!"

Fifteen miles to the west, Nakao entered a right turn and conserved fuel. Black smoke now towered over Midway, and, above them, high altitude winds carried it east. Far to his left, Maruyama saw Kure between breaks in the clouds. Lieutenant Kikuchi would make a water-landing there. Uninhabited. They'll probably spend the day sunning themselves. He informed the others.

"Kikuchi-san is nursing his sick plane toward the atoll to the west. They'll be rescued tomorrow, two days at most." Nakao glanced west to see for himself and nodded.

The *Sōryū* Type 97s joined up below in trail, and, alone or by twos, the *kanbaku* dive-bombers from the CarDiv 1 ships assembled. The *Sōryū* group seemed intact, and, for something to do, Maruyama counted them as he waited.

They all waited, a familiar experience. Wait for Tomonaga to rejoin and take them away from this place, then, after a long open-water transit, wait to land. Then wait to find out the next mission. Maruyama hoped it would not be back here, now an angry beehive of entrenched guns that still fired in the distance, despite the thick columns of black smoke rising from both islands. In the lagoon, he spotted the wake of a patrol boat. Studying it through the binoculars, he watched as the boat fired an automatic gun into the air.

Silhouetted by the smoke, sunlight glinted off the wings of three airplanes approaching them at level altitude. He found them in his glasses: black-nosed *kankōs*, surely Tomonaga-san. Nakao passed through west as Tomonaga maneuvered his formation on bearing line. Waves of *Zero-sens,* that Maruyama recognized by their crisp *shotais,* followed them from above. No American fighters were visible.

"Continue your turn. Tomonaga-san is joining."

Nakao acknowledged Maruyama and held his easy right turn as the others maintained position.

Tomonaga no longer trailed mist, and the lumbering Type 99s continued to straggle in from lower altitudes. A message group burst over the radio, one from the group leader. Maruyama recorded it, and his heart sank.

We must return here.

He kept this from the others as Tomonaga took the lead back and continued to circle over the assembly area so the returning *chutais* could join. He checked the time: 0705.

CHAPTER 7

FLAG SHELTER, USS *ENTERPRISE*, 0535 JUNE

Spruance pulled himself up the ladder and into the flag shelter as he scanned the horizon around *Enterprise*. Off to port was *Hornet*, about 4,000 yards he figured, and the screen positioning met his approval. Further to port the sun broke through the heavy clouds, and he assessed the calm weather and seas. Ingrained habit. On the flight deck aft, he heard an airplane engine chug at idle power.

Buracker and the others, their backs to the admiral, were hunched over the chart facing the radio speaker. Surprised by his admiral, Buracker stood up straight and was about to call attention, but Spruance raised his hand.

"Good morning, Admiral," Buracker said.

Browning and the others turned and stiffened to attention. "Good morning, sir," Browning said, his burning cigarette held in fingers along his trouser seam.

"Good morning gentlemen, and please, carry on. What news?"

Browning relaxed and stepped toward Spruance.

"Sir, we had a false alarm a half hour ago and had the pilots man the planes, but we've stood down. They're in the ready rooms. Deck's spotted for launch: CAP fighters followed by scouts and VB. Just waiting for the word now."

"Very well. Where's *Yorktown*?"

"North of us, sir. They've been flying this morning and we're maintaining visual on them."

Spruance stepped to the port gallery and surveyed the deck below. The after half of the ship was jammed with blue-gray airplanes, a deadly maze of wings and propeller blades. Except for a lone engine aft, they were quiet, and the men in the colorful jerseys walked among them like any other day. The irregular outline of *Hornet's* deck proved that she too had a deck-load of strike planes spotted aft. Peering over the rail he saw *Yorktown*, just visible to the north.

"Sir, we're monitoring the patrol aircraft frequency from Midway. They've had flying boats out all night. All we can do is wait."

45

Spruance put his maneuvering board on the shelf, and his aide, Lieutenant Oliver, handed him a cup of coffee. He sipped it and looked off to the west. *We'll find them soon enough.*

The staff was still huddled around the radio, staring at it as if it would talk to them, and, by the looks of the stuffed ashtray, they'd already smoked a pack of Chesterfields each.

"Miles, where are we from Midway?" Spruance asked.

Browning motioned a fix on the chart. "Admiral, we're here and Midway is about 230 miles south. We've been closing it during the night."

"How old is this fix?"

"Dawn, sir, backed up by the ship's dead reckoning plot."

"Where are we from the planned intercept point?"

"Southwest of us sir, but inside 200 miles."

"Very well. What do you think?"

"Admiral, given our standing orders, once we get a confirmed sighting report, we go. A problem is the winds, light from the southeast. We'll have to turn into it for launch, and if the Japs are where we think they are, we'll be opening."

Spruance nodded, imagining the triangle formed by two fleets and one island on the open ocean. Here and there disembodied voices broke through the radio static as Buracker and the others stared at the radio with arms folded, waiting for something to act upon.

More crackling static filled the silence in the shelter as the men pondered what was happening over the horizon. *How close are they? Have we been spotted?* Then, Morse signals in the clear.

...enemy carriers...

"Did you hear that?" an excited Browning said to no one.

"Yep, enemy carriers! That's from one of the *Catalinas*," Buracker said, smiling.

"Okay, where? What patrol plane?"

Spruance stood off to the side with hands behind his back, unable to do anything but wait. He had to hand it to the CINCPAC staff. *They were right.*

Minutes passed with nothing. *Enterprise* with her task force ships turned east to keep sight of *Yorktown*, which was in the midst of flight ops. Cigarette butts jammed the ashtrays as the officers tapped them out one after another. The time was 0545. The staff radioman listened...

...many planes...closing Midway three-two...one fifty miles...

"Was that *fifty* miles?" Browning barked, again to no one.

"No, sir, one fifty."

On the chart they plotted the bearing and range from Midway. Buracker pulled at his chin. "They're probably an hour away."

"Yes, but what kinds of planes, and how many is *many?*" Browning replied. Spruance assessed the back-and-forth of his staff, trying to piece together fragmented information as it came in on scratchy radios. The reports were both blessing and curse.

"And where are the damn carriers?" Browning growled in frustration. He looked at the radio as if expecting an answer.

"The planes are fueled and loaded?" Spruance asked.

"Yes, sir. Pilots standing by in their ready rooms."

Spruance nodded his understanding. His staff had been up half the night in nervous anticipation. Incomplete reports from pilots added to the tension. He glanced at Oliver, who jumped up to refill his porcelain coffee mug.

As the sun rose higher, the men sat waiting as the second hand on the bulkhead clock twitched with each passing second. The Jap attack group must have Midway in sight by now. Buracker stood to stretch as four bells sounded on the 1MC, followed by the bosun.

Reveille! Reveille! All hands heave to and trice up...

Spruance smiled to himself. *Enterprise,* and all the ships in the task force, were already wide awake, had been all night, and in relaxed general quarters. Minutes passed as his staff fretted in silence, like a wound up tension spring. The radio then crackled with a long Morse transmission, this time with clear and unambiguous words that tripped the release.

Two carriers and battleships heading Midway at high speed...three two zero, one eighty from Midway...[1]

Browning lunged at the dividers as all crowded over the chart. One officer plotted the bearing, and with a straight edge, ran a pencil line out to the northeast. Browning measured the range – and measured it again to be sure.

"That's a different *Catalina,*" Buracker offered.

Browning nodded. "Yeah...okay. Two carriers...where are the others?"

Spruance wanted to know that too, but for now he had positive identification on two carriers. *Whaddaya know. Right where Chester Nimitz said they'd be.*

While his staff plotted the sighting report and their current ship's posit, Spruance unrolled his maneuvering board. Baffled, Browning and Buracker watched. They had never seen anything like this admiral, a recluse who carried

---

[1] LT H.P. Ady, VP-23

a blank mo-board with him at all times, like some security blanket. Spruance then took a pencil from his pocket and marked the paper with an "N" on the top before asking for the ranges and bearings from Midway. Oliver watched him plot the information as if he were an officer of the deck, an ordinary lieutenant. Halsey barked orders and demanded answers; Admiral Spruance did it himself. *Does he think we can't plot a sighting report?*

The staff was dumbfounded as they watched Spruance silently mark the paper and measure the distance with the thumb and index finger of his hand.

"Is the contact report authenticated?"

"Yes, sir," Browning answered.

Spruance took the measure on the scale and thought out loud. "One seventy-five, and we're closing."

The others waited for a decision.

Spruance then rolled up the maneuvering board and faced Browning.

"Launch everything you've got at the earliest opportunity," he said quietly.

"Aye, aye, Admiral!" Browning said. He then pointed at Buracker. "Have the bridge signal the task force to steam us west at twenty knots. Get the group commander and COs up to the bridge. Pilots, man your planes. Oh yes, suggest to the captain that we go into GQ."

"Expected launch time?"

Browning looked at the clock: 0610.

"We'll shoot for zero-seven-hundred. Comm-O, signal *Hornet* and TF seventeen with blinking light: *'Steaming west at twenty to launch full complement at zero seven.'*"

"Aye, aye, sir."

While some officers left the shelter to accomplish their tasks, others passed orders on the voice pipe and sound-powered phones. Spruance motioned for Browning to sit beside him.

"What's your launch plan?"

Browning forced himself to be patient. Halsey would know, would have directed it himself. The staff knew what *he* was thinking, and he knew what *they* were thinking. The sequence and the why behind it was evident to all – all except this new admiral. Queer. Peculiar. This *is the best we've got?*

"Sir, we'll launch our CAP fighters first and then the VS and VB – our dive-bombers, sir – already spotted on deck. We'll launch them, the SBDs will hold overhead, and we'll bring up the escort fighters and torpeckers – ah, torpedo bombers sir."

"I understand all the nomenclature, Captain. Please continue."

"Yes, sir. *Hornet* will do likewise, and we'll go at them with a coordinated attack of dive-bombers from above and with TBDs coming in on the deck to finish them off. Mister McClusky has the group lead, and I find him dependable and aware of the importance of this first strike. Stanhope Ring over on *Hornet* is top drawer. We're going to get those two carriers, and chances are the other two are nearby and just missed by the PBY."

"Very well. What are the shortfalls?"

Browning bristled at being second-guessed by the black shoe. This wasn't some management job interview. *We're attacking the Japs, sir!*

"Admiral, I see none at the moment. In 45 minutes we we'll launch two deck-load attacks of over 100 airplanes, and they should arrive by 0930. Even if the Japs move at flank speed, that's only 75 miles from where they are right now. Our SBDs can scan quite a bit of ocean from high altitude and can lead the slower VT to them. We have plenty of firepower to attack four carriers, and more than enough for two."

Spruance wasn't convinced. *Something always goes awry.* But orders were orders: attack at first opportunity with everything he had.

"Admiral, we're manning the planes now and running west. I'd like to increase speed and run southwest until ten minutes prior to launch time. We should be able to shave fifteen, twenty miles before we turn into the wind to launch. That'll take no more than 30 minutes. Then we turn southwest and close them again. That should put us inside 150 miles for their return leg."

"Very well," Spruance said as he got up. Under him the deck tilted as *Enterprise* turned west, and he felt the *thrum* of her screws as the bridge increased turns. To starboard, the obedient screen ships matched the flagship's turn. Spruance assessed them, then the weather. Clouds seemed to have broken up since dawn. Light seas.

The 1MC sounded.

"General Quarters, General Quarters! All hands man your battle stations..."

The sounds of beating feet and shouted orders floated up from below. Hatches were dogged closed with metal clanks and gunners dropped ammo cans next to their light guns on the gallery decks. The flight deck burst with activity as dozens of men in multi-hued jerseys scrambled amid the maze of aluminum. Helmeted men lined the catwalks, their blue chambray shirts rolled down to cover forearms sunburned from months at sea.

"Ding, ding, ding, ding, ding..."

The time was 0630, and the task force ships bounded west with bones in their teeth.

Spruance peered down and saw Murray and Browning on the bridge wing below speaking with their aviators. The pilots – *commanding officers!* – were practically boys, with lieutenant bars on khaki collars that peeked out of their yellow Mae Wests. They each carried a plotting board to make dead reckoning calculations with grease pencil as they flew at dizzying speeds toward the enemy. He shook his head at the wonder of it.

Across the water was the shaded side of *Hornet*, the fleet's newest ship. *How are they doing?* he wondered.

A nervous Marc Mitscher stood on *Hornet's* starboard bridge wing and looked west.

Nagumo was out there; the patrol boys had found him as predicted. Now *his* boys were manning planes to smash Nagumo before he could counter. The Japs would discover the Americans before lunch – he knew it – and hoped Fletcher and Spruance did, too. He wished he could send more fighters with Ring but could not spare them.

Stan Ring was about to lead the greenest pilots in the fleet against the most experienced in the world. Would 59 airplanes be enough? He crushed his cigarette butt against the ashtray in disgust. *It was never enough.* Nagumo had a superior fighter, and Mitscher could only send half a squadron of *Wildcats* to protect Ring's three squadrons, one separated by altitude. Was Johnny Waldron right? Too late now.

With their pilots in the ready rooms, he had Ring and the squadron COs summoned to the bridge.

VF-8's Mitchell arrived first, and his eyes locked on Mitscher immediately. *Oh, oh,* Mitscher thought as the fighter squadron CO walked toward him with purpose.

"Captain, please, sir," Mitchell spoke in a low tone. "Let us go in with the VT."

An agitated Mitscher shook his head.

"No, Pat, we've been over this," he said, impatient with his petulant lieutenant. "You are needed and can perform better up high. You'll support Commander Ring and the dive-bombers. Do you read?"

"Aye, aye, sir," Mitchell answered, dejected. *Those poor bastards won't have a chance.*

Ring and the others arrived, and Mitscher motioned for them to come into the charthouse with him. He faced Ring.

"Your boys ready to go?"

"Yes, sir, Captain. Loaded and ready," Ring said, his helmet cinched tight. Mitscher noted his necktie, perfect dimple in place. The others had their collars open.

"Ruff?"

"Yes, sir, pilots are confident, planes in the pink," Johnson answered.

Mitscher nodded his understanding and turned to his VS skipper.

"How about your scouts, Walt?"

Rodee nodded. "Yes, sir. Ready."

Mitscher turned to Waldron. The pilot's eyes were determined, piercing. Not accusing, but impatient. *Johnny wants to kill something.*

"We're ready, sir," Waldron said, before Mitscher could ask.

Mitscher sensed Waldron wanted to say more, was holding it inside. He caught himself before asking Waldron to spill it. *There's no time.*

"Good. We'll launch the first CAP at zero-seven, then Walt's scouts, then you, Ruff. We'll get all of you off except half the VT. Then we'll bring you up, Johnny, and get your guys airborne as soon as we can. Nav plotted their position and our expected launch posit. A heading of 240 should bring you to them if they hold their course and speed. If there are changes, we'll blinker them to you, but right now 240 is your course. We'll close you after you depart, and I expect the flagship will have us on the reciprocal just outside 100 miles. They're launching their own attack, and you may encounter them en route, but, Stan, you're only responsible for your air group. Got it?"

"Yes, sir, Captain."

The squadron COs nodded. Mitscher noted Waldron breathing through his nose like a prizefighter in his corner, waiting for the bell.

"Johnny?"

Waldron couldn't hold it in any longer. While he still had a chance, he had to fight, to fight for his men.

"Captain, may we have *one* fighter to escort us?"

Before he could finish, Mitscher was shaking his head in pent-up frustration as he looked down at the deck. Perturbed himself, Ring took a step forward.

"Skipper, we've been through this!" Mitscher snapped. "The F4F handles better up high, there are more than twice as many planes than you up there for them to escort, and once Pat's fighters slash through their CAP, they'll be heading down to help you on the deck."

"Captain, we need *help*. This is their crackerjack team, *four* carriers from the intel – which has so far been right. We'll put fish in them, but my guys are flying a jalopy truck at 110 knots. Please sir, we can –"

"Johnny, I said no! And we are not discussing it anymore. Am I understood, Commander?"

Waldron's tight lips betrayed him, and he looked away. The entire bridge was silent as all – from COs to watch officers – were taken aback by the exchange. *He's arguing with the old man, Oklahoma Pete!*

Mitscher took a moment to compose himself as the embarrassed aviators stood waiting to be dismissed. Outside, the first *Wildcat* starting cartridge popped, a reminder to all that minutes were ticking away.

"Sea Hag, what are you flying?"

"Sir, I'll be in one of Ruff's bombers and will lead both SBD squadrons in a group. Johnny and his boys will be underneath. We'll join overhead until the last TBD gets airborne and joined, then head out as a group flying 240 as ordered."

Mitscher nodded his approval. "What if you don't see them at the end of your leg?"

"Sir, I'll bring us south to follow their track toward Midway –"

Conversation stopped as Waldron shook his head vigorously. Ring glared at him, and Mitscher's annoyance was evident. With everyone waiting, Waldron piped up again, facing Mitscher.

"Sir, they're gonna find us soon, and, when they do, they'll be coming northeast. Besides, they can't get too close to Midway because of the air threat."

"Waldron, you're guessing!" Ring snarled. "They don't know we're here, and they're focused on mopping up the island. They'll stay 100 miles off to soften it up and support the landing tomorrow."

"Sir, we would do that, but they don't have to! Their *Zeros* and Nakajimas can easily attack Midway from 200 miles. They risk too much by closing Midway, and I'm telling ya, sir, they're going to find us. Captain, I recommend an outbound heading of 250, at least 245. And once we get to the end, search north. It's imperative for my guys – and Pat's fighters – that we go right at them and not burn fuel in a search."

Ring was both dumbfounded and incensed by Waldron's insolence. He had never witnessed or even heard of such insubordination. And from a fellow Annapolis man! In public, on a ship's bridge, junior officers within earshot! There was no time to deal with this now, minutes from launching to destroy the Japanese task force. Below them, more cartridges fired, and more engines coughed to life. Johnny Waldron would not get his own group. Ring would make sure of it.

Mitscher placed his hand on Waldron's shoulder and could feel the tight muscles and tension within the pilot. Seeing one of his COs ready to explode caused him to try another approach. It dawned on him that this could be it for

Johnny. Before him stood a warrior. Waldron's conduct could be dealt with later. There'd be time for that after the battle.

"John, Commander Ring has the lead, and 240 is the heading we've been assigned by the flagship."

"Captain…"

"Skipper, we're all tense. You and your boys can do it; the VT boys on *Lexington* and *Yorktown* did well in the Coral Sea. We have a plan we've trained to, and we have our orders. We must man the airplanes now."

The time was 0639, and *Hornet* sprinted toward the southwest at 25 knots with the rest of the task force.

Mitscher, his ire gone, smiled as he shook the hands of each squadron CO, wishing them good luck. He squeezed Waldron's hand a bit longer, to convey support.

"Good hunting, Skipper."

Waldron nodded as their eyes met, professional enough to know he had fought the good fight. "We'll find 'em, sir, and we'll get hits." He nodded emphatically, as if convincing himself, already in the cockpit and leading his men. Mitscher grabbed Waldron's arm before letting him go. A foreboding came over him. *Johnny's not coming back.*

Ring allowed the others to leave the bridge ahead of him.

"I'm sorry, Captain."

"We're all tired. They can be forgiven."

"Sir, you were justified…"

"Stanhope, go. We'll discuss later. Good hunting."

Ring saluted and said, "Yes, sir. By your leave, sir." He then departed through the hatchway. Outside, four dozen reciprocating engines spun deadly propellers into a deafening roar as the pilots manned the airplanes. Mitscher sensed that the watch standers on his bridge were afraid to move. He needed to cut the tension, and stepped toward the 1MC microphone.

"Officer of the deck, report."

"Captain, we're steady on 240, making revolutions for 25 knots. Flagship orders next turn at zero-six-fifty to a launch heading."

"Very well," Mitscher replied. He rehearsed in his mind what he was going to tell the crew about the upcoming action. He motioned his readiness, and the bosun blew a four-note signal on his pipe into the microphone, signaling a message from the captain. Once the last note faded, he handed the microphone to Mitscher.

"*Hornet*, this is the captain," he said, looking ahead off the bow to the southwest.

CHAPTER 8

VMSB-241, NORTHWEST OF MIDWAY, 0655 JUNE 4, 1942

Through a hole in the clouds, Iverson saw it.

A Japanese carrier, at their eleven o'clock and fifteen miles.[1] Flat, with no superstructure that he could see, and a strange deck color. It turned away at high speed with an escorting destroyer crossing its wake.

"We've got 'em, Reid! Look for CAP!"

"Yes, sir!" the private shouted back, charging the gun.

Major Henderson gave the hand signal to descend to eager wingmen on either side of his cockpit. Glidden passed the signal, and Iverson relayed it down the echelon. He was puzzled. Why wasn't Henderson going for the carrier? He then saw why: another carrier, closer, on the nose.

Splashes erupted around the far carrier. *The Navy guys in those new Grumman torpedo planes?* He scanned the air around the carrier and to the west. Nothing.

A hole opened up in the clouds below: a ship! A big one with a huge pagoda mast and two massive turrets forward. *A battleship!* Muzzles blazed from its guns amidships before the behemoth was again covered by cloud.

Henderson pushed them steeper, increasing their airspeed to over 200. The carrier was inside ten miles and turning left, showing its broadside. On the hull and across from the little tower in the middle stretched a strange black slash. An airplane was on the flight deck. Taking off or landing? He couldn't tell.

"*Zeros!* Four o'clock!"

Iverson jerked his head right as Reid opened up with the .30s. All the gunners fired on three attackers who appeared as silent as barn owls, in for the kill. They went for Henderson, white mist from their machine gun rounds marking their killing paths.

As they pulled off, Henderson's *Dauntless* burst into flame.

"*Seven o'clock!*"

---

[1] HIJMS *Hiryū*

54

Three more enemy fighters roared over, and the sharp reports of their cannon produced terror inside the American cockpits. Major Henderson held on in his burning *Dauntless* as the SBD next to him sliced down with its left wing on fire. The *Zeros* zoomed up into the brilliant blue, red meatballs on wings that gleamed white in the sun. Iverson whipped his gaze from the Japanese to Henderson, then back to the carrier. It seemed to recede even as they approached at near redline airspeed.

Tat tat tat tat...tat tat tat tat tat tat tat

"Mister Iverson, we got one! We got one!"

Iverson felt punctures on the aluminum skin and heard the snaps of rounds passing by his ear. One ricocheted round rattled inside the fuselage. Wisps of gun smoke from cannon rounds formed translucent rings to mark their flight paths as the *Zeros* ripped another one of his mates from the sky. The carrier turned hard away, lengthening the run in. *We'll never make it.*

Henderson's burning plane spun out of control in a slow roll down, trailing heavy smoke. Others, either smoking or flaming, followed him. Iverson was too busy to count them. Three? Four? Elmer Glidden moved up to take the lead, but, at 4,000 feet, they were in among the puffy clouds and had lost sight of the carrier. They had to get lower.

Iverson entered the cold mist of a cloud, and, for a moment, felt secure. *I'm invisible; they're invisible.* He broke clear again, and the whole of the Japanese fleet spread out below him. Wakes large and thin inscribed white curves on the blue surface. Here and there flashes of gunfire erupted from the escorts, and the *Zeros* reappeared.

"Reid, there's lots of ships down here!"

"Lots of Japs up here, sir!" Reid bellowed before squeezing off another burst. Iverson then heard him shout, *"Motherfuckers!"* above the roaring engine.

The punctures on the wings – which sounded like pencils jabbed through foil – and the snaps outside were followed by the guttural roar of the attacker. Each hit registered in their spinal cords. The gunners fired back feverishly. Iverson saw the gunner next to him grit his teeth in fury and fear as he fired. Iverson closed up the formation and took peeks at the carrier. It had a red ball painted on the forward flight deck. Overhead, a plane circled lazily.

"You okay, Reid!"

"Yes, sir, but I'm low on ammo!"

They were running on the nearest carrier, which was running from them. Glidden leveled them off at 2,000 and shouted something into his throat mic. Iverson couldn't receive it, but he knew what to do.

His bomb was armed, switches set. Only ten SBDs remained, and the overwhelmed lieutenants flew formation while trying to skid away from the *Zeros*. At the same time, they had to make a glide bomb run in an unfamiliar airplane.

Iverson's left arm was locked, balls to the wall, damn the redline! Black AA puffs burst around him with loud detonations. Sparks flew off the prop and a chip appeared in the right quarter panel of the windscreen. He couldn't hold steady for Reid. Had to jink. Had to stay with the captain.

Whuff, whuff, whuff

"What the hell was that?" Reid cried.

Iverson didn't know himself. A shell burst behind the SBD to his right, and the pilot flinched into him. Iverson pushed down to avoid a midair and saw holes in their fuselage. No smoke.

Whissshhh

Fragments riddled the back of his plane, like a handful of gravel thrown against it, and Reid cried out.

"Sonofa*bitch! Fuck!*"

"You okay, Reid?" With the carrier under their nose, they were seconds away from release. Glidden kissed off his wingman and pushed over into his run.

"I'm hit! *Dammit!*"

"Where you hit? We're goin' in now!" Iverson shouted.

"In the foot sir…bleedin'…I can still fire."

"Okay – fire then!"

Iverson nosed over 10 degrees and left the throttle up. *To hell with the dive brakes. Don't know how to use the damn things, anyway.* The carrier was still turning left and presented its stern to them. Definitely a *Zero* on the big, yellow deck. Sudden flashes along the edges. He sensed lights float toward him and then zip past.

Whuff, whuff, whuff

It was antiaircraft! *Big!* The eerie sound was formed by shells piercing the air.

Passing one thousand feet, Iverson concentrated on his bombsight crosshairs, holding them steady on the wooden deck as his dive angle shallowed. The SBD shuddered from more punctures, more impacts. Glidden was off right, hosed by the carrier's machine gun tracer fire.

Eight hundred feet… men visible on the deck. Below, the raging rapids of a powerful wake churned the sea white.

Six hundred feet… Iverson had his hand on the release. Hold it steady… 230 knots… individual planks visible… That red circle… Flashing muzzles…

Iverson heaved on the release and felt the *Dauntless* lift as 500 pounds fell away. In back, Reid gave out a whoop before Iverson suddenly yanked the plane over on the right wing and pulled. A massive geyser from Glidden's bomb erupted next to the ship. The explosive spray came within mere feet away as they flew past. Arcs of tracers curved underneath them as Iverson found Glidden and another *Dauntless* hightailing it east. Another geyser. And another. Iverson could no longer assess his hit. The *Zeros* were back.

Iverson's left arm strained against the throttle, and he whipped his head around to search for fighters. Two of them bore in from the left, co-altitude, leading edges flashing. Iverson pushed down to the wave tops before resetting back up. The *Zeros* roared overhead before three more of the Mitsubishis came in from the ship. Iverson waited for the first to position before he stomped on the rudder to skid. The *Zero* missed high and boiled the water ahead of Iverson into a froth. *There's a* Dauntless. *Follow it. Captain Glidden or no, pick your way through the ships and get out of here.* He shouted over his shoulder.

"Reid! *Reid?*"

"Yes, sir!"

"You with me?"

"Yes, sir."

"If you can shoot something, shoot it!"

Iverson flew on instinct. *Sun. Fly to the sun.* Antiaircraft splashes raised geysers on the water ahead while smaller splashes from the spent machine gun rounds of the fighters stippled it. Ahead was a gray plane with a star. *Go with it.* The rudder pedals twitched under his boots like a nibble on a fishing line. *Bullet hits?* He checked the pedals, and felt relief when they responded. *Southeast to the sun. Run southeast.*

He flinched when the canopy frame on his left exploded. He felt a tug by his neck and reached for the microphone cord: *severed.* Useless anyway.

"Mister Iverson! There's one coming at our four!"

Iverson saw the *Zero* and turned into it. Saddled in, the enemy fighter pumped out cannon rounds as it maintained distance and pulled lead. Iverson pushed down, making the rounds miss high. Flying above the waves with nowhere else to go, Iverson pulled back in as the fighter repositioned. By instinct, Iverson chopped his throttle and selected the dive brakes. As the stubby SBD "stopped" in midair, the *Zero* roared past, unable to stay inside. As soon as the nose was off him, Iverson retracted the brakes and firewalled the throttle, looking for someone to join on.

He picked on open lane between two screening destroyers. Another *Dauntless* had the same idea a half-mile ahead. To his right were geysers around the battleship they had flown over. The *Vindicator* boys! Black smoke marked the flight path of one nosing down to the ocean.

The destroyer was at what he thought was a mile; he hadn't had enough experience around ships to be confident in the distance. A *Zero* swooped down to strafe his mate ahead, missing long as water churned up around the SBD.

Iverson's plane was shot up bad, and Reid wounded behind him. The engine ran rough, but the oil pressure held steady. Once Iverson got past the screen, there'd still be the fighters to contend with.

"Reid!" he shouted over his shoulder. "How're you doin'?"

"Okay, sir!"

"The gun work?"

"It's…sir."

Iverson couldn't hear his answer and craned his neck to check Reid's condition. Behind him, the carrier emerged from a curtain of smoke, evidence of at least one hit. He turned to get a better view, and saw he was trailing mist. *Fuel?* His gallons remaining indication was fine. *Must be oil from the sump.*

Somehow, he was heading southwest and crossed the destroyer's bow, looking down the barrel of its deck guns as he did. To the left were some *Vindicators*, which, like him and the rest of VMSB-241, scrambled to get out of there. Every man for himself now. A *Zero* came out of a cloud and blasted one of the hapless SB2Us with cannon. Engulfed in flames, it fell into the sea like a stone. He heard a metallic click behind him.

Tat tat…tat tat tat tat

What's Reid shooting at? He twisted his head left and picked it up at once – a black nose pulsing yellow from the cowl as rounds flew in front of them. Iverson lifted his nose up and stomped on the left rudder to spoil his aim. The Japanese pulled off and reversed over him. For an instant, their eyes met as the enemy pilot looked into Iverson's cockpit. *He's just a kid!*

The *Zero* flew off south, now attracted to a small covey of *Vindicators* clawing their way home. The old hand-me-down dive-bombers seemed to be pasted against the sky. Iverson banked left to join on them. Iverson's best guess for Midway was southeast toward the sun. He stayed on the waves as he looked for airplanes, gray ones to join on and khaki ones to avoid.

Are the Zeros gone? Around him were his marines, singletons or in section. Now, everyone was leery of everyone else. Better to escape and defend alone than to fly wing on someone and attract attention or not see an assailant coming.

They continued on a heading of 150. Clear of the screen, clear of the CAP fighters. In the shot-up bombers, men kept their heads moving to search for threats. Some of the marines began a shallow climb, and Iverson joined them. An SDB approached on his left wing. It was Captain Fleming, who pulled acute and took the lead on the left. Relieved, Iverson let him, and communicated his condition as best he could, showing the frayed end of his earphone cord. Fleming gave him a thumbs up as his gunner looked at Iverson's shredded plane with mouth open.

They climbed above the clouds, where others joined on them. Iverson counted only six. *Hope the other guys make it alone,* he thought. He knew all would not. He had seen the flaming scout bombers. Seen one explode. They got at least one hit on the carrier. Maybe it was his bomb. *Who won't be at chow tonight? Did the Navy fellows in their new planes make it okay?*

Would he and his squadron mates come back here today? Tomorrow?

An engine cylinder missed. Iverson had little choice but to ignore it; they were at least an hour from home with nothing below but water and cloud. Another SBD trailed faint smoke, but it seemed to be flying well. He had lost sight of the SB2Us, slower in the best of times. Iverson was just glad he wasn't flying one of the old canvas-covered beaters.

"Reid?"

The private shouted something back. Iverson nodded his head to show Reid he had heard him. *Still with me.*

Far down on the horizon, a column of black rose through the clouds. Midway. Iverson guessed at least fifty miles. His left-hand fuel tank indication was low – one tank probably holed and empty – but he figured he had 30 minutes, enough for fifty miles. He'd save some in the descent.

Now Glidden moved up to take the lead. Its prop feathered, one SBD fell out of formation, and Iverson watched it as long as he could. *A flying boat will find them.* He made a note on his plotting board.

"Reid!"

Behind him, Reid moaned something, as loud as he could in his weakened state. *He must be bleeding bad.* Iverson now saw the breaking surf on the north shore of the atoll. The engine chugged, and a puff of black flew over the windscreen. *C'mon.*

Sand Island was closer, and with the fuel low and engine acting up, he wasn't sure he'd make Eastern. Ditching short with a wounded Reid in back was the last resort. He made the decision – Eastern.

"Stay with me, Reid! Another ten minutes!" Iverson shouted.

"I'll make it, sir! I...all right."

As the other *Dauntlesses* sped ahead, Iverson flew over Sand Island. A heavy black pall rose up from the burning fuel tanks and the Navy seaplane apron. Below them a gun emplacement opened up with two half-hearted shots before it went silent. Next to it another emplacement smoked from a direct hit.

Iverson swung over the channel to line up on the runway at Eastern, itself burning near the arming area. He dropped the flaps. *Nothing.*

Cycling the switch didn't help. He groaned. A no-flapper…he could do it. Had to. The ailerons were holed but responding. So was the rudder, and he skidded left – *easy now* – to bleed off airspeed and line up.

With his right hand, he pushed down on the gear handle. The airplane yawed right as the gear lowered. Iverson sensed the reason, and the cockpit gear indication verified it. The left wheel was still up, or at least not down and locked. He needed to land *now.* Gear be damned. He inhaled to shout.

"Reid, we only have one wheel and no flaps. Hang on!"

"…sir!"

Iverson didn't see a green light to land. *Hell with it.* One SBD was rolling to the end; Iverson wouldn't get that far. He was committed now, and as he lined up, he saw men on their gun mounts stare up at him. He felt fast. *Hold it up as long as possible.* Once he had the runway made, he eased back on the throttle. A cylinder misfired… engine vibrating but running. *We're gonna make it!*

He held the nose down until near the runway threshold, then cut the engine and applied back pressure to the stick. The *Dauntless* floated in ground effect for a long time, still flying and not slowing. *Patience. Don't prang it.* He was committed: plenty of runway left. He began to settle and waited for the right main to touch. It kissed the runway – *hold it, hooold it* – and Iverson edged the stick right to keep the wing up. Without warning, the left wing fell and dug in, and the two marines were thrown to the right as the wounded plane made a violent and dusty half-loop to a stop.

In the distance, men cheered, and coral dust kicked up by the landing choked Iverson before it dissipated. Without the engine and slipstream noise, he could speak in a normal tone. He wanted water. And food.

Iverson unstrapped and cut a finger as he pulled himself up on the jagged metal canopy bow.

"*Sonofabitch*…You okay, Reid?"

"Yes, sir."

Iverson's empennage was a tattered metal mess, with most punctures inward and some metal shards splayed outward. Below, a stream of fluid splattered on the runway.

"How's yer foot?"

"Damn bullet or shrapnel cut the boot on the laces, sir. Bled for a while but I was able to stop it with my handkerchief. Guess the corpsman will hook me up with some mercurochrome or somethin'... Just hurts a lot."

Iverson inspected Reid's foot: torn up leather and blood. Didn't seem too deep. On the runway another SBD chugged past them after their landing, pilot and gunner waving. Iverson waved back, noticing the holes in their tail. *Is that Elmer?*

Reid hoisted himself up. The floor of his cockpit was littered with casings and smears of blood. Felt good to stretch. Good to be alive.

Iverson helped him out, and Reid tested the foot on the wing root.

"Good to go, sir. I'll live."

"Good man, Reid. Let's see what the head shed got."

Iverson jumped down and winced. Too long sitting.

"We got that carrier, sir. It was smokin' heavy."

Iverson nodded. "I thought Captain Blain was with us. You see him?"

"About halfway home I saw them fall out. Think they ditched, sir."

Iverson nodded again. He had made it. Major Henderson, Al Tweedy...they hadn't. Fell right in front of him. *Exploded* right in front...

They walked stiffly across the coral and matting toward the Operations tent as a fire from the arming area continued to blaze. Iverson scanned the sky to the east and saw a covey of dive-bombers. The SB2Us. *They made it!* He tried to count but they were weaving too close to each other to get an accurate number. *Looks like most made it. More than us anyway.* He shook his head at the thought of it. The canvas-and-bailing-wire *Wind Indicators* had just won the war.

Captain Fleming met them at the tent.

"Danny, was that you with the one-wheel landing?"

"Yes, sir."

"How's your plane otherwise?"

"Has some holes."

Fleming looked at Reid's blood-stained leg.

"Do *you* have some holes, Danny? You men okay?"

"We got nicked, sir."

Reid stepped forward. "A Jap bullet cut the lieutenant's earphone cord, sir." A sheepish Iverson grabbed the frayed end dangling from his flying helmet to prove it.

"Criminy sakes, Danny! You *sure* yer okay?"

"Yeah, I'm okay. Never knew it happened. We didn't have any radio or interphone anyway."

For a moment Fleming stared at Iverson's earphone cord in disbelief. *"You never knew...?"* He then turned to Reid. *"You* okay, Private Reid?"

"Yes, sir, good to go."

Fleming shook his head in amazement at the men.

"Okay, get the doc to bandage up your wound, and, if you can fly, we'll prob'ly go again this afternoon, so go easy on the sauce. Here come the *Vibrators*. Maybe they'll have more word."

Iverson and Reid turned to watch the clattering dive-bombers approach, close enough for a better count. Fewer than ten.

Fleming could only shake his head. "Yep...one ride I am *glaaad* is over."

Chapter 9

Navigation Bridge, HIJMS *Akagi*, 0700 June 4, 1942

Vice Admiral Chūichi Nagumo stood imperious as his chief of staff, Rear Admiral Ryūnosuke Kusaka, took the message from the orderly and read it as Genda watched him.

"Hmmm," Kusaka groaned. "Nagumo-sama, the group leader signals that another attack is necessary."

Nagumo absorbed the message and gave a nod of understanding. It had been folly for Combined Fleet to expect that one attack, even with 100 planes, could neutralize the American fortress. With the time built into the schedule, he could mop up the islands' defenses before Kondō landed his forces in the morning. The message from Tomonaga implied heavy resistance. *How many have I lost?*

A bugle sounded. *Air raid!* As gazes snapped south, gunfire commenced from the ring vessels. One of them made smoke. By instinct, the staff looked above the horizon to catch a glimpse of the attackers. What were they, and how many? Genda searched the sky with binoculars. *Trigger-happy gunners on the escorts must be frightened of a returning floatplane.* On the flight deck, crews ran to their stations as the entire *Kidō Butai* put their helms over to port.

"Americans. Looks like torpedo bombers. Four? Five? Can't see any others," Genda said.

Mere dots in the distance, diving *Zero-sens* pounced on the enemy planes and set them aflame one by one. The Americans had targeted *Hiryū* to port. As the *Zero-sens* scored, cheers erupted on the bridge and from flight deck galleries. One American[1] turned away toward *Nagara*, and Fuchida saw its planform in the distance and sensed it was bigger than the American Douglas torpedo planes. The last of the Americans burst into flames and splashed into the sea short of *Hiryū*. As *Akagi* sailors roared in elation, the lookout above them shouted a warning.

---

[1] ENS A.K. Earnest, AMM3c H.H. Ferrier, AMM3c J.D. Manning, Torpedo Eight Midway detachment.

"Starboard side! Six medium land-based planes approaching! On the horizon!"

Nagumo and the others stepped around the helmsman to observe as Captain Aoki maneuvered *Akagi* away from this new threat on their quarter: twin-engine bombers, hugging the surface.

"What are those planes? More *Mitchells?*" an incredulous Kusaka asked.

"Martin B-26s, Admiral," Genda volunteered. Mesmerized as the Americans bored in on the Mobile Force, straight at *Akagi*, he counted only four. Plane handlers on deck froze as the enemy approached while gunners fired for their lives. As flak burst around the Americans, *Zero-sens* tore into them. One attacking Type Zero flamed up and plunged into the sea, downed by American fire.

As the *Zero-sen* exploded on the water in a shower of spray, Genda's eyes widened. These twin-engine planes were fast, and not breaking off. Gunners in the catwalks and galleries opened fire on their assailants, and thunderous *booms* from the heavy guns rattled the bridge windows. Nagumo, too, felt the concussions, as he had from outgoing gunfire throughout a career spent on ship bridges. The sleek planes grew larger and did not drift. *Constant bearing.* A worried Aoki ordered the helmsman to shift his rudder, and the nervous sailor manhandled the ship's wheel in the opposite direction.

As they approached, one bomber exploded and rolled headlong into the sea. Cheers and shouts rose amid the staccato bursts of automatic fire and the deafening reports of the ship's main battery. Fuchida watched the remaining three continue, bearing down on *Akagi, bearing down on me!* Spray from antiaircraft mixed with CAP fighters pelted the water underneath the attackers, who showed no signs of retreat as they faced a full broadside of *Akagi's* antiaircraft fire.

"Are those torpedoes?" Kusaka asked. Aoki bolted to the bridge window to see for himself

"Hard right rudder!"

"Hard right rudder, aye, Captain!" the helmsman responded, pulling on the wheel. It came to a stop, hard over.

"Captain, my rudder is hard right!"

"Very well!"

Helpless to contribute, Nagumo's staff could only watch and wait for Aoki to deliver them. *Akagi's* heel increased as she turned toward the Americans. Through the spray on the surface, Aoki tried to discern torpedo wakes. He struggled to think among the roaring chatter of his guns. For now, he could only estimate a torpedo attack.

"Rudder amidships!"

The helmsman furiously complied, but everyone else on the bridge was still as the lead American bomber bore in at flight deck level – down their throat – without a single degree of heading drift. Tracers from the starboard bow gallery bracketed the plane above and below. As *Akagi* steadied out, her gunners could no longer bring even their automatic weapons to bear on it. Fuchida, a spectator, held his breath.

"Seppuku," Nagumo muttered, loud enough for Genda to hear. The American was going to hit the pilothouse and take them with him.

"Hit the deck!"

As some ducked behind the thin plating of the pilothouse, others faced the American madman with stoic resolve. Awestruck, they watched the strange craft race down the length of the flight deck. Men dove for cover as a gunner in the nose fired bursts from a single-barrel gun. Those on the bridge looked into the American cockpit and saw that the pilot and co-pilot wore cloth flying helmets and goggles.[1] The co-pilot grimaced in defiance as they roared past with engines at full power. Their big wingtip, with a navigation light they could almost touch, flashed only a few meters away. The strange bomber had a huge white star on the fuselage and a giant single tail, mangled from a hit. Damage from running the gauntlet of *Zero-sens* and antiaircraft was evident elsewhere on the aluminum skin, and the rear turret gunner was still. It was as if the bomber were taxiing aft, but at blinding speed. Witnesses on the bridge and flight deck gawked in wonder.

As the first speeding monster cleared *Akagi's* fantail, another followed it. Genda could only watch dumbstruck – *we're dead* – before the plane veered away from the bridge at the last second. Once the bomber cleared the ship aft, ready gunners tore it to pieces in a cacophony of automatic weapons. A huge fireball erupted as the speeding bomber nosed down and exploded next to the wake, sending up a giant shower of spray, flame, and twisted metal. Deep and raging animal cries and epithets rose from the men on deck. The cries were the only signal those on the bridge received that the threat was gone.

Aoki picked up the torpedo wake. His estimate correct, the torpedo bubbled down the port side and away. He shouted at the watch and lookouts to search for other torpedoes from the surviving American bombers that now fled from fighters and cruiser gunfire to the southwest. The unnerved captain rushed

---

[1] Lt. J.P. Muri, Lt. P.L. Moore, Lt. W.W. Moore, Lt. R. Johnson, S/Sgt. J. J. Gogoj, Cpl. F.L. Melo, Pfc. E.D. Ashley, 22nd BG

about the bridge as he scanned the horizon for threats and assessed his flight deck.

Nagumo was prone to acting. *Tomonaga was correct.* Nagumo's staff huddled with him near the chart table as he spoke.

"Kusaka, we can see that Midway remains a threat. We literally dodged a torpedo from capable land-based bombers the Americans fly as if one of our agile *Zero-sens*."

"Force Commander, I agree for the need to restrike, and soon, so they cannot rearm. It only takes one to get lucky."

"What can you send soonest?" Nagumo asked.

"Our own level-bombers and the dive-bombers in CarDiv 2 are fueled and loaded, but with torpedoes and armor-piercing bombs. We can rearm them with land-attack weapons within an hour. By then, the Midway aircraft will be arriving here for recovery."

"We must recover them."

"Yes, Admiral, and, with luck, we may be able to load and spot the planes we have in readiness. We'll close Midway another 20 miles. The first wave has a fuel reserve to circle while we launch."

Genda was skeptical – the morning attack had never been called "the first wave" – and his eyes met those of Fuchida. Rearm and spot for launch in an hour? *If all were perfect, it could not be done.* Nagumo explored another option.

"Could we recover this wave, reload them, and send fresh pilots?"

Kusaka was quick to answer. "We could, but we lose time waiting for their arrival, recovery, striking below, loading…and then the reverse."

He closed his eyes and counted on his fingertips before he continued.

"It would be well past noon when our second wave could reattack Midway, giving the enemy even more time to prepare. And if a third wave is required, we risk nightfall for our group recoveries and may not accomplish the goal of neutralizing the atoll for the landing tomorrow."

Nagumo held his jaw with one hand as he contemplated the chart. Outside, men shouted orders as they manhandled a Type Zero into a launch spot.

"I'm inclined to agree with you. The schedule must not be altered if we can avoid it."

Genda couldn't remain quiet.

"Force Commander, we can radio Admiral Kondō if required. The Americans *know* we are here."

Kusaka frowned at his subordinate. *Know your place, Genda!*

"Our orders are to remain *silent*, Genda. Here we saw a handful of American planes escape after a feeble and unsuccessful attack. Chances are that our escorts and CAP fighters downed the survivors minutes ago. It is unlikely they radioed accurate position reports."

Genda could not stay silent.

"Kusaka-san, they *know* we are here, have known it for over an hour from their flying boats that still shadow us. After we recover our attack planes, which may have wounded aboard, my recommendation is to consider a withdrawal north or west to regroup. We'll get a first-hand account of the damage and intact targets remaining from Tomonaga and our own pilot-observers. We can then attack at noon, and, as we did this morning, from a longer range that shields us from their threat. We are fortunate the winds favor us. Besides, we've not heard from the scouts yet."

Kusaka shook his head. "*No*, Genda! We cannot allow the Americans time to regroup and refortify; otherwise, we will suffer more losses from another half-strength attack. We have planes and crews at the ready; hitting them soonest is vital. Attacking two hours from *now* is much better than *perfect* in five or six."

"Kusaka-san, I agree we must restrike, but we've not heard from the scouts who should be approaching the ends of their outbound legs. Perhaps send the dive-bombers in CarDiv 2…"

"*Commander Genda!* Enough of this! In warfare, fortune favors the bold!" The impatient and perturbed Kusaka scowled at his impertinent junior. Nagumo watched and listened, somewhat amused by the exchange. Fuchida also listened from his folding chair against the bulkhead.

Genda held his ground. "Chief of Staff, if we recover, withdraw, and reassess with the knowledge of our searches, we can and should hit Midway with another full-strength attack. I believe we could accomplish that in four hours. And with our finest pilots, whom we held in reserve. We just saw enemy torpedo planes… a carrier-based type of a new, modern design…"

"Yes, but they were without fighter escort, without coordination – even from their own medium bombers within visual sight!"

"What if they came from a carrier, Kusaka-san? They've shown innovation and courage. We–"

"There are no carriers nearby," Nagumo murmured, which shocked all into silence. Minutes counted, and he had to end this.

"There are no carriers in these waters. If there were, we would have received warning from Combined Fleet. Scouts have been airborne for three hours and nothing. Genda, you are prudent and wise, but Kusaka-san is correct that we must act now and attack as soon as possible, at full strength, with the proper ordnance for land fortifications."

Nagumo turned to his chief of staff.

"Give the order. Reequip our CarDiv 1 level-bombers for land attack, and the CarDiv 2 dive-bombers with suitable land weapons."

"*Hai*, Force Commander," Kusaka said as he came to attention and saluted. His eyes swept past those of Genda before giving orders to the Communications Officer and Air Officer. The officers saluted.

Amid a flurry of shouted orders, Genda stood on the bridge wing and gazed at *Hiryū* 6,000 yards to port. Her deck was clear.

We are contravening an order, and too soon. And sending the "second wave" too soon.

He sensed someone step behind him. Turning, he saw the understanding face of his Force Commander.

Genda stiffened and offered a slight bow. He expected a rebuke.

"Genda-kun, you are right to argue your position, which is sound. These discussions are important for me to weigh courses of action."

"I serve at your pleasure, Force Commander."

Nagumo put his hand on his shoulder. "You are a brilliant planner and wish things to go perfectly, with every detail addressed. But now we are in it, and it falls on me to act without the luxury of peer review and superior critique. Time does not allow it."

Genda nodded, his lips tight from frustration and embarrassment. *I am correct!*

"We all want the same thing, Force Commander."

Nagumo smiled and squeezed Genda's arm before he walked to the other side of the cramped bridge. Genda fought back tears. *Why did I argue? What chance did I have?* He reflected that he should have whispered his fears to Kusaka-san instead of taking him on in public. Men of action, none of them had time. Orders given were obeyed at once, to the letter.

Except this order from Combined Fleet...

Fuchida sat near a window, a soft smile on his lips as he met the gaze of his friend. Genda returned it with a gentle tilt of his chin. *Yes, I too wish we were out there instead of in this prison cell.* It was easier out there. Just fly and fight. *Follow orders.* Turning back to the horizon, Genda had a sudden urge to go below and sleep.

The time was 0719.

Chapter 10

Flight Deck, USS *Enterprise*, 0710 June 4, 1942

Lieutenant junior-grade Bud Kroeger gave a thumbs-up to the Bombing Six ordnanceman who crouched next to his left wing.

The 1000-pound bomb secure, the red-shirted sailor looked for a way to scramble clear amid the spinning propellers and choking exhaust fumes from the SBDs ahead. The CAP fighters were already airborne, and the scouts were taking off from spots abeam the island. Kroeger's SBD was spotted on the Number 3 wire as *Enterprise* ploughed into the gentle seas to generate 25 knots of wind over the deck. The *Dauntlesses* in VB-6 would need it, carrying their heavy cargoes. Kroeger, flying with Skipper Best, would have a roll of 650 feet to the bow to get airborne. Signal flags snapped from the halyard: plenty of wind.

The SBDs of Lieutenant Lanham and XO Smith were acting up. Lanham's wasn't even started, and an impatient director motioned the mechs under the engine to clear away to push him out of traffic. The chief was standing on the wing next to Lanham as he cussed out the director, both shouting in rage. The deep *whirrr* of dozens of reciprocating engines around them was deafening, a vibration felt in their bones. Up forward, the roar of one of the scout SBDs at take-off power peaked and then faded as it became airborne. Even with the noise, the XO's plane wasn't sounding good, and looked like it was burning oil.

The CO was ahead in *Baker* 1. With unflappable calm and confidence, he nodded his approval to pull chocks. Fred Weber would go next, then Kroeger flying *Baker* 2. Plane pushers removed the tie-downs as Kroeger went over the takeoff checklist again. Relentless gusts of sea air mixed with gasoline exhaust swirled about his cockpit.

To the northeast, *Hornet* conducted her own launch with her own dangerous buzz saw of deadly propellers spinning over crouching men and live bombs. Kroeger wondered if they were going to launch their VT squadron as *Enterprise* would do once the VS and VB were launched. Bringing them up and spotting them would take time; Kroeger hoped it wouldn't be too long as he and the others burned fuel as they waited. Going out together with some 100 planes was something he had never seen. The *Devastators* would have a hard time keeping up, and *two* squadrons of the old clunkers would be near impossible.

The director appeared and Kroeger gave him a thumbs-up. "Halterman, here we go."

"All set, sir!" the radioman said over the interphone.

Lieutenant Best held his brakes and went to full power as the launching officer waved his flag in furious motion over his head. Kroeger watched his skipper give the controls a wipe-out as helmeted gunners along the catwalks and officers on the bridge gallery also watched and waited. Satisfied with the strong sound of *Baker* 1's engine, the launch officer lunged and pointed forward. At that, Best released the brakes and the SBD bolted ahead. With purposeful movements of the rudder, the CO rolled toward the gently rising bow. Kroeger and the others watched close to determine where his main wheels would leave the deck before reaching the end. As it approached the bow, *Baker* 1 levitated into the air. *We'll make it,* Kroeger thought.

Following his director's signals, Weber eased ahead and lined up for takeoff. Another director taxied Kroeger behind him, and Weber's exhaust flowed into and through the open cockpit. Off the bow to the right, the CO cleaned up and reversed left into the sun to initiate his rendezvous turn.

With his prop spinner mere feet behind Weber's rudder, Kroeger held his brakes in wait. Prop wash from *Baker* 3 at full power buffeted Kroeger's wings as he and Halterman bounced in their seats. Weber roared away, revealing the launch officer who now motioned to Kroeger to taxi forward before Weber had cleared the bow. He signaled a slight turn and Kroeger tapped the right brake as he modulated the throttle to taxi.

Enterprise rose and fell on the long swells, and with the flight deck empty before him, Kroeger carried a half ton more than he normally did. Skipper Best and Fred were safely airborne, but, in his mind, Kroeger prepared himself for any number of events that could put *Baker* 2 in the drink with a speeding carrier bearing down on them. His fingers grazed over the jettison handle to jog his muscle memory, and he pushed hard on the brakes in anticipation.

Impatient, the launch officer waved his flag and pointed at Kroeger, who jammed the throttle to the firewall. Manifold pressure – good. RPM – good. Oil pressure – good. His *Dauntless* bucked and strained as he held it in position on deck. Kroeger sensed the men along the island and the officers in the island galleries watching him. *Ready.*

He waited for the launch signal as his leg muscles burned to keep the SBD in place. Satisfied with the engine revs, the launch officer knelt and pointed into the wind.

With his left arm locked against the throttle, Kroeger released the brakes and his bomber jumped forward. His taps on the rudder pedals to maintain alignment down the deck were as natural as walking. Now past the island, he noticed the faces of men in the bow catwalks, some with arms held high, waving encouragement. It reminded him of a track meet. *Running free to the tape!*

Through his seat, Kroeger felt each plank and expansion joint his tires rolled over. His tail wheel came off, which allowed him to see the deck edge race up. With gentle pressure on the rudder pedals, he maintained his heading and soon felt resistance on the stick. The bow disappeared under his cowl, and, as it did, he sensed lift. He rolled to the deck edge, then bunted the nose to gain airspeed. *Baker* 2 was carried aloft by the warm North Pacific air.

Veering right, he slapped up the gear and flaps and entered a gentle climb. To his left, he saw Weber join on the skipper in a left-hand turn. He reversed into them as a sleek destroyer passed underneath.

The time was 0718.

Once on bearing line, he glanced around him. Above, Scouting Six were almost all joined; Group Commander McClusky was somewhere in that gaggle. To the east, a swarm of planes orbited over *Hornet* her air group mirrored their launch. *Yorktown* was around someplace, but he couldn't find her and concentrated on his join up.

He slid under the CO and popped up on his right. Best signaled him to check fuel: 285 gallons remaining. He signaled that back to Best, who answered with a thumbs-up and a nod.

Others joined, and once the rest of Bombing Six was aboard, Kroeger and his mates could only wait and watch the deck. An SBD near the island had men milling about – *XO's plane?* – and another pushed forward. They took it to the elevator to strike it below. From the midships elevator, a TBD rode to the flight deck. Overhead, the SBDs circled in lazy, fuel-burning turns as the pilots watched the delays on the flight deck below. After another wide circle, only two more VT-6 planes were on the deck, pushed by the sailors to their starting spots. Across the circle, Kroeger saw that the sky over *Hornet* was full of planes. *Are they going to wait for us?*

Minutes dragged, nerves frayed, and gallons remaining dwindled. Next to him, Skipper Best fumed. The torpeckers were nowhere close to being ready for launch. Outside of the turn, Kroeger closed the canopy to reduce drag and flew close to Best so as not to burn more fuel than necessary. Flying form, he admired the thousand-pounder his CO carried under him, a big weapon he also carried. He glanced down and saw 273 gallons. *C'mon guys.*

The time was 0745.

The pilots fidgeted in their cockpits as they flew easy circles, annoyed and then exasperated at the delay and already worried about their return fuel states. Behind them, their gunners sat and waited, resigned. Kroeger could only fly form. *It's always something.*

Now the fighter escorts for VT-6 were coming up on the two forward elevators. *Wish we had them,* Kroeger thought. At least he and his wingman SBDs had a chance against a Mitsubishi. Tying the *Wildcats* to the torpeckers was the right thing to do; he didn't resent them. What he did resent was holding, now for a full thirty minutes, the scout bombers even longer. He checked *Hornet* – and saw no planes over her! Incredulous, he scanned around the ship and caught her big gaggle of SBDs heading southwest, their VT squadron below them. *Those guys are leaving on their own!*

All 18 Scouting Six birds were up, and Kroeger wondered if the XO and the others down there would join Bombing Six on this attack. *XO's gonna be hacked if he misses out.*

Another circle, another two gallons. It was the waiting that killed him. Hurry up and wait. The wait in the ready room, since long before sunrise, had been interminable. Silent, each man alone with his thoughts as they sat shoulder to shoulder.

Kroeger saw Skipper Best nod emphatically. *What's going on?* The scouts rolled out to the southwest and entered a climb. The CO motioned with his hand to steady up, then signaled for a climb. Kroeger noted *Enterprise* with planes still cluttered aft, but the SBDs were heading out now, no question. He selected interphone.

"Guess we're pushing out, Halterman. The rest will have to catch up best they can."

"Yessir. I saw a Morse signal from the ship. Think they told us to go."

"Good, we don't have gas to wait all day."

"Yes, sir."

The time was 0754.

Stabilized, Kroeger noted the time and the heading: 231 magnetic. He pulled out his plotting board, marked the heading, and figured a ground speed in the climb of 130 knots. Checking the sea surface through gaps in the clouds, winds were light with only an occasional whitecap to discern direction. Once level, they'd accelerate to 150. Another hour. One more hour of waiting.

Passing 8,000 feet on the way up, they were met by a layer of white puffy clouds that stretched west to the horizon. Thirty-three SBD *Dauntless* dive-bombers of the *Enterprise* Air Group, armed and loaded, flew over the gleaming clouds and into the sunlit blue. Searching around him and through the breaks, Kroeger found no other planes from *Hornet* or *Yorktown*. *Enterprise* had sent her SBDs alone.

Bud Kroeger flew on his CO's wing, monitored the engine instruments, and thought about what they would meet over the horizon.

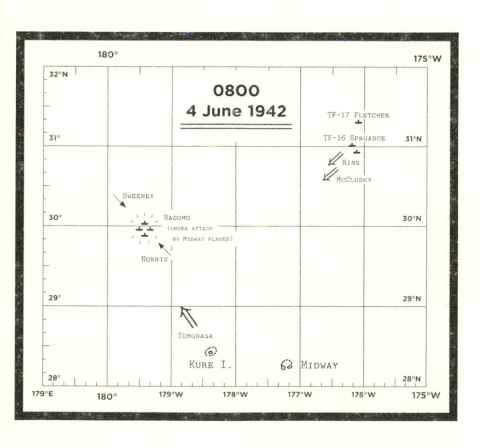

CHAPTER 11

HIJMS *AKAGI*, 0800 JUNE 4, 1942

Nagumo considered Midway as he stood at the port bridge window. On the flight deck behind him, a Type Zero recovered from patrol chugged and popped as it taxied forward to the elevator. His secretary Nishibayashi handed him a glass of water, and someone shouted that another CAP fighter was circling overhead for landing.

He would hit Midway twice: first with the reserves now rearming and then with Tomonaga's group sent back in the late afternoon to clean up any remaining resistance. At dusk he would retire northwest, then circle south to support Tanaka tomorrow. Not having perfect information gnawed at him. *How many planes had Tomonaga lost?* He wouldn't know for at least an hour.

His mind distracted, Nagumo stepped to the forward windows for a change in scenery. Staff and bridge watch standers, aware of his presence at all times, moved aside in the crowded space, then filled in behind as he passed. Off the starboard bow, *Tone's* blinker sent something to the flagship. He could read it himself but would let his staff inform him. Their job.

Nagumo stopped next to Aoki, who surveyed the screen ship positioning and his available sea room. The idling fighter on the forward elevator suddenly disappeared into the hangar bay below.

"That was a close shave back there," Nagumo murmured to him.

"Yes, Force Commander. I just received word that two of my men perished from machine gun attack."

"Loyal sons of Nippon. They died in great glory."

"Yes, Force Commander."

They stood in silence as *Akagi* and the Mobile Force continued southeast toward Midway – and Tomonaga's returning attack group.

From the chart table, Kusaka groaned in frustration, loud enough for Nagumo to hear. He stood impassively, as was the custom of admirals. Kusaka would inform him within a half-minute, and he heard him approach.

"Force Commander, *Tone* Number 4 plane reports as follows: Sight what appears to be 10 enemy surface units. Bearing 010 degrees, distance 240 miles from Midway. Course 150 degrees. Speed over 20 knots."

Nagumo brushed past Aoki and the helmsman toward the chart table. Lieutenant Commander Ono, the intelligence officer, plotted the position as the rest of the staff huddled along the table edges.

"Ten enemy surface units, but what kind?" Nagumo growled to no one. With the dividers, Ono measured the distance to the *Kido Butai*.

"Ha! Only 225 miles distant! We can hit him."

Nagumo needed more.

"Ascertain ship types and maintain contact! Radio him. At once!"

"*Hai*, Force Commander," Kusaka answered, and ensured that the message was transmitted.

An apprehensive Genda stood near the hatchway. *Ten ships to the northeast? Heading southeast at high speed...*

It then hit him. *Into the wind!*

With no time to confer, Nagumo acted. "Kusaka, Aoki. Belay rearming. Put torpedoes back on all planes. Message CarDiv 2 to load planes for ship attack."

The staff, now electrified, swung into action, and signalmen blinked the message to *Kaga* and *Hiryū* from the Morse lamps topside.

Nagumo and his brain trust remained at the chart table. Genda spoke.

"Force Commander, ten ships...by themselves? There *must* be a carrier among them."

"Our scout planes cannot discern a carrier?"

"Admiral, it is a possibility we must consider."

"Yes, and, by this chart, we can see that we are between two enemy forces. We'll deal with the ships to the northeast first."

Kusaka jumped in.

"Wise, Force Commander. Even if a carrier *is* present, at this range their torpedo and fighter planes cannot reach us, and their dive-bombers are at their extreme range. They must steam at least an hour to give them a chance. It would be foolhardy to attack with no fighter escort. We have time to prepare. Besides, their reported course and speed indicates they are steaming away from us."

Genda saw the flaws at once. He warned himself to be diplomatic and lowered his voice so the watch standers could not hear.

"Kusaka-san, we just saw them attack us without fighters, and they are steaming *into the wind*. We *know* we've been spotted, and they could have a shuttle-bomb attack planned at extreme range followed by landing at Midway."

"All the more reason to neutralize Midway, which you opposed thirty minutes ago," Kusaka replied dismissively.

Nagumo raised his hand. "We are closing the enemy and preparing to strike him. If the scout spots a carrier, we'll be ready, and I want frequent reports from him. Masuda, when can you launch the strike?"

The Air Officer was fast on his feet.

"Force Commander, we could launch what we and CarDiv 2 have in readiness right now by...0830, allowing for spot and warm up. My estimation is that only half our torpedo bombers are still configured with torpedoes. We could launch them and the dive-bombers of CarDiv 2."

"Fighters?" Genda asked.

Masuda's pained expression betrayed him.

"Twelve...maybe twenty. We'll need a similar number for our defenses here. But we must keep in mind the Tomonaga force. They'll return in 45 minutes. To get this attack wave off, we must order it at once or wait until after the Tomonaga force is recovered and struck below. If all goes well, we could launch by 0945. This would give us added time to configure all the *kankōs* with torpedoes."

Nagumo and the others considered Masuda's assessment of what their carrier flight decks could actually accomplish. Even the battleship men knew these things took time. *The Americans are so close!*

Lookouts reported gunfire from screen ships to the south. All craned their necks and narrowed their eyes to see the action on the horizon.

"More Americans?" Ono wondered.

A lookout burst into the bridge.

"*Sōryū* reports enemy high-level bombers sighted to the northwest!"

A coordinated pincer attack? Genda wondered to himself. Fuchida pulled himself up to look aft.

Through their binoculars, Aoki and Kusaka scanned the southern horizon.

"Another attack from Midway? Can you see them?"

"No, Kusaka-san, too many low clouds, but the screen sees something." On the horizon, a destroyer blinked a message Aoki could not decipher. Overhead, a *shotai* of fighters roared southeast.

Out of the clouds, a flaming plane trailed black smoke to the sea.

"Action to the southeast," Kusaka said.

Another flame fell straight out of the clouds and disappeared once it touched the horizon. The men watched in silence, unsure if the plane was American or Japanese.

Squinting, Fuchida observed the skies to the northwest. He gave a play-by-play report as would a baseball broadcaster. "Boeing high-level bombers," he said. "*Sōryū* is taking evasive action."

"There they are!" Ono pointed off the bow.

A formation of American dive-bombers emerged from the clouds, one of them burning and trailing black smoke.[1]

Genda studied them through the binoculars. "Carrier-based dive- bombers – but coming from the direction of Midway," he offered.

"They are attacking the CarDiv 2 flagship." Oishi said.

Genda made a face. *Ineffective glide bombing. Americans such as these are who defeated CarDiv 5 in the Coral Sea?* The staff had professional contempt for their fellows in *Shokaku* and *Zuikaku*, but was *this* amateur attack the level of skill that had turned them back, postponing the southern operation? He remained quiet and watched the inept display. The burning plane, in a steady parabola, plunged into the sea with a visible splash.

Unnerved, Nagumo watched the surviving Americans approach *Hiryū*. "Where are our CAP fighters?" he asked. No one answered, spellbound at another suicidal Yankee attempt. The tight formation pulled off over the carrier, and all held their breath.

In close sequence, geysers erupted around *Hiryū*, climbing to over 100 meters high. For a moment the entire ship was obscured by the heavy spray.

"*Please,*" Nagumo whispered.

Hiryū emerged from the veil, unscathed.

With broad smiles, Nagumo's staff let out their collective breath, and Oishi joked about the close call. "*Hiryū's* laundry will be working overtime tonight!" The men laughed.

Zero-sens culled the American formation as a fascinated Genda watched with professional interest. Outside, *Akagi's* captain scanned aft, monitoring the B-17s high to the north.[2]

The bomber formation drifted apart. *Three are coming at me*, Aoki thought. He handed the binoculars to his Air Officer. The aviator had better eyesight.

"Masuda, watch them. Are their bomb bays open?"

After a few seconds of study, Masuda answered. "They are open, Captain." *Zero*-sens on the deck behind them warmed up to relieve the CAP.

---

[1] VMSB-241 SBD attack, Maj. L.R. Henderson
[2] Lt.Col. W.C. Sweeney, 431st BS

"Very well. Let me know at once when you see bombs falling free." Aoki stepped around the island aft to check for any escorts close to his starboard beam. *Good. Open water.*

"Here they come, Captain! Falling free!"

"Right standard rudder!" Aoki shouted as he stepped back into the pilothouse. "Right standard rudder!" he repeated so the helmsman would respond.

"Captain, my rudder is right standard!"

"Very well, increase your rudder to right full! Maintain ahead standard!" Nagumo and his staff kept silent in professional courtesy. Genda checked the seconds tick by on his watch.

As both helmsmen responded, Aoki joined Masuda outside. *Sōryū* and *Hiryū* also maneuvered hard to throw off the aim of the Boeings.

"You have them?"

"There," Masuda pointed.

A cluster of heavy bombs floated down toward them. They held position on each other as they fell through the air. Silent. Seconds from impact, both officers perceived they would explode close to their still-roiling wake. *Akagi* heeled hard from the turn.

The sea next to the wake exploded in a tightly packed line of gray smoke and white spray. Water was still climbing into the air when the rapid-fire thunder from the explosions met their ears, shook them, and echoed off the hull. To the east, *Hiryū* heeled starboard as it turned to evade. Keeping a wary eye above, Aoki watched the bombers turn south, unconcerned about the few *Zero-sens* that followed.

Inside, the admiral and his staff stared at the chart, their only dependable source of information. Nagumo pushed his hand across his forehead.

"Kusaka, I *want...to...know* the composition of the American surface force! What's the delay?"

"Admiral, during the attack we received a report that they turned to 080."

"Very well, Chief of Staff, but *what are they?*" Nagumo fumed under his breath, struggling to maintain control so as not to cause undue concern among the ship's sailors. Unforgivable. He clenched his teeth tight. *We are behind schedule.*

"*Haruna* is under attack," someone pointed out.

Genda welcomed the perverse respite from the tension as he watched *Haruna* maneuver. Flashes and cordite smoke seemed to cover the battleship's superstructure as it defended. Genda shook his head. *More lackadaisical Americans in another pathetic glide bombing attack.* One bomber flamed up and exploded halfway to its final resting place.[1]

"A carrier dive-bomber of an obsolete design, Force Commander," Genda informed him.

Nagumo said nothing. How many more planes did Midway have? An existential threat, the atoll had to be dealt with. The American ships? Maybe a threat if a carrier was among them, maybe not. Midway was more known than unknown, and the air group leader was little help. *Restrike?* With no amplifying information? Nagumo pondered the options he had before him, all urgent and all necessary *now*. Midway and the American ships both had to be dealt with, but what truly was the priority? He needed double his force. He had to act...his responsibility. Doubt crept in. *Did I act too soon?*

Kusaka left him, and though surrounded by his staff and watch standers on the overcrowded bridge, Nagumo felt alone with his thoughts.

It felt good.

---

[1] VMSB-241 SB2U attack, Maj. B.W. Norris

Chapter 12

Torpedo Eight, Southwest of USS *Hornet*, 0810 June 4, 1942

Belted in the seat of his cockpit, an agitated John Waldron looked as if he would explode.

From his position three miles below the rest of the *Hornet* Air Group, Waldron monitored the SBDs and *Wildcats* while he worked the navigation problem on his plotting board tray. Evans sensed Waldron was angry. No, irritated. No, frustrated. He went over a list of words that could capture the emotions of his CO as a scowling Waldron peered down the echelon of his TBDs, beginning with Evans. The skipper glanced right and assessed, then back to the plotting board. They were holding 238 magnetic. Evans remembered hearing a base intercept course of 240 before they had bolted from the ready room. *Is that close enough?*

High above, through breaks in the clouds, the bombers and fighters flew a double vee formation and edged ahead of Evans and his mates. They looked like a flock of geese flying south for the winter. He couldn't tell the exact heading of CHAG Ring and the SBDs, but it was basically southwest. Pilots on the ends of the formation jockeyed their throttles to remain in position. Evans was glad he didn't have to. As they flew, the VT pilots stole glances skyward. They had only been gone 15 minutes and had at least another hour to go…if the Japanese were there. *What had happened to the* Enterprise *birds?*

Waldron could not keep still in the cockpit, and, seated behind him, Chief Dobbs pressed his throat microphone at regular intervals. Evans assumed they were having a conversation. Waldron kept looking to starboard. Evans looked off his nose to see what his CO was eyeing. Nothing but empty horizon.

"We're going in the wrong direction."

The sudden radio transmission jolted Evans, and he looked over at Hal, who did not appear concerned. On Waldron's left wing, Moose maintained formation with no reaction.

A minute passed. No answer. Was he hearing things? Did the CO mean to use the interphone with Dobbs?

"You're going in the wrong direction for the Japanese carrier force."

That was *the skipper!* Evans grasped. No doubt. On the radio, and for every ensign and radioman to hear. For the *Japanese* to hear. A new and terse voice answered: *Sea Hag.*

"I'm leading this flight!" Ring barked. "You fly on us right here!"

Evans and the rest of the formation pilots exchanged glances. Next to him, Hal repressed a grin, and Moose was indifferent. Evans, however, was shocked. *Is this how commanders talk to each other?*

"I know where the damn Jap fleet is," Waldron answered, defiant.

Evans couldn't believe his ears as he watched Waldron transmit, practically barking the words as his head moved with emphasis. Holding his position on the CO, he took peeks at the vee high above. A seething Sea Hag answered.

"*You fly on us!* I'm leading this formation. You fly on us!"

Above them, the giant formation continued on, as did Torpedo Eight on the surface. All the pilots and gunners, except Waldron, were astonished by the very public argument. Evans held his breath and imagined that everyone on the net was holding theirs, too. The profane backtalk was too incredible, too *unfathomable* to comprehend. Evans searched his memory. Had he ever heard of public arguing with a coach over a play selection? A professor over a letter grade? A supervisor over work assignments? What did this mean? What was going on between these two men?

A silent minute passed, another two miles passed, but the old man wasn't done. Waldron's eyes met those of Evans before giving a head nod toward him. *The skipper is turning us!*

"The hell with you," Waldron transmitted.

Evans felt a cold and electric sensation run the length of his body. By reflex, he tweaked the throttle and moved the controls to maintain his position in formation as the CO turned into him. If Sea Hag responded to the rebuke, Evans didn't hear it. *Where is the skipper taking us?*

He remembered Waldron's word when he said that if he had to find the Japs by himself, he would. *We must find them and hit them first. If we fail, there won't be a ship to come back to.*

Waldron rolled out, signaling with the tomahawk chop signal Evans had learned in flight school to steady up on a given heading. Waldron then clenched his fist in front of him, his silly signal for attack. To Evans, it seemed as if he were grabbing the Japs by the throat.

Evans checked the formation around him. Fourteen TBDs held position. *What just happened?*

Genda noticed the quiet.

As the last of the Americans flew off – almost fifty enemy planes had attacked the *Kido Butai* in the past hour – the bridge of *Akagi* returned to order and watch standers went about their duties with calm efficiency. Below decks, arming crews continued to rearm the *kankōs* two at a time. Soon, the force would turn into the wind to recover the morning strike. Genda reflected that he was standing at the nerve center of the finest carrier strike force in the world.

Fifty airplanes of all types – *and the Americans have not so much as scratched the paint on our hulls.* Half of the Americans had been either shot down or had escaped to limp home with their dead in damaged and wheezing wrecks.

Nagumo radiated tension, and *Tone's* enigmatic float plane dominated his thoughts. He was powerless to make this plane report, to reach into their cockpit and shake some urgency into them from 200 miles away. Genda realized the search plan was one *he* had devised, starting with what the Force could spare, authorized with a cursory nod from Kusaka. He didn't know if the Force Commander had ever seen it. The float plane pilots would receive training once this ended. He would see to it. Like his admiral, Genda was uneasy. *Maybe we should have...*

A message came in and Ono read it aloud. "Report from *Tone* Number 4…the enemy is composed of five cruisers and five destroyers."

He smiled in satisfaction. "Just as I thought. There are no carriers."

Not so optimistic, Nagumo said nothing. A suspect report from a junior pilot in a creaky float plane. He turned to his chief of staff.

"What do you think, Kusaka?"

His face strained, Kusaka struggled to answer. "Admiral, he reported ten ships and has now identified them. That said, I'm still unconvinced. The report does not mean a carrier is not nearby."

Nagumo nodded, frustrated at the truth in Kusaka's words. He wanted to scream. Oishi approached them.

"Message from the screen, sir. The Midway strike force is approaching." Genda took a step toward Nagumo to hear better. Kusaka began.

"Admiral, once we launch the CAP relief, we must recover them. It will take thirty minutes, forty at most. Then we can swap out the ready attack aircraft."

"To attack what? I'm inclined to hit the ships."

"Midway remains a threat, but for now we must recover," Kusaka answered.

And steam west, Genda thought, hoping that his admirals could somehow hear his thundering mind. Too many unforeseen variables! His plan with its rigid timeline had not survived first contact. *Throw it out!*

Like the First Air Fleet staff, the Mobile Force ships were confused and thrown off-balance by the unusual American attacks with all manner of planes from all points of the compass – except east. Now the Tomonaga force was back, and someone had reported a periscope sighting as destroyers raced to the attack.[1] *We must take a breath and think,* Genda thought.

Another message came in from *Tone.*

"The enemy is accompanied by what appears to be a carrier."

Nagumo slammed the table with his open hand, and the tension on the bridge shot through the overhead.

"What *appears* to be a carrier! A *carrier!*" Nagumo bellowed. "We needed this information thirty minutes ago!"

Embarrassed and fearful, no one spoke. Kusaka collected himself in the nervous silence.

"Force Commander, you are correct. However, they remain well over 200 miles away. We can now properly load our ready planes as we recover the Midway planes. We can then spot them, and launch a coordinated strike against the enemy carrier from all our ships."

"When!" Nagumo thundered.

Kusaka swallowed as he thought. "Not long after 1000, Force Commander."

Genda stepped up. "I agree, Force Commander, and if it's not a full complement, it will be close. We should launch each deck load as soon as they are ready. No delays for stragglers."

Nagumo breathed through his nose, trying to control his rage. The Force needed to close Midway in order to recover the planes airborne, then sprint to the northeast and close the American carrier from 200 miles. If he were still outside 200, so be it. He had to strike now. *What is an American carrier doing here?*

Form battle line. Admiral Togo did so 37-years earlier at Tsushima to defeat the Russians, *a western navy,* signaling the arrival of Japan as a world power. A decisive battle all the officers of the *Kido Butai* had studied in detail. A battle fought by the commander in chief himself. From the bridge of *Mikasa,* Togo just swirled his fingers over his head and his column crossed the Russian "T." Simple. Effective.

Nagumo nodded to himself. *Yamamoto-san wants that, to cross the American "T" when they come out of Hawaiian waters. To share in the glory. To turn back time.*

---

[1] USS *Nautilus,* LCDR W.H. Brockman

To be young again. He caught himself nodding in thought. *The staff is watching you!*

Some forty years later, *everything* was different. Now flimsy flying machines ranged 200 miles – *almost half a day's steam!* – to find and then *sink* ships on the open ocean. *Submarines* added an even more lethal dimension to naval warfare. After Etajima, he had become expert in naval rifles and torpedoes. None of his professors could ever have imagined *this*.

Ono stepped between Kusaka and Oishi, his eyes submissive. Nagumo sensed he was about to be disappointed again.

"Admiral, another message from the *Tone* scout: Two additional enemy ships, apparently cruisers, sighted. Bearing 008, distance 250 miles from Midway. Course 150. Speed 20 knots."

Nagumo threw up his hands and scowled at Kusaka. Ono took the dividers and plotted the sighting report, thankful to busy himself away from the heat directed at the chief of staff. Kusaka had not yet answered when he was handed another dispatch.

After he read it, Kusaka spoke in a low tone, knowing he was about to deliver a message the Force Commander did not want to hear.

"Admiral, from blinking light message relay Commander CarDiv 2: Deem it advisable to launch immediately."

At his limit, Nagumo exhaled and turned toward *Hiryū* and its junior admiral. *Yamaguchi cannot wait to take my job.*

"Noted…and no response," Nagumo said, frowning at Yamaguchi's flagship across the waves while she recovered her CAP. Your *ship is still* my *ship!* He felt a growing tightness in his chest.

I need to get off this bridge, for just a moment.

Akagi's flight deck was clear, waiting for their dive-bombers and fighters to return. Below, in the hangar bays, the armorers toiled reconfiguring his planes in the rising heat of mid-morning. Nagumo had to stay at his post, even with the privileges afforded a force commander.

Musada spoke into the loudspeaker. *"Clear Deck! Commence landing the attack group!"*

Formations of his planes arrived overhead and took landing interval on each other in a manner Nagumo still did not understand. They just did, and somehow landed without crashing. He could appreciate the dangers. Battleship gun turrets were dangerous. Torpedo attack was dangerous. He well understood why.

Nagumo watched as the first Type Zero snagged a wire, was freed, and taxied forward, a strange machine from outer space.

CHAPTER 13

TORPEDO EIGHT, NORTH OF MIDWAY, 0825 JUNE 4, 1942

Bill Evans could not get over it.

Skipper Waldron had just told off Sea Hag, and on the radio, so the whole Pacific Fleet could hear! Without even answering, Ring and the SBDs had continued southwest.

He glanced to his right. His roommate Hal held position in the formation. Down the line, the others maneuvered in a manner that resembled an accordion as they maintained their places out of the turn. Behind Evans, the XO's division flew as one in trail.

What's the skipper doing? he thought, still stunned that the CO had left the group formation. The rest of the squadron followed him; not to do so was unthinkable, but what *was* he thinking? In the TBD next to Waldron, Moose concentrated on flying form. By instinct, Evans checked the time: 0825.

Stretching his neck in both directions, Evans counted all fifteen *Devastators*. High to the left, the scouts and VB continued on in their big vee formations. Through breaks in the clouds, he saw the fighters in trail.

Waldron was head down in the cockpit, glancing up only to stay level, as he worked his plotting board. Ahead was a crisp – and empty – horizon, covered by scattered clouds. Any clouds were welcome. Evans checked their heading: west. Sea Hag led the SBDs and fighters southwest. *Where is the skipper going? We'll miss them to the north.* Now finished with his plotting-board calculations, Waldron looked straight off his nose, not moving a muscle.

"Mistah Evans, what's going on?" Bibb asked over the interphone.

"We're followin' the CO. No change."

"Sir, somethin's not right."

Evans agreed but remained silent.

The hell with you!

Evans and Bibb had heard it. The whole squadron had heard it. *The* Hornet *Air Group* had heard it. Bibb deserved an honest answer, but, just as dumbfounded, Evans didn't know what to say. He turned his head to Hal who shrugged as if to say, *hell if I know*.

"We're stayin' with the CO, Bibb. Nothing on the horizon, but I bet we're inside an hour from the Japs. Anything more and we'll have to turn back for fuel."

"Yes, sir."

"Relax for now. Still see 'em?"

"Yes, sir, nine o'clock high. Can barely make them out. All the TBDs are here."

"Good. Track the VB as long as you can. The Japs may find them first."

"Yes, sir."

Waldron motioned for them to continue straight ahead. He then turned to Evans and, with an open hand, pushed him away. Evans passed the signal to Hal, who passed it down the line. The TBDs opened up to form a scouting line, each aircraft scanning the sea ahead for anything: a mast, stack gas, AA puffs. Evans had seen the black marks the *Hornet* gunners had formed in training, had seen the newsreel images of the pockmarked sky over Pearl Harbor. He had never seen *enemy* antiaircraft but imagined he would in the next hour.

Once the XO's division moved into position and took station, the entire 15-plane squadron was steady on 270 in a line abreast. In the middle of it, Evans was confident. He and his mates had flown this formation before. *A scouting line.* Find and kill the enemy. They were spread out over a mile, and Waldron led his obedient pilots below 1,000 feet. There, they would better pick up any irregularities on that stark line where the sea met the sky.

Evans's senses were alive. He was aware of every cylinder firing, every wisp of slipstream that entered the cockpit. The sky between the clouds was the clearest he had ever seen, the sea a crystalline royal blue velvet. He was in a warplane, shoulder-to-shoulder with fourteen fellow pilots, the gunners behind them shoulder-to-shoulder with their fellows. All scanned the skies, checked the navigation, their manifold pressures, the gallons remaining, their guns, and the time. Evans couldn't wait to write about this day, in detail, with the clarity of one who had been there, one who could *remember with advantages*.

The skipper would find them for sure; the old Oglala Sioux was never more determined. He sat composed in his cockpit, scanning the horizon and his wing placement with a technique learned in flight school, a technique passed down to Evans and the others in Pensacola, a technique Evans himself would one day teach to the hordes of men cramming the recruiting offices to join him out here in a scouting line of armed aircraft. He glanced left and right, up and down the line. Torpedo Eight flew as one, not one plane drifting, maintaining perfect position on each other. Waldron led them into battle as he had trained them, modern day *Zouaves* marching to the sound of the guns.

The 2,000-pound Mk 13 below him swayed in place. Evans found he could handle this new sensation and trimmed T-3 as a natural extension of his being. His plane felt strong, poised to strike. *Deadly*. American steel, delivered by his hand, would strike against Japanese steel – and the men on the other side of it – sending them and their ship to Valhalla. *One thousand yards, eighty feet at eighty knots*. Evans was flying with his CO, the fightingest man on the ship. If only one man were going to get through, that man would be Skipper John Waldron, and, if Evans stayed close, he would have his best chance too. He would go back to Wesleyan, having done his duty here, to tell the next generation about the youth of *this* generation, condemned as slackers by the old-timers, thrust into war, into battle, *for them*, to save them and the society they all stood for. At that moment, it hit Evans that they were not fighting for the folks back home or America. Not for Sea Hag or Captain Mitscher. At that moment, he realized that he and Grant and Abbie and Whitey and XO Owens and Hal and Rusty and Moose, Bibb behind him and Chief Dobbs – and especially Skipper Waldron – were fighting for each other. He now understood what warriors through the ages had understood. And he sensed that here, over the trackless North Pacific, he had earned a place in their company.

The minutes droned on, and he wondered if there was anything out here. Maybe they had missed them. What would happen to the CO if they had, after he had told off Sea Hag? What if Sea Hag and the dive-bombers got to the Japs without having the TBDs to finish them off? It dawned on him that, either way, the CO had signed his own professional death warrant. *Public insolence to the air group commander! And on the common radio circuit!*

Still nothing visible anywhere on the horizon. He squeezed the interphone.

"Bibb, see anything back there? Any trace of our VB and VF?"

"Nothin' sir, and I lost sight of them a way's back."

"Very well," Evans answered. He checked his fuel flow; he couldn't lean the mixture anymore lest he fall out of position. Their outbound leg would take them to the limit of their range, but *Hornet's* expected Point Option position would make the return leg at least thirty miles shorter. Maybe closer to forty. Evans was confident they'd make it okay.

After 0900 and still nothing. Skipper Waldron hadn't moved off heading as he led them at 112 knots. Evans twisted his torso to scan his rear quadrants. As he was trained, he focused his eyes on a patch of sky to better detect movement.

Empty. Between breaks in the puffy clouds, the setting moon remained their only company as it beckoned them forward.

More fuel calculations. They had enough for another forty miles, but Evans *knew* that Waldron would press on, squeezing more range out of their charges and betting the ship would be at the designated recovery point. Or not. The skipper had said running out of gas was a possibility they had to prepare for. He scanned behind him, another habit.

Movement, a plane at five o'clock and over a mile. Evans watched as it overtook them, flying a parallel heading, and his heart beat faster. His eyes widened and he subconsciously pointed at it. Hal then turned to see what Evans was looking at.

"There's a fighter on our tail," Waldron radioed.

Evans couldn't take his eyes off the enemy plane, painted green and moving fast. It looked big for a fighter, but it was fast. *Everything* was faster than a TBD.

"Bibb, four o'clock going to three. We've got company. Look down our wing line."

"Lookin', sir… Okay, ah've got it!" Evans felt their TBD lurch as Bibb adjusted himself to charge his guns. Next to Evans, the CO was padlocked on the intruder, keeping the unknown aircraft in sight as it continued ahead. They were at 600 feet; Waldron took them lower.

"What is it, sir?" Bibb asked.

Evans could only give his best guess. "The *Zero* canopy is big, but that's a long canopy… Could be a Nakajima." He focused his eyes, and made out a red mark on the fuselage.

Evans was fascinated. *The enemy.* Surely it had seen them. *It?* No, Japs. Japanese boys were in that plane, and no doubt alerting more Japanese boys. Were they ahead? How many? How many ships, planes, boys? By now, every crew in the formation watched as the interloper flew away. The horizon ahead was empty. Evans checked the clock: 0910. With nervous energy he reached down to wind it.

Japanese.

Evans knew in his heart they were human, far removed from the buck-toothed caricatures of recruiting posters. But they were alien. With an alien culture, an alien tongue. *Eastern.* Evans was from the Midwest: Indianapolis, Indiana. Where were these Japs from? The only Japanese city he had heard of was Tokyo. He remembered his mother admonishing him for digging a deep hole in the backyard. *You'll dig through the earth to China!* Tokyo must not be too far off then. Evans wondered what kind of people they were, what was going through their minds now. Indianapolis. Tokyo. *Though they come from the ends of the earth.*

Waldron pointed ahead and clenched his fist, pumping it with excitement. Evans followed his eyes forward.

And he saw them, tiny indentations on the horizon, like jagged rocks on a ridgeline. Wisps of shadow, appearing stationary, yet seeming somehow to move with methodical purpose. He noticed a light, a blinking light, as if it were from one of the tin cans that escorted *Hornet*. Drawing closer, the indentations changed shape as the ships maneuvered in a formation that took up most of the horizon. Some of the features were long and flat…

They had done it!

Skipper Waldron had done it! The CO pushed on the stick and his pilots followed, gaining airspeed as they descended to the wave tops. Where were the VB, the scouts? Evans looked south and up through the cloud breaks. Nothing. Next to him, Waldron signaled for attack formation, and Evans passed it to Hal who relayed it down the line.

"Stanhope from Johnny One. Enemy sighted."

Evans searched for the rest of the air group. He couldn't help it. Since the split, the distance between them had opened what he figured was fifty miles. Hell, the *Wildcats* could cover that in ten minutes, the SBDs in fifteen. Maneuvering into attack position on the Japs ahead would take most of that time. *"Stanhope from Johnny One… Answer…enemy sighted."*

Behind him, the XO's division slid aft into position and provided the mutual support of the defensive triangle the CO had briefed. Evans fell back into a right echelon, making it easier to fly form on the skipper *and* see the enemy formation ahead.

It was impressive.

The strange ships were pale gray in the sun, many maneuvering hard with white water flying off their bows. Evans counted three carriers; the biggest was the farthest away. A plane was landing on one of the nearest ships, and no CAP fighters were visible. He looked over his shoulder at Hal, who smiled back.

"Stanhope from Johnny One…"

Leveling at 100 feet, they charged ahead at 120 knots, the fastest they could get with the fish they carried. Waldron led them to the nearest carrier, low and sleek, some ten miles ahead.[1] To Evans' left, a Japanese destroyer appeared two

---

[1] HIJMS *Sōryū*

miles off, surprising him. It fired its bow gun, and Evans was transfixed by the yellow bloom from a gun trained at *him*. He wished he could somehow stop and write notes but realized how ludicrous that was. No, he would remember every second of this experience for the rest of his life. Torpedo Eight had penetrated the outer screen of the Jap fleet! All the training, all the ready room talk. This was it – *torpedo attack* – maybe their only chance, maybe *his* only chance. *Where is the CAP?* Waldron then transmitted, clear and composed.

"We will go in, we won't turn back. We will attack. Good luck."

Evans and the others held their positions as they absorbed the message. He and the others searched in vain for friendly fighters to help. He saw no VB or scouts high above ready to plunge on the Jap carriers, to draw their fire, to wound them, to open a lane for Evans and the rest of the torpeckers.

But Evans felt no fear. Heck, the *Lexington* boys had done it, and with these same TBDs! VT-8 would, too. December 7th was a stroke of luck; *the Japs had caught us with our pants down.* Evans had confidence in himself, the TBD, and the squadron. And Skipper Waldron. *He had done it!*

Waldron turned in his seat and pointed over his left shoulder. Fighters. *Zeros!* Evans picked up three of them in a left bank, with three trailing. They maneuvered to come out of the sun. *There are three more, and another three!*

"You see 'em Bibb? Looks like a whole squadron of them passing down our port wing."

"I got 'em, sir!"

High to the southwest Evans picked up many more dots, all converging on the Americans. The first group of *Zeros* were swinging their wing line, in no hurry, setting themselves up. Evans watched them while he maintained position, and behind him the second division of TBDs had stepped down from the first. Glancing right, he saw the echelon weave as nervous TBD pilots, distracted from formation-keeping, watched the fighters set up behind them, now in hard, knife-edge turns.

"Johnny One under attack!" Waldron radioed.

The *Zeros* to this left closed in, still banking hard, and to Evans's estimation about to overshoot the entire American formation. *Maybe they aren't that good,* he thought, and in an instant considered that the skipper had positioned the TBDs like a porcupine, quills ready to strike any predator that got too close. *The Japs are just watching, afraid to mix it up with us!* Evans then looked up. He was shocked to see more *Zeros* – seeming to dive straight down on them! He checked his six.

Oh my gosh!

Amazed, Evans watched the lead *Zeros* go from 90 degrees off to nose-on in a flash, tighter and faster than he had ever seen a *Wildcat* turn. In unison, they fired on one of the second division planes, with yellow flashes blinking from their noses. Around him, the TBD gunners fired back as the pilots held course. When Bibb opened up, the chatter of the twin .30s was louder than Evans had ever heard but was soon drowned out as the three-plane of *Zeros* roared overhead and off right.

Once off, the high fighters were in, and they swooped down on a trailing TBD, setting it ablaze with accurate high-deflection gunfire. Back to his left, the swarming fighters took their turns, and, out of the corner of his eye, Evans saw a large splash with a black smoke trail behind it. Another *Zero* dove down, and streaks of light reached out to one of Evans' friends.

No!

The Japs swirled about them like khaki-colored sparrows, the rising sun "meatball" on their wings easily visible. Their black nose cowlings hid guns that shot synchronized yellow flame between spinning propeller blades. As they pulled off, Evans could make out their human faces through the closed cockpits, *alien* faces that looked at him with calm detachment. *Your turn will come.*

Terrified, his head swung with wild-eyed fear to pick up the next attack. Behind him Bibb blazed away at the Japs as the skipper shouted something on the radio. He looked over to Hal.

Hal!

Nagumo's staff peered through their binoculars as guns from the screening vessels to the east opened fire on unseen attackers. They observed faint silhouettes of carrier planes diving and climbing. Fuchida admired the performance of the CAP fighters. A flash, followed by a thin, black smoke trail, appeared, then another. On the other side of the bridge, Captain Aoki ordered a port turn.

"Enemy torpedo planes… Carrier based," Genda offered.

Nagumo turned to him. "Are you sure?"

"Yes, Force Commander. An obsolescent model, painted gray as all of them are, and coming from the east."

"The scout report was correct," Kusaka said with a smile. "This is all the evidence we need."

Genda was captivated. "There goes another… Looks like ten enemy, maybe more." *They look like waterfowl on a faraway lake.*

All were captivated by the scene that had caught the attention of flight deck crew. They looked off to the east as *Akagi* heeled to starboard, unable to help themselves. The planes appeared stationary on the horizon as sunlight glinted off their wings. With increasing frequency, black marks appeared among them, trailing down to the sea as the fighters swooped about in their grisly ballet.

Fuchida stood behind Genda and murmured, "Again, no fighter protection." Genda nodded as he continued to scan the horizon. Over the American formation, *Zeros* dove and climbed like eagles on a millpond. Cruisers and destroyers laid smoke and above the enemy – who kept boring in – black AA bursts dotted the sky. None on *Akagi's* bridge had witnessed such slaughter as they had for the past two hours, and still not one hit.

"Looks like they're running on *Sōryū*. Are they brave or just desperate fools?" Fuchida asked, not expecting an answer.

Genda had no answer to offer. Unease grew inside him; they must be from the carrier that *Tone's* scout had spotted. The carrier everyone thought was far outside the range of these obsolete Douglas torpedo planes. A carrier that was supposed to be riding at anchor in Pearl Harbor.

They aren't supposed to be here yet.

Evans twisted in his seat to track his assailants, now coming from all sides. Bullets stitched the water near a smoking TBD behind him, and, across from the CO, a *Devastator* climbed away from the formation as it rolled left. The burning plane continued in a slow and graceful roll on its back as the fiery nose fell through. Horrified, Evans watched the gunner fall – or jump – from the bomber and follow it as the TBD dove headlong into the waves, sending up a high spray that caused those in the formation behind to veer out of the way.

"*Is that a Zero or one of our planes?*" Skipper asked on the radio, to anyone who would answer.

"*Devastator,*" Tex answered him.

They continued ahead, the high RPM roar of the *Zeros* growing in volume then fading just as fast, again and again. Bibb continued his fire, but, even between the rapid *pops* of the .30s behind him, Evans heard the chattering machine guns and slow booming cannons as the *Zeros* worked them over.

Skipper Waldron continued toward the carrier, just a flat slab, but Evans, now panting in a fear beyond terror, didn't think that at this rate any of them would make it there and back. To his right a TBD exploded, and frag sprayed the plane next to it and set it on fire. He fought the human instinct to flee, to leave the formation, to run in scared retreat as an infantryman could. But he could not, afraid to leave what meager support the shrinking formation could provide, to remain stable for Bibb to shoot, to follow the CO as he had trained them. *If there is only one man left...*

Surrounded by the cacophony of deafening fire, Evans gripped the stick and throttle harder than he ever had, gritting his teeth with shoulders hunched and squinting his eyes. He didn't look back anymore...too terrible. *Ahead* was terrible enough with fields of froth from missed rounds, *Zeros* darting about like bats, ships on the horizon with yellow blooms from the heavy stuff and small caliber winking from the lighter. Some of the fighters attacked head-on with rhythmic flashes from their wings. The sea around him was now white with spray and sudden geysers that looked like full-grown oak trees jumping out of the sea. In his peripheral vision he detected flashes – his friends.

"I'd give a million!" the skipper transmitted. Evans was unable to decipher the rest through the combined and desperate sounds of 45 inches of manifold pressure ahead of him, Bibb firing behind him, screams on the radio, Jap rounds snapping past the canopy, and his jackhammer heartbeat.

"My two wingmen are going in!"

Waldron's engine exploded and fire cascaded over his windscreen. In back, the chief wasn't moving, and as the plane nosed down, Waldron threw the canopy open and bolted himself out on the right wing. Evans watched in horror as his commanding officer stood next to his burning cockpit, no longer able to fly, but still leading the way to the enemy. Waldron stood resolute as the North Pacific rose up to meet him, and disappeared in a shower of spray and debris.

"Skipper!" Evans shouted.

Beyond where Waldron went in was empty water. To Evans's right...more empty water. He saw a few TBDs behind him, tail-gunners blazing away against the incessant fighters.

Ensign Bill Evans was alone and in front, heading to the carrier now turning to port. By the geometry, if he could overtake it in the next five minutes, he would attack it from starboard, as the CO had drilled into him. *Go in and get a hit.*

"Ow!" he shouted as a round thudded into the armor plate against his back. Another exploded against the instrument panel above the throttle quadrant. *"I'm hit!"* Bibb cried, and Evans turned to see the guns pointed up with Bibb's head moving.

"Mistah Evans, I'm hit!"

"Hang on, Bibb!" Evans yelled back while oil smeared the left windshield. Pressure and RPM were holding, but his airspeed and altitude instruments were out. He would have to best-guess 80 feet and 80 knots.

Zeros pulled abeam for another attack in an approach run that seemed to take an hour. At least two TBDs were in trail, and, with Bibb wounded, he could skid his plane to throw off the Japanese aim. The Mk 13 made the *Devastator* fly like an ox cart, but he had to keep it, had to drop it on the carrier ahead amid smoke, spray, and tracers that filled his view.

"Mother? *Mommy!*" Bibb shouted, loud enough for Evans to hear.

"*Hang on, Bibb! We're approaching the target!*" Evans cried, fighting back tears of fear and frustration, of panic and shock. *Please, God!* And realization. *We don't have a chance!*

Bullets slammed into T-3 with metallic punches to the corrugated metal skin of the wings – and to the engine. Evans's windscreen shattered in front of him as the antenna mast was shot off – *Oh please, God!* – and the slipstream buffeted his face with gray smoke. The engine bucked in its housing, and Evans instinctively retracted his throttle.

Except that he couldn't. His left arm wouldn't move, and when he looked down another round exploded through the glass canopy. He pushed on the left rudder to maintain balanced flight – but his leg wouldn't move. He reached over with his right hand to reduce the RPM, but the engine would not respond. Frantic, he firewalled it back, but nothing.

More staccato aluminum punctures, more spray kicked up ahead, and, without warning, the vibrating engine belched black smoke from the left cowl flaps. Evans was losing consciousness, but a calm spread over him. It was quieter now, the sounds of combat muffled in the background as images appeared in his mind: that fun day on the Wabash, tackle football in the front yard, standing next to pretty Doris Smith for the 8th grade class photo, cranking the neighbor's Model T and jumping back from the…

Bang!

Sparks and flame gushed from the smoking engine that then sputtered and seized. Evans felt tired but no longer afraid. Beyond the motionless propeller blade, the water approached. *It is like they say,* he thought, comprehending, accepting, beyond fear, his eyes now focused on the swells ahead. Flying fish jumped out of one swell and dove back into another. Enthralled, he wanted to see more, and drew closer.

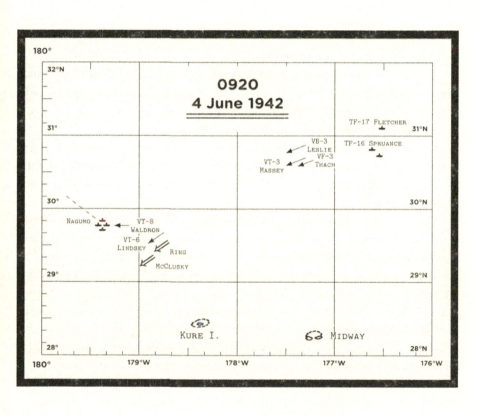

Chapter 14

LCDR Wade McClusky, Northwest of Midway, 0930 June 4, 1942

McClusky felt the tension in his gut.

The air group commander had a decision to make. His SBD was below half fuel, and the 31 *Dauntlesses* of VB-6 and VS-6 probably had less. He had already passed where he thought he would sight the Japanese carriers, and, at 19,000 feet, should have been able to see for dozens of miles.

Except for the damn clouds! Cotton balls scattered or broken over the water as far as he could see. To the south was a black column that rose skyward until it was carried away to the west by the high-altitude winds: Midway. Little over 100 miles, he figured.

The rubber oxygen mask, brittle from the cold, added to his discomfort. He couldn't remember the last time he had used one. Hard to talk. Behind him, Radioman Chocalousek said nothing. Like the other gunners, he tried to stay warm as he too searched down through the clouds. Conversing on the interphone wasn't something McClusky did as a single-seat fighter pilot. No one to talk to. And the current situation didn't lend itself to a conversation with an enlisted man he didn't know, whose job was to operate the radio and free guns. Chocalousek and the rest of the pilots and gunners in the *Dauntless* formation depended on one man, their group commander, to lead them.

McClusky sensed the resentment. Dick Best and especially Earl Gallaher were experienced SBD pilots. McClusky knew dive-bombing, but he was VF, not VB like them. They had to get *hits*, but first they had to find the Jap carrier force. Earl was the scout squadron CO. Who better to lead this gaggle? To McClusky, however, leading was never a question. He was senior – and responsible. He had to lead, and could not delegate it.

He was comfortable leading, had led long open-water navigation legs, but had never led such a large formation of SBDs, certainly not two squadrons worth. He liked the Douglas: decent climb, honest handling, rock stable in a dive. With little experience in the newer SBD-3, he welcomed the help from a radioman-gunner. The SBD was no darting falcon, but it was tough, and if need be McClusky could maneuver it for a high-deflection shot with his fixed guns. If some *Zero* pilot got slow in front of his wing line, McClusky would flame him.

Most of his planes had been airborne for two-and-a-half hours. Together they had departed *Enterprise* over 90 minutes ago, the aviators sucking rubber in freezing cockpits. McClusky checked the position of the sun: high to his left. A fighter-pilot habit. *Zeros* could get up there, above him, but he didn't consider it likely. The rays warmed him. *Thank God for the sun.*

Five more minutes. About twelve more miles. That would put him 36 miles beyond the planned intercept point directed by Captain Murray on the bridge. There must be planes out here somewhere: a PBY, Army bombers from Midway. McClusky had never wanted to see a *Zero* so bad in his life. Even if it came out of the sun…his home must be nearby. McClusky was already beyond the point of no return, and the 63 men behind him knew it, too.

The minutes counted down, and the unsettling black column to the southeast was both welcome and foreboding. Midway was underneath it, but McClusky did not know the extent of damage. The column looked to be hours old. Between every nook and cranny of cloud were only shadows and empty blue water.

One minute to go. The decision he'd been dreading for the last half hour was upon him. *They aren't here!* Which way to turn? If only the clouds would open up. If only a "speck" of an airplane outline would appear against one of the white buildups.

McClusky wrestled with his options. He could turn them south toward Midway, toward the inviting column that marked evidence of the Japs. They were there a short time ago – and could be still. He checked his plotting board again: too close. No admiral would put his fleet within 100 miles of a known air threat. Unless he knew it was no longer a threat. McClusky didn't know.

North was where he had told Captain Murray he would go, along the course they had been spotted at dawn. It made more sense and gave the Japs plenty of sea room from which to attack Midway. Or *Enterprise* – if they had found it.

At 9:35, the sweep-second hand on his watch swept past 12. He'd flown his allotted extra fifteen minutes – and nothing. He checked the eight-day clock in the cockpit that he had synchronized with his watch when he strapped in: also 9:35. He selected the interphone.

"Chocalousek, we're comin' right. Look down there and find 'em."

"Yessir, Commander."

McClusky nodded to the right, then eased the stick in the same direction as his formation followed.

Trailing McClusky in VB-6, Kroeger flew wing on his CO while taking peeks at the scouts ahead and the surface underneath. He felt lightheaded, and took big gulps of oxygen through his ill-fitting mask. Was the oxygen system broken? He gutted it out as long as he could before he signaled the CO that he and Halterman were struggling to breathe. Skipper Best just shook his head in disgust. Kroeger didn't know if Best's ire was meant for him, or the airplane, or the situation.

Taking Bombing Six down to fifteen, Best showed his pilots they could breathe without supplemental oxygen. All that gas to lug their 1000-pounders up to twenty grand…wasted. Kroeger watched his fuel and wondered where McClusky was taking them now, and so damn fast at 190 knots, chewing up their fuel to keep up. All of them were in extremis.

It's time to hit the Japs or go back.

Each man knew what was at stake. Go back and recover with their bombs? Maybe, but chances were the Japs would roll in on *Enterprise* before they could even get off the flight deck. Kill or be killed. Two hours ago the Jap snooper had found Task Force 16. *They must know we are out here by now. That scout must have gotten off a report.* Who knew if *Enterprise* was still there? Kroeger reckoned the odds were even that, one way or another, he'd end up in the water on this flight.

The dark plume to the south dominated his thoughts. The Japs had hit the Marines at Midway, hit the island like they had Pearl Harbor. Australia. India. With impunity. *They were just down there!*

Kroeger wanted to close throttle to save fuel but needed to stay with the CO. Best told them to fly south forty miles after they hit the Japs before heading home to throw off a Jap tail. Figuring his fuel again, he would shave that. Had to.

The formation above veered right. Skipper Best mirrored them from below. *We must be heading back*, Kroeger thought. Miles ago, beyond the point of no return, he had wanted to go back. Now, he wanted to attack something. He was going to run out of gas – knew it, all of them did – but maybe they could attack the enemy task force and at least make it back to the outer screen. He'd ditch next to the closest destroyer he could find.

Had to find the Japs first. Wade McClusky had to find them.

Leveled at 19,000 feet, Ensign Clayton Fisher felt a foreboding he had never felt in his life.

Almost two hours after they had left *Hornet*, he flew wing on Ring's miserable SBD. CHAG held course, taking peeks between the clouds below. He seemed steady now…the bad business with Skipper Waldron had been over an hour ago. Fisher couldn't wait to talk with the others about it, and especially the guys in Torpedo Eight.

Skipper Waldron on the radio again. How could Sea Hag not have heard him a while back? *Attacking? Planes in the water?* Sea Hag didn't move in his cockpit. He just continued on, oblivious.

Who could blame the fighters for leaving? Twisting in his seat, he looked behind the Scouting Eight SBDs and couldn't see any Fighting Eight F4Fs in trail. Low on fuel, all had gone back to the ship.

Maintaining his parade position, he checked the time: 0920.

Then, out of the corner of his eye. The VB were leaving! *My squadron!* Skipper Johnson was taking them southeast! Fisher checked below for wakes and saw none. He looked at Ring, who didn't notice. To his right, Skipper Rodee slid the scouts into trail. Bombing Eight continued in an easy turn away, toward the black column of Midway.

First the VF, and now the VB! Fisher felt naked and alone, even with Radioman Ferguson sitting six feet behind him, even with Scouting Eight behind him. In growing distress, he sucked on his rubber oxygen mask, high over the very middle of the Pacific with nothing but the impassive sun and the moon…and that black column to the southeast. Death was surely under that column. American men…no, boys. Like him. Had they fought back, or was it like December 7th? He shifted in his seat to relieve the pain in his shoulder joints from the cold. Or was it tension?

VB-8 headed toward Midway, and Fisher counted them in quick glances as he held position. They were heading for a sure thing when ahead of Fisher was known oblivion. Could the Japs have moved this far from the sighting report? The ready room teleprinter had relayed that report almost four hours ago. Maybe they were ahead. Desperate, Fisher fidgeted in his seat as he looked for the enemy. Ahead, only the midmorning sun reflected off his spinning propeller. His eyes were then drawn to his fuel gauge, as they would be for each remaining minute of the flight.

He was down to 135 gallons.

He was going in the water, all of them were. Should he break and run after his squadron? They were still in sight. No. He'd be stripped of his wings. But Skipper Johnson took his squadron out of formation as Waldron had, as Commander Mitchell had. They just up and *left*, and only Commander Waldron had said anything on the radio. *Are they all chickening out? What the hell is going on?*

He studied Ring, wished he would turn to him, look at him, reassure him, *just acknowledge him*, and lead him home, something, *anything*. Commander Ring scanned the sea surface as before, focused on nothing else.

A minute later Fisher got his answer.

CHAG looked at Fisher, then pointed at the scouts. He signaled for a scouting line, and motioned to Fisher to fly down and pass the signal to the scouts. With a thumbs-up, Fisher nodded his acknowledgement before he slid back and away to join on VS-8.

As he broke free, Skipper Rodee turned the scouts left. *They're leaving!* Fisher thought. Scouting Eight flew in a collapsed vee formation as they passed through 90 degrees of what Fisher knew was a 180-degree turn for home.

"Mister Fisher, the scouts are leaving," Ferguson said over the interphone. *He must be freezing back there.*

"I know!" Fisher answered in frustration. In apprehension. In dread. The plane he was flying and the man behind him were his responsibility. He worked to the inside, in trail and burning fuel, in between, trying to keep an eye on Ring behind him as his best chance for home flew away in front. He was the pilot, a commissioned officer. Accountable. A man, no longer a carefree boy. Ensign Clayton Fisher. *I'm just a damn kid!*

His breathing increased as he struggled to decide. Go home with the scouts or join back with Sea Hag? *It's now or never!* Scouting Eight was almost out of their turn for home. If he didn't go soon, he never would join up with them. Or even find *Hornet*. Over his shoulder he looked for Ring and couldn't find him in the blue. *Where'd he go?*

Almost hyperventilating with indecision, Fisher knew this was his last chance, and with a deep breath – *I have to!* – he pushed down in a scooping turn that would buy him some knots to catch up to the scouts. Taking one last quick search for his flight leader, he pulled away to the east.

Commander Ring, now abandoned by all of the 58 planes he had set out with, continued ahead into unlimited visibility, unable to see a thing.

CHAPTER 15

HIJMS *Hiryū*, 0945 June 4, 1942

Maruyama was starving.

On the mess deck he scooped some rice balls into a napkin and stepped aft onto the passageway. The mess men stepped aside with a curt bow as a sign of respect for their returned warrior. The ship heeled port and then starboard to maintain position in the formation. Ignoring the deck motion, he popped one rice ball into his mouth and cradled the rest to share in the ready room.

Upon recovery some 45 minutes earlier, they had learned that *Hiryū* and the entire force had been under attack for most of the morning. The Americans had thrown everything they could at them, including the planes from Midway that had escaped before the attack. Fighter pilots back from the morning CAP spoke of downing wave after wave of ham-fisted and cowardly Yankee Doodles, all but helpless against them. Maruyama wondered if the real action was here instead of Midway to the south.

An American carrier had been spotted far to the northeast, which electrified the aviators. Sadly, Maruyama would miss the action. The Tomonaga strike force would sit this one out as CarDiv 1 had claimed the glory, again. *Kankōs* from *Akagi* would lead the attack, and *Hiryū's* dive-bombers would have a major role. High above on the flight deck another Type Zero roared aloft.

He climbed a ladder and stepped onto the lower hangar bay. Fat *kanbakus* waited with armor-piercing bombs. Crewmen cleaned their windscreens with rags as others inspected control surfaces and weapon sway braces. The aft elevator was down, and handlers rolled a fighter onto it for the trip up to the flight deck. For a few minutes, brilliant sunshine illuminated the corners of the dark and enclosed bay.

Walking forward several frames, Maruyama ducked into a vestibule and climbed three more ladders to the ready room. As soon as he stepped inside, Lieutenant Kadano stopped him.

"Did you see Miyauchi-kun go in?"

Maruyama didn't answer at first. *I could almost touch him.*

"No. Shot down by an unseen Grumman above us. He was on fire and fell out of the formation as we passed their airfield. I didn't see him go in… We were in our run." *He looked at me through the flames.*

"None of us did either," Kadano said. "How about Kikuchi?"

"His engine was smoking, and we saw him head for Kure atoll to the west," Maruyama answered the lieutenant. He craved sleep.

Kadano nodded. "Yes, a probable water landing in the lagoon. We'll make a pass there on the way back this afternoon."

"This afternoon, Kadano-san?"

"Yes. After our mates deal with the American task force, we'll hit Midway again. Tomonaga-san radioed for a restrike."

Maruyama remained silent. Half of the attack unit planes were lost or damaged; five hadn't made it back. The number of remaining Grummans on Midway was anyone's guess, but there were a lot of guns down there. Big and effective. The mood in the ready room was grim; none had experienced such losses.

"Lieutenant Hashimoto is compiling the accounts; give him your report at once and then take a cat nap. Doubt we'll get back much before sundown."

Maruyama answered with a crisp bow as Kadano scowled at the rice balls the junior airman carried.

"Duty *first*," the pilot murmured. Chagrined, Maruyama nodded as Kadano left. He popped another rice ball in his mouth and handed the rest to Nakao, who sat on one of the benches.

It then hit him. *Where is everyone?* He answered his own question as soon as it entered his mind.

"Come on down, Jim!"

Like the other pilots in his torpedo-plane division, Lieutenant (Junior Grade) Robert Laub searched the sky above after Skipper Lindsey called on the radio for the Fighting Six *Wildcats* that would defend them. "Come on down" was the signal for the F4Fs to get down on the waves and engage. They *had* to be nearby. Since VT-6 had departed *Enterprise,* the CO had flown the briefed heading, at the briefed airspeed. The SBD boys had pressed ahead: that Jap floatplane must have spooked the bridge.

Laub also looked for the dive-bombers because – *There they are!* On the northern horizon he saw the Jap task force, but the only smoke was from stack gas, no burning ships from SBD bomb hits. Could Mister McClusky have missed them to the south? He scanned above the enemy ships for a glint of sun off a wing, specks of dark *Dauntlesses* peeling off in their dives. Nothing. Laub and the others searched for their promised *Wildcats* as tension – and fear – rose inside them.

"Jim! C'mon down!" Skipper Lindsey radioed again, nervous pleading in his voice. Seated behind him, Chief Grenat scanned above for deliverance. *Where is Fighting Six?* The CO could barely fly, and needed help to get into the cockpit and strap in. He had limped around the ready room, wincing in pain, and struggled hard to climb the ladder to the flight deck. Anyone else would have been in traction after that flight deck crash last week. Laub was already sore from just two hours in his *Devastator's* uncomfortable seat. *The skipper's back must be on fire right about now.*

However, what was on the horizon ahead had their full attention. *Four carriers! Battlewagons! Cruisers! We got 'em! Where's the VSB? Where's the VF?*

Lindsey led VT-6 toward the now-alerted enemy, who was running north-west. He picked out *Kaga*, the big one. Pilots like Laub had studied images and silhouettes of the giant carrier. Through their windscreens they saw it, *the real thing*, huge, heeling hard through west in a starboard turn. Now in a stern chase, Laub kept an eye on the other flight decks off the nose to his right, and watched for any *Zeros* lifting off.

"Come on down!" Lieutenant Ely barked on the radio to back up the CO.[1] No *Wildcats* in sight. No bombers rolling in. The Japanese carrier was ten miles ahead, trailing a white wake as it ran for safety. The torpeckers realized it would take almost fifteen minutes to pass it and build acceptable launch angles off its bow. Behind Laub, Radioman Humphrey cleared his free guns.

A fight was coming.

Blooms of gunfire blazed from the cruisers. *Big* guns trained at them. Lindsey detached the XO, who veered north for a classic anvil attack against the biggest Jap carrier: *Kaga* herself. Laub marveled at the other carriers falling off his right wing: tall and thin, with tiny little islands up forward. Some sent blinking light messages that Laub wished he could understand. What were they saying? *Shoot the Americans?*

Geysers in front and to the right. Big geysers from big shells. To the left, a destroyer laid smoke.

---

[1] LT J.S. "Jim" Gray, CO of Fighting Six and returning to *Enterprise* at the time, never heard these radio calls.

"Mister Laub, here they come! Port side nine o-clock!"

Laub saw them – two formations of three coming down their left as the plodding TBDs penetrated the screen. *Zeros*, painted khaki against the blue. He looked for others and found them high at his ten in a descending turn, taking their time, padlocked on the American torpedo planes. From a distance of only a mile, the mechanized wolves stalked their prey. Laub felt like prey, felt like a dumb pheasant flushed from an open field. And shot. Fast and quick, with the dogs howling after them and the sharp reports of the guns echoing off the tree line. Some escaped.

Some.

The first six fighters peeled off one by one, putting their noses on him, pulling lead. Petrified, Laub could only watch as he flew formation, unable to run. Staying in formation was all he knew, all any of them knew. Attacking a carrier? Hangar talk. Lines on a ready room chalkboard. Yellow chalk on a green board.

A Georgian, Humphrey screamed a rebel yell Laub heard over the engine noise. Over his left shoulder, Laub picked up an attacker. At that moment his whole being focused on the black prop spinner pointed at *him*. Humphrey was no less focused, and when the *Zero* was in range, he opened up on it.

Bup,bup,bup,bup,bup...bup,bup,bup,bup,bup,bup,bup

Humphrey then held his fire as the fighter roared over, a deep and throaty roar from a big and powerful engine. Skipper's plane was the target. Lindsey's TBD survived the onslaught, and Chief Grenat moved behind him. No time to look for damage.

"Yeeeeeeaaaaahhhhh!"

Humphrey squeezed his .30s again, and the TBD vibrated from their contribution to the hail of defensive fire from all seven in the division. The *Zero* shot past in another slashing swipe at the *Devastators* – big, dumb pheasants unable to escape.

Fire and black smoke to his left. *Skipper? Is that Tom?*

"Mister Laub!"

More *Zeros* zoomed by, markings on the tails, numbers like his, spitting bullets from the nose, their pilots concentrating on the deadly work before them. Cannon fire ripped through the formation like a mace. Once all the Japanese had taken their turns, Lindsey's formation remained intact in their desperate stern chase.

Laub couldn't believe they were all still flying and watched the determined *Zeros* circle in a daisy chain for another run. He selected his interphone.

"Humphrey! How you doin'?"

"Okay, sir! They're comin' around!"

"I see 'em," Laub answered. He studied *Kaga* ahead, growing larger. The bearing drifted right, but too slow.

"Another five minutes, Humphrey, at least."

"Doin' my level best, sir!"

"I know! We'll make it!"

In the middle of the enemy task force, the TBDs received antiaircraft fire from all quadrants – and cannon fire from above – as *Zeros* made run after run. One flaming *Devastator* in Ely's division climbed into a wingover – smooth and controlled – before it plunged into the sea. Seconds later, another of Laub's friends in a burning torpedo bomber flashed flame and nosed down with a large splash.

We're gonna make it, dammit!

Ahead, a plane lifted off *Kaga* and turned hard. Then another. And another. *Zeros!* Next to him only two of the six Jap fighters worked them over with machine guns. As the gunners returned fire, Skipper Lindsey's division continued into the teeth of the enemy flak. *Kaga* now fought her assailants with her port side five-inchers that belched bright flame. On the flight deck gallery, the smaller guns winked at them. Tracers floated off the ship before they whizzed past, and the sea became white with spray. Laub heard his engine, the jackhammer sound of Humphrey wailing away behind him, and the aluminum punches of machine gun rounds through his tail.

"I got one, sir!"

To Laub's right, a *Zero* flamed from its underside, the pilot pulling up and away. The flames spread fast, and the fighter entered a sharp turn, rolled level, then slowly inverted. In a power dive, it smacked the sea next to *Kaga's* wide wake.

Ely's division lost another TBD that caught fire without warning and broke up. The left wing fluttered away while the burning fuselage spiraled down to the water. A trailing *Devastator* maneuvered to avoid the splash.

Both divisions now ran parallel to the carrier, well inside a mile, each facing a broadside of antiaircraft guns. To Laub, *Kaga's* entire port side was on fire, as rows of tracers arced above and kicked up spray below the Americans. One of the gunners in a TBD to his right fired at the carrier with his free guns. *Stop wasting ammo*, Laub mentally admonished. On the other side of the ship, *Zeros* dove and climbed; Laub was glad he could not see the grim results.

Kaga then swung hard to port, into Laub, bow guns blazing from under the huge flight deck overhang. He could hear the gunfire, continuous muffled thunder, set against a steady chatter from the small stuff. Now too close, Lindsey veered them away, and Laub, with combat instincts learned only minutes ago, didn't want to throw a wing up and present a bigger target. *Kaga's* bow filled his field of view, white water lifting above the anchor deck as it cleaved the sea.

With the carrier bow-on, Laub and the others could now only see three of their fellows as they fled to the south. The TBDs ran for their lives and one smoked. Laub saw that they were clean – *they dropped!* – and waited for an impact on the big hull. But there was none, and soon the ship reversed to parallel his division. *Kaga's* attention shifted to him…and the *Zeros* returned.

Having overtaken the ship, Lindsey needed to open distance for the attack and continued on through the fire. Laub glanced from one side of the formation to the other to pick up the fighters that would surely pounce. *Where were they?* He couldn't see anything near, and his frantic head-whipping didn't allow him a chance to really see the threat. He had to fly form on the skipper. He had to remain steady for Humphrey. He had to drop his fish and *get out!*

With *Kaga* again presenting her broadside, Lindsey took his men as far as he could. Laub saw the signal and passed it down the line. They were turning in, attacking. They had come so far, their only chance. *Where are the damn* Zeros? He couldn't afford to scan for fighters, he had to set up, stay in position, slow to eighty, hold fifty feet, 800 yards *but no closer*, 70 degrees off the bow. Or whatever they could get. *A lucky hip shot?*

"Out our tail, sir. Zero deflection!"

In his right turn, Laub twisted his neck all the way right and picked them up: three of them, nose on, and stationary. Their wings pulsed yellow. *Cannon fire!* The wispy streams of their trails indicated a miss high.

Laub whipped his head back in time to see the CO's plane burst into flame as the cannon rounds tore chunks out of the wings and empennage. Lindsey fell away from the formation at once and into the maelstrom, a frenzied spray of errant cannon shells and machine gun rounds. Horrified, Laub watched Lindsey's plane explode on the water in a fiery splash.

Their leader gone, the formation loosened up, the confused pilots unsure of whom to follow. Another TBD pulled up in an easy climb, streaming smoke, and released its torpedo as it burned. The torpedo climbed and wobbled away from the stricken plane. Laub watched, fascinated and shocked, as it reached its apex, for a moment suspended in midair before gravity took over. On its back, the burning *Devastator* nosed over and down, exploding on the water seconds before its torpedo followed it in.

Every man for himself. Line up and drop. Rolling out, Laub throttled back and skidded his plane to slow. He was both furious and fearful, his teeth clenched to the point of pain, concentrating on his run, the only one he would get. He'd hit it, and he wasn't ever going to come back. The huge carrier filled his field of view, and he saw a man running on the flight deck, a clear ridgeline above flashing pops of gunfire and a moving fog of cordite smoke.

Next to him Irv McPherson dropped his fish and banked hard away to the right. Laub felt alone. He *was* alone, in the lead even if there was no one behind him *to* lead. He took aim on the forward part of the gray steel wall as fireflies of tracers floated by or shot past in every direction. Radio calls of fear and confusion. Somebody is hit; another has sight. *Eighty knots! Now!*

Flushed with adrenalin, Laub yanked up on the release handle as the Mk-13 fell free with a welcome lurch. Safety was to the right, but he again feared throwing up a wing, especially only 500 yards from dozens of guns, all shooting at him. Point blank.

With his throttle firewalled, he overbanked anyway – *no choice!* – and pulled his nose across as the carrier turned away, showing its stern and the huge girders that held up the flight deck. The engineering of this strange vessel amazed him even as a fusillade of tracers ripped past. *What am I doing?* he thought and got as low as he dared, overtemping the engine, manifold pressure be damned.

Irv was still flying, and somebody else further west was, too, as the TBDs fled south amid splashes of bullets. Laub looked back and saw no plumes of water high against the carrier's hull, no fires, *nothing. Did all of us miss? Not one hit?* A mile to his left were three gray planes like his, low on the surface. The cruel Jap fighters slashed at them without mercy. Three of the seven. *Three.*

"Humphrey, you okay?"

"Yes, sir! We missed, sir."

"I know. How's yer ammo?"

"Half a can left, sir!"

Laub scanned the sky. He was safe for the moment. A destroyer cruised two miles to his right, firing at them, but from only one gun.

"Make 'em count. We gotta fight the way we came in."

The Americans escaped as singles, and Laub noticed one of the planes to the east was too close to the water. *Pull up*, he thought, but it continued down in a shallow trajectory. The *Devastator* pancaked in with a splash that resembled a stone skipping on a pond, pieces flying off and tumbling through the air before they, too, fell back and slapped the water. No flame. No smoke. *Were they already dead?*

His TBD felt like a fighter without the Mk-13 but accelerated slowly through 140 knots. McPherson and his unknown mate were a half mile at his four o'clock, all going for the same opening in the screen. To his left, a big ship charged at him, a cruiser. As he looked down the barrels of her bow turrets, the ship did not seem to take interest.

Movement above the cruiser caught his eye. A *Zero* banked hard right. Toward him.

"Humphrey, nine o'clock at a mile!"

"Got him, sir!"

Laub stayed low, both he and Humphrey padlocked on the enemy fighter. It was alone, painted gray with red dots on the wingtips, and Laub watched it approach. Maybe it didn't see them...

When it overbanked down a second later, rage welled up inside, from a place Laub did not know he had. This pilot was going to execute him, a motherless fawn in the open, the unfairness of it, the savagery of it.

"You sonofabitch!" he bellowed, and yanked the stick left. He would engage and kill him. Kill. That bastard Jap. Right damn now.

His *Devastator* rolled into the *Zero*, which now reversed to deliver a medium-deflection shot. This was single combat, but Laub's TBD, though more responsive, would not do what he wanted it to do. He couldn't meet the Jap head-on in a game of machine-gun chicken. Patient and focused, he held his bank, stayed low, watched the black nose approach from over his left shoulder. *You are not going to get me!*

When the *Zero's* nose lit up, Laub leveled his wings and pulled. The *Zero's* short ranging-burst missed low and the pilot repositioned as Laub banked into him again. Humphrey opened up with his free guns, and rows of bullets crisscrossed the deadly space only a football field wide. Laub's rudder pedals vibrated from a hit.

Laub rolled level again and pushed; behind him he heard Humphrey cry out from the sudden negative g-force. The Jap also pushed underneath, the composed pilot looking up at Laub, who then reversed back as the *Zero* switched over to McPherson on the wave tops. Laub's alert wingman had turned toward the action to help Laub and also jam the fighter's shot. After a half-hearted attempt at his friend, the *Zero* reversed north and back to the carriers, McPherson's gunner firing off a burst as it did.

"Damn, sir, when you did that, the ammo can floated up and hit my elbow! It flew overboard – good thing it was empty."

"Sorry, Humphrey... How much do you have left?"

"This belt has a coupla small bursts or one good one. That's it, sir."

"Okay…clear for the moment. Keep your head on a swivel."

An excited Humphrey was jubilant. "Yes, sir, but *damn*, we got one of those fuckers!"

Laub smiled to himself. They had made it. Far from safe, but alive. He checked his fuel and manifold pressure. The two TBDs to the east were turning for home. On the horizon behind them the enemy ships steamed on. Intact. Not one hit.

"Sorry for the obscenity, sir," Humphrey said over the interphone.

"Forget it."

McPherson crept up Laub's right bearing line, and the trailing *Devastator* crossed behind them to cut the corner for home. *Is that Ed?* With McPherson almost aboard, Laub rolled left in an easy turn. All ten men in the five planes kept watch to the north as they breathed deeply of the salt air. Laub wondered if the XO was flying one of the TBDs ahead of his spinning prop. One misted from its underside. Skipper Lindsey hadn't had a chance, torn to pieces right next to him. *Who's in command of the squadron now?*

And where was Fighting Six? *Numbskulls!* Why hadn't they come down when the skipper called? *All that and no hits!*

He thought about *Enterprise*, and wondered if she was still there.

Chapter 16

McClusky, Northwest of Midway, 0950 June 4, 1942

As the minutes counted up and fuel counted down, Wade McClusky replayed his decision.

Fifteen minutes earlier, he had turned his formation northwest to fly up the Japanese approach course. They *had* to be off his right nose, and he spent most of his time looking in that direction. With his binoculars he again scanned a break in the clouds before he methodically moved on to the next one. The breaks opened up as the formation passed overhead. Nothing.

He sensed the nervousness of his pilots behind him. *He* was nervous, and it wasn't because the Japanese were nearby. The high fuel flow to maintain altitude dominated his thoughts. If his fuel flow was high, those behind probably had higher flows to maintain position. He mentally calculated fuel flow against fuel remaining for the time and distance it would buy him. *Enterprise* was some 180 miles off his right shoulder, and he figured a rough Point Option course for home; 075.

As each search of water came up empty, doubt crept in. *Did I maintain a steady outbound course? Was the sighting report accurate? Did I calculate airspeed properly?* From 20,000 feet, there was nothing but low scattered clouds and barren ocean, nothing from which to take a fix. Their fuel state was desperate, almost as desperate as a gasping man unable to breathe, and he had seen one SBD fall out of formation and glide down to the surface, probably due to empty tanks. McClusky sensed his formation was already in extremis. Searching for enemy fighters was secondary. They all scanned below for anything to hit. They could then escape…and breathe.

Another minute passed. In five more minutes, it would be 1000, the time he gave himself to turn. He referenced his plotting board again. Ninety right was 045. On that heading, if they didn't find anything once he calculated 150 miles from *Enterprise*, he'd turn for home. Cold, frustrated, and tense, McClusky placed the binoculars against his goggles and scanned two breaks to the west. *Nothing.*

McClusky then searched a break off his nose. Above it, a rainbow hovered over the sea, vivid and pleasing. For a moment he admired it – all he could do – as he waited for the break to open.

Whoa! What's that?

He lifted his goggles and put the binoculars against his eyes. A ship trailing a big wake. He focused. A single ship, the size of a light cruiser. Heading north.

And Japanese.[1]

It was a Jap ship all right. McClusky waggled his wings to get the attention of his wingmen before he pointed to ensure they saw it, too. With Ensign Pittman's enthusiastic thumbs-up, he got his answer. Next to him was Earl Gallaher, and, after catching his attention, McClusky pointed down to his right. Earl's vigorous head motion confirmed that he, too, had a tally on the enemy ship. McClusky's fighter pilot instincts compelled him to scan the horizon at altitude for CAP fighters: clear. The Jap carriers must be nearby. But where? *Why is this guy out here alone? Might be a destroyer…but where is he going so fast?* He selected the interphone.

"Choc, I think we found 'em. We're gonna see where this guy is headed, but I think he's gonna lead us to 'em."

"Yes, sir," Chocalousek answered, and readied the radio for use.

The ship left a wake that resembled a white arrow as it steamed alone at flank speed. McClusky paralleled its heading as he followed it off his right side. He peered into the next cloud break as it revealed, slowly, what it hid on the surface.

His heart rate increased when he saw them: multiple dark specks trailing white slashes, steaming in all directions on the blue tabletop. Two carriers with light-colored decks resolved themselves as their escorts dashed about. The break opened up further to reveal two more flight decks and a battleship closer to him, escorted by more destroyers and cruisers. At least a dozen ships. *We found the bastards.* He selected the transmit button as relief washed over him.

"This is McClusky. *Tally ho!* Have sighted the enemy."

He checked his watch: 1002.

Spruance glanced at the clock. The dive-bombers had been gone for over two hours, the *Hornet* planes longer than that. The only transmissions received were

---

[1] HIJMS *Arashi*, a destroyer which McClusky mistook for a light cruiser.

garbled radio snippets from a jittery pilot. Browning said they were from one of his fighter pilots. Nothing from the torpedo planes.

Browning lit another cigarette and leaned over the chart table with a scowl on his face. At least he had stopped his pacing. It was as if *he* were the admiral, prowling and growling and rubbing his neck as he looked out to sea through narrow eyes.

"Signal *Hornet* and ask if they've heard anything. *Anything*," Browning snapped at one of the staff officers. As the order was passed to the signal bridge, he went back to the DR plot he kept on the chart, busying himself measuring distances, checking the bridge repeaters, plotting new courses. Spruance sat and watched, keeping his calm. Somebody had to.

Had he done the right thing, countermanding his staff and sending the dive-bombers out alone, before the fighters and torpedo planes? He had stepped in to take the conn many times in his career, sometimes for confused junior officers unsure of how to take station, or unmindful of shoal water when entering a harbor. Having to assert himself with his chief of staff, a *captain*, was unexpected. They were spotted, time was of the essence, yet Browning had not acted when it was clearly called for, stubbornly holding out for a perfect launch composition. *Perfect* would have taken another thirty minutes, at best, and the launch was already thirty minutes late with most of the planes holding overhead and burning fuel. Spruance smiled to himself that he, although inexperienced in the ways of carriers, had to step in. His eyes met those of Oliver, who took his measure. Caught in a moment of reflection, Spruance smiled at his aide before he stood and walked over to Browning. The chief of staff took a drag on his cigarette as he searched the skies to the west.

"What do you think?"

Browning exhaled, and the sea breeze directed his cigarette smoke into Spruance's face. His mind over the horizon, Browning didn't realize what he had done. Spruance ignored the slight.

"He's either in his attack or still searching. I'm worried about the fighters, though. They've gotta be coming home, or they've gotta prepare for water landings.

"When will we know?"

Browning grimaced at the question.

"Admiral, my guess is that unless McClusky finds something and transmits a sighting report, some of them, probably the fighters and torpeckers, will come back in an hour or so. The dive-bombers have another ninety minutes, tops."

"What if they're unsuccessful?"

"I've considered that, sir. They get back here at eleven, eleven-thirty, we'll have to recover them – which will take 45 minutes – turn them around, maybe reload…I'm thinking a 1400 launch, maybe 1330 at best. We'll have to use many of the same pilots, and they'll only have time to hit the head and scarf down a sandwich and gulp a glass of water before they go again."

Spruance nodded his understanding, but how could over 100 planes from two carriers *not* find the enemy? And Fletcher had launched a strike an hour ago and still nothing? The radios remained silent.

"Nagumo will be hitting us in that time," Spruance said, keeping his voice low.

"Yes, sir. Another concern. I'm considering a move east."

Spruance, also facing west, remained expressionless. Such a movement was in his command domain. He knew enough to know that moving east would make a long flight longer for his airborne pilots. However, moving east would increase his chances of avoiding an enemy attack. Would Browning recommend, or would he suggest command decisions?

Enterprise and *Hornet* were all but empty. TF-16 had shot their bolt and Spruance would not get another chance until the afternoon. He felt vulnerable, and Browning was not radiating confidence. Like listening to Jack Benny on a Sunday evening while sitting in their own parlors, the anxious men looked at the radio speaker, waiting and hoping for something to come out of it.

Then, a weak, crackling transmission.

"…running low on fuel…return…"

"Who'zat?" Browning barked.

"Sounds like Jim Gray, the VF skipper," Buracker answered. All turned their ear to the speaker, again waiting for something to emerge from the static.

"Enemy sighted, two carriers…"

Spruance strained to listen as Browning stepped toward the microphone.

"Two carriers!" he said. "Okay, he's escorting the VT, right?"

"Yes, sir," Buracker said.

Browning scowled at the speaker and muttered under his breath. "C'mon. *Come on!*"

Another minute passed. Unable to restrain his tension any longer, Browning snatched up the microphone.

"McClusky Attack! Attack immediately!" he shouted into it, breaking through 150 miles of static.

Long seconds passed, and nothing.

"Why aren't they attacking, for crying out loud?" Browning fumed to no one.

Spruance wished he knew the answer, too, but remained silent, knowing that an attack had better happen soon.

Wonder if Nimitz is monitoring these transmissions?

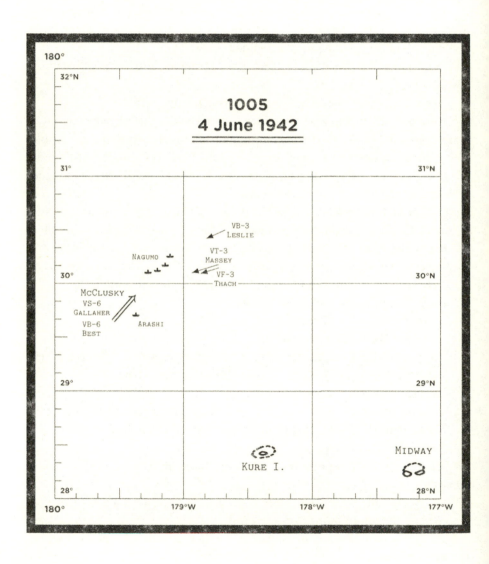

Chapter 17

LCDR Max Leslie, Bombing Three, 0940 June 4, 1942

"Dammit, dammit, dammit!"

Max Leslie slapped the dashboard. As soon as he had flicked the switch to arm his thousand-pounder for electrical release, he had felt the familiar jump of a bomb falling from his *Dauntless.* He couldn't believe it. He ground his teeth and pounded his fist on his thigh in frustration as he cruised toward the enemy at 15,000 feet. He wanted to explode. *How could this have happened?* And of all times *now*, leading his squadron toward the Jap carriers that were probably at their most vulnerable recovering planes.

Why?

Leslie seethed at the thought of going into combat unarmed, of leading his men with nothing. Did some bonehead screw up the wiring, connecting arming to release? He had always armed his bombs manually, but, today of all days, he had used the newfangled electrical method. Modern 20th century technology over tried and true. Should he go back to *Yorktown?* He selected the interphone to discuss it with his radioman.

"Gallagher, do you know what just happened?"

"Yes, Skipper. I felt the bomb come off. What for?"

"The damn electrical arming switch, that's what for! I'm wondering about going back to reload," Leslie snapped back, thinking aloud more than asking for his radioman's opinion.

Still boiling, Leslie scanned behind him and saw a splash on the surface far below. *Another bomb?* He looked at his wingmen, and noticed an SBD in the second division was missing his. Furious, he turned to the third division in time to see another 1000-pound bomb fall free to the North Pacific.

Dammit!

Leslie had to break radio silence or the whole squadron would be unarmed.

"Do not, repeat, do *not* arm the electrical release! Arm manually!" he barked on the radio. Having checked his wingman on either side for thumbs-up signals of acknowledgement, he continued to berate himself in silent rage – and again slapped the dashboard in frustration.

Below, among the twelve *Devastators* of Torpedo Three, Lloyd Childers flinched at a sudden tall geyser of spray off to starboard. He shouted to his pilot, Harry Corl, and lifted his head skyward to find the reason.

"Harry, you see that? Are we under attack?" Surprised and anxious, Childers continued to scan about for the enemy.

Corl nodded before he answered on the interphone that he, too, had seen the splash. Both men checked between the scattered clouds above them.

"I think that must have come from the VB up there," Corl said. Next to them, other TBD crews searched for more unexpected missiles coming out of the clouds. Off their right, they saw evidence of another impact seconds earlier: a plume of mist hovering over a white mark on the surface.

What are those guys dropping on? Childers thought. Between the clouds, he caught glimpses of the *Wildcat* escorts[1]. Only six, with two trailing the torpedo planes. It was something. The VB boys were way up above in the teens. For the moment a spectator, Childers was charged with anticipation. *We're gonna sink a carrier!*

He and the others in his compartment had been awakened at 0400. Grateful to have slept, he felt a calm confidence. After waiting for what seemed like forever in the radioman ready room, the order had come down for pilots to man their planes. He had run out to the flight deck and met Corl by their TBD. Once inside and strapped in, Childers pressed the interphone. "Harry, today is my 21st birthday. Theoretically I'm a man. Let's celebrate."

Flying on the skipper's wing, they had an unobstructed view to starboard. On the CO's left wing, Chief Esders held position. Behind him, Bobby Brazier had his hand resting on the canopy rail as if on a Sunday drive.

Childers's eye picked up *another* falling bomb and watched it smack the surface a half-mile off their wing. *What the hell is going on?* Through a break above he identified a formation of specks – SBDs – before they were hidden by another cloud. Skipper Massey had seen enough and veered the formation left as his nervous pilots followed.

Soon the excitement faded, and monotony returned as they droned ahead to the southwest. Childers liked flying with Harry, an experienced Warrant,

---

[1] VF-3, LCDR J.S. Thach

but, to him, a fellow sailor. It was different with the commissioned officers: the chasm of separation present even inside a TBD cockpit. Officers got the briefing from the bridge, and gunners like Childers just jumped in the back, not knowing where they were going. The gunners weren't expected to ask. Just operate the radio and shoot the enemy. *Ours is but to do and...*

Harry he could talk to. Though filled with respect for him, Childers could ask Harry what they were doing and why, as an equal. With him, Childers felt part of the team. Some of his fellows had strong relationships with their pilots, even the Annapolis officers. Some didn't. One guy had a report chit written on him by his own pilot and got busted down to seaman. Then he had to save his pilot in combat or lose his own life. The unfairness of it.

As Corl held position on the CO, Childers continued to search in the direction of the explosions. He knew enough about navigation and fuel to know they would find the Japs in the next thirty minutes, or they would go home empty-handed. Though he was apprehensive about his first taste of combat, he was now a twenty-one-year-old man in a torpedo bomber cockpit flying with the best pilot in the squadron. Sinking a carrier would be a great birthday present.

He scanned off his right wing...and saw something. A small disturbance on the horizon. And another! Waves? *No.*

"Harry, got somethin' to starboard, about thirty degrees off our nose."

Corl turned his head and soon nodded. Dark smudges. He counted them as he maintained formation. Signs of ship stack gas or screening smoke, lots of it, about 25 miles away. He gave up counting.

"You got 'em, Lloyd. I'm tellin' the CO."

Corl rocked their wings as a signal to Massey, and Childers caught the attention of his wingmen and pointed to the contacts. He received knowing nods and thumbs-up signals in return as the sighting was passed down the line to the excited pilots and gunners. Within a minute, the skipper turned the formation northwest and put the enemy off their left nose.

This is it!

Lieutenant Commander John Thach – everyone called him Jimmie – struggled to keep visual on the formations above and below him as he led his four *Wildcats* of Fighting Three.

The bomb splashes next to the TBDs startled him. They must have come from Max someplace above. A switch snafu? He couldn't see the bombers, but

Lem Massey was turning his torpeckers north. Maybe he had something off to starboard. Thach followed the TBDs…easier to see. Two more of his F4Fs were tied on to VT-3. It was better than nothing, and if they were near the Japs, at least he had some gas left to mix it up.

Lem and his TBDs were easy to track, only occasionally obscured by the scattered, puffy clouds. They rolled out north, and Thach scanned the horizon ahead and above. Nothing. As a fighter pilot, his world was one of silent pondering. Though he had his mates in their charges next to him, each man was alone. Alone with his thoughts. Alone in his cockpit. Thach thought about the admiral, Captain Buckmaster, his friends, Lem below him and Max above. The captain and the admiral were too damn stingy with his fighters. Thach and his fellow COs had devised a plan. Would it work? Next to him, his wingmen wondered the same – but about their own skipper and his new way to fight the *Zeros*.

They continued ahead, and Lem took his boys closer to the surface. There must be something on his nose, but the clouds obscured the horizon. Thach checked his fuel…and continued to scan.

Then, an antiaircraft burst off his right, yellow. And then another. A blue one. Through a break he saw a ship, a destroyer trailing a big wake. On its fantail a turret fired.

Lem found 'em!

Thach then picked up the CAP, a formation of *Zeros*. A bunch of them, slicing down from above, inside two miles. Shocked, he called out a warning.

"This is Jimmie! Bandits at ten high!"

"Tally!" Macomber answered.

A sudden flash to their left, and Red Dog's F4F flared up[1]. He nosed over as unseen *Zeros* from below streamed past them toward the *Devastators* ahead. Red Dog never had a chance. The air around Thach was unexpectedly filled with agile enemy fighters, and he found himself flying through faint lines of tracer smoke made by his attackers seconds earlier.

Holy shit! he thought as he struggled to get a count: at least twenty. The Japs seemed to be falling over themselves to take turns at his puny formation. Macomber cried that he was hit, and Tom Cheek escorting the TDBs yelled about something. The swarm of fighters Thach faced overwhelmed him more than he had ever been in an airplane. Lem's screams for help broke through the confusion as Thach fought off one Jap after another.

Sonofabitch!

---

[1] ENS E.R. Basset, VF-3

Thach tried his beam defense maneuver and pulled hard into the threat. Once his assailant took its nose off to reposition, Thach reversed into it. Each of the *Wildcats* scissored back and forth to defend itself, with both sides taking snap shots. Macomber was there but no longer transmitting. The nimble Japs pushed them around, but one got slow as he corrected his angle on Macomber. As Thach reversed, a shot fell into his lap. This *Zero*, painted khaki, appeared to hover in front of him as it pulled lead on Macomber. Thach lifted his nose and squeezed. Rows of tracers raked the fighter from bottom to top, and Thach kicked left rudder to avoid the growing cloud of black smoke.

More *Zeros* rolled in. Voices screamed on the radio, one of them Lem. Thach twisted in his seat to keep sight, grunting as he pulled, gasping for breath as he let off, then bracing for another high-g turn. He had never experienced such sensory overload, but he surprised himself that he could fly and track and talk. *Gotta* do *something.*

"Ram, slide right, and act like a section leader!"

Ensign Ram Dibb pulled away and into the tracer lines as he was ordered, with two Japs in pursuit. Thach avoided a *Zero* and was now free.

"I've got two on my tail! *I need help!*" the desperate ensign shouted.

"Reverse left!" Thach answered, pulling his *Wildcat* across Dibb's extended six as Macomber, his radio out, held on.

Thach saw a high deflection shot develop, just like in training off Point Loma. He kept his pull in as Dibb flew across his nose with a Jap in trail. Assessing range, he bunted for a moment to close it, and squeezed again as the *Zero* touched his canopy bow. The enemy's cowling blew off as the engine burst into flames.

"Reverse!" Thach radioed to Dibb as he stabilized abeam, and, at that moment, Dibb got it. With another on his tail, he pulled into the skipper, who was maneuvering for a repeat high-side attack. *Yes!* With the *Zero* out of range for the moment, Dibb allowed himself to float, which sweetened the angles for the CO. As the enemy cranked on a turn to align, Dibb pulled into him and stepped on top rudder. Across from him the CO opened up, and his rounds stitched across the Jap, cutting a wing off and sending the burning fighter spinning to the sea.

Thach rolled out to check his belly. *Sonofabitch!*

A *Zero* was in for its own high-side shot. Once its nose lit up, Thach leveled and pulled up, and the machine gun rounds missed low. The enemy overshot and Thach reversed, perplexed that Macomber was a thousand feet below them. Below him the slow TBDs continued on the surface, one on fire. Behind them, a white parachute bloomed.

Dibb was in, and the Jap, belly up to him as it went after the CO, didn't see him coming. When Thach reversed back, the *Zero* followed into Dibb's gunsight. Dibb, fascinated, tracked the beige-colored plane with the strange cage canopy in front of him. In the cage was the bastard enemy who had just shot Red Dog. He didn't know Dibb was behind him. For a moment, Dibb felt as if he were an executioner, holding a pistol to a man's head. Despite flying through space, the head was stabilized in front of him, for an instant not moving. Steady. Deserving. Zero deflection, like the textbook. Pull a little lead... *Now!*

Dibb fired, and the first rounds flashed on the fuselage before the *Zero* exploded in front of him. He snatched his *Wildcat* up and away as flames filled his windscreen, and rolled over to watch the burning plane that carried the pilot he had summarily executed nose over. Finished. Revenge for Red Dog. *Die, you sonofabitch!*

He twisted his body to check his six and, seeing nothing, twisted back to check his other side. The Japs were gone. After bigger game.

"*Hiryū* reports enemy formation approaching from the east."

As they'd had to do all morning, the First Air Fleet staff scanned the reported quadrant to assess the attack, and watch the CAP do its lethal work.

Genda's practiced eye was the first to identify them. "More Douglas torpedo bombers," he said, loud enough for all to hear.

"Carrier based?" Kusaka asked.

Genda kept the glasses to his eyes as he answered. "Yes, Chief of Staff." Low on the water and over ten miles distant, the dots seemed to be running on *Hiryū* to the northeast. One burst into flame, as the reckless American planes had in each attack.

Nagumo was now more worried than angry. He had just beaten back a torpedo attack, and the Americans were attacking him *again*. As long as they did, he was unable to strike back. His carrier captains had to defend their ships, which hindered spotting and warm up. Save for a few fighters, his flight deck was clear, all of them were, and his impatience turned to alarm. This level of resistance was not anticipated, and it was more than the slipping timeline that unnerved him. There *had* to be another carrier to the east. No submarine sighting reports of a large task force? No reported intelligence? He sensed a need to run northwest and regroup as Genda had counseled while concentrating his floatplane scouts to the east. Once definitively located, he'd send the iron gauntlet to smash the Americans. If CarDiv 2 could escape another attack. *What's out there?*

"Kusaka!"

"*Hai*, Force Commander!"

"What do you recommend?"

Kusaka looked about as he gathered his thoughts. Genda was close enough to hear, as was Fuchida, who looked up from a bench.

"Admiral, after we defeat this attack, we run north and bring the attack groups up. Once spotted and warmed up, we'll launch. And, if we cannot send all the escort fighters we wish, we'll proceed regardless. In the event CarDiv 2 lags behind, so be it. They'll launch their planes as soon as possible. I'd say no more than twenty minutes after we do – if we change course now."

"When do you expect our CarDiv 1 carriers to launch?"

Kusaka swallowed. "With all required preparations and the turn to launch heading…1100, Force Commander."

Nagumo shook his head in disgust. *An hour.* An hour ago Kusaka had said it would be an hour.

"Admiral, the Americans are exhausting themselves in these futile, piecemeal attacks. We've repulsed each one. We are superior in equipment and training. They are no match for us. We'll run to get clear, bring up the attack force, and send it the moment it is ready."

"And what of our fighters?" Nagumo growled. Genda leaned in to hear the answer.

"Admiral, if we cannot recover them, and some must land in the water, so be it. We all agree that time is the most important factor now. Recommend consider that we designate one of the CarDiv 2 ships to serve as a recovery deck for all of our CAP fighters until we can redistribute them to their own ships." Kusaka seemed confident in his answers.

Genda had to agree. It made sense. Some of the *Zero-sens*, out of ammunition and fuel, would have to be sacrificed as the attack group was spotted aft on each deck. It was vital to get them airborne. Extra Type Zeros in the hangar bays, earmarked for the Midway defense force, could be pressed into service of the First Air Fleet. Priorities. *Akagi* and *Kaga* steamed north to minimize their exposure, the top priority.

Nagumo had been disappointed by events – and misled by his fliers, junior and senior – all morning. Now, he could only acquiesce.

"Proceed as recommended," he said to Kusaka, holding his gaze. *You had better be right.*

Chapter 18

LTJG Bud Kroeger, Bombing Six, 1005 June 4, 1942

Kroeger studied the ships off to the northeast and eased away from the skipper for a better view. Many white wakes, some larger than others. Going in all directions, mostly south, and some east. His eyes darted back and forth from the enemy warships ahead to flying form on the CO. Across from Best, Fred Weber seemed to spend more time assessing the ships than flying wing. Looking behind, Kroeger sensed the others in their cockpits picking their targets, excited, checking their switches, their engine readings, fuel, and making one last calculation on their plotting boards – an initial steer for home.

Awestruck, he focused on the two closest carriers. No islands to speak of, they looked like big yellow planks on the water. Their high freeboards gave an impression of being top-heavy. One was huge: *Kaga* by the recognition photos. Checking the VS – the *Sails* – above, it looked to Kroeger as if they would go for the one a few miles further to the right. Skipper Best was as cool as ever and scanned below with no indication of excitement. His own mouth dry from adrenalin, Kroeger looked across the skipper for enemy fighters and saw none. Yes, they were going for the big one, *Kaga*.

"Halterman, there they are. One o'clock about fifteen miles. Ready back there?"

"Yes, sir," the radioman answered. Kroeger heard him stow his guns in preparation for the dive.

More ships came into view as the cloud break opened, screen vessels to the south. How big was this fleet? *There's gotta be CAP up someplace.* The sun blazed above his right shoulder and the geometry became clear. The CO would roll them in left from out of the sun. Perfect, just like training, just like Skipper Best had said he'd lead VB-6. Best fishtailed his plane, the signal to take column as his gunner stowed his free .30s. Kroeger nodded when Best glanced at him, and closed his throttle to adjust. He'd follow his CO down the chute as number two. He'd follow him down to hell and back. And Dick Best would get him home.

The *Sails* were still in their vee, on top of him, but angling toward their carrier to the right. *Ten miles! Where are the* Zeros? The ship types were visible now: destroyers and cruisers. *No, that fat one must be a battleship.* Targets galore, but today Bud Kroeger was going to hit a carrier, the biggest damn carrier in the Jap Navy! It headed northeast, and he squinted to see if it had any planes on deck. There were a few parked aft, probably getting ready for launch. Too far away to tell, but, if they were, he'd lay his bomb right on the flag man. He rechecked that his weapon was armed. Fixed guns – charged. Canopy – back. Blower – low. Prop pitch – low. What was he forgetting? At least another five minutes. Below, the sun reflected the ripple texture on the blue surface. *There's a plane!* He followed it as it flew east, a mere speck and in no hurry. Alone. He looked for others and caught himself breathing in the thin air, mouth open from anticipation and repressed fear.

Two more amber flight decks to the north: *four carriers!* On *Kaga* he made out a red dot on the bow. The Japanese rising sun. The rest of the deck was all but empty. Maybe they were recovering; he scanned the sky again. Nothing. Were the Japs already headed for *Enterprise*? *Damn, did we get here too late?*

McClusky transmitted his intention to Skipper Gallaher. *"Follow me down, Earl."*

Kroeger heard no instructions for Skipper Best as he watched him stretch his neck up to assess the scout formation that was coming closer. They, too, were setting up, but in echelon. *Kaga* turned through west and the other carrier turned south. That one must be *Akagi* – the flagship. With a little Jap admiral on it. About the size of *Enterprise*. From his trail position, Kroeger couldn't see the skipper's head anymore, only his gunner scanning from one side to the other. Best's voice then filled his earphone.

"Attacking according to doctrine..."

Yes, the trailer, big fella Kaga, *while the Sails go for the far ship. Kaga* slid toward his left wing as Kroeger approached, and he was surprised to see only a single *Zero* parked aft. Far to the right, *Akagi's* deck was clear. Maybe a few planes, but only a few. *We missed 'em!*

"Take the one on the right..."

McClusky and the *Sails* headed for *Akagi*. The timing would be textbook. Sun over their right shoulders. Perfect! Best eased his formation left as Kroeger and the others followed, keeping their target visible in front of their wing. It turned toward them now, a turn that would force Kroeger and the others to be steep and minimize ranging error. *Steeper is better.* Armed. No CAP up here – or anywhere! Light winds...*we got 'em! Gotta get a hit. Gotta press it.*

Best opened his dive brakes to slow his approach. The perforated flaps across the trailing edge his wing – painted red on the inside – reminded Kroeger of the open maw of a hungry starling waiting to be fed. When lead's dive brakes opened, Kroeger opened his, as did the eleven remaining SBDs of Bombing Six. Below, *Kaga* reversed her turn. Kroeger was impatient for Best to dive. *Hurry up!*

As Best pulled his nose left across the horizon, Kroeger and the others matched him. Cutting the sea and trailing a massive wake as it turned to starboard, *Kaga* was directly underneath with elevators up and deck clear. Ahead, the CO pulled into it before he pushed over, and Kroeger pulled to...

Whoa!

A *Dauntless*, brakes open in a vertical dive, shot past the CO as he pushed his nose down. Then another, belly up to Best's formation. *Holy shit!* They had almost hit the skipper. Kroeger stayed with the CO and overbanked to follow him down as another SBD whistled past! He whipped his head back in time to see a row of dots in column above, diving down on him. *Dammit! Sails are gonna hit us!*

Best closed his flaps and waggled his wings as he pulled off right. *What is he doing?* Kroeger wondered as he matched in a panicked pull that put him underneath Best and his armed 1000-pounder. Kroeger climbed back into position as Best signaled in wild gestures for the rest to abort. Kroeger twisted to look behind him. *There's Fred...but where are the others?*

"Halterman, you see where the others went?"

"They're in their dives, sir!"

Looking back at *Kaga*, he saw an orderly column of SBDs below, with a swarm of them following from overhead, all diving on the point of water that the great carrier would occupy in thirty seconds. *Sonofabitch!*

Skipper Best flew toward the other ship, *Akagi*, as his two wingmen hung on, both gasping lungfuls of air after the near collision with the *Sails*.

Kroeger, now confused and fearful, scanned for fighters as the three American planes and their slingshot bombs flew toward a duel with Goliath.

Pressed against a window on *Akagi's* bridge, Genda couldn't believe it. *More?* he thought as yet *another* formation of Douglas torpedo planes approached CarDiv 2 from the southeast. The CAP would deal with the outclassed Americans as they had since the morning watch, but the tired *Zero-sens* would have to be recovered at some point, refueled, and rearmed. The Americans were gaining time – time to make repairs at Midway and to gather forces to defend against the next Japanese attack. But *this* level of opposition? No one had foreseen it in planning. Was there another enemy carrier closer to Midway? *My plan didn't foresee it.*

The helmsman kept his eyes to his task while Captain Aoki and the First Air Fleet staff scanned the horizon for additional threats and tried to organize the formation. It had long ago broken down, with the four carriers spread out in a line as screen ships opened up to keep them inside. Gaping holes would allow the Americans to enter unmolested until the CAP showed up.

A lookout shouted into a voice pipe. "Enemy dive-bombers high to the south!"

Genda stepped to the port bridge windows with Aoki, Kusaka and Oishi. Even Fuchida pressed close to get a view of this new threat. *Yes, Midway still has fight.* Dive-bombers in glide attacks had been ineffective and the men searched the skies to the south as Nagumo fumed. Nothing was visible until Fuchida, looking higher than the others, spotted them.

"There, through the clouds...over *Kaga.*"

Genda easily saw them, a huge formation of Douglas dive-bombers. The numbers in the swarm stunned him. They were high, and the lead aircraft were already in a dive on *Kaga* some four miles away. This was not a glide bomb attack; these American dives were steep. Professional. Now alarmed, Genda watched as *Kaga's* antiaircraft opened up.

Please, no...

McClusky rolled out and bunted, hanging by his lap belt. He was off his seat a bit, as uncomfortable as Gallaher had said he should be. *If yer not uncomfortable, yer not steep enough.*

He stabilized and put the carrier in his telescopic bombsight, crosshairs on the bow. His goggled eye pressed against the padded end of the tube as he dove on it. The carrier turned to starboard, and he repositioned with aileron to keep the crosshairs on it. No planes on deck, no ack-ack...

"Eight thousand!" Chocalousek called out.

The carrier seemed to float up to him, growing in the bombsight. Lines painted on the yellow deck, a lone *Zero* parked aft. The big red ball on the bow held his attention as his hands and feet moved the controls in minute corrections to keep the crosshairs on the turning ship. McClusky fought to concentrate as he noticed the powerful wake to port, the shadow from the island sweeping along the deck.

"Six thousand!"

With half of *Kaga* now in his bombsight, his *Dauntless* stabilized as his ears popped from the pressure. Centered ball. *Keep it centered!*

"Four thousand! Thirty-nine hundred, thirty-eight…" On the interphone, Chocalousek now called out every hundred feet to help his pilot.

Muzzle flashes pulsated from the galleries: the light automatics. *They see us!* Small lights floated up and then rocketed underneath his SBD. The carrier's turn forced him to bunt and reposition the wings. He felt as if he were on his back, *uncomfortable*, timbers, yellow tire-stained flight deck timbers…he could almost count them, hovering over the ship with his prop windmilling easy. Hand on the release…

"Three thousand, twenty-nine, twenty-eight…twenty-five hun'rd sir!"

With tension in his voice, Chocalousek kept the calls coming as the altimeter spun past 2,000. *Now!*

McClusky yanked up on the release handle. The nose quivered and the crosshairs jumped. *Damn! I threw it!* He felt a familiar jolt, followed by a shudder, as 500 pounds fell away toward the men running across the yellow deck. With the sea rushing toward him, he tensed up his body and pulled.

Nine g's of crushing force fell on McClusky and Chocalousek, pushing their heads into their shoulders and flattening their legs against the seats. McClusky's vision grayed and tunneled under the strain as the swells rushed toward him. His heavy left arm struggled under the g to push the throttle to the firewall. Close the dive brakes, nose above horizon, ease the pull… *Vision opens and color floods in. Breathe! Run!*

McClusky felt the SBD lurch as Chocalousek whipped his seat around to face aft. They came off north, and McClusky scanned fast to get his bearings. Nothing but ships to the east, and he snap-rolled hard away from them. *Kaga*…water curtain next to it, and another plume rising off the far side as a bomber pulled off with streamers from the wingtips.

You threw it, dummy!

An opening in the screen to the southeast. *Zeros to the right. They don't see me. Unload to the deck.* Tracers zipped past on the right, splashes. Roll left. Clear. *Keep the airplane moving!*

Smoke on *Kaga!* Someone scored! Jink. Head on a swivel. Carrier three miles to port – the one Dick is supposed to hit. *Where is he?* More flattops on the horizon. Hornet's *group left before we did. Where are those guys?* Cruiser firing main battery at something: sudden columns of yellowish water off to starboard.

"Holy shit, sir!"

McClusky looked back to see thick, black smoke rise from fire that lined the length of *Kaga's* flight deck. As he did, a muffled flash from inside the ship blew the forward elevator off. He was transfixed for a moment as the huge wafer careened and floated at the apex of its flight hundreds of feet over a towering sheet of flame.

"We got that fat SOB, Commander!"

"Sure did! I got bandits at three! Nose on!"

"I see 'em, sir!"

McClusky and Chocalousek watched them cross aft, then peel off on the trailing SBDs that had just pulled out of their dives above the flaming carrier. Keeping his throttle firewalled, McClusky held his course for the opening in the screen. They'd join on him once clear, and McClusky wasn't about to feint south. *Akagi* was turning hard through west. Intact.

Where the hell is Best?

The First Air Fleet staff watched spellbound as a sudden column of water from a near miss shot into the air next to *Kaga*, then another.

"Thank goodness they are ineffective," Oishi said. Unconvinced, a pensive Genda looked on. The Americans only had to get lucky once.

A groan went up as an orange flash transformed into a black smudge that bloomed and rose over *Kaga*. "Blast!" Kusaka cursed, and Genda turned to see Nagumo's tight lips and fierce eyes fixed on the horizon as Aoki and Masuda shouted orders to their gun crews and lookouts. Another flash and a new column of smoke arose from the forward half of *Kaga*. Stoic, Genda could only watch as more American planes dove on the wounded carrier. *We should have regrouped,* Genda thought.

"Hell divers!" a terrified lookout screamed.

Dick Best was almost at full RPM as his two wingmen held on. Kroeger was worried now and guessed Fred was, too. A moment ago they had arrived unmolested over the entire enemy task force with the CO leading them on a textbook run against the biggest Jap carrier in the fleet. Perfect geometry, perfect conditions. It didn't get any better – not even in training. He was reminded of a routine training attack on *Enterprise* off Lahaina on a crystal blue morning.

Kroeger thought about their close call. *As soon as we entered our dive, the Scouting Six boys cut us out...on* our *target!* Idiots! *Lucky we didn't collide with the dummies.* He still couldn't fathom it. *The carrier to the left was ours!*

Akagi was ahead, with a *Zero* in take-off position amidships and two behind. *C'mon, Skipper!* The planes were not moving, but they would be soon. He hoped the CO would push over a little shallow, to attack ASAP, *to get them before they get us.* Fishtail signal, get in column, number two again. Trim tabs, carb heat, mixture rich. Kroeger went over checklist again in the seconds left.

"Halterman, ready?"

"Yes, sir! We're still clean!"

"Good."

No CAP. Can't believe it. Cinch belt down... Gonna press it. Only three of us. Gotta get three hits. *Damn, how could we have gooned this up?*

Best didn't have time to set up to the south. Doctrine called for simultaneous attack. *Kaga* was already hit, fore and aft, with more SBDs diving on it in an ordered column. Another hit forward...Wow! *Gotta hit this one now. We're late.*

Seconds from their push, Kroeger forced himself to scan a patch of sky for movement. Nothing. The only planes were down there on the surface, some in a loose wedge, others solo. Screen ships were shooting at something, but what? To the northwest were two more carriers, ten miles at least. Kroeger pressed the interphone.

"Halterman, get ready!"

"Yes, sir! All set!"

"Okay, Skipper's gonna push soon."

Best came up on the radio: *"Don't let this carrier escape!"*

The skipper's plane slowed again, and the open flaps caused it to almost stop in midair. Kroeger, and Weber in trail, matched him. Far below, *Akagi* waited, holding her fire. *We're above their range...for the moment.*

For the second time in five minutes, Best lifted his plane up then pushed down. Sliding to the inside, Kroeger watched him go and counted.

One potato...two potato...

Still leaning forward from the deceleration, Kroeger pulled, pushed, and kicked, his nose falling through in a tight arc as he dove down on his target. *Akagi* seemed alone except for the CO in his dive above her. A white wake followed the carrier, a scar on the pristine ocean surface. Airspeed built into a rising crescendo of cold air that shrieked past the open canopy. His pushover, *good*. Following the skipper was easy. Stabilized at 240 knots, aiming ahead half a ship length. Engine idling and prop blades flickering in the sunlight in front of him. CO holding steady.

Now gunfire, cordite drifting off the galleries. To Kroeger it was silent proof of lost surprise. There goes a *Zero. Damn, too late!* Red circle on the flight deck forward: huge. Red and yellow timbers. Gaining on the CO…airspeed good. Hold it there…ship's turning into the crosshairs. Fireflies in the gun sight, a row of them… Ignore them! CO's bird drifting into view, don't get in his wash.

"Six thousand, sir!"

Ship's turning hard to starboard. Lead it… Gonna be a beam attack, dammit! Strange island, strange funnels, all the elevators up. Turn needle, ball. A bit more trim to sweeten. Hold it steady…

"Four thousand!"

CO should come off any second. This is a good one. steady… Just a little aileron to correct…

"Three thousand!"

Damn, Skipper's pressin' it! Pull, sir! Nothing but deck and that queer little island. Lay it on the island. Automatic guns blazing, no let up.

"*Twenty-three, twenty-two…*"

Crossing rows of tracers – *Oh, shit!*

"*Mister Kroe – !*"

Kroeger mashed the release button and welcomed the seat-of-the pants jolt as the hooks opened. Tensed and ready, when the bomb swung free at the second jolt, he pulled with both hands into an instant wall of unseen force, squeezing him, crushing him, blinding him as his tunneled vision sped across the blue surface. Behind him, Halterman grunted under the high-g load. Kroeger's face drooped down and his elbows were pushed into his sides by the 9-g pull. With vision obscured by dark streaks due to the high-g pooling of blood, he strained in desperation to get his nose up. He let off to unload, and his full vision gushed back in. Through his earphones, he heard it: a crackling sound…automatic gunfire! Flaps in… *Where's the skipper?* Tracers above. *Dammit!* Snap right. *Balls to the wall and get out of here!*

Skipper off right, his prop blades practically in the water. Turn to follow. Clear area southeast. Look for *Zeros. Fred?*

Kroeger picked up Weber over his right shoulder, and behind him saw something on *Akagi's* deck: smoke, but not much. A soaring geyser erupted next to the carrier's stern – Fred's bomb.

"I think we hit it, sir!" Halterman crowed.

Kroeger had no time to evaluate; he was keeping sight of the CO, looking for the CAP, and avoiding the defensive screen ships in a frantic effort to break free. He would run out of gas, all of them would, but a water landing far from the enemy vessels would give him a chance.

"WOW!" Halterman shouted.

Chapter 19

Navigation Bridge, HIJMS *Akagi*, 1023 June 4, 1942

Captain Aoki stuck his head outside the window and picked them up off the port bow. *"Right full rudder!"*

Fuchida saw three planes coming at them – at him! An object floated clear of the lead plane. *A bomb!* Fuchida's whole being focused on it as it grew larger, silent, not moving off its trajectory toward him.

"Take cover!" someone shouted, and Fuchida curled up next to a mantelet in an absurd yet instinctive effort to save himself. Outside, gunfire, seemingly from everything *Akagi* had, thundered and chattered amid shouted orders and cries. He felt Genda crouch down behind him as the American bomber pulled off with a fearsome roar that drowned out the cacophony of defensive fire.

A faint whistling sound rose in volume until it became a shriek, and a thundering explosion shook *Akagi's* frames as the flagship raced ahead. A giant column of water, accompanied by a rumbling sound none had ever heard before, lifted high over their heads. Seconds later the deluge slammed into the bridge and drenched everyone. *Akagi* heeled as the rudder bit in. *Near miss! We might make it!* Fuchida hoped.

Another marrow-rattling roar as the second plane pulled off, followed by another faint whistle. Crouched on the deck, Fuchida's midsection hurt, and dirty seawater sloshed down the deck plate as his mind struggled to grasp this new sensation amid the piercing scream of the hurtling bomb.

A thunderous explosion erupted from behind as shrapnel lashed the island and tripod mast. Fuchida felt the jolt in his hands and knees as shock from the blow shot through *Akagi's* steel decks, and he sensed the flash despite his closed eyes. The men on the bridge were knocked off their feet by the force, then ducked instinctively as another bomb whistled in. It exploded aft and rocked *Akagi* to the keel. Genda noticed the antiaircraft guns were silent – and wondered about the severity of the hit amidships.

As he rose to his feet, Fuchida was relieved. One hit; not too serious. On the flight deck men ran to the hoses as Masuda shouted, and a hose-team from starboard streamed water on the conflagration. As they crept closer, a thunderclap from below blasted out sections of deck. Men were again knocked off their feet as the shockwave blew through the bridge. With foreboding, both Genda and Fuchida waited for more secondary explosions they knew would follow. On deck, the hose snaked in wild oscillations, the only evidence of the firefighting team mowed down seconds earlier.

Now anxious, Aoki shouted at his terrified helmsman, who had the wheel over hard left with all his weight, frantic that the helm did not respond. Genda did the tactical calculus. While the damage to CarDiv 1 was devastating, at least CarDiv 2 was intact. In spite of the destruction around him, Genda gazed spellbound at the horrible and unimaginable sight of *Kaga* to the west.

At Halterman's excited shout, Kroeger whipped his head back in time to see flame and black smoke shoot high over *Akagi* as debris fanned out from an induced explosion inside the ship. Out of the corner of his eye, he noted *Kaga* on the horizon, giving off heavy smoke the length of it. A muffled flash amidships, and another aft, lifted visible pieces of the ship into the air. Slowly, they tumbled, like a pinwheel on fire. *Holy cow!*

He forced himself to keep sight of his jinking CO, to stay with him but not too close. *Gotta be CAP down here.* Best pointed them to an opening, and, miles to his right, Kroeger saw gray specks hugging the water and also running to the southeast. *Zeros* pounced on them. *Run.*

He drifted acute on the CO. *Heck with it!* Kroeger hoped Best would see him and add every inch of manifold pressure he could. Regardless, Kroeger kept his throttle firewalled. *Where's Fred? There he is, running hard.* His gunner fired at something. Alarmed, Kroeger searched for a threat. Nothing. Behind him, smoke from *Akagi* billowed high. A bright light flashed from inside it, then another. The middle of the flight deck was covered in flame.

We did it!

Max Leslie assessed the two carriers below him. He'd have to dive all of his planes on the nearest one. *Where the hell is Wally Short and Scouting Five?* They must be nearby, and, when they showed up, would take the smaller flattop to the west. They couldn't help but see it. *They're missing out!*

Lefty Holmberg held position next to him, and Leslie envied the 1000-pounder slung underneath his plane. Regardless, he'd dive on this carrier[1] with its strange starboard island, and his boys would pummel it. He patted his head so Lefty could see, pointed at the carrier, and popped his dive brakes open.

Just then, his gunner opened up off the left. Surprised, Leslie saw tracers zip past, missing forward due to the sudden change in airspeed. Radioman Gallagher held the hammer down, and the *Zero* that appeared out of nowhere flamed up as Gallagher continued to blaze away at it.

"Got it, sir!"

"Dammit, Bill, where'd that come from? Here we go!"

Leslie rolled in on top of the carrier that was in a starboard turn and closed the throttle to idle. With his fixed .50s, he'd strafe the damn thing to keep their heads down. In unison, gunfire erupted from all sides of the flight deck; though the deck was a rectangle, it now resembled a ring, a ring of fire. It was nothing more than a high-deflection shot, and Leslie held the gunsight just forward of the bow as Gallagher called out their altitude. The red ball on the flight deck was a perfect bullseye, and Leslie let his gunsight fall on it as he opened fire from 5,000 feet, kicking the rudder to spray the deck with bullets. With his trigger squeezed, Leslie's .50s clattered in front of him as his tracers jumped from the barrels and floated down on the blond timbers of the Jap flight deck. The scent of burned gunpowder filled the cockpit.

After four seconds of fire, his guns jammed. *Dammit!* Leslie held his dive and attempted to clear them. *Dammit!* Since Gallagher could take a shot on the pull off, Leslie allowed the great ship to move out of his sight before he pulled up so Gallagher could shoot it.

Recovered, and with Gallagher giving it to them, Leslie twisted his neck back in time to see Lefty's hit.

The bomb entered just forward of the island, and a mix of flame and debris shot high into the air. A white concentric shockwave burst from the ship as it heeled hard to starboard. The fireball rose into the sky and dissipated, and the ship charged ahead with flames pouring from the hole in the flight deck.

"Yeah!" Leslie cried as he pumped his fist and noticed that the guns on the forward half of the ship had gone silent. However, a big battlewagon nearby fired with all but her main battery, as did the screen ships. The water underneath him was covered with splashes as the sky above was filled with crisscrossing yellow lights and spotted with black puffs. In this confused whirlwind he was

---

[1] HIJMS *Sōryū*

now afraid, more than when he had approached the fleet. No longer *thinking*, he could only react, overwhelmed from the roaring engine, Gallagher firing at something that may be firing at them, more and higher splashes, the thudding, and airplane control reactions to rounds ripping through the tail. Antiaircraft puffs, splashes, and tracer trails filled his windscreen as he held the SBD steady. *Just pick a direction and go!*

Leslie found an opening of a few miles between two destroyers in the screen and went for it, thankful it was to the southeast, toward safety. He had a general idea Holmberg was behind him but saw no others. To the west, smoke... *Stack gas?* No, smoke – *and flame* – from hits! *Must be the* Enterprise *and* Hornet *boys!*

Clear, Leslie rolled left as Lefty maneuvered to the inside. Other SBDs ran for their lives, taking fire as they escaped. Looking over his shoulder at the carrier, he spotted sheets of flame high over the length of it that undulated like harvest-ready wheat in the afternoon breeze. Transfixed, Leslie eased his turn as his boys flew past, oblivious to their lead and focused on survival. They ran hard away into the safety of the desolate blue wilderness of water, the promise of home somewhere far down to the east.

Leslie could not turn himself away from this terrible and magnificent sight, and orbited clear to behold it, to sear it into his memory. Flames from the carrier snapped at the sky hundreds of feet above as muffled flashes from inside foretold unspeakable destruction. To the west, two more carriers gave off huge columns of black that climbed thousands of feet into a sky dotted with flak smudges. Antiaircraft rounds arced and burst over a sea churned white – alive with the evidence of death.

As Best's three *Dauntlesses* clawed their way out of the Japanese crossfire, Kroeger throttled back and maintained position on the skipper's wing. The *Zeros* were no longer interested in them, and flak from the screen ships lagged behind as the SBDs crossed them at ninety degrees. Skipper Best seemed unconcerned as stray tracers and spent machine gun rounds slapped the water around them. He was interested in something to the northeast, and pointed in that direction to show his wingmen. On the horizon, heavy black smoke rose from fires covering the length of a ship, one Kroeger could not identify. *Is that a carrier?*

Whatever it was, Kroeger scanned for threats to them, held position on the skipper, and *ran*.

Miles to the south, Childers and VT-3 fought for their lives.

Not long after Massey had steadied his formation on an attack heading, the *Zeros* pounced as a flock: firing in unison, slashing at the Americans, and almost hitting each other. Their attack was so sudden, so *violent*. Childers turned his gun on a gaggle of them to his right, shooting in the middle of the group, spraying more than aiming, flinching as tracers snapped past him. More lined up, and Childers forced himself to aim. Three were in, angled toward the lead, big cannon balls ripping through the skipper's formation. Childers led the first *Zero* and fired, his rounds missing low and behind before he frantically swung to its wingman as the deflection increased. Despite the deafening hammer blows of his own .30 cal., Childers heard the gunfire from the TBDs around him along with the steady drumbeat of the *Zero* cannons that added to the background clatter as the Japs pulled off less than a football field away.

At intervals, the assassins kept coming and Childers kept firing, as did Brazier, Darce and Phillips next to him. Their pilots held steady on the CO as he pressed ahead. For a moment, Childers had nothing to shoot, but saw the Fighting Three F4Fs in a swirling fight high above. *Where are the* Zeros? *Okay, two setting up on the right.* Just then a flaming *Zero* – in a vertical dive and trailing heavy smoke – smacked the water off their tail, less than 100 yards away. Startled by its sudden and fiery appearance, Childers recovered to defend the stabs and slashes from the new knife fight he was engaged in.

As soon as the *Zeros* had finished a run, Childers looked for more, then saw Darce next to him. Smiling, Darce patted his gun and mouthed, *"You owe me, Okie!"*

A sudden row of tracers from below shot toward the second division. Childers looked down and fell back as the deck of a Jap cruiser passed below. Harry had flown over it at masthead height, still flying on the CO who led them ahead at 100 knots. With a clear line of fire, the cruiser's port side gunners opened up with a broadside of light AA, and Childers felt two hits on the left wing. *Damn it, Harry!*

Now inside the screen, three carriers in column, Skipper going on the closest, escort ships churning the waters, heeling hard with muzzle flashes on their superstructures, and puffs from bow guns breaking over their bridges. Taking a quick glance, Childers noticed they were still a few miles from the separation point. Antiaircraft bursts over the task force. *Where are the Zeros?*

Their target carrier[1] ran from them at flank speed… An agonizing stern chase. Childers searched for *Zeros* and found none. Antiaircraft fire whizzed past, rounds punching the corrugated metal skin. A cry from Harry. Turning right… Second division veering left. An unseen *Zero* roared overhead 90 off. One from the high side, then another, both turning and rolling like bats on a summer evening. Childers scanned to his left, awestruck as two jagged holes appeared on top of the wing with no accompanying sound.

"Look at the skipper!" Harry cried.

Childers looked to port in time to see Massey's flaming TBD nose down to the water. Horrified, he saw the quizzical look on the gunner's face turn to panic when he realized what was happening. At impact, the *Devastator* exploded and tumbled in churning fire that sent spray and debris high over Childers and the other TBDs as they flew past.

The second division was losing planes, *somebody bailed out*, a cannon round to the tail, *can't see up ahead*. Frantic, Childers shot at what he could from his bucking mount.

"We're not gonna make it," Harry said on the interphone. Matter of fact. Resigned.

Fear gripped Childers as he absorbed Harry's words. He remembered the CO and his chief radioman in their doomed TBD moments earlier. Fear. No, *terror!* Childers's TBD was nosing toward the water as Harry fought to control it, cursing as he did. *Was this it?* A *Devastator* next to them caught fire as the rest continued into the blizzard of dancing yellow dots and red bursts of AA that turned to black stains. *Darce!*

"Let's get outta here!" Childers shouted.

Harry struggled for control as Childers scanned for threats in the rear. The *Zeros* were off – too close to their own flak. *"Can't control it,"* Harry cried, but soon Childers noticed they were turning right, to north, and away from the target. The nose came up, and Harry seemed in control now. Chief Esders was ahead. *Stay with him!*

Anxious because of the lull, Childers had nothing to shoot – until he checked below. He was shocked to see a *Zero* camped out underneath, flying formation on them, the unruffled Jap pilot's eyes visible through his goggles. They could practically shake hands. Alarmed and scared by the impassive face of a human being bent on killing him, Childers assessed this sudden threat. *Is that SOB gonna cut our tail off?*

---

[1] HIJMS *Hiryū*

Without thinking, Childers raised his gun as he stood, firing it *down* on his unwelcome wingman as soon as he had a bead. The Jap recoiled and pushed away. *Gone.*

Childers checked around him for enemy fighters. *Where are the rest? Where are they, dammit?*

The *Zeros* returned in force: methodical, determined, taking turns to pour fire from classic high-side attacks into the surviving Americans now running for their lives. Their target carrier charged ahead unscathed. Childers matched their discipline with effective bursts, gaining confidence with each push of the trigger. Two slugs tore into his left thigh. Too engrossed to notice the stinging burns, Childers kept up his fire.

To avoid him, the Japs came in from the beam, and Childers pushed the guns 90 degrees to broadside and twisted his body to get behind the gun sight. With a foot outside the cockpit to steady himself, a round slammed into his ankle bone.

"OWWW! *Damn...sonofa-bitch!*"

"You okay?" Harry shouted over his shoulder.

"They hit my ankle! *Damn!*" Childers barked back, angry and wincing from the searing pain. He bled from both legs, but continued to fire. *Conserve ammo. Don't just spray them out of range!* A Jap came across from right to left and Childers led him. At the right moment, he pressed the trigger.

Nothing.

"*Dammit! Mother-,*" Childers bellowed, now panicked with a jammed gun. It wouldn't clear, and another Jap lined up on him.

He was beyond terrified. Unarmed. *Naked.* Childers's mind raced through options. He unstrapped his .45 pistol and, with one hand, placed it on top of the gun sight as he aimed with the other. A *Zero* came in from the quarter, and, just before it opened up, Childers squeezed off three shots. The Jap pulled up. Another rolled in, and Childers adjusted as the enemy's black nose grew larger. Harry lifted their TBD up and fired at something ahead with his fixed guns. At the same time, Childers squeezed some more rounds at the Jap who had scored hits on the wing and engine. Another, and Childers emptied his magazine. *Now what?*

Two *Zeros* climbed to the right and headed back toward the task force. On the horizon, the sky was dotted with black puffs that to Childers looked like an upside-down bowl over the enemy ships. Big caliber fire, black smoke, white spray. He looked for his fellow TBDs and saw none. No, wait...two second-division birds veering off north, one misting. *Barkley okay?* Ahead, Harry joined on the chief.

Childers realized he was panting as adrenalin pulsed through his body. Pain from his legs gripped him, and his dungaree pants were soaked in blood. He used a bag on the cockpit floor to tie around his ankle to stop the bleeding.

The *Zeros are gone...where are those two guys going? Home is to the east, follow us...engine sputtering, now quit, son of a...caught back to life...still flying.*

Chief Esders joined next to them, shot up. Brazier. *Brazier! You okay, shipmate?* Head moving...not much. Chief Esders signaled Childers to ask if he had a good homing signal to the ship. *No, the set's shot out. Engine quit again...back to life. Still flying. Oil streaks on left canopy...Chief climbing away. Brazier, look at me! Please!*

Corl and Esders nursed their wounded planes and wounded gunners back to the east. They dropped. They missed.

Childers wasn't worried about failure. He was exhausted and, with his remaining strength, held pressure against his left thigh to stem the flow of blood. His head rested on the canopy rail as he contemplated the blue sky and white clouds from the back of his drafty TBD. Shell casings and Jap shrapnel rolled about the cockpit floor smeared thick with his blood. They had escaped, and the steady vibration of the engine comforted him.

CHAPTER 20

HIJMS *Hiryū*, 1035 June 4, 1942

"Mina-san, come quick! Flight deck!"

Maruyama and Nakao were relaxing in the ready room when their excited squadron mate burst in to alert his mates. *Hiryū* steamed at flank as it had much of the morning, and gunners aft fired at another wretched American torpedo attack. Maruyama would have watched the spectacle to assess the American technique, but he and the others had orders to remain in the ready room.

The man showed fear. Maruyama could not resist following him topside, as all did, unable to control their curiosity. The passageway became crowded as the Type 99 pilots and gunners in the adjacent compartment also hurried to the catwalk hatch to take a look.

Gunfire continued aft and Maruyama's eyes were drawn there, but not for long.

On the flight deck, clusters of men gaped, their eyes transfixed on the western horizon. As Maruyama stepped onto the gallery deck, he saw the black columns first, and, when he moved between the men on the catwalk, had an unobstructed view of the CarDiv 1 carriers. *Akagi's* bow and island identified her, but the after half of the carrier was covered in flames – flames which gave off black and brown smoke that climbed hundreds of meters into the air. Farther down, what could only be *Kaga* was all but unrecognizable, on fire the length of her with billowing smoke and roiling flame amidships. Antiaircraft fire burst about the carriers, leaving black scars as witness to the American presence. Low on the churned-up water, he saw two enemy airplanes, then a third. Stunned, his mouth hung slack.

"*Look!*" someone shouted as several sailors pointed to starboard.

Maruyama and the others climbed up to the deck forward of the island to get a better view. Two miles away, *Sōryū* was on fire from the main deck up. Bright flame gushed from openings in the hangar bays, and fire shot from the bow as if from a blowtorch. Like Miyauchi that morning, Maruyama felt as if he could touch *Sōryū*. As they stood aghast, a tremendous explosion blew off a huge section of her flight deck aft, and the men gasped in horror and amazement.

"Induced explosions...that was probably a Type 91," someone said. Seconds later a thunderous *boom* reached their ears. Maruyama and the others stood in awe at the destruction. Uncomprehending...yet understanding. Maruyama thought back to *Oklahoma*. Powerful ship-killing torpedoes now detonated inside *Sōryū*, ripping it apart from within the way Maruyama and his wingmen had ripped out the hull plates of the great American battleship. Two more explosions in quick succession tore through *Sōryū's* after hangar bays as *Hiryū's* dumbstruck aviators watched. Maruyama turned, and next to him stood a grim Tomonaga. Ignoring Maruyama's shocked gaze, he contemplated what this meant for the Mobile Force – and *Hiryū*. More terrifying detonations from *Sōryū* echoed across the water amid the rumble of gunfire and the constant hum of airplane engines droning all around the *Kido Butai*. Aboard *Sōryū*, the intensity of the raging fires increased, and the burning ship fell aft as *Hiryū* charged ahead. Who could survive such a holocaust? The loudspeaker blared the voice of the angry Air Officer.

"Spectators get below! All not engaged with the launch off the flight deck! Spot and warm up the strike group at once!"

A bell sounded as the amidships elevator lowered to the hangar bay to retrieve a dive-bomber. Farther aft, another elevator brought up the first Type 99 with an armor-piercing bomb slung below it. The *kanbaku* pilots next to Maruyama appeared confused, and some ran along the edge of the flight deck edge to parking spots aft as others returned to the ready room to retrieve their gear and plotting boards. Maruyama and his mates cheered them with cries of *banzai!* and exhortations to take revenge on the savage American killers.

"Get below!" Tomonaga barked at his torpedo pilots. He grabbed the arm of one and shoved him toward the catwalk ladder. Maruyama filed behind the others, with his eyes on *Akagi* and *Kaga*. Red blooms of flame opened and then disappeared inside the hideous black columns over each. On the southern horizon, *more* Yankee airplanes dodged the screening cruisers as they fired, and the uneasy men scanned for threats. Before he stepped off the flight deck, Maruyama lifted his eyes to the bridge. Above the cluster of mantelets were windows he could not see inside, revealing only dancing reflections of the sea on the glass as the ship raced over the waves.

Are we doomed?

The deck shuddered and another shockwave of warm air blew through *Akagi's* bridge as Fuchida struggled to the ladder. The induced explosions had been coming from further aft, but this one was much closer. *Fresh planes and weapons.*

Aoki, more enraged than Fuchida had never seen him, shouted orders to the helmsman and into the voice pipe as Masuda led the firefighting effort on the flight deck. It appeared hopeless. A hose-team spraying water on the midships elevator was blown up and overboard when the flight deck below them erupted into flaming fragments. Fearful survivors refused to pick up another wild hose that whipsawed across the hot deck, its gushing water turning to steam. Shrapnel tore into the hammock mantelets along the island and set them on fire. White smoke drifted into the bridge from the ladder well next to the chart table. *Akagi* circled as Aoki fought to control her. A realist, Fuchida knew she was dying. *I will die today, too.*

The horizon around *Akagi* was filled with flame, fire, and death. Black trails led to concentric circles on the water that signified the violent destruction – *ours or theirs?* – of warplanes carrying one or more young men. Reverberations of gunfire from screen ships and airplane engines – *ours or theirs?* – filled the bridge, as did the cracking of timbers and the roaring fires on *Akagi's* flight deck. To the east, destroyers made smoke as nearby cruisers fired at unseen attackers with their main battery turrets. Fuchida stopped.

Oh, no...

One of the CarDiv 2 carriers erupted in towering flame as fiery debris fanned high above. Across the water, *Kaga* continued to blow herself apart. Fuchida considered her finished. But the ship he saw on the eastern horizon was just a low slab covered by a bright flare the length of her, as if she were carrying white-burning magnesium. The smoke that spewed from above the long flare was black, gray, brown, *red*. Could any survive on that blazing and gruesome funeral pyre? The intact carrier turned, and Fuchida could make out the island to port. *Hiryū* was still alive.

Sōryū was dying, then. No, it was already dead. *Take me, too.*

Shock and thunder from below jolted everyone. After they steadied themselves, Kusaka argued with the commander to abandon. Nagumo refused, not willing to concede defeat, *unbelieving*. Fuchida knew the real reason. Pride.

Genda stared speechless at *Sōryū* in her death throes, and sensed Fuchida studying him.

"We goofed. *I* goofed."

"Genda-kun, we broke off too much at once." Fuchida said. Another blast from behind sprayed the island with splinters as the men flinched.

"Engines stop," Aoki commanded, unable to control his ship. Masuda stood behind his captain. Others on the bridge held their breath as they waited for the unthinkable.

"Pass the word," Aoki muttered to Masuda before resuming his position near the starboard windows. Resolute, he wished that the next blast would kill him. Behind him, Masuda relayed the command to abandon.

Off to port, *Nagara* hove to, waiting to embark the commander of the Mobile Force and his staff. Near her, an escort ship closed on the derelict to pick up survivors. With a bright flash, *Kaga* convulsed again, throwing off another giant section that lifted clear. Half the size of one of His Majesty's destroyers, the twisted steel structure slapped the sea and disappeared beneath a huge wave. The concussion from it raced across the water and shook *Akagi's* bridge windows with a deep *ba-boooom.*

"*Hiryū* is left to fight," Fuchida said, forgetting for the moment the pain in his side.

"If I were Yamaguchi, I'd run," Genda replied, standing like a statue amid the chaos. To Fuchida, the bright eyes of his friend had turned black.

Best checked Kroeger and Weber in position. *Good.* He left his throttle alone as the three sprinted toward the outer ring for safety. Two thousand feet above, two sections of three *Zeros* crossed from right to left. Best saw what they were going for: TBDs attacking a carrier to the east, two or three miles away. Two of the *Devastators* blazed up as a swarm of fighters worked them over. *Is that Gene and VT-6?*

Searching all around him, Best scanned for threats as he bumped the throttle, then checked to see if the others could keep up. Ahead, he saw a speck that grew larger on the windscreen. It was a floatplane that resembled a fighter with two big feet for floats. The enemy plane bore down on them for a head-on shot. Best pointed at it, and Kroeger nodded. The three SBD pilots lifted their noses at the intruder and, when satisfied with the range and deflection, fired their fixed guns in a fusillade of tracers. The floatplane pulled up and away, and Best watched it fly off to the northeast – toward the burning carrier.

"*Holy shit, Skipper!*"

Best turned around to see what had caught Chief Murray's attention. A huge explosion had blown *Kaga's* elevator into the air and transformed it into a burning and smoking table top that seemed to float above the carrier before falling back into the maelstrom of fire and smoke. Next to *Kaga*, *Akagi* was still moving. Inside her, muffled flashes from induced explosions lit up both existing openings and new ones made by the destructive force. Best assumed most of the planes were in the hangar bay, and probably loaded.

Three carriers burned with fierce intensity, but a fourth was untouched. *Who hit that one to the north?* Best wondered. *Whoever it was, they nailed it.*

Behind him, Murray was awestruck by the scene they had created. *"Whoa, sir!"*

Max Leslie made sure that all his chicks headed east. One after another, internal explosions from the carrier they had attacked flashed their destructive power. In mere minutes, the ship had been transformed into a molten inferno, laid to waste by *his* boys! Lefty stayed with him as the others egressed east. Gripped by the scene, Leslie was unable to leave. His pilots shouted their excitement, taking peeks over their shoulders and marveling at the damage they had inflicted.

To the west, two carriers gave off heavy smoke. Leslie didn't know if it was Wally or the *Enterprise* guys who had done it. Maybe *Hornet* got in their first licks. Then, a massive blast from one doomed ship generated a fireball that bloomed into a mushroom-like cloud. On the radio, pilots howled with shocked amazement at the spectacle, followed by primal screams of revenge, of retribution, from boys, some of whom two years ago could not have brought themselves to shoot a crow resting on a rail fence. *"Bobby, didja see that fat mother explode! Die, you yellow bastards!"*

The cloud rose high through the existing black column of smoke, as if lifting the dying ship and supporting sea into the air along with it. More shouts of excitement, the bloodthirsty and racial cursing of hated enemies, hundreds of whom had surely just perished. With the cloud, a release, a euphoric cleansing of stored tension, an almost sexual tension of conquest followed by *loving acceptance* that the men sensed deep inside. Loved by warfare, the ancient competitive human achievement.

They had been tested, after months and years of preparation, days of anxiety, pressure, growing hatred, pointless worry, and the raw fear of death before they'd even had a chance to really live. They'd manned up on their wooden decks in their flimsy planes with unreliable guns and flown west over a desolate expanse where a tested enemy waited for them in a fight where neither gave quarter. They'd met the test, *in the clinch*, an uppercut knockout of a schoolyard bully – *an enemy vanquished* – but more than that, they'd gained acceptance, a chance to live. *I'm gonna live!*

Each man sensed he was forever changed, the scene indelibly etched in their memories for as long as they *would* live.

Maneuvering hard in his own fight for his life, Thach noticed carriers blaze up in the distance. Max and Lem had scored, but he could only discern the black columns for a split-second before dealing with the *Zero* crossing his nose. The poor torpeckers were on their own, had been for almost ten minutes, and when the last *Zero* disengaged, he looked around for the TBDs to escort any survivors back.

During a lull, he saw the dive-bombers attack the eastern carrier, sun glinting off them as they rolled and dove in practiced order, one by one. The carrier didn't seem to see them, running to the aide of her stricken mates to the west before being ambushed and pounced on by Bombing Three. Thach soon saw hits on the deck, along with near misses that lifted great geyser columns of water high alongside the carrier. The shimmering water fell back in a curtain of spray on the flight deck. Another unseen bomb then tore it open with devastating flame and blasted fragments thrown high. Mesmerized, he watched the ship shudder from the blows, as it was also consumed by flames that spread faster than he could imagine. Like campfire tinder soaked in lighter fluid, the fire suddenly bloomed into a bright and crackling inferno, fully involved.

After circling east of the Japanese, he turned for home with only three of his *Wildcats.* On the way, he spotted a lone TBD, shot up and misting, the gunner not moving…maybe dead. Thach joined, and the pilot waved a greeting. He didn't look like Lem, but it was a *Yorktown* bird. What about the others? Surely more TBDs had made it than this one derelict. To Thach, the torpedo bomber next to him would never fly again, and the forlorn pilot inside it could only fly back and hope to save his gunner and be reunited with his squadron mates. The pilot, older and probably enlisted, kept his eyes on Thach, almost accusingly. *Where were you?* Behind him, the gunner's head moved. *He is alive.*

Thach's F4F's couldn't stay with the wounded torpedo bomber due to fuel considerations, but the poor SOB was flying in the right direction. Should find the ship in another hour. Along their flight path floated clouds suitable for cover, and after a thorough scan Thach saw no enemy. He pointed off his nose, gave a thumbs up to the VT pilot, and waved good-bye. The TBD pilot, carrying his half-dead gunner behind him, could only wave a response.[1] Thach and his wingmen pressed on.

Thach thought about Lem and VT-3. Though he and his wingmen had had their hands full with at least two squadrons of *Zeros*, he cursed himself that he couldn't have defended the TBDs better than he did. *Maybe this one got spit out from Lem and the formation,* he rationalized...not believing it himself. Who was he kidding? *The Nips had a field day back there.*

Though together in formation, each *Wildcat* pilot, from the solitary cages of their own cockpits, reflected on what they had been through over the past hour. For the next hour, with only the clouds and North Pacific swells to keep them company, they transited back to *Yorktown* in silence.

Sure hope Lem made it, Thach thought. *I'm sorry, Lem.*

---

[1] CAP W.G. Esders and ARM2c R.B. Brazier, Torpedo Three

Chapter 21

Navigation Bridge, USS *Hornet*, 1140 June 4, 1942

Marc Mitscher couldn't take it anymore.

On the bridge since the launch, he smoked cigarette after cigarette. He was mentally with his boys out there, imagining the open ocean, the sudden squalls that required deviation from course, the droning of radial engines over the vast sea. Jap fighters, barrage-fired antiaircraft. And time melting away. Did Stan get them through? Did they hit them? Or was a formation of fifty enemy planes coming for *him*? Across the water *Enterprise* had recovered her fighters some time ago, but where were his? They had launched and departed with the bombers at roughly the same time. If they were still airborne, they were on fumes, but he saw nothing on the horizon. *What happened out there?* Conscious of the OOD and quartermasters observing his nervous fidgeting, he stepped into his at-sea cabin and closed the door.

Removing his duck-billed cap, he rubbed his hand over the smooth skin of his bald head. He felt 100 years old. And looked it. Getting *Hornet* ready for sea, the dash through the canal, the onload and rushed delivery of the Army B-25s to a launch position deep in enemy waters, an imagined periscope behind every whitecap… All had added more lines to his sunburned neck and subtracted more hair from his spotted head. He needed rest. He needed shore duty, and was ready to relinquish this command, the pinnacle of any aviator's career, as soon as this operation was over. More than anything, he needed a drink.

At a knock on his door, he placed the cap back on his head.

"Enter."

Apollo Soucek, his Air Officer, opened the door. Soucek passed for a friend at sea, if ship captains were allowed to have friends.

"Sir, our planes are returning."

"Good, good," Mitscher said, grabbing a fresh pack of cigarettes before leading them back to the bridge. He stepped out onto the port bridge wing as a formation of SBDs roared overhead. Leaning over the edge, he saw *Enterprise* a few miles behind him, recovering her own planes.

"How many, Apollo?" Mitscher asked him.

Soucek winced. "Not as many as I was expecting, sir. About twenty SBDs."

Taken aback, Mitscher pressed for more. "No fighters? They must be out of gas."

"No, sir – maybe they jumped on the nearest available deck," Soucek said, pointing at *Enterprise*, an offer of hope that they all weren't shot down.

If the fighters were out of gas, the TBDs were near empty. The corrugated rattletraps were slower, but all his planes had been airborne for almost four hours. He thought of John Waldron, who had been standing right here five hours earlier. Both of them knew he was going to die. Waldron had all but begged on his knees for fighter protection. One damned fighter. When Mitscher refused him, Waldron set his face. *You couldn't even give him one*, Mitscher thought, condemning himself, wishing he could go back in time and grant the last request of a dying man. He'd never forget Waldron's determined visage, the fire in his eyes. The boys said he was part Sioux Indian. *Did he find the Japs? Is he still out there?*

The first dive-bomber approached the ramp, and Mitscher noticed it was still carrying its 500-pounder. Alarmed, he cried out, "Is that bomb hung?" Before anyone could answer, the *Dauntless* took the LSO cut and plopped down on deck as it snagged a wire. Once freed, it taxied up, and Mitscher recognized the face of Walt Rodee as the dive-bomber passed the island. *Where's Stanhope? Was he shot down?*

The next plane rolled wings level, and Mitscher's heart sank. It, too, had its bomb affixed. *Oh, no!* Mitscher thought as the young pilot taxied forward. Another scout – with another bomb – trapped aboard. Mitscher walked over to Soucek's station and spoke in a low tone. "Get Skipper Rodee up here right now."

The SBDs recovered in thirty second intervals. Mitscher watched them as his lookouts scanned the skies around *Hornet* for more of his aviators. All the SBDs carried their bombs. They hadn't dropped, obviously hadn't tried. But where were Bombing Eight, the fighters, and Waldron's torpedo planes? Tension gripped him, and he fought to remain calm. *The first report is always wrong.*

A lone SBD came into the landing circle and dirtied up, armed like the others. With no other airplanes overhead, Mitscher followed it off the abeam, assessed the quality of its approach, watched it slow as it slid toward the ramp and the LSO's outstretched arms. Roger pass, and as the LSO flicked the paddle across his throat, the *Dauntless* sat down on deck with a little bounce. *Hornet's* landing pattern was empty.

Mitscher focused on the cockpit as the plane taxied past. Stanhope! He waited for Ring to look up to catch his wave, a thumbs up, a smile. Ring didn't acknowledge the bridge as he taxied to his spot, concentrating instead on his director. Mitscher inspected Ring's plane for damage and found none. *None* of them had any holes or torn fabric. Had they even *found* the enemy? All went off together; why had only the scouts returned? In his wake, *Enterprise* continued to recover planes – and Mitscher recognized the planform of a TBD. *Maybe Johnny went over there.*

Ring deplaned and found the nearest catwalk hatch to go below. At that moment, Walt Rodee stepped onto the bridge wing.

"Lieutenant Commander Rodee, reporting as ordered, sir."

"Walt, why didn't you guys drop?"

"We didn't find them sir."

Mitscher let it sink in as a tense Rodee stood, waiting for the next question.

"Did Ruff find them? Where's he?"

"Sir, I don't think so. Last time I saw him, he was headin' to Midway."

"You saw Midway?"

"Yes, sir, the smoke from it anyway. Guess the Japs beat it up. Ruff took his boys in that direction, and that's all I know, sir."

"And Waldron?"

"Don't know, sir… He left about thirty minutes after we left here."

"He *left?*"

Rodee's perspiration was from more than the midday heat. A feeling of foreboding then came over Mitscher.

"Sir, we were pretty much leveled off at altitude, and it was hard to see him with the cloud cover, but he told the group commander he was goin' to the Japs."

Mitscher was stunned. A squadron commanding officer just up and left the group formation. On his own. Unheard of. *What the hell?*

"Did Commander Ring approve?" Mitscher asked, his face frozen in disbelief.

Rodee struggled to answer. "No, sir…"

His patience spent, Mitscher sensed there was more and stepped toward Rodee, whose lip quivered.

"Lieutenant Commander, tell me, *now.*"

Rodee looked from Mitscher to Soucek, who listened from behind Mitscher's shoulder. The old aviator's eyes narrowed.

"Now!" Mitscher barked.

"Sir, Johnny said he knew where the Japs were."

"On the radio?"

"Yes, sir. Sea Hag told him to pipe down and fly form, but Johnny kept at it. Pretty much told Sea Hag to jump in the lake."

Mitscher was incredulous. Waldron was aggressive, but *this*? Public insubordination? Open defiance?

"What did he say exactly?"

"Commander Ring or Johnny, sir?"

Mitscher exploded. *"Waldron!"*

Rodee braced up, eyes locked on his fuming captain.

"Sir, Johnny told Sea Hag to go to hell, that he knew where they were. He veered off right, about thirty degrees I'd say – pretty much west. I followed him for about five minutes before I lost him."

"What did Commander Ring do?"

"Nothing, sir. He and the rest of us continued on our heading for about another hour and a half. Actually, the fighters didn't stay that long."

"Where'd they go?"

"Sir, they left in singles and small formations before Pat finally turned to catch up with them. They were all low on fuel, and I thought they'd be here, sir."

Mitscher tried to comprehend it all. At this point, if his planes weren't on a flight deck, they were in the water – or Midway. And where the hell was Ring? He had recovered over ten minutes ago, then scampered below. Enough with the petrified scout CO.

"You wait here," Mitscher said, sent his orderly to summon Sea Hag to the bridge at once.

As Rodee waited in the sun, Ring arrived on the bridge. Mitscher sat in his chair, weighing several explanations for Spruance and Fletcher. At the moment, only Waldron, by leaving the formation, may have found the enemy. *Did he get hits like he'd said he would?*

Behind him, Ring cleared his throat. "Cap'n? Reporting as ordered, sir."

Mitscher turned and scowled at Ring, noting his combed hair under his fore-and-aft cap and his fresh khaki shirt. After several seconds, Mitscher finally answered.

"Come with me."

Mitscher led them outside onto the bridge wing gallery, where Rodee waited, with Soucek as witness.

"Stanhope, we've been waiting to hear. *What happened?*"

Ring nodded with a nervous look in his eyes. "Sir, we couldn't find them. We flew down the assigned bearing, but they weren't there."

"Navigation error?"

"No, sir, I watched it like a hawk, and the winds were light on the surface. We had okay visibility, but it was tough to see between the broken layer below us."

Mitscher held Ring's gaze.

"*Where* is VF-8?"

"Sir, I don't know. I was leading us on course, and when I checked behind me, they were gone."

Mitscher nodded. He said nothing, his annoyance evident.

"Where is *Torpedo* Eight?"

"Sir, Johnny Waldron just took 'em someplace without my direction. We had left the ship about thirty minutes earlier. I don't know where he went."

Mitscher nodded again. Ring was holding back.

"Your scout CO here says you had an argument with Waldron on the radio." Rodee looked ashen.

"Sir, Johnny said we were going the wrong way but, Captain, I stayed on the course you gave us that we all agreed on. Waldron didn't agree, but once you gave your order that was it, and I wasn't about to hash it out on the radio with a squadron CO. I told him to stay in formation, and the next thing I knew he was gone. He's a wild card, sir. I've tried to work with him, but I must recommend disciplinary action when he returns."

Mitscher felt as if he were transported in time back to Annapolis, a Firstie bracing up two plebes discovered out of their room at lights out.

"So that leaves Ruff. Did you argue with him, too?"

Ring shook his head in vigorous motion. "No, sir. Bombing Eight was with me until I turned back. I think they went to Midway." Mitscher noticed Rodee was unable to maintain eye contact. *Who to believe?*

At that moment Soucek was handed a dispatch. As he scanned it, the others waited for his report.

"You're right, Sea Hag. Just got a message from Midway; Ruff took his boys there. Once the Marines fuel 'em, they're comin' back here."

Mitscher breathed a sigh of relief, but that still left his fighters and torpedo bombers unaccounted for. And unless Waldron found the Japs and sank them single-handedly, *Hornet's* entire strike had been a failure. No, a *disaster!* Ring had taken 59 planes out with him, and only these 17 bombers had returned!

Seventeen! No reports of hits, not even a damned sighting! Insubordination? More like mutiny. Whole squadrons just *leaving.* Unheard of. Mitscher needed time to think. He needed a warrior like John Waldron – the confident flight leader Waldron, not the high-strung hotheaded Waldron whom he couldn't trust. Whom *could* he trust? He had little in the two aviators facing him. Were the Japs stirred up and coming? Defending from that was the priority; the accounting could wait. *What really happened out there?*

"You two are dismissed. But get ready to go again this afternoon."

"Where's the damn ship?"

Wade McClusky's shoulder burned in pain, and, while his fuel needle wasn't touching E, it was close. He was wounded but could fly. The SBD was holding up. Between his VF experience and Chock's marksmanship, they had held off the two *Zeros* that jumped them once clear of the enemy screen.

His thought back to the attack. There was an intact carrier out there – that he had missed. Too many dive-bombers hit one, planes that could have been diverted to attack that fourth carrier. *Hornet* or *Yorktown* got the ship far to the northeast; he had seen dive-bombers recover from their dives on the hopeless ship. Some TBDs were in the mix. *Gene? Or some other squadron?* He couldn't tell.

He had taken too long to find the Japs, and that one remaining flattop could retaliate. His airplanes had fallen out of formation all morning. Way too many losses. As flight lead and group commander, the attack was his responsibility. *Failure.*

He called for help. The ship was 60 miles east. *Sixty miles!* Thirty minutes at best, and into the wind. He'd have one chance or make a water landing in *The Big E's* wake.

A carrier came into view, on a recovery heading. He turned toward it and made a recognition turn. Something was strange… *Darn it, Yorktown.* Wasted time and wasted fuel. To his right, he noted a splash on the surface. Someone had ditched short of the task force. *Failure.*

Five miles east were two more flattops, and, recognizing *Enterprise*, Mc-Clusky pressed on. His boys circled for landing. The fuel needle was holding, and he wasn't sure he could trust his landing ability with his wounds. He'd let the young guys recover first. He had to report to the admiral, the captain: the Japs would come, gotta regroup, set the CAP, and rearm the bombers. As he circled in wait, he felt weak and dejected. He took too long to find them...found them too late.

With most of his chicks aboard, McClusky lined up on the flight deck. One of his SBDs was still in the pattern, and McClusky cut him out. He hadn't seen him. Too bad. The LSO rogered his group commander, then waved him off. At the signal. McClusky shook his head. *Sorry, pal. Can't do this again.*

After almost five hours airborne, an exhausted and bleeding Wade McClusky took his own cut and slammed down hard aboard *Enterprise* at 1150 with three gallons remaining.

Taxiing forward, he noted Dick Best, heading toward the island. After the director inched him ahead to a spot and they chocked him, he cut the throttle and the engine sputtered to a stop. Painfully, McClusky pulled himself out, retrieved his plotting board, and eased down the wing to the flight deck. *Home.* But no time. *They'll be coming.*

Driven, he ignored the men staring at his bloody sleeve as another straggler dive-bomber taxied forward out of the landing area. With tunnel vision he strode to the island hatch to climb the steps to the bridge and report to Captain Murray and Admiral Spruance. He didn't see any TBDs on the bow. *What happened to them?* Only a handful of Best's SBDs were aboard, and many of the *Sails* from Scouting Six were absent. He scanned the western horizon – clear. *Did I screw up?* McClusky asked himself. *Hornet* was recovering planes. Maybe they went there, or found *Yorktown.* Any port in a storm.

Inside the island, Best climbed one ladder and turned to the next when he encountered Captain Browning, waiting to intercept him. *Pompous ass.*

"Best, what happened?"

"Sir, I'm coming up to tell the captain and admiral."

"I know, dammit! Tell me what happened!"

Exasperated, the lieutenant bit his tongue before answering. "We hit two carriers, and somebody hit one to the northeast."

"You hit two?"

"Yeah, and they were burning hard."

"Sunk?"

"No, sir...*burning.* Like hell."

Browning was impatient. "Dammit, man! Are they out of action?"

"Yes, sir, far as I can tell."

"Best, are you sure?"

"Sir, I'm *tellin'* ya, there wasn't an inch of flight deck that wasn't burning when I left. Huge explosions. They aren't gonna fly any more today."

"Which one did you hit?"

"*Akagi.* Positive. Three hits, two amidships and one aft."

"Only three hits?"

"Yes, sir, three for three," Best answered, arrogant condescension spilling out. Browning studied him, suspicious.

"You attacked with only three planes? Why the hell only three?"

"Because the group commander took my carrier! I led my guys to the far one, which was *Kaga,* I swear, according to doctrine. And just when I'm pushing over, the *Sails* shoot past me in their dives. Almost hit me, and most of my guys were already committed. So I took my two wingmen a few miles away over to *Akagi.* Three for three."

"You're *sure?* How many hits on *Kaga?*"

Frustrated and exhausted, Best answered. "Sir, I *don't know*, but it looked like newsreel film of Pearl Harbor: black smoke, everything blowing up. *Kaga* and *Akagi* are done for today, and there was a third carrier to the northeast on fire from stem to stern. Best bombing I ever saw."

"The torpeckers?"

"Sir, I *don't know* if they were involved, but I saw SBDs dive on that one to the northeast, and I do know that when I left there were three ships on fire and one carrier undamaged, up to the north. Recommend we rearm and hit it ASAP."

When Commander Walter Boone joined the impromptu intelligence debriefing on the ladder well, McClusky struggled up. His left arm hung limp as he pulled himself using the handrail with his right, plotting board wedged against his elbow. Boone was shocked at the sight of his blood-soaked left side.

"My God, Mac, you've been shot!" he exclaimed. Best helped Boone steady McClusky against a bulkhead. Browning stepped forward.

"McClusky, how many carriers did you hit? Where are the TBDs?" he demanded. Because McClusky was obviously ambulatory, Browning ignored his wounds.

Panting from his exertion, McClusky took a breath. "Three are burning, sir. I hit one... Dick, you got that one to the right?"

"Yes, sir," Best said.

"And somebody got one to the northeast. Is Gene Lindsey back yet?"

"No, none of the VTs yet," Browning answered, then added, "Are you *positive* the carriers you hit are out of action?"

Winded, McClusky nodded. He looked as if he were about to collapse. Boone had seen enough.

"Mac, we gotta get you below." He grabbed a sailor who was held up by the officers crowding the ladder well. "You, help me get the commander down to sick bay."

McClusky didn't argue as Boone and the sailor helped him below. Browning focused again on Best.

"Did you see any *Hornet* planes? Could you have just seen stack gas from the carriers?"

Best was at his limit. "Sir, the only other planes I saw out there were the ones shooting me after I pulled off, and the SBDs that hit the carrier to the northeast. And, sir, I know the difference between stack gas and black smoke from a fuel-fed fire the length of a ship. Three ships are out of action – and I'll bet sunk by now – but one escaped. Recommend we go back at once, *sir.*"

Browning scowled at the cocky lieutenant. Before ripping him, he needed him to go out and kill again.

"Message received; go below and stand by for orders. Wait, who's the senior squadron commander?"

Best tried to be respectful. *He should know the answer to this.*

"Willie Gallaher, Scouting Six."

"Okay, go below. Go."

Disgusted, Best did as he was told, wondering what Browning would convey to the captain and the admiral.

CHAPTER 22

FLAG BRIDGE, USS *YORKTOWN*, 1150 JUNE 4, 1942

Fletcher watched the last of the scout bombers clear the bow and fan out on their assigned search tracks. Reports from Spruance and his own dive-bombers indicated three carriers hit. A fourth was reported undamaged. The Japanese would retaliate, and twenty minutes earlier Fletcher had learned that he had been spotted. Spruance had sent him an updated sighting report, but attacking with only one scout squadron of SBDs was risky. He and Spruance would recover and regroup while his scouts found and maintained contact. In a few hours both task forces could launch the hammer blow.

The deck now ready, two SBDs entered the landing pattern while others circled. Spence Lewis squinted as he scanned the sky.

"Admiral, I count fifteen bombers overhead, plus these two. All of Max Leslie's planes are back. Looks like the VF lost one."

Fletcher nodded. Losing just one plane, and the man inside it, passed for good news in carrier combat. But what about the TBD planes? Spence would have the answer.

"Don't see any of the VTs," Fletcher said. "What do you think?"

"Sir, they're slow on a good day, so I'm not too surprised. They'll probably show up in the next twenty minutes or so."

Fletcher nodded again as the first plane caught a wire. As it rolled out in the gear, the engine sputtered and stopped.[1]

"Whoa! That's an *Enterprise* bird!" a surprised Lewis informed him.

As plane pushers manhandled the fuel-starved SBD over the barrier, the two officers noted the damage to the tail. Big chunks missing due to cannon fire. The right wing was peppered with bullet holes. The second one down also belonged to Spruance, his ships barely visible to the south. It, too, was shot up, the wounded gunner bleeding from the mouth.[2]

---

[1] ENS G.H. Goldsmith and ARM3c J.W. Patterson, Jr., Bombing Six
[2] LTJG W.E. Roberts and AMM1c W.B. Steinman, Bombing Six

"Guess these guys went to the first carrier they found," Lewis surmised. "That means all of Max's planes *aren't* back yet." From his station above, Murr Arnold shouted orders to strike the refugees below and bring the pilots to the bridge at once.

While the *Wildcats* took their turns at landing, General Quarters sounded.

"Uh-oh. Let me find out why, sir," Lewis said. Fletcher waited for him to return with a report. A nervous lookout or a real attack? He suspected the latter.

High above Fletcher, the giant radar antenna turned, sending and receiving invisible energy that could detect planes farther than any lookout could see. The fall-of-shot tower masts on his carrier, and on the old battlewagons at Pearl, were anachronisms, useful for the last war but not this one, where flying machines and "circling bedspring" antennas determined the next move. If you could wait for it. At least he could know when something came at him from over the horizon.

In furious haste, gunners loaded their catwalk guns and snapped closed their kapok jackets as the last F4F recovered aboard. Fletcher recognized the kids, initiated to combat only last month. Bloodied and tried, yet still fearful, knowing better than those on *Hornet* to the south what was coming. The bogeys were at twenty miles, and the group commander vectored fighters to meet them. Lewis and Buckmaster directed the ships in screen and their air defenses to prepare for the onslaught. How many? What kind of planes? He stepped to the chart table and retrieved his tin helmet. Wash basin with a chinstrap. He could do nothing more than consider the next move while all around him defended TF-17 and its vital carrier. *I have nothing to do.*

He studied the chart. Nothing but black latitude and longitude lines on a cream background, with two black dots to signify Midway on the bottom. Penciled-in fixes of sighting reports. Who knew how accurate they were? Fletcher thought about Nagumo far to the west – both were fighting with paper and pencil and fragmented information. He wondered if Nagumo's carrier was the intact one, if he, too, was hostage to his fliers, those advising him on his staff and the farm boys in the airplanes. The fighting farm boys.

Thach arrived on the bridge, and Lewis motioned him over.

"Admiral, Commander Thach has a report."

Fletcher turned to face Thach, his sweaty face lined by combat.

"Sir, Lieutenant Commander Thach, CO of Fighting Three," Thach said.

Fletcher extended his hand, and Thach took it. "Welcome back, son. What happened? Spence, can we get this man a cup of water?"

Thach nodded, impatient to report. "Sir, three carriers are burning. We found them pretty much where we expected. Max Leslie's boys plastered one, and two more were burning to the west. Not sure who got them."

"Was it the VT?"

"No sir, not ours anyway," Thach answered. Fletcher saw he was troubled as Lewis handed Thach a paper cup filled with water. The exhausted fighter pilot downed it in one gulp.

"Sir…we couldn't protect them. Lem Massey found the Japs and turned north to attack…we were with him. As soon as we steadied out they hit us, about twenty *Zeros*, I never got an accurate count. My guys had their hands full defending themselves – lost one of my wingmen."

"Torpedo plane losses?"

Thach nodded, preparing him. Fletcher's heart sank. *Oh, no.*

"Yes, sir, at least half. They all went in. Didn't see any hits, and that carrier was still out there when I left. Some TBDs got away, and I came across a survivor headin' home, shot up pretty bad. Saw another one to the south. I couldn't stay with them. Too slow. We tried, sir."

"But the dive-bombers sank one?"

"Don't know if it sunk, sir, but it was *solid* flame, the length of the ship. I watched the VB dive on it… Sun off their wings. It looked like a beautiful silver waterfall," Thach said, smiling. "That ship is done. Wouldn't be surprised if it sank."

Fletcher nodded. *One down*, confirmed by a credible eyewitness.

Lewis pressed Thach. "And the burning ships to the west, Jimmie? You *sure* they're carriers?"

"Yes, sir, you can tell by their high flight decks over the bows, which was the only part of them not burning. Huge explosions, and the condition of one of them looked like the carrier Max bagged. On fire from stem to stern, huge columns of black. I'd say ten miles west. Not sure who got them, but they weren't from *Yorktown*."

A watchstander shouted so all could hear. "Inbound raid at the screen edge!" Fletcher turned toward the horizon, then back to Thach.

"You better stay put with us, son. Well done."

"Thank you, sir," Thach said, unsure of what to do next or where to stand on the unfamiliar bridge.

Fletcher felt the pace quicken, the terse commands, the tension, the building fear as they all waited. CAP fighters engaged the bogeys, and his ships ran southeast. Lewis returned, and somebody yelled, "Ten miles!"

"Let's go watch," Fletcher said, as Lewis and the rest of the staff moved outside and on to the flag bridge. Thach followed.

Leaning over the starboard rail, they saw them: sudden dark splotches of AA against the sky. A pinprick of fire appeared and fell to the surface, trailing black. An airplane. The western screen ships had opened up, and amid the bursts, Fletcher made out the enemy formation, a row of dots moving in slow motion. Faint streams of tracers lifted skyward toward them. White contrails inscribed small arcs that revealed CAP fighters turning hard before they disappeared into the abyss of blue. A dot glinted in the sun, then two, and nearby, a formation of dots. One blew up, and another black smear streaked down.

Binoculars against his eyes, Lewis recognized the fixed undercarriage of the enemy planes. "Dive-bombers, sir…and not all that many. Ten?"

"Will the CAP and screen get them?"

"Yes, sir, but only one has to get lucky."

Scattered and culled by the *Wildcats*, the Japanese formation broke up into smaller groups. Fletcher saw them clearly now. He could not hear them yet over the rumble of gunfire from his western screen, but they were coming. Fletcher was no aviator but he'd seen this less than a month ago. Even if the *Wildcats* were on them, some of the enemy planes would get through.

"See any torpedo planes?"

"No, sir!"

"Good."

One gun fired, and then all of *Yorktown's* guns opened up at once: a hurricane of lead, sheets of tracers sent aloft by a unified engine of defensive fire. Inside the freight train of chatter and howling metal could be heard the crew-served five-inchers, their sharp *booms* rattling the ship. It sounded like a twister on the plains, sudden and all-enveloping, but, unlike a tornado, it did not abate, did not recede as it cut its deadly swath. Fletcher stood fast in the middle of it, traveling at 25 knots as *Yorktown* sprinted to avoid the blows of telegraphed punches.

Surrounded by antiaircraft bursting around it, the first bomber peeled over, and Lewis shouted, *"Let's go inside!"* The bulkheads would offer them 3/8 of an inch of steel to protect them from splinters and flash. Chances were the bomb would miss, or hit some other part of the ship. *Yorktown* was big, but it wasn't that big. Fletcher could only huddle under the chart table. It was unseemly, he thought subconsciously, especially with his silly doughboy helmet. Better than nothing. Outside, the kids stretched their necks to the sky under their tin hats as they fired at the hated Aichi's and screamed at them in fear and rage.

The first bomb whistled through the cacophony of gunfire and hit someplace aft. The power of the blow transferred through the decks and jolted all on the bridge. *Yorktown's* defensive fire continued unabated, and Fletcher's eyes met those of the young fighter squadron CO. To Fletcher, they conveyed sorrow, as if Thach had let him and his shipmates down. *Don't be too hard on yourself. This is war.*

The second bomb exploded with a thunderous roar that knocked everyone over. A shock wave pushed them, and anything not bolted down, against the forward bulkhead. All sensed the missile's trail of destruction deep inside, right below them. Sickened by the sound of death, Fletcher expected heavy casualties, more than last month. Lewis went to retrieve the chart, blown off the table and now damp as it lay on the deck. *Yorktown's* defensive fire continued as heavy smoke flowed into the bridge.

Another hit, this one forward, a knife puncture through siding, followed by a muffled boom. Smoke filling the space, on all fours to breathe. Gunfire subsiding, must be done. The crackling flames sounded as if they were coming from the other side of the aft bulkhead. Fletcher felt the ship slow, a familiar feeling. A sickening feeling.

"We gotta get out to weather deck, sir!" Lewis shouted, as he and Thach helped their admiral to his feet. The men had stopped firing the small caliber, and soon all the carrier guns fell silent as the rumble of gunfire from the screen ships continued.

"We're clear, sir!" Lewis said as they watched the last of the Japanese attackers claw their way west through their screen. Heavy smoke poured from the uptake vents and shrouded the aft end of the ship in darkness. Fletcher checked the water surface some sixty feet below. Only a small bow wave flared out as *Yorktown* coasted to a stop.

Dammit.

The flight seemed never-ending.

Puffy white clouds drifted behind Childers as he studied their shapes, the same way he did as a boy on the plains, lying on his back in the dirt. He faced aft, sun burning the left side of his face. No longer sweating, he felt cold as if he and Harry were at 10,000 feet.

Harry said something about the screen, the ship. Childers didn't understand. He was thirsty, and his canteen empty. His legs hurt, especially his right ankle.

He couldn't help anymore, and he shivered in the heat. *Sun so hot, ah froze to death. Suzannah, don't you cry.*

"Comin' up on home, but she's not moving. Smokin' kinda bad, too."

Home? *Yorktown?* Childers had to prepare for the arrestment…but slumped back in pain and exhaustion. He selected the interphone.

"Where? How far?" he rasped.

"Off to starboard. Almost right over her."

Childers pushed himself up to look. Nothing.

"Where? I don't see her?"

"You can't see her, Lloyd? She's right next to us. They're reparin' some hits on deck. We can't land on her."

Childers first thought was of Wayne. "Wayne! Is he okay?"

"Dunno, probably," Harry answered as they flew past their damaged ship. "She's not in a real bad way, got some VF spotted forward, crew all over the place. Deck's clobbered, Lloyd, we gotta press on. Two flattops ahead…if we can make 'em."

Now beyond caring, Childers thought of his brother down there. *Wayne!* The Japs got him, too! Weak and half-blind from blood loss, he could only sit and wait for Harry to take them to another ship. He hoped it was *Hornet,* where he had a friend in VT-8. Wayne. *Mother.* The engine sputtered and caught, sputtered and caught.

"We're not gonna make it, Lloyd. Prepare to ditch. Stow yer gun."

Prepare to ditch. Ditch in the sea… Why is it called that? *Ditching.* Childers and his brother dug ditches in Norman, the red clay of their childhood. *I'm twenty-one today. It's my birthday.*

Did Wayne make it?

Harry dropped the tailhook. *We're gonna land!* Childers thought. Land on a carrier. The engine sputtered and died, and all he heard was the wind whistling through the canopy. "Get ready, Lloyd!" Harry shouted, and Childers braced himself for landing. USS *Hornet* would have a doctor; it was a new ship. Maybe the doc was already helping Wayne.

"Brace yourself!"

Childers felt their plane twitch as Harry corrected for the LSO. The engine was silent… *Why is the engine off?*

The first slap stunned him, but, before he could think, the second impact slammed him forward. Spent cartridges propelled off the floor and pelted him from below as water doused him from above. Their TBD had stopped and Childers wondered why he was wet. *Why is the engine off?*

"Get out, Lloyd!" Harry cried as he unstrapped to help his wounded gunner. Out on the wing of the sinking TBD, he reached into Childers's cockpit to unbuckle his lap belt. "Dammit, Childers!" Harry cursed before trying again.

He felt Harry's hands pull at him. "Oww!" Childers cried as Harry forcibly lifted him up and over the side.

"Here, hang on while I get the rubber boat!" Harry shouted as Childers hunched over the rear cockpit. "There's a tin can next to us that's gonna get us! Hang on, Lloyd!"

Childers felt the plane wallow in the swells and winced as salt water sloshed against his right ankle. On the floor of the cockpit he saw blood mixed with seawater. *Sharks!*

The raft inflated with a whoosh, and the calm seas allowed Harry to keep it next to the wing. Childers patted the fuselage. *Thanks for gettin' us back.*

"C'mon, Childers!"

Childers then became puzzled. *Why are we standing on the wing?*

"Lloyd, they're comin' in a whaleboat! Just a few more minutes."

Childers felt Harry grab his waist and pull him back to the raft. Rising on a swell, Harry pushed him, and Childers fell into the raft, bellowing in pain. *Harry, you sonofabitch!*

On his back, eyes stinging from saltwater and the sun, Childers heard the whaleboat motor up and saw Harry catch a line thrown to him. Childers could only close his eyes and listen.

"What ship, sir?"

"*Yorktown!*"

"Is he bad?"

Childers cracked open his eyes as he waited for Harry's answer.

The pilot nodded. "Yeah, pretty bad."

"We got a doc aboard," the destroyerman said, then ordered his coxswain. "Back off a bit...watch the damn tail. Bring us left; *no!* Yer military left."

"What ship are you guys?" Harry asked as Childers felt the boat bump the raft.

"USS *Monaghan*... Sir, can you help us with him? Smitty, help the sir pull him over. Easy."

Like a child, Childers was helped over the gunwale of the whaleboat and winced again as his tailbone landed on the wooden deck. The sailor talking with Harry seemed older, like a chief. *Thank goodness a chief has me.*

"Sorry, buddy! We'll have you aboard in two shakes of a lamb's tail! The damn Nips left about ten, fifteen minutes ago. Looks like they beat up *Yorky* bad. How'd you guys do out there, sir?"

Harry hesitated. "Think we hit one or two of them. Most of our guys got shot up, though. Did you see any more of us torpedo planes?"

"Sorry, sir, all planes look the same to me... Okay, cast off! Clear... Let it drift a bit. Okay, Smitty...starboard accom ladder. Go."

As the coxswain gunned the throttle and the whaleboat accelerated and turned, Childers sat with his back on the center console: in the sun, drenched, spent, no longer caring. He craved sleep, even though every pounding swell jarred his back and his tailbone. Harry was nearby with the salty chief. They'd take care of him. Harry took his hand and squeezed it hard.

"We're comin' alongside a destroyer, Lloyd. Just a few more minutes. Hang on. Don't sleep, dammit."

Childers nodded, unable to talk.

"You saved us, Lloyd. You saved our lives."

Childers nodded again and passed out.

CHAPTER 23

FLIGHT DECK, USS *YORKTOWN*, 1230 JUNE 4, 1942

Fletcher walked the flight deck as he had that hot, sunny day in the Coral Sea four weeks earlier, to see the damage for himself. He had seen death before, too many times in his career…didn't want any more images of dead kids in his memory. But he had to assess – and had to be seen assessing.

Smoke poured from the hole next to the island as crewmen darted about clearing debris and dragging both timbers and plating forward to patch the other hole near the elevator. Emerging from behind the smoke, medical personnel carried a man in a stretcher to the port catwalk. A crowd of men had gathered aft of the island, and, ahead of Fletcher, a man – more boy than man – was down on all fours. Retching. Another boy walked away from the scene, crying from a sight he would never forget.

"Watch where you step, sir," Lewis warned as they approached the group, and Fletcher scanned the deck ahead of him. Amid wooden splinters and unidentifiable debris was a hand with half a forearm: cut clean and palm down. Fletcher stopped and gathered himself while a corpsman retrieved the part, placed it in a bag, and continued his search for other remains. Men tended to the wounded on the 1.1-inch gun mount, the gun tub riddled with shrapnel. One dead sailor was slumped over the barrels, the back of his kapok jacket shredded and bloody. The man was decapitated. Fletcher averted his eyes to maintain his composure. Nearby, a chief directed the men to remove the gun's ammo cans and heave them over the side.

The mood differed from that after last month's attack. As *Yorktown* wallowed and smoldered, Fletcher sensed fear in the crew. Their ship lay prostrate: in the open, a column of towering black smoke marking their position. The Japs had at least one – maybe two – carriers out there. They'd be back to finish *Yorktown* off. Sailors scanned the horizon for help. Only one of their torpedo planes had made it back, *only one*, and seeing the ship immobile and the deck holed, flew on to find another flight deck. Fletcher glanced up at the radar antenna on the spotting tower. Dead, not moving. No early warning capability. Communications out.

"Spence, we can't fight from here. We've gotta transfer."

"Yes, sir. *Astoria?*"

"Yes. Have them send a boat."

"What about *Yorktown*, sir?"

Fletcher had thought of little else since the attack. The Japs would be back. He considered options: Make a stand here with Ray, or send everything east to regroup and wait for a report from either his scouts or the Midway PBYs? Around Fletcher the sunburned sailors shouted to one another as they hammered in timbers and deck plates in the event *Yorktown* could raise enough steam to operate planes and escape. *A miracle.*

The order to *Astoria* was passed as Fletcher strode forward toward the repair party near the elevator. Already the men had dragged steel plates to cover the wooden frame they had built over the hole as chiefs continued to bark their orders. He and Lewis looked south for signs of Spruance. Only a few destroyers and some planes were visible.

"My eyes are gettin' old, Spence. You see him?"

"No, sir, but I did before the attack. He's just over the horizon, probably recovering."

Fletcher nodded as the deck rolled gently under him. Ahead on the brilliant sunlit sea: friendly ships, *his ships*, and their promise of salvation, making best speed toward him. Behind him: black smoke and blood, worried kids hammering wood and moving debris, chiefs and officers spurring them on, pushing them. The combat-experienced men scanned west with a wary eye. A chief caught them. Fletcher heard his salty bellowing, familiar, and, in a way, comforting. *"Knock off the skylarking, dammit, they'll be comin' back!"*

Fletcher smiled at the chief's language. *Chiefs.*

Instinctively, Fletcher scanned the western sea. Nagumo was out there, bloodied. And dangerous.

Kroeger stepped into the ready room. *Where is everyone?*

He knew, of course. Had seen his mates fall out of formation and ditch before they found the Japs, had seen them fall from the sky in flames after they had. Not many of the *Sails* were back either. A handful of the torpeckers were aboard and in the pattern. The one he saw on deck was shot to hell. Maybe the others had found refuge over in *Hornet.*

What a cluster! The forever launch, chewing up gas with a wasted climb to altitude, nothing to see but clouds, bad oxygen, and the damn ship over fifty miles from the expected Point Option! Half the squadron in the water. Then a break... *There they are!* Practically the whole Jap fleet, the attack geometry perfect. And then, the knucklehead *Sails* just about hit us as we push over on *our* target! Thank God the skipper took us over to the other carrier. Hit, but probably not bad enough to sink.

Weber walked in and dropped his parachute where he stood. With eyes closed, he breathed through his mouth. Deeply, to calm himself.

"Fred, you okay?"

Eyes still shut, Weber nodded. "Jus' need to let it all out." To Kroeger, Weber seemed to have aged ten years.

"Where's the CO?" Weber asked as he removed his cloth helmet and Mae West.

"Think he went up to the bridge."

"Yeah... And Bud, you hit it. Did you see your hit on the pull off?"

Kroeger looked at Weber with skepticism. "I saw a fire and a geyser aft when I looked back. Halterman thinks we hit it. *Akagi*, I'd say."

"You did hit it. I saw the CO's hit, and it scraped their paint close aboard the port side."

"Hell, I dropped just as he did, with him in my bombsight as I pickled."

"Yeah, and I was still tracking when the first bomb exploded, huge geyser just off the port side forward, an' the ship moved right into the splash. But your hit, Bud...as I released, I saw yours explode amidships."

"I just saw smoke and a geyser aft," Kroeger answered.

"Then I must've missed short, *darn it*, but you hit it, because I swear the first bomb was a near miss. Did you see it burn?"

"It was burning, but not like that guy to the west. Think that one was *Kaga*. Pretty sure of it."

"Yeah, no wonder, with practically two whole squadrons of SBDs to plaster her. Did you see that one giant explosion? Looked like a mushroom."

"Yeah, felt it. Did you?"

"Oh, yeah! And didja see that ship to the north? *Whooo-wee*, it looked like a blast furnace. Musta been the *Hornet* guys!"

"Or *Yorktown*."

"You hit a moving, turning carrier – the darned *flagship*, you lucky SOB! And how about that Jap floatplane that ran on us? It was like the CO just swatted it out of our way!"

Kroeger allowed himself a smile, but he and Fred were still the only ones in the ready room. They heard planes taxi outside, *Dauntlesses,* hopefully their squadron mates. Maybe the scouts.

"I'm sure you and the CO holed it," Kroeger said. "But there's still one more out there. It was to the north as we cut through the screen, between us and that burning carrier to the northeast. You see it?"

"Yeah," Weber nodded. Both men considered what that meant.

Best entered the ready room and leveled his eyes on Weber.

"Weber, you gotta stay in position or yer gonna get shot."

"Yes, sir."

His message delivered, Best changed his tone. "Nice bombing, you two. Three for three. Have you debriefed yet?"

"No, sir," Kroeger answered.

"Tell them we hit *Akagi* forward, midships, and aft. She's not going to fly anymore today. I saw two other burning carriers and one untouched. I just relayed that to Captain Browning. Have you seen any more of our guys?"

Kroeger and Weber shook their heads. The reciprocating coughs and chugs of another plane taxiing forward filled the room.

"They may have gone to the other ships. Your radiomen okay?"

"*Yes, sir,*" the pilots answered in unison.

"Good. Okay, get some food, and be ready to go again. I'd say in another hour. Stay close to the ready room."

"Yes, sir."

Bob Laub was the first to enter the VT-6 ready room, empty save for the enlisted phone watch. Skipper Lindsey, the XO, Tom... He had seen them go in, had seen them get hit and struggle to control their burning planes. Each of them had tried well past that sickening point that all hope was lost. Doomed. *Did they know?* Laub had thought about it most of the way back.

Tom Eversole – *the nicest guy in the squadron.* Gone.

McPherson walked into the ready room and slumped into the nearest chair.

"You okay, Irv?"

The ensign nodded.

"How about Ed? Didn't he land before you?"

McPherson closed his eyes, fighting to keep control.

"Irv...?"

"I saw him go into the head. To piss…or throw up."

Laub sat down across the aisle. He didn't know what to do. Skipper and XO…gone. Was Lieutenant Riley the one guy in the second division who had made it?

"Irv, did you see that second division guy ditch after we cleared the Japs?"

"Yeah, but don't know who it was. Then that one guy who wouldn't join on us. Not sure who he was. Think it was the XO?"

"No, I maintained contact on the XO as we went in. He was shot down. As sure as I can be."

McPherson nodded. Both men were spent. Starving and thirsty, they were too tired to get a cup of water, too exhausted to debrief. They were stunned by what they had just experienced: shell shock, they had called it in the Great War. They could only sit in their grimy, sweat-stained flying togs. Laub loosened his necktie, then pulled it off and let dangle from his fingers to the deck. Damn neckties. *Must be in the proper Uniform of the Day.* For Torpedo Six, officers' ties were only good for tourniquets.

From the passageway, Laub heard a scuffle. *"I'll kill him!"*

Laub and McPherson turned to listen to a commotion from outside the ready room.

"Where's Gray? – *Get your damn hands off me!"*

Laub bolted up and into the passageway. Chief Smith struggled against three men as they tried to restrain his rage. He had a .45 pistol in his hand with his finger on the trigger. Grunts and shouts, and Smith's wild eyes…

"You bastards were afraid to shoot the Japs, but shoot me? Sons of bitches!"

Laub lunged at Smith. *"Chief Smith!* Put it down! Give it to me!" he bellowed.

"No, sir! The VF let us die out there!"

McPherson now joined the fracas, as five of them struggled to restrain Smith, who was looking to kill the CO of Fighting Six.

Inches from Smith's face, Laub unloaded at the top of his lungs.

"Now, Chief! *Now!* Gimme the gun, *right now!"*

Surprised by Laub's ferocious outburst, and pinned against the bulkhead, Smith slacked off as two of the pilots pried the pistol from his hand. His foul breath assaulted Laub in quick pulses as the chief relaxed his muscles. Smith's eyes narrowed and focused on Laub: one of them. *Worthless officers!*

Fighting tears, Smith fumed at Laub. "Mister Laub, you heard the XO, didn't you? *'Come on down, Jim!'* Well, where were they, sir? I didn't see a single fighter!"

"Chief Smith, you are to secure to the Chiefs Mess!" Laub recognized another chief who was helping to restrain Smith. "Can you get him down there?"

Smith wasn't finished.

"Then, sir, I come back here, shot to hell, do my damn recognition turn, and *still* one of these VF assholes shoots me! We're all half dead, and they don't know their ass from third base!"

"Chief Smith, that's enough!" Laub thundered. "You are relieved! Secure to the Chiefs Mess and stay there! That's an order!" Shocked sailors watched the spectacle from either end of the passageway.

"Yes, *sir,* Mister Laub," Smith muttered with open disdain.

"Damn you, Chief, not one more word or yer on report! Go below, now! *Now!* You two, make sure he gets there and stays there."

Smith glared at Laub in contempt as the men released their hold, allowing him to turn for the ladder well. Laub held his gaze as he did, not backing down.

Laub spun for the door, took the pistol into the ready room, and dropped the magazine. No round chambered. Smith wasn't that out of his head, but this incident could not be forgotten. The squadron maintenance chief then entered the ready room.

"Mister Laub?"

The pistol still in his hand, Laub turned. The chief's eyes fell to the weapon, then back to Laub. Laub set it on a cabinet, barrel facing away.

"Yes, chief."

"Sir, the captain ordered us to push *Tare* 11 over the side."

"Captain Murray?"

"Yes, sir, it was leakin' fuel and oil all over the deck...what little it had. I don't know how Smitty got it back."

"Chief Smith's plane?"

"Yes, sir. Don't even know how he kept it airborne – the tail looked like Swiss cheese. Said our guys shot him on the way home, too, after the Japs roughed him up. Madder than I've ever seen him when he climbed out."

Laub nodded. He'd forget the passageway incident. Officially.

"Sir, what happened out there?"

Laub grappled with the memories: burning *Devastators,* tracers and spray, crunching metal, the torpedo floating in mid-air. *Fire.*

"We saw...four carriers and ran at one. Set up the anvil attack, but the *Zeros* tore up the XO's division. Then us. We dropped, but our angles were poor." *The CO's plane exploded...*

"Are they going to send you back, sir? The dive-bombers say they want to get another flattop they saw. We've got just three flyable planes, sir, two on deck and one in the hangar bay." McPherson stood behind the chief, waiting for Laub's answer.

But he couldn't answer. Couldn't find the words. Go back? That decision was above his pay grade. *Go back?* Today? Back out there?

"Dunno," Laub answered, pained, unsure. Overwhelmed.

"Mister Laub, sir, as far as I can see, you are the senior officer in the squadron."

The chief's words stunned Laub, and he recoiled in disbelief, as if stung by a wasp. McPherson waited too, expectant, his face dark. Was it too much to ask? *Go back?*

Laub dug deep, eyes downcast. Thinking about Tom. Fatigue fell on him like an avalanche.

"No. We're done," he answered, not lifting his eyes, his mind still out there. "I'll report to Commander McClusky. We're done."

"Sir, I saw some men taking him to sick bay. He got shot."

Laub's nod was weak and barely perceptible. He'd stay in the ready room, in his chair next to the bulkhead. It was too much to ask – of him or anyone. Three planes…the Japs would splash them all in one pass. Suicidal to go back. He needed food but was too tired to go below. He needed a moment. Just a moment. A catnap. He was alive, and took deep breaths to prove it.

The acting commanding officer of Torpedo Six sat in his ready room chair and wedged his head between the seat headrest and the bulkhead. With his eyes closed and mouth open, he fell asleep under a second avalanche – one of responsibility.

CHAPTER 24

FLIGHT DECK, HIJMS *HIRYŪ*, 1320 JUNE 4, 1942

Hurrying behind his mates, Maruyama burst out of the catwalk hatch into the sun. Crewmen crowded the catwalk, slapping his back, exhorting him. Maruyama was annoyed by the bottleneck they made, especially when one man stopped one of the pilots to deliver a personal message. Pushing past, he popped his head over the level of the flight deck and saw why; hundreds of crewmen had jammed the catwalks, waving their caps and lifting their arms in a *banzai* send-off for the pilots. Instead of the confidence of that morning, the faces of the men now showed desperation, pleading. *Please avenge us!*

The deep guttural sound made by the warmed up *Zero-sens* drowned out Maruyama's Type 97s that belched and purred from their spots aft. He checked overhead; a tiny *shotai* – a *shotai!* – of dive-bombers had returned and circled for their turns to land. Climbing the small ladder to the flight deck, he followed behind the others as they all dashed to their planes, conscious of the hundreds of eyes on them. Some searched the sky in anxious anticipation of another American attack.

The fliers ahead of him stopped at the base of the tower, and Maruyama craned his neck to assess the hold up. *The admiral!* Tomonaga-san was speaking with him, their hands clasped. Admiral Yamaguchi then turned to the gathered men and gestured to the three black columns on the horizon, their dark shapes resembling tall trees in the open, their branches intertwined. Raising his voice to be heard above the idling engines of the parked planes, he spoke.

"Sons of Nippon, the war situation is as you can see. I look forward to your further efforts to recover this defeat. I ask each of you to go now, and take revenge."

The admiral then took the hands of the man in front of him, a *Zero-sen* pilot, then moved to the next, speaking briefly to each. Maruyama waited his turn as Yamaguchi moved through the men, eyes clear yet grave, delivering his message. When the admiral got to Nakao, Maruyama tried to hear but could not. The admiral them turned to Maruyama, who stiffened with a crisp bow.

Yamaguchi took his hands and locked eyes with him.

"I ask you."

Maruyama replied with a sharp *hai* before the admiral moved to the next man in line on *Hiryū's* wind-swept flight deck.

As Maruyama trotted aft with the others, one man ahead looked over his shoulder, transfixed by the southern horizon even while running toward the spinning propellers. Maruyama stole a glance: the three black pillars towered above the scattered cotton ball clouds over the Mobile Force, their tops sheared by winds high above any altitude Maruyama had ever flown.

The fighter pilots lowered themselves into their cockpits. As they did, the torpedo men scampered under their wings as they too entered the dangerous maze of idling airplanes parked for takeoff. Foreboding filled him as he recognized one of the Mitsubishis was from *Kaga* – an orphan out to avenge his family.

Maruyama found his *kankō* on the aftermost spot, port side. Nakao was already inside strapping in. Slung underneath was a Type 91, like the torpedo he had carried that morning. *Oklahoma* had been a sitting duck, groggy from sleep, but whatever was over the horizon now would be moving, alerted and escorted. As he crouched under the wing along the deck edge, he saw *Hiryū's* frothy wake flare out on the water as the carrier turned to the launch heading.

Exhaust fumes filled his nostrils as Maruyama jumped onto the wing and bounded up and into the middle seat. His torpedo bomber vibrated against the chocks, and the flags above the bridge snapped and fluttered as they matched the crew's tension on deck. Maruyama and the grim faces in the cockpits felt it. The desperation. The uncertainty. Nine hours earlier, every man in the force had experienced supreme confidence. Now, the black scars on the southern horizon served as warning. *You can be beaten.* Even by the hapless Americans.

Standing straight out, the flapping flags aligned down the deck, and the ship steadied up on an even keel. Nearby were the escorts, many with sailors visible as white dots on their upper works – stationary, watching as *Hiryū's* assembled crewmen did – this desperate hope to avenge *Sōryū*.

Once strapped in, Maruyama counted the Type 99s circling overhead. *Five!* Only five of Kobayashi-san's force of dive-bombers! One of them misted from a wing tank. He also noted a lone plane circling, a *Zero-sen*. Like those warmed up on deck forward, a full *shotai* of *Zero-sens* had been sent to escort the dive-bombers, with only another orphan to return.

Lieutenant Tomonaga wouldn't have it. In the ready room, Ishii and Obayashi had pleaded with him to trade planes for this attack. Tomonaga-san had refused, said the Americans were only 90 miles away. He now sat in the pilot seat of his leaky plane, damaged from the morning strike. Old now at nineteen, Maruyama knew courage. *Ninety miles.* Bah! The brave strike leader wasn't coming back. Who could dare refuse to fly with him?

Behind Maruyama, Hamada strapped in and prepped his gun for battle.

"Maruyama-ken, the dive-bombers sank an American carrier!" the excited gunner said over the voice tube.

"What?" Maruyama answered.

"It's true! The *kanbakus* dropped a message. One carrier on fire and sinking. We'll get another one. Then we'll be evenly matched!"

In the pilot's seat, Nakao let out a whoop of delight, but Maruyama could only dwell upon the forlorn collection of planes overhead. And ahead of him on deck. Six fighters and ten carrier attack planes! Against two American carriers and their deadly Grummans!

The first fighter roared down the deck and into the air as the hopeful crew waved their caps in a wild send-off. On a nearby cruiser Maruyama noted the white dots doing the same as their bow knifed through the water toward the enemy.

The remaining *Zero-sens* rolled and lifted off the deck almost in formation, their takeoff intervals dangerously close. Tomonaga goosed his throttle and pivoted on the centerline, the animated crew waving with no letup. He gunned the engine and rolled, clutching his heavy torpedo as his *kankō* picked up speed. Maruyama and all the torpedo men assessed his takeoff roll. Tomonaga's wheels left the deck well before the end – nothing to fear on takeoff. Nine hours ago, it was all they feared.

The heavy Type 97s rolled for takeoff with a safer interval, and ahead of Maruyama a stray torpedo bomber from *Akagi* lined up. The *Akagi* plane roared off, rudder fluttering as the pilot worked to keep it on centerline aboard his new and smaller home.

Once the *Akagi* plane was rolling, Nakao eased to the centerline and pivoted. He waited until the *Akagi* plane cleared the bow, and Maruyama sensed they should be rolling. They were the last plane on deck, and, once clear, *Hiryū* could recover the circling dive-bombers. He was looking over Nakao's shoulder to see what the delay was when he felt the pilot gun the engine. The *kankō* shuddered in place as Nakao held the brakes, with hundreds of their crewmen cheering them on, waiting in heightened anticipation their majestic takeoff, as if – by their bellowing *banzais* – they could thrust them at the enemy themselves.

With a jolt, Nakao released the brakes and they shot forward, increasing speed, pulled forward by the human will of the frenzied men along the sides of the deck. As Maruyama sped past, he was amazed by their faces: faces contorted by a rage and fury and bloodthirsty *wrath* he did not know his people were even capable of. Boys who bared their teeth in screams of revenge that Maruyama could not hear over the engine, fists clenched, caps blurred from muscular and spirited waving, their bodies vibrating in savage ferocity. As they approached the island, Maruyama looked up to see Admiral Yamaguchi lift a salute, somber, unlike the self-assured confidence of the morning. Electrified, Maruyama noticed the admiral's eyes locked on *him* as Yamaguchi held his fingers to his cap bill.

I ask you.

Maruyama popped his arm up to return the salute, to honor his warrior leader. As the Type 97 reverberated past the island, Maruyama dropped his salute as the admiral held his, and the sound of the men met Maruyama's ears, a deep human roar, a rolling thunder, louder than the engine cylinders firing at full RPM.

The men lifted Maruyama up and threw him in vicious anger to the east, to vanquish the Yankee barbarians who had killed their mates, who had dishonored Nippon, and who had dared to oppose their divine rights. Nakao cleaned up and turned inside of the *Akagi* plane to join the *chutai*. For one last look at home, Maruyama twisted in his seat. As the carrier receded into the distance, the white-uniformed men along *Hiryū's* catwalks swayed like rows of day lilies in a windy field.

Ensign Johnny Adams walked forward with Ram Dibb along *Yorktown's* battered deck. Ahead of the *Wildcat* pilots, a damage control party hammered down the deck timbers that repaired the hole on the port side as two men drug a steel plate patch into place. A chief took a sledgehammer to one already positioned, driving it lengthwise before delivering the final blow that drove it flush with the deck. As they worked, the men took cautious glances to the west and then toward the two pilots ambling along the deck. Adams felt their accusing looks. The chief scowled at him. *Why can't you pretty-boy aviators defend us?*

Both pilots had tangled with Japs, but Dibb had flown in combat three hours ago with their new CO and his new way of fighting. Johnny wanted the gouge and listened as they continued forward, eyes on the deck for holes or metal shards. Using his hands as any fighter pilot would, Dibb described the morning fight as the sailors around them gleaned what they could.

"So the CO had me leave the formation, and now I'm exposed, scared outta my skin, and, sure enough, two of the SOBs roll in on me from my eight, little high, kinda flat, so I jammed the first one just as he reversed on me." Dibb stopped and picked up a wooden splinter in front of him. After a cursory inspection, he chucked it overboard in a sidearm motion.

"You turned with him?" Adams said, surprised.

"Had no choice. He was saddled in. But just then the skipper blasts him – *boom* – I mean, a huge fireball. The other Jap's eyes must've got big cause he took his nose off." Dibb's left arm scooped high out in front as he continued.

"Now he's on me, and the CO has me reverse *again*, back into him and I'm about, oh, 160...150 knots now, firewalled the whole time, and just as the Jap pulls to align, the CO nails him! Johnny, I'm tellin' ya, they just explode. You could hit their trim tab, and the damned things just light off."

Adams nodded. He spotted a metal shard sticking up from the forward expansion joint and pointed at it, a warning for both pilots to avoid it on takeoff. Next to them, plane handlers pushed the *Wildcats* on the bow back to their start-up spots aft of the island. He saw his plane, F-12, as they pushed it past. Dibb's hands continued to cut through the heavy air as they walked.

"Then a Jap comes at the CO from his flat side – I'm on the right now – and the CO sees him and pulls to jam him, but he's in trouble. As the Jap pulls lead on the CO, I'm in on *his* flat side and he doesn't see me. The skipper goes up and right in a wingover, and the Jap follows him – right in front of me, practically zero deflection. I mean, I could almost reach over the prop and grab his rudder. So, I pepper him with all six, and Johnny, my whole field of view becomes *fire* – headin' right for it – and by reflex I just yanked it up and away. Ya know, it's something to watch out for if you're zero deflection, the way they just blow up in front of you."

The last fighter was pushed aft, and the bow was now clear of planes and debris. Once they rolled past the patch, they'd be safe if they needed the whole deck for takeoff. To the south, the two low slabs of *Enterprise* and *Hornet* signified safety. Adams noticed the heat and lack of any breeze. Skipper Thach joined them.

"Boys, if you've got 30 gallons or better, take it. Not sure if we're gonna maintain CAP overhead, or if the captain is just gonna send us down to one of those two ships. Can you tell if they're flying?"

The men scrutinized the skies around the carriers, down by the hull. None saw any evidence of flight ops.

"Sorry, sir, can't see anything around them," Adams offered.

Thach nodded. "Me neither... Okay, let's man up and stand by to warm up engines ourselves. Not sure what they're gonna do... Just wait for the signal. Ram, you ready to get another one?"

"Yes, sir! I was jus' explainin' to Johnny how we went back and forth with the Japs this morning."

"Yep, that beam defense maneuver works...you tested it in combat, Ram. Adams, who's your lead?"

"XO Leonard, sir."

"Good. Once engaged, get abeam him, either side, and keep your eyes peeled. If one goes for him, shoot it off his tail. If one goes for you, jam him and the XO will get it. You ready? Feeling okay?"

"Yes, sir, all set."

From aft, near the island, they heard a cheer.

"What's that about?" Thach asked to no one. Around them the screen vessels circled and turned to defend their assigned charge, their captains also uncomfortable and nervous.

"Are we moving?" Thach asked.

Stepping to the deck edge, the pilots tried to discern any steerageway. A cruiser off the starboard bow paralleled their course as its bearing fell aft.

"We *are* moving, and turning," Thach said, answering his own question. "Okay, guys, let's shake a leg. I'll bet the captain launches us when we get fifteen knots over the deck. If the Japs attack us, stay in section, ignore the *Zeros* if you can, and go for the torpedo bombers or dive-bombers, whichever poses the greater threat."

The men headed aft as the wind force increased on their backs. From the flag locker, signalmen broke two signal flags and a pennant: Mike, Sugar, and Five.

"My speed five. Five knots," Thach muttered as his ensigns walked with him. "Better'n nothing, I guess."

As the pilots strode abeam the island, signalmen wrestled with another flag as four of them heaved on the halyard. Loud cheers rose up from the deck crewmen as it unfurled, and, from across the water, one of the cruisers gave a long blast from its horn before other escort ships joined in.

The stars and stripes flowed in the gentle breeze, the large battle ensign symbolizing *Yorktown's* determined spirit and the nation the grease-stained kids on deck were fighting for.

They smiled now, elated and confident they'd make it. The eight *Wildcats* were spotted, chocked, and tied down as men lugged fuel bowsers and ammo belts to fill them. Along the gallery catwalks, gunners remained at their weapons, keeping watch, joking and bantering with the deck-apes, mocking their "beer-barrel" fighters and each boasting about who would shoot down more Japs if the sons of bitches returned. *Next stop, Bremerton!*

As he got to his *Wildcat,* Thach stopped and turned to Adams and Dibb.

"And one more thing… If you have to, ram them. They cannot be allowed to drop. Got it? It's that important."

Taken aback, Adams nodded, "Yes, sir."

"I expect you to *ram* them, Ram," Thach deadpanned, "but only after yer bullets are gone. So make 'em count." With a wink he walked around the folded wing to man up.

"Aye, aye, sir!" Dibb shouted back, enjoying the CO's barb.

Yorktown crept to the east, keeping an eye to the west as its radar antenna rotated again. Adams climbed onto the wing of F-12 and was about to lower himself in the cockpit when he heard a commotion and shouts forward. He stopped to listen.

"Hot foot it! There's more planes comin'!"

CHAPTER 25

HIRYŪ B5N STRIKE GROUP, 1430 JUNE 4, 1942

Where is he going? Maruyama thought as Hashimoto slid closer to Tomon-aga. They had been airborne an hour. *The Americans must be nearby.* Maybe Hashimoto had a message for the group leader. Using his binoculars, Maruyama saw Hashimoto gesturing to the right, and Tomonaga looked in that direction. Maruyama also looked, and, through a break in the clouds, saw faint white marks on the surface. About thirty miles. *Ship wakes!*

Hashimoto returned to his position, and Tomonaga entered a shallow de-scent as he continued east. The ships were also steaming east, and Maruyama saw that Tomonaga was leading them to a cloud bank from which they could hide before pouncing. The cloud cover had abated somewhat since the morning, but it still offered concealment. Scanning the wakes, Maruyama found a big one in the middle – an intact carrier.

"There they are, mates, off our nose. Hamada, get ready."

"Tallyho!" Nakao cried, reducing power and holding his position as Tomon-aga descended his formation into warmer air. A column of cloud slid by on their left, its cottony protuberances gleaming white in the afternoon sun as it hov-ered in silent witness. Maruyama, concerned about fighters, warned Hamada. "Watch for Grummans!"

Tomonaga keyed the radio. *"Take positions in preparation for attack!"*

They continued their descent, airspeed building to over 200 knots. As they entered a clear area, the American formation turned right. *We've been seen.* Maruyama took one last record of their heading and time to help them get home if they became separated from the others.

"All go in!" Tomonaga transmitted.

Tomonaga then turned his understrength *chutai* toward the Americans, who now presented their sterns to him. Maruyama felt relieved when the *Zero-sens* stayed with his group. Hashimoto headed them up to the northern edge of a cloud bank from which they could circle around or penetrate in a desperate dash to attack. Once in, they would target the carrier's port side, opposite the large American superstructure – *if* they could get through the screen unscathed. Maruyama felt the pace quicken, and observed a gray airplane fly off the carrier's brown flight deck and turn right.

Hurry!

Hurry! Adams thought. He sensed the Japs were attacking from the fearful faces of the men on deck. Waiting behind the XO, he twisted in his cockpit to see if he could pick them up himself. Thirty-two gallons of fuel was all he had! Enough for one fight before landing, here or on one of the other task force carriers to the south. Overhead, the CAP *Wildcats* bustered north. Adams scanned ahead of their flight paths to see what he could. *C'mon!*

The battle ensign swayed in the breeze – plenty of wind over the deck. Skipper Thach was the only one with a full bag of gas, and would begin his deck run from abeam the island. *"Let me off!"* Adams shouted in frustration as he waited in line for takeoff.

The bullhorn boomed. *"Torpedo raid!"* Seconds later, one of the starboard-side five-inch guns opened up: sharp hammer blows that shook the whole ship. More followed, and soon the 1.1-inch guns rattled away on targets behind Adams in a thunderous crescendo. *What's goin' on back there?*

Then he saw them – a small formation of planes, knifing down from the starboard quarter. Torpedo planes, painted dark. Black AA puffs from the trailing screeners suddenly dotted the sky around them. Ahead, Skipper Thach roared off the deck – *finally!* – as *Yorktown* steadied up southeast. Behind Adams, the Japanese drew closer. And under the Nakajimas were torpedoes – slung like an osprey carries a fish. The formation separated, and two planes veered off east. *They're gonna anvil us!* he thought. As Dibb roared away, Adams hoped he'd be able to get airborne. Only one ahead – the XO.

C'mon!

Clear of the bow, Thach banked right as he raised his gear and accelerated. No time to climb or rendezvous with Dibb, and the radio was alive with calls from the CAP. They seemed involved with contacts to the north, but Thach saw the enemy formation off his right wing, about three miles and closing. He locked eyes on the first one, allowing himself to swing wide and build airspeed as he continued to crank the gear up. He figured he had a minute before the torpedo bomber could drop on his ship. *Whoa, they're fast for big planes!* A cruiser on the right fired at two of them with tracers and big guns on the bow. The Japanese continued in, relentless.

Thach flew his *Wildcat* by feel, less than 200 feet above the water, his eyes not leaving the lead Nakajima[1]. He would kill him, had to. Killing the squadron leader like they had killed Lem was all that mattered now. Guns charged. Airspeed building. *C'mon!*

Thach brought the torpedo plane to his nose. With shell splashes below and tracers arcing above, he focused on the speeding plane. The Jap showed Thach his gray underside. *He doesn't see me.*

The torpedo bomber raced along the wave tops with his wing still up. Thach watched the geometry build and positioned his nose on a spot the Nakajima would fly through. Flat-side and almost full deflection. *Now.*

Thach's guns chattered as he squeezed the trigger, watching his tracers converge on his target as it flew into them. The left wing blazed up at once with a bright yellow that turned into black smoke as it continued ahead. Thach pulled up and over, looking down on the burning wing, its ribs already exposed. The tail had yellow bands on a green base and giant red meatballs on the tip of each wing. Three men inside.

Damn! He dropped it!

Helpless, Thach watched the torpedo separate from the burning bomber and head toward *Yorktown.* As it slapped the water, the plane's flaming wing buckled, and after two quick rotations the bomber dove into the sea off *Yorktown's* starboard quarter.

The carrier's fire was on Thach now, small stuff bracketing him above and below. Thach braced himself and threw up a wing to escape. He descended to the water and ran up *Yorktown's* wake, away from her – and with another kill after only four minutes airborne.

As he skirted the enemy screen to the north, Maruyama watched Tomonaga's *chutai* split up.

"Lieutenant Tomonaga is attacking," he told his crewmates as Nakao maintained position and Hamada scanned for Grummans. Maruyama saw a Grum-

---

[1] B5N flown by LT J. Tomonaga, ENS S. Akamatsu, PO1c S. Murai

man approach the lead plane from the blind side – *watch out!* – before it suddenly flamed up, bright and pulsing. Tomonaga continued in. Would he dash himself against the carrier's hull? Then, without warning, the *kankō* fluttered down to the sea with a splash.

Should I tell them? Maruyama thought. *No, no need.*

Adams taxied into position, desperate to get his *Wildcat* off the ship. He stood on the brakes to rev up his engine, eyes on the launch officer who was vigorously waving his flag. Adams caught himself nodding at the lieutenant – *Engine's good! I'm good!* – to coax him to set him free. The launch officer nodded back – and lunged forward.

When he released the brakes, Adams's *Wildcat* jumped ahead, rolling toward the island as gunners in the port gallery opened fire. He guided the F4F just right of centerline to avoid the bomb-damaged deck as sailors on the island pointed aft. Past the island, the tailwheel was off, and the 1.1-inch battery forward was shooting *over* him at something. *Sonofabitch!*

A concussive shock wave from the port 5-incher swept through his open cockpit as the flash bloomed off his left. His moved his head back and forth to assess the deck as it rushed up to him and search for the unknown threat masked in water spray, tracers, black AA puffs, and escort ship gun fire. *What the heck am I flying into!*

Like the XO, he turned left off the bow – into the threat, the unknown threat. *What threat?* he wondered. *Everyone sees it but me.*

Struggling to fly his heavy dash-4 and crank up the gear, he ran the prop pitch up manually and cursed in frustration. He was behind - *not ready yet!* – and he still couldn't make out a threat in the confused scene behind him. He kept the turn in, furiously cranking up the gear, inside the screen, inside a wild crossfire of flak and tracers that only a crazy man would fly into.

Over his left shoulder, he saw it.

A single Nakajima, painted green, between him and a screening cruiser. The Jap hugged the deck, splashes lagging behind as the gunners tried to assess lead. It was damned fast, and going for a position off *Yorktown's* bow, from which it would turn in to attack. Adams roared over a destroyer that fired everything it had – at the Jap and at him. The constant roar of the ships' automatic guns and the thunderous booms of the five-inch filled his cockpit.

The bomber banked over another tin can that was firing like crazy, belly up to Adams. *He doesn't see me!* he thought and pulled hard into the Nakajima's flat side. Inside a mile now, the torpedo it carried was big, almost as long as the airplane. By habit, Adams rolled to check his own belly – nothing but the crazy destroyer gunners shooting at him – and pulled back in, guns charged and gear finally up.

He slid to the enemy's eight o'clock as it leveled its wings and flew even closer to the water. Adams pushed the throttle as hard as he ever had to close the range before the enemy plane dropped against his ship. As they raced, both flew inside a maelstrom of spray and yellow lights coming from every direction. A giant splash off his left made him flinch, and the Jap was inside 1,000 yards of *Yorktown*, where the torpeckers said they liked to drop. Adams had no time to track, to aim, and as he slid to the enemy's seven, he pulled his nose in front and squeezed a long burst.

He had been airborne two minutes.

Hits registered on the Nakajima, but it continued ahead, leading Adams into the teeth of *Yorktown's* fusillade of AA fire. Among the splashes and smoke, the bright impacts and confused tracers, the Japanese torpedo dropped free.

Damn! Adams cursed as he held the trigger down, hosing the Nakajima as it continued toward the carrier. It veered off on the wake as *Yorktown's* port side gunners fired at it in ferocious rage. The green airplane started to smoke as Adams closed it, now more afraid of the rabid-dog sailors in the catwalks. The plane's tail-gunner had so far ignored him amid the black puffs, spray and cordite, and the dancing, supersonic fireflies of death.

Adams kept hammering the torpedo-bomber as he followed the Jap further into the hailstorm of angry lead. The tail-gunner stood and raised his arm, seeming to shake his fist at *Yorktown*. At that instant, his bomber exploded underneath him. By instinct and with a startled cry, Adams yanked the *Wildcat* up and right, flying through an edge of flame as it turned into black smoke. He cursed in fear and frustration when a piece of metal smacked his windscreen and froze in place.

"It's me, you idiots!" he cried as he rolled his *Wildcat* inverted over the water, tracers all around him, his nose pointed at the waves before he scooped out above them, his shoulders hunched as if to somehow brace himself for a stray tracer that would take his head off. Through his seat, he felt hits on the airframe – *bullets or fragments?* – and spray from spent rounds lifted higher than his wing line. He sprinted to a hole between two destroyers that, by instinct, lashed out automatic gunfire at him and anything that dared to fly inside the angry beehive.

Their starboard side guns took half-hearted shots at him as he broke free of the defensive circle, and, for the first time in four minutes, Adams checked his fuel: under 15 gallons! He throttled back and lifted his plane into a shallow climb, glancing over his left shoulder at *Yorktown*, still fighting for her life. No longer able to help, Adams inhaled great lungfuls of salt air as he watched her.

CHAPTER 26

HIRYŪ B5N STRIKE GROUP, 1440 JUNE 4, 1942

Maruyama strained against the steady g-force as Nakao hung on the outside of the turn. This was it, a descending right-hand turn to attack just like his own *Hiryū* Type 97s had performed that early December morning, but, unlike that morning, turning in against an alerted and suddenly capable enemy, an enemy hell-bent on killing all the *kankōs* the First Air Fleet could muster.

In the cloud breaks above them, *Zero-sens* tangled with the Grummans. Maruyama could not tell who was winning. No matter. They were *in*, breaking free of the cloud bank along the screen's perimeter. They took fire from a destroyer almost at once, flying right over it. Hashimoto's vee of five *kankōs* were naked now, alone, pulling and sprinting hard into a dozen gray ships that fired defiant flame at the pitiful attackers.

Inside their defenses, Maruyama contemplated his target: a carrier, a moving carrier. Awestruck, he identified it as an *Enterprise* class, just like the recognition silhouettes, undamaged, its massive castle-like superstructure dominating the whole fleet...with Grummans taking off! The enormous ship glowed, swathed in a halo of white gun smoke.

Bright flame from the bow turret of a cruiser on the right surprised Maruyama as Hashimoto leveled his formation at 50 meters. Nakao hung on in position, fighting to ignore the sudden water columns created by big American shells that erupted to their left and right, blasting water into the air like giant fish nets placed in front of the *kankōs* to snare them. Ahead of the carrier, another cruiser did the same from her after turret. *"Watch out!"* Hamada cried as an arc of American lead shot over them from behind.

Maruyama crouched into the tunnel and picked up the gray carrier. The ship filled his computer's aim sight. Crossing 2,000 yards of range, he shouted *"Take us lower!"* Nakao descended to release altitude amid the rumble of gunfire. Maruyama felt more than heard the punches and plinks from small caliber hits as he lay prone. With a whoop Hamada fired at something – *A Grumman?* – but Maruyama could not see, could not assist. His station was here, under Nakao, his loins exposed, only a thin sheet of aluminum for protection between him and the enemy bullets and the 300 kilograms of high explosive their *kankō* carried. He watched the range count down, slow and agonizing. His subconscious wanted him to get up and *run* over the wave tops to safety, but it was overruled by his conscious mind. For now he was trapped inside this delicate aluminum insect.

"*Banzai! Hashimoto-san! Banzai!*" Nakao yelled out from above him.

Glued to the target computer, Maruyama concentrated on the aim point. Hashimoto must have dropped, and soon the others would release as they came into range. Maruyama had to wait, but he could not wait too long, lest they be blown out of the sky. Three hundred yards; he'd pull the release handle at 300. *Point blank.* Now a veteran, Maruyama would make the call. They couldn't afford a miss.

"Nakao, fly the plane! Left two degrees! *Level fifteen meters!*" he barked, and the bomber twitched left under Nakao's obedient control. "*Whoa!*" Hamada cried as an eruption of water jumped up behind them.

Through the viewfinder Maruyama could see the gallery automatics, and bigger crew-served guns on the bow, muzzle flashes and wisps of tracers. Splashes on the surface stitched a line and others suddenly appeared like fat raindrops from no known source. Concussions, more plinks on the *kankō's* skin, a thunder of gunfire from someplace ahead over the steady roar of Nakao's firewalled Hakari radial engine. *Seven hundred yards...*

"*You bastard!*" Nakao shouted as Hamada bellowed *banzai* from behind. Maruyama fought to assess the range and angle-off while surrounded by the chaos inside and outside his Type 97 bomber. He lined up on the bow, the port anchor his aiming point. The carrier ran hard, but Maruyama had seen His Majesty's ships run faster in training runs. He sensed the great carrier turn away from them. Hold it...hold it...*Now!*

Maruyama yanked on the release, and, with a familiar jolt, the torpedo fell away. Nakao whooped in joy as Maruyama extricated himself and lifted his head above the rail. A childlike Hamada again shouted, "*Banzai!*"

They were alone with the American carrier, nothing but a cliff of steel in front of them, the flight deck now above them. Through an opening in the hangar bay, a man stood, frozen, and, along the catwalks, the Americans delivered their murderous fire. Maruyama could see them, like those Americans on the moored battleships who had run confused, to something, anything, unsure of what was happening. But these Americans had the high ground, a wall of black shadowed by the afternoon sun, and every gun that could poured a broadside into Maruyama and his mates.

Nakao veered left and ahead of the ship as tracer rounds hurtled toward them. Sharp punctures to the empennage and Hamada cried out. "I'm hit!"

Maruyama turned to see Hamada writhing in pain, clutching his bloody hand as lightning flashes of tracers snapped past. He couldn't fire the gun, and Maruyama craned his neck to search for any Grummans on their tail. As they crossed the carrier's bow he saw the red faces of the frantic American gunners trying to get their weapons turned around on them as they roared past. Ahead, the *Akagi* bird was still carrying its torpedo and falling behind. *Why didn't they drop?* Nevertheless, it was now every man for himself, and Nakao took a heading between a destroyer and a cruiser as the carrier's starboard gallery opened up with sheets of tracers.

"*Banzai!* We did it! A hit! *BANZAI!*" Hamada cried, ignoring his wound and overcome with joyful, savage emotion.

Maruyama twisted in his chair in time to see a giant geyser lift high above the carrier next to a rain of falling mist from a previous hit.

As Nakao and the rest of Hashimoto's *kankōs* fought their way out of the cauldron, Maruyama sensed they had done it. Once clear of the anti-aircraft, and with no Grummans visible, he looked back.

The carrier no longer made a wake, and it appeared to have a list.

Fletcher and Lewis looked aft from the bridge wing as *Astoria* heeled to port, her batteries firing at the small group of planes attacking *Yorktown*.

"C'mon! *C'mon!*" Lewis shouted over the deafening roar.

Fletcher grimaced as the last five Japanese torpedo planes approached the carrier. They dropped – *Dang it!* Now it was up to Elliot to avoid them. With dread, Fletcher and Lewis saw he could not, despite the furious and confused crossfire that converged on the little line of Japanese planes.

The swift Nakajimas scurried west and away, but Fletcher ignored them, waiting and hoping.

"Oh, hell!" Lewis cursed as the first torpedo found its mark, sending a plume of spray hundreds of feet into the air.

"Hit her amidships. *Dammit!*" he added, and by instinct he looked south to assess TF-16. Fletcher kept his eyes on his flagship, still in a starboard turn.

Fletcher groaned when a second plume shot as high as the first, and also on *Yorktown's* port side amidships. "*Shoot!*" Lewis barked, and again he scanned the skies for threats – and for salvation.

For the second time that afternoon, *Yorktown* coasted to a stop. No flames, but she had already developed a list. Lewis gripped the rail and watched her before he exploded in frustration.

"The last two planes! Of all the damned luck!"

Spruance and Oliver watched the action to the north, another dome of black spots and flashing lights over *Yorktown* and her escorts. A sudden black line led to the water, marking a downed plane that both prayed was Japanese. Along the flight deck, gunners in helmets and kapok jackets stood at their guns, also watching their mates fight for their lives on the distant horizon.

On the other side of the shelter, Browning agonized. For two hours, this timid admiral had dithered, *waiting* for direction instead of actively seeking it. Content to let others find the Japs. Best and the other fliers said there was another ship out there, intact. *Can't always believe them...no, we got four carriers.* Browning was convinced there was a fifth or sixth Jap carrier remaining, and after they were done pounding *Yorktown* they'd be down after TF-16. *We should have launched at least an hour ago; Bill Halsey would have launched the damn float planes. Would've ignored Fletcher and sunk the Japs singlehanded.*

"*Yorktown's* net just went dead, sir."

Browning nodded. "Figures," he muttered, not acknowledging the radioman. *She got hit again, and if this bookworm doesn't get off his ass and take action, we're next.*

Spruance turned as Lieutenant Commander Ham Dow approached him. "Sighting report, sir, from *Yorktown's* planes."

Browning appeared from the other side of the shelter, irate that he didn't intercept it. "Where away?" he barked at the Communications Officer. "Range, bearing, and time?"

Spruance read from the sheet Dow had handed him, somewhat amused to receive it direct. He hadn't received a direct sighting report since he'd been a ship captain. Halsey ran a loose operation, and the chain of command was fluid. Spruance tried to fit in and not make too much of it. Absentmindedly, he felt the stubble on his face, proud that he'd adopted this brown-shoe "combat" practice. After two days without shaving his whiskers were longer than they had ever been.

Buracker stepped forward. "Admiral, one of *Yorktown's* scouts found another carrier, undamaged. This could be the fifth one."

Spruance read the dispatch and handed it to Browning, who devoured it like a starving man.

"Okay, sir...two groups, one with a carrier in it...two-seven-nine at one-ten from us. Admiral, recommend we attack as soon as practicable."

Spruance nodded. "How many can you send?"

"Sir, we've got fifteen of *Yorktown's* dive-bombers and about ten of our guys. *Hornet's* planes from Midway should be back aboard or close, but she should be able to put up about twenty-five with what she has on hand. Then there's our remaining torpedo planes..."

"No," Spruance said, shaking his head.

Browning remained silent. He'd let it pass. *Live to fight another day.*

"Then, sir, that's about fifty planes. We can easily hit two carriers, and there's gotta be another one in that second group the pilots missed. I'll give them orders to go off on the battleships and cruisers if the carriers are sinking."

"When can you launch?" Spruance asked.

Browning looked at his watch. "I'll coordinate with the captain sir, but we could go at...1530, in forty-five minutes."

"Very well, attack with your dive-bombers. Keep fighters here to defend this task force and TF-17 to the maximum extent."

"Concur, sir," Browning said before wheeling to call the bridge on the direct circuit. *Finally!*

Doctor Sam Osterlough stepped onto the bridge to find Mitscher on the starboard bridge wing. Mitscher watched the silent activity over *Yorktown* in the distance, lost in his thoughts.

"Captain?"

Mitscher turned to his senior medical officer. Osterlough noticed his captain's bloodshot eyes under the shaded bill of his cap. Mitscher knew why the Doc was here.

"Sam, what's the butcher's bill?"

"Five dead, sir. Twenty wounded." Osterlough then swallowed and added, "And sir, one of the dead is Lieutenant Ingersoll."

Mitscher recoiled inwardly, as if squeezed by a giant hand. *Admiral Ingersoll's son. Of all...*

Nobody could be blamed for such a freak accident. The wounded *Yorktown* F4F pilot had found refuge on *Hornet* when his own ship had been damaged during the attack two hours ago. The gear collapsed on landing, and, as the fighter skidded toward the island, it let loose with its .50s, spraying the personnel standing on deck near the island hatchways. By reflex Mitscher had ducked below the bridge wing gallery rail. He then peered down and saw the carnage underneath him, not knowing the boys, but knowing them. His boys. *Responsible.*

"Did he live?" Mitscher asked, afraid to learn the answer.

"No, sir. Killed instantly."

Mitscher nodded. He remembered an encounter with young Ingersoll at a Mare Island reception when Ingersoll was a midshipman home on leave from Annapolis. His father was a cruiser captain then. Almost ten years ago. Ingersoll was one of his wardroom lieutenants, a comer whom his father had helped steer to *this* ship. *My ship.* Gone now, no warning. *Responsible.*

"Captain, two will lose use of their arms, and one man his leg. We'll probably amputate once we come out of GQ. Some men inside were hit with splinters…afraid for one of the sailor's eyes."

Mitscher could only absorb the news as he strode across the bridge to the port wing as Osterlough followed. Casualties – from self-inflicted fire. Still no word from Waldron's squadron, nothing from Midway, nothing from Mitchell's escort fighters, no word of water landings or rescues. It was still early. Maybe they'd spot them later in the afternoon. With any luck.

Three burning Jap carriers evened the odds, and word of a fourth from a scout plane meant *Enterprise* would send orders soon. Mitscher readied his bombers anyway and thought of Ring as he watched his plane handlers push his available SBDs aft. Ordies with bomb dollies followed. Could Sea Hag handle this? Soucek stepped beside him.

"Captain, just got word that Bombing Eight took off from Midway an hour ago. Knowing Ruff, they'll be here in another ten or fifteen."

Mitscher closed his eyes and clenched his teeth as Soucek let him vent his frustration. When he opened his eyes, *Hornet's* flight deck was still a jumble of airplanes, most of them wedged aft and spotted for takeoff.

"How many?" Mitscher asked. *Even keel!*

"Unclear, sir…we got word that about twelve landed there…I'd expect ten or twelve."

The time was almost 1500.

Mitscher squinted and lifted his head to the sun as he worked a kink in his neck.

"Okay, Apollo. Let's hold this spot until Ruff shows up and we get definite contact with him. Then we'll break it to recover them and respot for launch. I expect *Enterprise* to launch in an hour, and we should make that, but no orders yet. Meanwhile, get Stanhope up here and keep loading the bombers."

"Aye, aye, sir. Captain, when we recover the bombers, can we swap out the CAP?"

"Good idea. Proceed," Mitscher said, confident that he'd be ready in time.

CHAPTER 27

SCOUTING SIX READY ROOM, USS *ENTERPRISE*, 1505 JUNE 4, 1942

"All right, listen up!"

The dive-bomber pilots stood among the high-back chairs and crouched around Skipper Gallaher in the jammed ready room as he briefed them on the afternoon's plan. Best stood next to him, assessing the junior aviators' attention, while Kroeger leaned against the forward bulkhead and listened.

"Okay, we've got a pickup team this afternoon to go against that one ship that escaped this morning. It's identified as a *Sōryū*-class carrier and its last reported posit was two-seven-nine at one-ten. Once we man up and launch, we'll rendezvous overhead. *Enterprise* planes at two thousand, and you *Yorktowners* at three."

Kroeger glanced at the faces next to him, many unfamiliar. Practically all of *Yorktown's* VB were here, and, like him, veterans of the morning strike. Many stood close together in their sweaty khakis, goggles perched on their heads, helmet straps dangling.

Kroeger wanted to go back and finish it – and he had never seen Best so fixated. But the VS boys were *mad* and wanted revenge, their dark and angry eyes not leaving their CO. They were no longer afraid, none of the pilots were, and Lieutenant Gallaher would now lead the whole gaggle back to the Japs.

"Once we all get aboard, we're going. Don't know what *Hornet's* going to do, but we're going. No fighter escort – just us. I'm going to take us up to fourteen, and we're going to get right after them at 180 knots. So, hang on."

Next to Kroeger, Fred nodded his understanding. So did Best, who stood next to Gallaher, a public acknowledgment of his intent. Once they departed the ship, they'd find the Japs within the hour – and even the bridge couldn't screw up Point Option as much as they had this morning. Chalk dust flew as Gallaher drew on the blackboard.

"Once we find 'em we're gonna come south and up sun and come at 'em like this in a right-hand turn, or left if the geometry dictates. Dick, you stay with me on the outside of my turn and follow us down. Watch for fighters and stay tight. Dave – where's Dave? Lieutenant Shumway?"

From the middle of his pilots, Shumway raised his hand.

"Okay, Dave, you float your turn about ten degrees off us before you guys push over. Everyone, solid dives like this morning, steep and balanced, and on the pull out we'll be headin' east for home."

Best interrupted. "Yeah, Dave, on my egress I was watching you guys hit that carrier to the east – best dive-bombing I ever saw." Shumway acknowledged him with a humble nod. Kroeger felt a twinge of envy; his fellows had never received such a compliment from Best.

Gallaher resumed.

"If there's two carriers, then Dave, I'll direct you. If near-far, expect the near ship, and if left-right, I'll make a radio call and back it up with hand signals down the line. Watch me, and take the other one – the one I'm not going on. We had some confusion this morning and want to avoid that. If we plaster one or both and it becomes overkill, go for a battlewagon or cruiser. Saw a few of those this morning. Go home in squadrons, and Dick, you can stick with us if you'd like."

"Thanks Willie, we just might," Best answered.

"Yeah, expect Point Option to be east southeast, and it's gonna be gettin' dark, so buster back here if you can and heads on a swivel. You may or may not see the *Hornet* guys, and again, I *think* they're comin' but don' know their plan. Any questions?"

Kroeger had none. At this range, 1000- or 500-pound bombs made little difference. He presumed the VS would carry their customary 500-pounders. The *Yorktowners,* like him, were VB pilots and carried heavies.

The speaker crackled. *"Pilots, man your planes!"*

With an explosion of activity, the aviators undogged the hatch and burst through it onto the flight deck. *"Go get 'em, boys!"* Gallaher yelled as they whooped and hollered like a football team rushing from the locker room to the field.

Inside their battered Type 97, an exhausted Maruyama reached for his canteen. It felt light as he lifted it out of its housing. *Did the plane captain not fill it?* Inspecting it further, he saw it was holed in the middle, by bullet or shrapnel, he wasn't sure. He had never sensed being shot...actually hit. He turned the canteen carefully to swallow the water that remained. He examined it again. An

American bullet forged by an American smelter had ripped open his canteen. His Majesty's canteen.

The cockpit seemed draftier than normal, and at his feet was a small patch of sunlight. He found two holes, metal shards facing into the cockpit, evidence of bullet entry. On the left side of the cockpit he found an opening with the shards facing out, into the slipstream. Fascinated, he realized a bullet must have entered and exited while he was on the floor aiming their torpedo. *Blessed by the Gods of War.*

Deep down, he and the others knew they would fly in the service of His Majesty until they died. Nobody got shore duty, certainly not lowly petty officers. But if Lieutenant Tomonaga and Mori and Miyauchi-kun could give their lives for the Emperor, Maruyama would gladly join them.

They had escaped from the Americans thirty minutes ago and had at least that long to go to find *Hiryū*. Next to him were four shot-up bombers and a few *Zero-sens*. The First Air Fleet was melting away, with only this sorry little formation, not even a full *chutai*, able to fight – if the mechanics could patch them up. They would, of course, and Maruyama and his mates would get inside these patched-up planes once they did. Like Lieutenant Tomonaga had, with a confident smile as he went to his death.

"Maruyama-ken, do you have water?" Hamada asked.

"I'm sorry, but no. Canteen shot open. How's your hand?"

"Hurts more. The bullet broke a bone and tore open the meat of my palm."

Maruyama twisted in his seat to see, and looked at Hamada's goggle-covered eyes. He seemed lucid. "Keep it bandaged and keep pressure on it. We'll be home soon."

"My foot too. They hit my foot – above the toes. Boot ripped open. I noticed once we cleared the enemy fleet."

"Did you wrap it?"

"Yes."

"I have water," Nakao said through the voice tube.

"May I please have a drink, Nakao-san?" Hamada asked.

Nakao shifted in his seat, and, without taking a swig for himself, handed his canteen over his shoulder to Maruyama who grabbed for it. The canteen was full, and Maruyama would have drunk more, but he opened the top and handed it back to the wounded Hamada.

"Thank you, mates! A toast to the sunk American carrier!" Hamada exulted. Maruyama admired the fighting spirit of their gunner.

Finished, Hamada handed the canteen back to Maruyama, who closed it and handed it up to Nakao. Maruyama had had his share of water. He was too sleepy to drink it now anyway. Many of his fellows had complained of exhaustion after a combat flight, short or long range, it did not matter. How could he sleep, knowing that Nakao must remain awake to fly and Hamada was wounded behind him? He passed the time by counting the bullet holes in the *Akagi* plane on his right, its torpedo somehow jettisoned. The gunner appeared to be taking a nap – or worse.

The waves rolled under them, endless and eternal. One moment a wave existed, then it didn't, gone, disappeared, *just like that*, before another took its place. And another, in a never-ending sequence. But they would end, to crash on the shores of Honshu, or flow into the Inland Sea, and finally meet the shore of Hashirajima. Yes, the waves, endless and eternal, would one day end.

Hashimoto closed his throttle to descend, and, with binoculars, Maruyama scanned ahead. In the distance *Hiryū* steamed away from them, making her wounded *kankōs* chase her. Closing her, he saw she flew a white flag and black ball, and the others cried in relief when Maruyama informed them the ship was ready to take them aboard. The outer picket ships fired single shots, and the carrier slowed and turned into the wind. As the planes entered the landing circle, one *Zero-sen* buzzed the bridge, impatient. *Hiryū* steadied on course, and Nakao took his sequence. The impatient *Zero-sen* was aboard and already on the elevator to go below as Hashimoto's pilot lined up for his approach. Around the carrier, screen vessels held position as silent sentinels, anxious, fearing they had overstayed. As they waited their turn, Maruyama contemplated the three black columns on the southern horizon, and, with a chill, sensed they were an omen.

Now dirty, Nakao rolled out for the long straight in, and Maruyama joined him in monitoring the landing light indications. Once they crossed the ramp, Nakao cut the engine, and the Type 97 dropped to the deck with a hard bounce. As the wire caught them, Maruyama bent forward from the sudden deceleration, then raised the tail hook. Gunners at their stations watched in silence as Nakao gunned the engine to taxi ahead as another *kankō* lined up behind. No one on the bridge greeted them as they taxied past. The ship's mood was grim, the crew spent and demoralized. Maruyama, out of character, raised his hands in a triumphant clasp for the entertainment of the starboard gallery.

The dazed men looked back at him.

"What?" Mitscher asked with dismay, looking over Soucek's shoulder to the horizon. *Enterprise* appeared to be in a turn.

"Yes, sir," a chagrined Soucek answered. "They're launching at 1530 on the contact to the west and want to know how many we can send."

Mitscher checked his watch: ten minutes from now! He clenched his teeth in disgust and looked away as the last Bombing Eight *Dauntless* taxied up to the pack on the bow. Always conscious of the crew, he had to mask his frustration. Next were the CAP fighters – another five minutes at least. *How could this have happened?* No orders from Spruance's staff, no consideration for half of TF-16's striking power. It would be at least thirty minutes before he could recover the CAP, spot the bombers, and get them off. He had gambled – and lost.

An upbeat Ring appeared with Rodee in tow. Sea Hag saluted Mitscher as he came to attention.

"Reporting as ordered, Captain. We're loaded and ready to go!" Behind Ring, Rodee was downcast, ashamed of the morning's debacle as he held his salute.

Mitscher returned their salutes. "Stan, *Enterprise* is turning into the wind to launch…in ten minutes."

Ring's head snapped west. No way could his dive-bombers launch with them. If the *Enterprise* planes waited overhead, they could match up and go out as one big strike with Ring in the lead.

Soucek offered what he could. "Sir, the VB and VS are loaded and most are warmed up in the hangar bay. Once we get these fighters aboard and strike 'em below, we'll spot the deck lickety-split so we can get our guys airborne ASAP."

A stung Mitscher struggled with the damage to his pride. *Does Spruance not trust me now?* Launching late, despite the lack of warning, would do nothing to endear him. He had to redeem himself and his ship – and turned to the only man who could do it.

"Stanhope, if we can get you off in time to join with them, or if you go out alone like this morning, we've gotta find 'em and hit 'em. They were reported a hun'erd miles away, maybe one-twenty now. Can't miss."

"Yes, sir. We'll cruise in the low teens and get out there in a jiffy. Forty-five minutes, fifty tops."

"Good. Commander Soucek will figure the assigned heading and Point Option."

"Probably somewhere between two-eight-zero and two-eight-five," Soucek volunteered. "I'll get it down to you, Stan."

Mitscher raised his voice to be heard over the first *Wildcat* that chugged up the deck.

"May be night when you return. Your boys up to it?"

Ring opened his mouth to answer but could not. Rodee rescued him.

"Captain, most of my guys haven't experienced a night landing. Don't see how it can be helped though."

Mitscher nodded. "Yes...moon'll be down, but this weather should hold."

On the horizon, a plane lifted off from *Enterprise*. Then another.

"They're launchin', sir," Soucek said, resigned.

Mitscher observed the flagship through the glasses and noted the time. *1525. He couldn't even spot me five minutes.*

Unable to control the operations on *Enterprise*, Mitscher focused on what he could. "Okay, Stan, brief up your pilots and I'll have you man planes as soon as we can. Their carrier *first*, then escorting ships at your discretion. And I'm sorry, but I can't spare any fighters for you."

"Aye, aye, Captain," Ring said. He lifted a salute that Mitscher returned. As Ring wheeled with Rodee to go below, Mitscher stopped him.

"Sea Hag, nothing yet from Torpedo Eight or Fighting Eight from this morning."

A tight-lipped Ring nodded. "Thank you, sir."

Mitscher held his gaze.

"Good hunting, Stan."

CHAPTER 28

HIJMS *Nagara*, 1615 June 4, 1942

From *Nagara's* crowded bridge, Genda had watched the *kankōs* alight aboard *Hiryū*. He counted five. *Is Tomonaga among them?* They reported another enemy carrier sunk, but the fleet air arm was now whittled down to almost nothing. Yamaguchi planned for *another* attack on the third carrier a captured enemy flier had confirmed was part of the American force. With maybe ten planes. At dusk. To Genda this was lunacy, not even worthy of discussion. Even the *bushido* code discouraged rash misjudgment in pursuit of an enemy. Foolish pride.

Nimitz was wounded, too, yet Nagumo had no sighting reports of retreat. And Midway was still there, beat up from the morning, but in the last nine hours, planes could have been repaired, refueled, and rearmed. *They could be heading here now,* he contemplated as he watched the lone *shotai* of CAP fighters overhead.

Genda was convinced the Mobile Force *must* steam west at flank until nightfall. Escape. Reassess. Cancel the Aleutians operation at once, and, together with the battle force, rendezvous, regroup, and reattack. Genda glanced at Kusaka and Oishi. They stood next to Nagumo, both observing *Hiryū* while their commander read dispatches. Their damp and soot-stained uniforms were reminders of their escape from the flagship, its smoke still visible with the others to the south. Kusaka's flash-burned face, covered in salve, had a witness mark across his forehead, evidence of the cap, now lost, that he had worn. With the First Air Fleet staff present as surprise guests, the cruiser's bridge watch standers could barely breathe. Who could blame them?

Genda eased closer to the admirals to hear their conversation. Surely they could not be considering a dusk attack. Oishi spoke in low tones to Kusaka.

"Chief of Staff, many of our destroyers are tasked standing by our burning carriers to the south. They will be needed to form a picket line to sight and harass the enemy as we withdraw to rendezvous with the Second Carrier Striking Force. Recommend consider we scuttle the derelicts and form this line in the next hour so they can take station in time for Admiral Kondō's main body to shell Midway and eliminate the air threat from it."

Genda could not believe his ears. *Are they still adhering to the invasion time-line?*

Nagumo looked up to see Genda's distressed face. He motioned him to join them.

"Genda," Kusaka began. "The Second Carrier Striking Force is coming down from the Aleutians to join us. We'll have more planes for your tasking in three days."

Genda was skeptical. *Three days – at least!* Outwardly, he remained optimistic.

"Good news, Chief of Staff. Are we now sprinting out of here to the west?"

Kusaka shook his head. "Yamaguchi says he can hit them again, at dusk. If another strike can hold the Americans, it buys time for the Kondō force and Main Body to join us in neutralizing Midway and engaging with the American task force – should they give battle. The landing schedule can easily slip a day or two."

"You recommend, then, we continue the assault on Midway?"

Oishi sensed a challenge. "Yes, and we've recalled our submarines to form a new cordon line east of us. The transport group is ordered to stand by to the northwest, out of danger, as Admiral Kondō joins us."

Genda couldn't restrain himself. "Oishi-san, the purpose of taking Midway was to force the Americans to come out. Clearly they have, and surprised us on our flank. What other surprises await?"

Oishi had little patience for Genda's know-it-all insolence, but Genda wasn't finished.

"Admiral, if I may, I recommend in the strongest manner that you consider we retire northwest at best speed. *Hiryū* is fighting well today, but no one can expect success with a meager *nine* attack planes, possibly damaged, and at nightfall."

Nagumo sat listening, and waited for him to continue. Genda turned to Kusaka.

"Chief of Staff, if we run hard and rendezvous with the Main Body, we can bide our time out of range of their land-based air and meet up with the Aleutians force as they come down. Once joined, we can conduct proper searches and engage the Americans on our terms."

An agitated Oishi shook his head. "What, we suddenly have unlimited time and unlimited fuel? So easy! And what of the soldiers on the transport force?"

Ignoring the sarcasm, Genda answered. "Send the transports home! They are no longer needed! The Americans have sortied, and we can lure them west before turning back to engage. Concur, Captain, deploy the destroyers and submarines, but in a moving picket to protect this force and the forces we are joining with."

"Out of the question!" Oishi shot back. "The invasion has not been canceled. Night approaches, and that plays to our strength."

Genda looked at the battleship man with contempt. The big-gun club would have their Tsushima. Even at the cost of the First Air Fleet.

Both Nagumo and Kusaka had grown up in big-guns and were sympathetic. Torpedoes to start, then heavy broadsides as the clumsy Americans charged into them at midnight. All to plan – just like this disastrous day.

Nagumo listened to the exchange in silence. He then spoke.

"Senior Staff Officer, he may have a point."

Stung, Oishi bit his lip. He wasn't giving up. Next to him, Kusaka remained silent. After taking a breath, Oishi made his case.

"Nagumo-sama, you've just destroyed two of his carriers which evens the odds. Help is arriving in hours, heavy firepower to augment ours, and more torpedo tubes to augment ours. They are wounded, too, and we've not been attacked from the vicinity of Midway since this morning. Admiral, *Kaga* and *Sōryū* haven't a chance; leave them now and consolidate your rearguard force to give us and Kondō's force an advantage later tonight when we engage."

Emphatic, Genda pointed to *Hiryū*. "And them, Oishi-san? Send them again, not even a full squadron complement for a dusk attack on a carrier task force – and *hope* they can find their way back and aboard? They're as exhausted as everyone is. Admiral, this is high risk and low reward."

Nagumo raised a hand. "Enough. I've made up my mind. Withdraw *Hiryū* now, at best speed. No strike. And yes, Oishi, I'll ask Combined Fleet for permission to scuttle the ships, but we must also transfer the survivors and wounded off the escorts and onto heavier units that can berth and treat them. No dusk strike."

Kusaka exhaled disappointment through his nose. *Why ask? Those ships are still yours to command!*

"Genda-kun, again your logic is sound," Nagumo said, his voice trailing off, dejected. He was drained. No, shattered. Genda had lost to him this morning; Nagumo wouldn't listen. The three pyres to the south were proof. Kusaka and smug Oishi, blind to the possibilities and costs, were desperate for a change of fortune and still thought they carried the initiative. Even Combined Fleet thought victory was at hand, or at least possible. Nagumo, who had the most to risk, thought otherwise. He spoke.

"Let's move northwest until dark. Then we can reverse south or southeast to intercept Kondō. At flank speed until nightfall; we'll deal with the fuel bunkers later. And draft the message for permission." Finished, Nagumo rubbed his eyes and looked off to starboard.

"What's that?" Oishi asked, pointing outside.

Caught up in conversation, they had not noticed that *Nagara* had turned slightly. Off the starboard bow, an object, red in color, bobbed on the waves. Drawing closer, they now saw the object was a raft with two men inside.[1] Keeping off 300 yards, the flagship sped past and dispatched a destroyer to rescue the men.

"Are they ours?" Kusaka asked of no one.

Genda suspected American. "I believe enemy. Torpedo plane or dive-bomber."

Separated by distance and culture, the men on the cruiser and the men in the raft watched each other with suspicious eyes. Genda pitied his fellow aviators, even if the enemy. They were American, no doubt. Their raft was like a wounded animal unable to run, unable to escape, resigned to its fate as an unconcerned lion sauntered up to it to deliver the *coup de grâce*. The destroyer hove to, and, soon, the Americans would be aboard. Once interrogated, death would follow. Mercy killing.

"See to the message, Kusaka," Nagumo mumbled, head down, spent.

"*Hai*, Admiral," Kusaka said. As he followed, Captain Oishi threw daggers into Genda's eyes.

---

[1] ENS F.W. O'Flaherty and AMM1c B.P. Gaido, Scouting Six

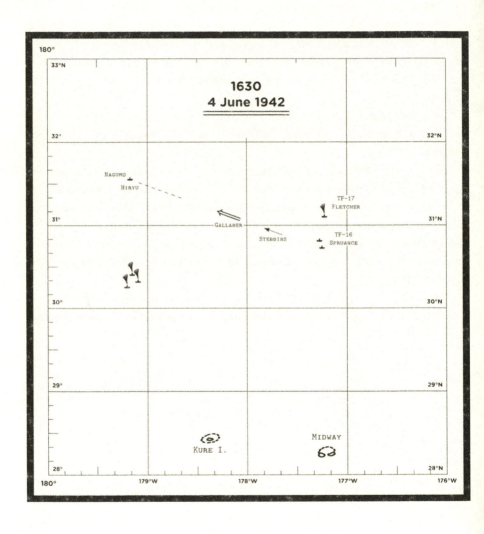

CHAPTER 29

SBD 6-B-2, 1655 JUNE 4, 1942

Kroeger's pulse quickened. Wakes in the distance, heading northwest. The pilots tightened up the formation in anticipation, and in the adjacent cockpits, gunners checked their firing arcs and twisted in their seats to see the enemy for themselves. The weather had cleared, and, to the left, the sun hovered over a layer of clouds.

Further left were three columns of smoke, pinpoints on the surface that expanded into broad clouds and trailed off to the southeast. He judged them to be about fifty miles distant. Ahead of him, the wakes – big and white – continued away from the Americans.

In the middle was a carrier, one that had survived the morning attacks. Kroeger flew again on Skipper Best's wing, at altitude with a 1000-pounder underneath. Ahead, Skipper Gallaher led the eleven *Enterprise* bombers on a heading that would take them south of the enemy formation. Kroeger understood the geometry and imagined a line from the wakes to the sun. That's where they would go to push over. Along that line he saw a cruiser in escort. They would fly right over it.

Over his shoulder, the *Yorktowners* maintained position on the outside. When Gallaher pulled into the Japs, Shumway would be in good position to float his turn and hit the other heavy unit on the carrier's starboard bow. Just then Gallaher came up on the radio.

"Dave, take the nearer battleship. Dick, follow me!"

Scanning north, Kroeger's heart jumped when he saw them: specks over the task force, level altitude.

"Halterman, they've got a CAP up! Two formations, just off the nose starboard, one o-clock!"

Halterman rogered Kroeger as Gallaher began his acceleration down to push over altitude. As he flew form on Best's left wing, Kroeger noted the disposition of the ships. The carrier was alone in the middle, the escorts in a wide circle. A loose screen, at least five miles across. Kroeger hoped he could pull off east; at the moment, an opening in the screen offered a clear escape route.

Kroeger counted eight SBDs ahead of him, seven of them from the *Sails.* Fred was tail-end Charlie again. "We've got company up here!" Gallaher radioed. *Good, he sees what I see.* In his plane, Best turned and gave Kroeger a thumbs-up as he waited for a response. In exaggerated motion, Kroeger nodded and pointed at the enemy specks to acknowledge. Best nodded back as Kroeger passed the signal to Fred. In response, the pilot held his thumb up high at the top of his windscreen.

They overtook the Japanese ships on the left, and Kroeger once more checked his switches, latched his plotting board, charged his fixed guns, and ensured his bomb was armed. His breathing became deep and rapid as adrenalin coursed through him. High to his right, he spotted five *Zeros*, all gray, orbiting three miles north. He checked south, pleased to see the horizon offered a cloud background that he and the other *Dauntlesses* could blend into. Kroeger sensed they were a bit over ten miles from their roll in. *Should be another five minutes...*

In unison – and with no warning – the ships turned left into the American formation. *Maybe they see us!* Kroeger thought, and monitored Gallaher's plane to see if he was reacting. The turn would force everyone to be steep.

"Halterman, get ready. Think they see us... I've got three *Zeros* high at our three."

"Tallyho, sir, I've got 'em," the gunner answered. Behind him, Kroeger felt Halterman swivel to the right.

The Japs continued their turns, yet Kroeger saw no gunfire, no sign of resistance. The *Zeros* to his right held in lazy circles, oblivious. The SBDs were going to come in under their noses, hit them, and run, like he had when he played doorbell-ditch as a kid. *Long ago. Yesterday.*

The ships steadied out, and he could see no planes on the carrier's flight deck, nor in the landing circle. Unlike the morning's targets, this carrier was smaller, just a slab of deck with a big red dot forward. An aiming bullseye. *Nice of them to do that for us.* Scanning the water, Kroeger noted a float plane approach the lee of the close cruiser, the one they would've flown over. By the time the crane hooked up the little fellow, Kroeger and his mates would be in and off on the carrier.

Gallaher initiated his turn and his squadron followed, echelon left. Best slid further outside, and Kroeger opened the throttle to stay with him. Fred held position, and, behind him, the *Yorktowners* fell back into trail. This was going to work out just like Lieutenant Gallaher had briefed it.

The right-hand turn allowed a full scan of the airspace over the task force. Above his lowered wing Kroeger saw them – *Zeros*, black dots, constant bearing and… *Coming at me!*

We've been spotted!

Kroeger overbanked for a moment to look down his wing line. Some two miles below, the same cruiser fired from guns amidships and on the forecastle. Beyond Skipper Best's plane was the carrier. Like an electric light switch, it suddenly lit up: two solid rows of lights along its catwalks.

"Under attack by fighters!" Gallaher radioed.

In a race to the push-over point, the *Zeros* swung their wing line, and an impatient Kroeger saw Gallaher had at least thirty degrees to go. *"C'mon,"* he muttered as he kept one eye on the *Zeros*. They'd be shooting soon, about the time he'd be in, diving down in column behind the skipper. Kroeger's head whipped back to the *Yorktown* bombers, easing away toward the big ship up north. Maybe the fighters would follow them. No, they won't follow them! *They know you – you! – are trying to sink their home.*

The CO signaled for dive brakes, and, ahead, the *Sails* followed Gallaher up and over. Antiaircraft shells burst below them like camera flashbulbs and turned to a black smudge in an instant. Tracers arced up like sparks of flame from the carrier and surrounding ships, too low to hit them – until Kroeger and the others dove into their grasp.

The AA beckoned silently. *We see you. Come, come!* All the ships around the carrier fired what they could, their blazing pulses a brilliant yellow in the late afternoon light. Skipper Gallaher was established in his dive. His dutiful wingmen, sequenced evenly, followed in graceful rolling pull-downs. Kroeger could not hear the guns or shell bursts below, only the high RPM of the engine as he held to the outside of Best. He found the scene fascinating. *I'll remember this moment.*

With the *Sails* all in, Best lifted his nose, up on a wing as Kroeger followed, as Fred must be following. The CO knifed down and Kroeger held it for a count as he was taught to, as he had been trained to do by rote. The *Zeros* closed the range, seconds to go. *We'll make it.*

"Halterman, stay on the guns. We're in!"

"I see 'em, sir!"

From his windswept precipice, Kroeger pushed down, on top of the carrier outlined by an oblong ring of steady yellow muzzle flashes, on top of Scouting Six, on top of the skipper…when Best suddenly rolled left and pulled up. *What the…?*

Alarmed and with the *Zeros* closing in, a frantic Kroeger scooped out to follow and searched above to avoid a midair collision. *What now?* Far below, two white circles formed on the surface next to the carrier. *Misses!* The ship turned hard into them trailing a huge wake.

He then saw why. The *Yorktown* squadron was in, about six of them, maybe more, converging in their own line toward the *Sails* in their dives. Best pulled up as Kroeger stepped on the rudder to match his roll and stay with him. Whipping his head back, Kroeger saw a *Zero* fire at Fred in a slashing attack. Another Jap yo-yoed up…

"*No!*" Kroeger cried as the fighters repositioned above them. In the CO's plane, Chief Murray fired at something over Kroeger's canopy. In front, the last of the *Yorktowners* were in their dives – *Those guys were supposed to go for the battlewagon!* – and Best with Kroeger tucked in behind followed them. Kroeger popped the stick to get some separation and pushed down, rolling again with rudder into a vertical dive behind his lead. Fighters above and flak below – into the valley of death.

Passing eight thousand, he was established, leading the target's curving track on the water. Smoke roiled up from the carrier's bow. A hit! A second massive explosion bloomed from the forward flight deck as another of the *Sails* – or *Yorktowners?* – connected. The SBDs ahead of him, underscored by their red dive-brakes, attacked in an orderly column over the dark water. Steamers of condensation formed on their wingtips as they pulled off in every direction. American kids dove their screaming planes in a headlong rush to hit the ship before the ship could hit them. Behind him, Halterman fired a short burst, and Kroeger flinched as he squeezed the stick in a death grip.

He heard them now, the shells: sharp pops all about them, close but not hitting. Tracers reached up, fiery fingers that swayed in slow motion to grasp him. But it was that *sound*, an eerie WHUFF, *whuff, whuf* of the heavy flak hurtling past his canopy. He knew what it was at once. *Will they explode behind Fred?*

Smoke covered the carrier's forward half and more condensation marked the pull out flight paths of the bombers ahead. The after half of the ship appeared undamaged. He aimed for that, holding his crosshairs on the pit of flame the forward part of the flight deck had become. He'd drop his bomb into it and expected the ship to move hundreds of feet as the weapon fell on it in mere seconds.

Flame poured out of the bow as the ship turned hard among geysers of near misses. The carrier's guns blazed away and tracers arced past. Kroeger flinched when fragments lashed his right wingtip, pebbles against tin. *We've gotta get outta here!*

Best released and pulled off. Kroeger was high and shallow, but wasn't willing to press it, not here, not into this hellish inferno. With one last correction – *Close enough!* – he mashed down on the release. Another half-ton of ordnance fell away, and Halterman let out a whoop that became a raspy grunt as Kroeger reefed the nose up. Eight g's fell on them like a breaking wave.

Kroeger jammed the throttle forward as he retracted the flaps, leveling on the wave tops as sudden splashes jumped up around him. Gasping from exertion and pressure, he looked for the CO. How could he lose him? Kroeger then found him, turning hard away, and rolled behind to follow. Best reversed back, and Kroeger had no choice but to slide to the outside as he overshot.

"Mister Weber!"

Kroeger looked back. A smoke trail led to a cloud of spray and mist that hovered above the water and veiled the bright gunfire of a ship on the horizon.

"*What?* Was that Fred?" he shouted over his shoulder.

Halterman answered him on the interphone. "Yes, sir…Mister Weber and Ernie! Didn't pull out!"

Kroeger and Best jinked out of phase as they made for a hole in the screen that an uneasy Kroeger saw was west. Around them the *Zeros* continued their attacks, and one of them suddenly lit up and fell into the sea, shot by a gunner. As Kroeger hung on, Best assessed the scene around them. *Cocky SOB. Indestructible.*

They burst through the hole into freedom, running away to the west even though home was to the east. Clear, Best then led them in a wide turn to the south. No *Zeros* in pursuit. The carrier burned from hits forward, yet still ran hard at flank speed. Nearby, cruisers and escorts twisted and charged in every direction as they kept up their furious gunfire. An anthill. They had knocked over an anthill.

Best throttled back and motioned for Kroeger, who eased up to his CO. Best pointed behind Kroeger and shrugged his shoulders. *Where's Weber?*

Kroeger made a motion of a plane flying into the water and raised his hands as if to say he didn't know the reason. Best nodded and continued ahead. Behind him, Chief Murray signaled to Halterman, using his hands in semaphore code, a personal message between the gunners that Kroeger didn't try to decipher.

Fred. They'd both flown the search west of Pearl Harbor that awful morning, flown combat together in the Carolines. The beer busts at Ewa Beach, mocking the CO behind his back in the bunkroom. Throughout, Fred was like a kid brother…closer than a brother. Gone, culled away seconds ago by a Jap that, by Divine Grace, selected *him* from all the blue planes. Slow and heavy, dive brakes out – Fred didn't have a chance. Must have been an execution. Or was it flak that got him? Kroeger looked back at the burning carrier, and, for a moment, shocked himself when his subconscious mind asked the unthinkable. *Was it worth it?*

As the others raced out of danger and back to *Enterprise*, Best and Kroeger flew south toward the three black columns. It was too early to mourn. That would come later. The Japs were out here, and what was left of Bombing Six still had a job to do, and probably at first light. *Compartmentalization,* they called it. Keep to the task at hand and sink the damn Japs. The ceremonies – and tears – would come soon enough, and Kroeger had already seen too many. Put it out of your mind! He got slow. He wasn't looking. Tunnel vision. Pulled too late. It happens…it happens.

The CO entered a shallow climb as they approached the burning carriers. Near each one, escort destroyers stood off. While Kroeger and the two gunners looked for enemy fighters, Best swept his head left and right along the surface. Kroeger joined him. *Maybe we'll find Johnny or Norm, or the XO in a raft.* He scanned the waves below, but no rafts. Nothing.

Ahead, lights flickered from the burning hulks. Except for their flight deck overhangs, they were unrecognizable as carriers. The two SBDs approached them inside ten miles. The sun was now hidden by a ridge of cloud that revealed only shadows of the ships. Kroeger counted five tin cans, all of which gave the derelicts plenty of room. One of the carriers flashed up for a moment, adding another black appendage to its already substantial smoke column.

Best got as close as he dared and veered left as Kroeger followed. The four Americans got a good look at what they had helped create only seven hours earlier. Kroeger wondered if anyone was still aboard the doomed ships, ships that had sailed with hundreds of men on each. Like his ship.

Kroeger remained to the outside as Best banked left for home. The threat was to the north, and the carrier they had just bombed flashed from induced explosions. Steady flame blazed on the forward half. Antiaircraft guns blinked here and there.

Halterman changed the coils and got a good signal from *Enterprise*. The skipper was right on it. *Good.* Should be home in an hour or so. Kroeger realized he hadn't said anything to Halterman about his lost friend Ordnanceman Hilbert. Long periods of time could pass before a pilot and gunner would say anything to one another. Some men liked to be alone with their thoughts, even though separated by only six feet.

"Halterman, I'm sorry about Hilbert. He was a good man."

Awkward seconds passed, and Kroeger wondered if he had somehow offended his gunner. Halterman then keyed the interphone.

"I'm sorry about Mister Weber, sir. He was tops and treated us great."

Kroeger shook his head up and down in vigorous motion so Halterman could see his strong agreement. Fred would be missed by all.

High above, in the lowering light, Kroeger picked up a formation of dark specks, about a dozen, heading west.

Must be the Hornet boys.

Gripped with fear and shouting nervous encouragement, Maruyama and the other pilots hurriedly climbed the ladder as smoke swirled about them. Through the opening to the weather deck, dense gray smoke raced along the catwalk, and the men pushed and jostled to reach fresh air. Bursting free, they climbed onto the flight deck and into a suffocating oven forward. Rising to their feet, they were at once knocked down by a shock wave of heat and a deafening blast from another induced explosion.

They had been inside the ready room – some dozing, some stuffing themselves with rice balls – when the antiaircraft opened up. Hashimoto woke up at the sound, his eyes meeting those of Maruyama. Both men stood as all in the room looked at each other with foreboding. Outside, a man shouted.

"Hell-divers! Port side!"

They were back, not giving up, even after *Hiryū's* planes had just sunk two of their carriers! How many did the Americans have? In the Type 97 ready room, nobody had the answer, and all they could do was wait. "Bend your knees!" Hashimoto commanded, and all crouched with their arms out for balance, like Hawaiian surfers.

The first explosion rocked the ship close aboard. *Hiryū's* turbines propelled the great ship through the light seas as she heeled to starboard. Another near miss. And then another amid the chattering automatics and painful reports of the heavier guns amidships. The aviators could only wait.

The first hit was a crunch forward followed by a booming explosion and shock wave that pushed the men aft and rattled *Hiryū's* frames. Seconds later, another thunderous boom caused dust and debris to fall from the overhead. The shock of the impact transferred throughout the ship, and every man felt it in the soles of his feet.

Another hit and another wave of invisible force knocked them down. Some of the pilots crouched under a table. The room filled up with smoke and heat blew through the space. Maruyama noted a bulkhead seam forward was cracked, with smoke gushing through.

Another devastating detonation forward, followed by shouts and screams outside. The ship heeled hard under the sledgehammer blows, and Maruyama wondered if it was capsizing. Fearful men huddled together coughing, eyes squinting through the acrid smoke, in anticipation and dread of the next...

A thunderous *BOOM* blew out the bulkhead wall, spraying debris and heat into the room. "Topside! All go topside!" Hashimoto bellowed as the compartment filled with smoke. Those who could dragged those who could not out of the space and into the smoke-choked passageway clogged with men, fallen pieces of overhead piping, and arcing wires.

Once on deck, a stunned Maruyama saw the forward elevator *above* him, resting against the starboard side of the bridge. The warped and smoldering steel was hideous to behold, and thick, dark smoke flowed from the gaping hole of the elevator well. Behind it, burning timbers of flight deck were curled up like a bamboo mat.

The wounded and the dead lay on the deck as firehoses were dragged across them. The ship's XO screamed at Hashimoto. "Get your fliers! Help cut down the mantelets!"

A thunderclap from below blew more of the flight deck up and over on itself. Maruyama fell to the deck and covered his head with his hands.

Hashimoto grabbed a man by his collar and pushed him forward. *"Get up!"* He then saw Maruyama also get to his feet.

"Maruyama! Grab a fire ax, your survival knife, anything to cut down the mantelets before they burn! Throw them over the side!"

Now focused, Maruyama found a shard of tie-down track to use as a makeshift knife and bounded up the aft ladder to the Air Platform. In frantic motion he cut the binding ropes as deck sailors below pulled on the mantelets. As one row of hammocks broke free, Maruyama moved to the next. Together, the men, unfamiliar to each other, improvised to save their ship.

The elevator acted as a shield from the smoke and heat as *Hiryū* pounded through the waves at full speed. Looking aft, Maruyama saw smoke coming out of openings along the flight deck as the winds fanned the flames in the hangar bay. To his left, the bridge windows on his side had been smashed. He would have to enter the bridge to cut more.

Another thunderous explosion from below caused the gigantic elevator platform to shift against the island. Maruyama had had enough. He returned to the flight deck, and saw smoke now coming up through the timbers and tracks. An injured and immobile man – *a boy like him!* – cried as a sudden spot of flame drew near him. With superhuman strength, Maruyama grabbed the man's arm and, as the apprentice sailor screamed in pain, pulled him over his shoulder in a fireman's carry. Aided by the wind at his back, he trundled down the smoldering and boiling deck to a safer area aft while hose-teams slogged forward. An explosion shook the deck behind him, and he fell.

The wounded man shrieked as he rolled off Maruyama's shoulders. Before he could help him, two petty officers appeared and dragged the crying apprentice off. Maruyama watched from his knees, gasping for breath as smoke raced along the flight deck.

He never saw the young sailor again.

CHAPTER 30

ENSIGN CLAY FISHER, BOMBING EIGHT, 1720 JUNE 4, 1942

Aided by the lowering light, Fisher saw the flashes ahead from over twenty miles away. Tiny black puffs dotted the sky, and here and there a flash appeared before it turned into a puff. Some were co-altitude. *Holy shit!*

Combat. All the big talk at the Royal Hawaiian, in the bunkrooms, even in letters home. Aviators like Fisher were held up as heroes before they had fired a shot. Going off to fight the Japs! *Lick 'em good, Clay!* Older men – veterans of the Great War – sent boys like Fisher off with their respect. *After you see the elephant for the first time, sonny, it'll make you a man.* Their matronly wives hugged his neck, wrung their hands, and said they'd pray. When they looked at him, their eyes welled up with what? Fear? Admiration? *Please save us from the Germans, Clayton. Be a good boy and come home soon.*

They would gladly offer their daughters to him, but they didn't have to – the girls did that themselves. All the hotshots had a photo of a girl they carried a torch for, were "pinned to," a girl, real or imagined, who had "said she'd wait." Some jumped the gun anyway, and, inside the bunkrooms, they swapped steamy stories of rolls in the hay with a big-bosomed farm girl they met on leave or of the good-time floozy who invited home the last guy on her dance card. Deck seamen on liberty in Alameda had a doll on each arm. If you wore a uniform, all you had to do was catch what was thrown at you. Anything for the war effort.

Many of his chums would not reach thirty years of age, some of the gunners not even twenty. With the end of life weeks or days away, there was pressure, urgency. *This might be it. My only chance!* Then guilt, shame, fear, and forgiveness…if sought. *Have mercy on me, Lord, a sinner.*

Mortal sin. Eternity. Fisher and the others had already faced it. All had seen death, sudden and fiery. *You can die in this business.* Like the lieutenant and plane pushers who had died on the flight deck hours earlier when a wounded VF guy from *Yorktown* had crash-landed with live guns that went off. Sprayed the island with fifty cal. Killed six in a second, no warning. Poor guy.

Lieutenant Stebbins of Scouting Eight led the reduced formation. Another screwed up cluster! The *Enterprise* boys were practically rendezvoused when Fisher's plane was spotted aft, and it took forever to get the rest brought up and pushed back, then warmed up. Everyone was mad at everyone else, and all Fisher could do was grit his teeth as the *Enterprise* bombers set out to the west without them. The *Big E* birds were long gone before *Hornet* got her first SBD off. *What were the heavies on the bridge thinking when they sent us off without the COs or Sea Hag to lead?*

Fisher's own Bombing Eight planes were led by Fred Bates, a jay gee, not even a full lieutenant. Everyone else was an ensign! He put it out of his mind. Having flown in the morning's flubbed attack, Fisher had as much "combat" experience as any commander aboard.

He mashed down on the interphone.

"Ferguson, they're up ahead. About five minutes to go."

"Aye, aye, Mister Fisher. All set back here."

"We got 'em, and I'm lookin' for CAP. Don' see any up here," Fisher added.

"Keepin' my eyes peeled, sir."

As they closed the fleet, a carrier was in the middle, on fire the length of it. *We missed out*, Fisher thought. It was clearly done for, and, though it ran hard, no longer a threat. With the sun in his face, it was difficult to see any CAP fighters over it. Maybe they had all run out of gas. On the surface, escort ships, many of them big, fired AA that exploded high over the task force.

As tail-end Charlie, he needed to stay tight. Alone, he'd be ripe for the picking. Ahead of him the tail-gunners searched the skies behind them for threats, as did Ferguson, their free guns pointed skyward. Waiting. *When did the Enterprise guys get here?* Twenty, thirty minutes ago? Then a glint, a movement on the surface, in front of his right wing. He opened a bit off Jim Barrett to study it. A *Dauntless*, alone heading east. Seemed okay. *What happened to his wingmen?* Fisher searched for them. *What happened here?*

Fisher triple-checked his switches. He could *not* screw this up, especially after the morning failures. Too many VT and VF guys lost; he and the others *had* to come through. Not getting his bomb off was a fear on par with getting jumped by a *Zero*. A lesser fear was not hitting a Japanese deck. He had to make his bomb count.

The carrier flashed as it raced to the northwest: induced explosions. Near it was a cruiser and two big boys, with the pagoda masts, just like in the recon card deck. Stebbins didn't seem to be going for them, and ahead, Fisher noted two cruisers, both in hard turns and firing at something. He searched for more *Enterprise* planes. Nothing.

Stebbins veered them left, and up the line Fisher saw signals exchanged. Bates eased away from Stebbins and signaled for left echelon step-down. At once Fisher deduced the plan: We'll come out of the sun. What's left of it. Two cruisers, and Bombing Eight will take the far one. Textbook. *And there's no CAP!*

As they set up, Fisher had time to study the carrier. The forward part was smashed in, completely aflame, and gave off heavy smoke. He could see inside it. Fascinated, he noticed it turn and slow a bit behind a cruiser as destroyers stationed on each quarter escorted it. A float plane came into his field of view, heading for the cruiser. It was a Jap, the red dots on the wingtips visible even in the late afternoon. His first enemy plane sighting. *The elephant.*

With a sudden pitch up, Bates was in, opening his dive-brakes as he went over. *Whoa!* Fisher thought, not expecting him to go so soon, expecting he'd continue another 30-40 degrees. One by one, his squadron mates followed, and, on the surface, the cruiser opened up. Barrett pushed over, and Fisher was next.

"Ferguson, we're in!"

Fisher lifted the nose and deployed his own dive-brakes as he overbanked down behind the others. Gunfire along the length of the cruiser, defiant.[1] He placed his sight on it and brought the throttle back at idle. Outside, the slipstream roar increased as the prop turned easily in front of him. He was fast, gaining on Jim, and he held the flap switch. Too late – too much airspeed! He tapped the rudder to get out of Jim's slipstream and gain separation. Huge bomb explosion on the target – dead center! Watery blooms to port. *Whoa! The real thing!*

Glued to his bombsight, Fisher saw two lights float toward him. Startled, he looked around the tube and saw a row of flaming balls loom up, then rocket past Bates, past Barnett. Toward him. He held his position and saw that they would miss high, ripping the air with rapid pops. They sounded like the snaps of a pajama shirt pulled open fast.

"Four thousand, sir!"

Antiaircraft fire poured out of the cruiser into fountains of flame that Fisher and all his mates were flying inside. He was fast, behind, ball leaning left, and scared shitless. Now hyperventilating, and, with his bombsight on the cruiser's

---

[1] HIJMS *Tone*

anchor chain, he'd drop a little high. He fed in a tad of left rudder as he pickled using electrical release.

Nothing. Pickle again! No jolt. Realization and dread gripped him at once. *Hung bomb!* Seconds from death, the altimeter raced toward zero.

Mother of God!

As the angry ship and the Pacific Ocean rushed up to smack him, a desperate Fisher pulled – *hard* – snatching back on the stick with two hands in terror. At near redline airspeed, he carried an extra half-ton of unwanted weight. Shoved down and squeezed like a vise by the unseen force of ten g's, Fisher blacked out. Still conscious and with eyes open, he couldn't see, but held his pull as he strained and struggled to breathe, guessing when he should ease off and "see" again. *Dive-brakes!* He closed them as the g continued to crush both men.

His *Dauntless* jumped ahead once the flaps retracted, and Fisher eased his pull as much as he dared. From a soda-straw-sized tunnel, his vision widened to full view. In that full view was a destroyer, firing furiously at them. *At me!*

Driven by fear and adrenalin, and still at the redline limit, Fisher opened the throttle all the way and flew over the ship's fantail. He pushed down to the water, now faster now than he had ever flown a plane, tracers missing behind while others ripped the surface near him. He was terrified to be carrying the bomb off target and fearing the wings tearing away from the fuselage. And being hit by the flak around him. For a moment he was alone – just running, flying, breathing. *Escaping.* He picked up SBDs to his right and turned to follow. He hadn't heard from Ferguson. *Is he hit?*

"Ferguson, you okay!"

"Geez, Louise, sir! Think I blacked out!"

Fisher nodded. "Me too! And I'm flyin' this thing! The bomb's hung. Once we clear, I'll try to release it."

"Yes, sir."

They joined up with Barrett and Friesz and climbed away from the area as the Japanese shot after them in a half-hearted effort. To his left, a *Zero* fired at two of the scout SBDs who fought back and drove him off. Scared himself, Fisher snapped his head behind and above to pick up any more enemy. *They do* have *a CAP!* Satisfied they were unmolested and clear of the last destroyers, Fisher eased away from the others. Over…just like that. Barrett pointed at him and made the hung bomb signal. Fisher nodded his head in vigorous agreement.

"Ferguson, I'm going to slip back and forth and porpoise the nose to kick this thing off."

"Yes, sir!"

Fisher bunted to increase his airspeed and stepped on each rudder pedal in turn, yawing the dive-bomber back and forth. The bomb remained attached. Then it hit him. *Pull the salvo release handle, idiot!* Relief flooded over him as the bomb fell away.

On the way back, Friesz found Bates, and, ten minutes later, they all found Stebbins's flight. Headed for home and all accounted for. They had hit that cruiser![1] Fisher cursed the fact that he had played no role, but he had been there, part of it. He had seen the elephant.

Before long they saw an occasional yellow raft float by them on the surface, silent reminders of fate he would never understand. Their friends were down there. Poor bastards. *Mark? Johnny? Bill Evans from VT-8? Nice guy, that Bill.*

Fisher and Ferguson plotted the raft positions, times, and wind/currents as best they could. Hopefully, a PBY could rescue them tomorrow. Maybe a small boy would find them tonight. *Hopefully.*

Twenty minutes later, the formation came across *Yorktown*, dead in the water and listing hard – and at an angle Fisher didn't think possible. He was both fascinated and sickened by the scene. A carrier – *like mine!* – dark and quiet, bobbing on the sea next to a lone destroyer that stood watch. Given up for dead, it looked as if it could roll over any second. The *Hornet* aviators inspected her, lost in their own thoughts as they flew past, and powerless to help.

Again waiting for word from his pilots, Spruance wondered if he had sent enough. Wondered what to do next. Fletcher had abandoned *Yorktown* but she was reported still afloat. Browning seemed to think there were *five* Japanese carriers, although three were burning and one reported intact, the one his planes were attacking at the moment. Mitscher had sent only half his strength. But why? A comm snafu? Ship casualty? *Is it enough?* For the moment, Spruance's carriers could only maintain a defensive CAP, and wait.

Fletcher was in *Astoria*, steaming his task force east. That sounded like a good idea to Spruance once his planes recovered aboard. Then what? What about the heavy groups approaching Midway? How to deal with *Yorktown*? Spruance hadn't heard from him and needed his guidance.

"Admiral, as requested," Browning said, handing Spruance the draft message.

---

[1] No American airplanes hit HIJMS *Tone* at Midway.

HORNET AND ENTERPRISE GROUPS NOW ATTACKING FOURTH
CARRIER REPORTED BY YOUR SEARCH PLANES X HORNET
NOW ABOUT 20 MILES EAST OF ME X HAVE YOU ANY
INSTRUCTIONS FOR FURTHER OPERATIONS?

Spruance nodded and handed the paper back to Browning. "Approved. Transmit on the TBS circuit."

Once Browning handed the message off to Ham Dow, he returned to Spruance. "Admiral, what are you thinking?"

Spruance was unaccustomed to such a direct question. "I'll let Admiral Fletcher task us, but I think we need to stay in this vicinity and defend Midway – regardless of the outcome of the attack."

Browning gave him a pained look. "Admiral, while that reasoning is sound, I expect our boys will put the carrier they find on the bottom, or at least out of action. But there might be another. If the Japs lose the services of four carriers, they'll likely withdraw tonight and call off the invasion. We must pursue, sir, and be in a position to attack in the morning."

Spruance withheld judgment. "And leave Midway unguarded?"

"Sir, Midway has plenty of airplanes – they can defend themselves. This is an opportunity, sir, to knock out the Jap striking force. We can end the war in an afternoon."

Spruance was quick to respond. "I recall an officer who once said he could *lose* a war in an afternoon."

"Admiral, this isn't Jutland. They're on their heels now, sir, and, if they have a carrier we missed, we can hit it at sunrise. Or, if there is no fifth carrier, we'll have free rein and can attack them at will."

Dow returned. "Admiral, response from Admiral Fletcher."

Spruance read the scrap he was handed.

NEGATIVE X WILL CONFORM TO YOUR MOVEMENTS

A smile formed on his lips. "Well. Admiral Fletcher just handed us tactical command."

Browning beamed. "Congratulations, sir! Shall I have them join us for the evening's formation?"

The radio crackled. "Red Base, Red Base... Single carrier on fire. Not – repeat not – operational. Escort consisting of two BBs, four CAs not – repeat not – damaged. Returning to base. Out."

Browning plotted their position. "Sir, they should be back in an hour. Would be tight to turn them around for a night attack. So, Admiral, my recommendation is to continue west at a 15-knot speed of advance, spot the deck for a 0330 launch, and go after whatever is in retreat."

Spruance considered it. Browning, after all, was the expert. But what if? What if Nagumo came at him with his own strength of battleships and cruisers, significant even apart from the heavy group spotted west of Midway and running hard to join him? Spruance would lose a night engagement against their Long Lance torpedoes and superior nighttime optics. He was outgunned as it was, and what if he did come upon them at dawn? No, he needed to stay clear.

"I'm inclined to withdraw us east."

Incredulous, Browning protested. "Sir, they're...*just* outside our grasp, only hours away. If we move east, they will *certainly* escape to fight another day. Admiral, we...you...cannot pass up this opportunity before us."

"And how do we regain contact without ourselves being ambushed?"

"Sir, we'll send destroyers. We have more than enough for a squadron to scout ahead. In the wee hours we'll launch float planes, and again, sir, we have well over ten to search 180 degrees, with more to spare. We'll have fixes on them and their dispositions, and the VB and scout squadrons will know right where to go from 100 miles, max. We *must* do this, sir. It'll shorten the war."

Spruance didn't like the thought of being tied to a course of action – and steaming into the unknown was anathema. *No way.*

"No. I want to be where I can defend Midway and deal with the enemy surface ships, which, I concur, may include another carrier. Once the pilots are back, we need to move east."

Browning exhaled his disgust, which Spruance detected. Spruance would have brought one of his own staff officers up short, would not stand for such rudeness, but Browning was Halsey's man, the aviation expert, and Spruance needed his expertise. He had no time for smoothing ruffled feathers – didn't have the energy. Could be dealt with later.

"Captain, put me someplace where I can deal with them in the morning," Spruance said, impatient.

"Aye, aye, sir, but I don't know where they're going to be. They can go any direction at any speed." Browning shrugged and turned up his hands. Spruance maintained his composure. *I'm not sailing with him again.*

Spruance stepped over to the chart table. *Fine, then.* With his thumb and middle finger Spruance measured off a distance, then took the dividers to measure the distance to Midway. He measured off another distance, then thumped the chart with his finger.

"Once all planes are recovered, take us east at twenty knots. At midnight, turn north for an hour, then back to the west. I'm going to the flag mess for a bite, then to bed. Wake me with a sighting report or anything unusual."

For a moment, an expressionless Browning said nothing. *I can't believe the Japs are slipping from us.* He then spoke.

"Aye, aye, Admiral."

"Good night," Spruance said, and went below.

CHAPTER 31

MIDWAY, EASTERN ISLAND, 1740 JUNE 4, 1942

Iverson tossed his C-ration tin into a garbage can and downed his canteen of water. He filled it from the barrel spigot, took another gulp, and refilled it to the brim.

"Danny, you ready to finish off that carrier you winged today?"

Iverson turned to see Dick Fleming step behind him to fill his own canteen.

"Yep...if we can find it out there."

"Oh, we'll find it. Moon'll be up round midnight, but we'll find it with starlight if need be."

As the pilots walked over to the makeshift Ops tent, they observed a dramatic sunset, one marred by the black column of smoke from Sand Island's still-burning fuel tanks. Frigate birds flitted about in the tropical breeze as the marines lugged ammo boxes and manhandled empty fuel drums to the lagoon docks. The men were dirty and sweat-soaked; none of them had let up since dawn. Far to the west, they heard a faint *bupbupbupbupbup* from a gunner on Sand and instinctively scanned the sky above.

Fleming stopped. "What are those guys shootin' at? See anything?"

"No, looks clear to me," Iverson answered. "Trigger happy, I guess."

Three carriers on fire to the north. The B-17 crews bragged that they had hit them, ducks in a barrel. *Stuffed shirt prima donnas.* Flying four miles up with five gunners firing twin fifties. Even the Japs were smart enough to not get too close. Marine aviators would get no argument from the Army B-26 boys, who were shell-shocked after losing half their planes. At least they went in and looked 'em in the eye. The Navy fellows had lost all but *one* of their newest planes, flown back by a dazed ensign who had no idea about what happened out there. Iverson had seen the bird...almost as many holes in it as his.

"With luck we'll have clear weather, Danny. Glad we're goin' at night, too. Don' ever want those guys to see me again."

"You *like* night? I never met anyone who did."

"Danny, I'll fight this whole *war* at night so long as the Nips can't take a shot at us. Actually, at night I'm more afraid of *you* runnin' into me, but I'll take my chances."

The pilots sat on picnic table benches as they waited to brief. Iverson felt the difference right away...only half of his fellows from the morning. Like him, they had been up since midnight and were exhausted, too keyed up from the morning strike to nap. Now, as night approached, they wanted to sleep but could not. *Need to drive a stake into the heart of the Japs while they're down.*

There was at least one carrier out there, and possibly more. Who hit the others? Maybe some Navy guys got lucky: some of their newer model SBDs had diverted into Midway around noon, but they said they hadn't seen a thing. Regardless, burning ships would be visible for miles, day or night.

The two aviators took their seats on one of the back benches. Iverson preferred them to the front row, where one could get called on or volunteered for something. The lineup was on the blackboard: Captain Tyler would lead the *Dauntlesses*, with Captain Glidden in his division. Iverson liked Elmer. Calm under fire.

Major Norris, waiting with folded arms, suddenly popped to attention. *"Tension on deck!"*

In one motion, the men sprung to attention as Navy Captain Simard entered the tent, with Lieutenant Colonel Kimes in tow.

"Seats. Take your seats," Simard enjoined them.

The men sat back down, and Fleming whispered, *"Pregame pep talk from the Navy."* Simard removed his Brodie helmet and began as Kimes scanned the rows of pilots.

"Men, we've hit three Jap carriers that are burning northeast of us, about a hun'erd and fifty miles. You guys can further damage them tonight – and maybe even put them on the bottom. It's an open secret now that we've got our *own* carrier off to the northeast. I believe their planes added to the damage you guys inflicted this morning, and now you can finish them off. So, your new CO – Major Norris – will lead you, and, to preclude them having an intact carrier nearby with fighter protection, we are going at night. Now, it goes without saying that if you come across an intact carrier, bomb that one first, but you had better know in your military mind that it's a Jap and not one of ours. Any damage you guys can add to their fleet means less for us to deal with if they invade tomorrow."

Simard stopped and assessed the pilots.

"You men did well this morning, as did the Army and Navy. That said, it is going to be you dive-bombers who can deliver the punch we need to disable them. I know that you saw their defenses firsthand, you've been through a lot, but we need you to go tonight – and probably tomorrow and the rest of the week. I heard one of you had your throat microphone cord cut by a bullet. Is that man here?"

Iverson raised his hand, and saw that Kimes, his jaw set, almost smiled.

"Yes, quite a story for the grandchildren. Heard you had some holes in your plane."

"A few, sir," an embarrassed Iverson answered.

"More like a few *hundred*," Fleming added. A wave of laughter helped relieve the tension.

"Well, then," Simard said with a smile. "Hope your luck holds."

A hush came over the tent. Iverson felt foreboding, as did the others.

He just jinxed Danny.

Simard sensed he had overstayed his welcome, if a Navy captain ever was welcome. Kimes looked at his boots.

"The major will now brief you. Good hunting and Godspeed."

"Ten-hut!"

The pilots jumped to attention again as Simard and Kimes departed with a terse, *"Carry on."*

Norris was all business.

"Take off time: 1915. Five SB2Us followed by you SBDs. Everyone has 500-pounders loaded. If at all possible, I'll take off to the southwest and turn easy right so you can have the last of the twilight to join on me. They're reported north-northeast, and hopefully we'll have an update before we walk to our planes. We'll climb to angels ten and go out in a stepped-down right echelon. Zach Tyler, keep close to Dick Fleming's wing in my formation, and the rest of you SBDs, follow your lead. We'll cruise at 135 knots, pretty much the best us old *Vibrators* can do."

Iverson did the math. Like the morning…about an hour and a half to get there. If the Japs hadn't moved. Norris motioned with his hands as he spoke.

"When we see the Japs, I'll try to offset right and roll in left in a glide bomb attack as we did this morning. If there are two carriers, I'll take the far and you SBDs the near. If aligned right or left, Zach, your SBDs will take the one on your side of the formation and I'll take the other. Rendezvous the best you can, stay away from the water, and come back here together if possible or as singles. We should be able to see this raging fire for miles, and Captain Simard told me they'd illuminate searchlights for us to guide us home, so thanks to the Navy."

Night was a challenge, but a formation of *Zeros* in sunny skies posed a greater one. Once the American bombs went off, the Japs would shoot wildly into the night air, hoping to get a lucky hit. Iverson was last and would have to face the barrage fire, but at least he'd be able to see his target by the muzzle flashes.

"No position lights… Goes without saying. Keep tight so you can maintain position and not get strung out where you have to jockey the throttle. Once we're back here for our landings, illuminate your lights and do your recognition turns. Check the windsock for the runway and the Aldis lamp for landing permissions. Again, no lights until you are over the lagoon on the way home. Questions?"

Glidden raised his hand. "Sir, when does the moon come up?" he asked.

Norris nodded that he understood. "Not until about midnight, Elmer. Depending on when we find them, probably not until we're back here. The good news is that it'll be dark over the target. Again, the Navy is going to have the lights on for us. What else?"

"Radio discipline, sir? Will we use it?" Tyler asked.

"Stay off the radio until you're back here, and *only* if you need it," Norris answered. "And if anyone makes a call, it will be me with a sighting report. The Nips can triangulate, so stay off the radio. Vital that we do."

The briefing ended and the pilots rose from their benches. Most headed for the latrine. Iverson checked his watch: 1835.

"Hey, look out there," Fleming said. "Wow!"

On the eastern horizon they saw them – a line of green Army bombers well over a mile long. The low sunlight and clear air highlighted every detail as they set up to land. The B-17s were huge, and they seemed to hover and float as they approached the runway.

"Sure would love to fly something like that one day," Fleming said.

"You don' like throwing yourself at the ground?" Iverson asked.

"Hey, I like to get up close and personal as much as the next guy, but look at those babies!"

Iverson counted the Army bombers parked on the apron. "These guys are new. Reinforcements from Hawaii, I guess."

Each bomber, painted a fresh olive drab, touched down in sequence. The marines watched them roll past, bristling with guns.

"Them fancy paint jobs ain't gonna last long in this dusty furnace, but those are still nice lookin' ships," Fleming opined. He couldn't take his eyes off the big planes. Iverson looked at him in wonder.

"Good grief, Dick, you wanna marry one?"

Fleming gave him a playful shove. "Hell, no! Can't cook, for one thing!"

Flying into the twilight, Iverson joined on Glidden's wing from the inside of the turn, manipulating the trim wheels and fuel mixture controls by feel, his eyes glued to his lead. The sunset beyond Glidden's SBD had turned the sky a deep red, streaked with yellow as the sun's last rays reflected off cirrus clouds over Kure atoll. Between him and Glidden was Bob Bear, flying parade like a good second looey.

Once Glidden rolled out behind Tracy, he eased up the bearing line to get in echelon. Ahead, Norris had his charges in formation, stabilized and heading northeast.

Norris's wide turn took them west around Sand Island. Its black pall had not abated since the Jap attack. Below them, surf broke against the big bell-shaped reef north of the two main islands. Before night cloaked it, the atoll revealed vestiges of turquoise along the sandy strips of shoreline. A stationary PT boat floated in the lagoon, and a PBY water-taxied out for an all-night patrol. The eleven Marine Corps dive-bombers continued up in a shallow climb, in formation flying as one.

To the north they found weather. Not scattered storms, but a solid wall of cloud. Maybe they could punch through it and find the Japs by their fires, even at a distance. Iverson could hope. He selected the interphone.

"How ya doin' back there, Reid?"

"Okay, sir. Foot's okay."

"Lemme know when you can't see Midway anymore."

"Yes, sir."

Now stabilized northeast, they approached a gray wall that darkened with each passing mile. As they neared it, the pilots drew closer to their leads. If they lost sight, finding them again would be dicey. On the other side of the wall, if they found the other side. And if they were lucky.

They flew under a ledge of cloud, a porch overhang that obscured the stars to the north. Off their left shoulders, the last glow of the late-spring dusk formed a dull ochre swath to the northwest. It ended where the weather began.

After almost an hour airborne, Iverson could barely detect the outline of Glidden's *Dauntless*. He knew that wouldn't last. They would go in; Norris was going to punch through. The glow of engine combustion through Glidden's cowl flaps and the dim backlighting of the wet compass on his canopy bow would soon be Iverson's only references.

And then they were in it – thick cloud, wisps of it visible as they flowed past Glidden's illuminated cowl. Iverson bounced in his seat as the clouds buffeted his plane. With no horizon, he concentrated on his lifeline, Glidden's two light sources in the pitch darkness. Glidden himself had to fly on Tyler's wingman and on up the echelon. Norris was ahead someplace, and the entire formation was jostled in the moisture-rich air. When Reid said he couldn't see Midway anymore, Iverson checked the time. An hour out. Feeling himself stable, Iverson took a peek at his fuel tanks. Time to transfer the left, and he reached down and found the knob by feel.

He focused on Glidden's two blurred luminosities, evidence that a plane was next to him. He held them steady, his hands making minute corrections on the flight controls. With his left, he felt for the trim wheels and turned the aileron a hair before going back to the throttle.

He glanced up at the heading, then glanced again. They were turning, and he hadn't noticed. Vertigo. *Fight it, Danny.*

"What time is it, Reid?"

"Twenty forty-five, sir," Reid answered.

Iverson sensed they were straight and level. But the compass heading continued to move. Iverson felt the tightness of his hand on the stick grip. They had been in the goo for thirty minutes, and his neck throbbed from the tension. Elmer Glidden's cowl was alive, and keeping it in sight meant life for Iverson and Reid. He sensed a climb. *Why are we climbing? To get out of this?* He checked the altimeter and saw the needle unwind. No, they were descending. *We're descending!* Iverson's surprise turned to fear as vertigo raged inside him. Hang on to Elmer. *Hang on!*

"Keep an eye on the altimeter, Reid."

"Yes, sir. We attacking now?"

"Not sure," Iverson replied, concentrating hard.

Clay Fisher was exhausted. And upset.

What a goat rope today had been! Even though a combat newbie, Fisher knew one when he saw one. Almost two hours flying to the southwest, and they hadn't seen a thing. *Everyone* had abandoned Sea Hag. The memory of him flying alone into the vast Pacific was indelibly etched into Fisher's mind. No fighters or torpeckers had shown up for the recovery. Not one. *What happened to them?* Not knowing gave Fisher a chill.

Brief again in the afternoon, a chance for redemption. Another fumbled launch: late, and only half strength. The *Enterprise* guys got a fat carrier, and Fisher almost killed himself pulling out with a hung bomb over a Jap cruiser firing everything but the Master-at-Arms pistols. When he got back, his jaw dropped when somebody told him that a formation of Army B-17s had released on the same cruiser at the same time – almost through their formation! He'd never seen them, never heard anyone call out a warning. All he'd seen was steady fire and raging water, black pockmarks in the air, and glimpses of SBDs in front of him as they hightailed it to safety. Confusion, fear, unease. *We're gonna go back!*

But the Americans had burned at least three carriers, probably four. Though he and everyone else aboard *Hornet* had botched it, he sensed he had just been through a great battle – one that would be remembered – like Dewey at Manila Bay. The aviators had stood down for the night, but despite his exhaustion, Fisher was too pumped up to sleep. He climbed the ladder to the ready room, and, taking the passageway forward, looked into VT-8's pilot ready room.

The room was empty, and all the bulkhead pegs that held the pilot parachutes and life vests were also empty. On the chalkboard, someone had written ATTACK! in big letters.

In the Bombing Eight Ready Room, he found his roommate Ken White, sitting at his chair, writing.

"How's it goin', KB?"

White looked up. "Hey. Doin' alright. How about you?"

"I'm bushed, but can't sleep. Thought you'd be in your bunk."

"Have you taken your shot? That'll do it."

"What?"

"Yeah, Doc Osterlough is passin' out bottles of Old Crow. Little ones. Told us to have a belt and hit the sack. 'Bout thirty minutes ago he came by our stateroom."

Fisher tried to recall where he was thirty minutes ago. Couldn't remember, but he remembered that cruiser.

"Why are you here then?" Fisher asked.

"Same reason as you, I guess."

The men were silent, wanting to talk about what they and the ship had just gone through, but not knowing how to begin. Their friends were missing. Maybe dead. Maybe out there in rubber boats. The uncertainty wore on them.

White broke the silence. "Heard any scuttlebutt?"

Fisher nodded. "Four carriers burning, at least three. May have another one out there. Did you see *Yorktown?*"

"No, you?"

"Yeah, dead in the water and listing hard. I mean, the flight deck was almost in the water. About sixty, seventy miles from here when we landed."

"Some *Yorktowners* aboard. Heard most of 'em went over to *Enterprise.*"

The men were again silent for a moment.

"Doin' okay?" White asked.

"Yeah. Thinkin' about the VT guys though."

White nodded in agreement. "Yeah… Did you see them go?"

"Yeah. After Skipper Waldron told Sea Hag to go where the sun don't shine, I looked down and saw 'em veer off right. You didn't see 'em?" Fisher asked.

White studied the bulkhead. "No, guess I was flying wing too close to watch. They all went. And no one knows what happened. Hal, Tex, Whitey, Rusty… No one knows. Same with the VF, but they turned back."

"Maybe they're all in rubber boats."

"Hope so. At least some. Gotta be some that made it. Skipper Waldron is a madman to just break off and leave. Guess he'll probably be court-martialed, if he's alive."

Fisher had to agree. *All* the senior leadership he had seen on this floating cheese box was suspect. The afternoon launch had been like something from a Keystone Kops movie. Everyone was yelling to hurry up, gesticulating, falling over bomb carts. *Goat rope.*

"Yeah. Maybe," Fisher replied. "Hey, us juniors did as well or better against that cruiser."

"I'm with you, Clay. Think we'll go tomorrow?"

"Yeah. Mop-up search, if nothin' else."

At that moment Commander Osterlough stopped in the doorway.

"Hey! You two. Hit the rack. Captain's orders. Right now."

White got up as Fisher stood there, not sure if the ship's doctor was going to put them on report.

"I'm waiting," Osterlough said, glowering at him.

Fisher bolted through the door. "'Scuse me, sir."

White followed, and, as Osterlough watched, the ensigns slid down the ladder rails and went up forward to their staterooms.

The passageways were lighted red for night adaption. Empty, even now before taps. They could discern frames ahead as they strode forward. Abandoned, as if a ghost ship.

The 1MC sounded: *Now stand by for the evening prayer.*

Fisher was in the lead but was now motivated to stop and listen. Tonight, this one time. It seemed appropriate. To starboard was an athwartship vestibule. He stepped in and motioned for White to do the same.

"Let's listen to the padre. Expect he's given this one some thought."

The men waited with their heads bowed, expectant. Chaplain Harp's familiar voice soon followed.

"Father in heaven and author of life, we have witnessed war today and are again reminded of the depravity of man. Tonight we grieve for our lost and missing shipmates who did their duty in the embrace of Your unlimited grace. We do not yet know what tomorrow will bring; allow us to face the trial with courage, secure in the knowledge that we are blessed by the gift of Your eternal mercy. Allow us to do our earthly duties to our utmost abilities in the service of our great nation founded in Your love and goodness. Give us humility in victory, and offer prayer for the souls of our fallen comrades and those of the enemy vanquished. Guide our blows that they may quickly lead to peace for all mankind. We ask a special prayer for our flying men who must navigate great distances as they fight for all of us, here and at home. Be with them always in the air, in darkening storm and sunlight fair. In Your name we pray, Amen."

After the chaplain finished, Fisher and White stepped into the passageway and resumed their trek forward. Fisher looked over his shoulder and saw Doc Osterlough ten frames behind, also heading forward. Osterlough recognized Fisher, and, without saying a word, pointed forward with a stern look – like his dad would have. *Get to bed!*

They entered their stateroom and flicked on the red light. On each desk was a cordial bottle of Old Crow. White picked up his.

"See? Take one of these and man your plane in the morning."

Fisher took his and unscrewed the top. Both sat down in their metal desk chairs.

"Shall we toast? *To our fallen comrades.*"

White unscrewed his bottle. "Our fallen comrades." Both took a swig.

"To Fighting Eight and Torpedo Eight," Fisher offered.

Both took another gulp.

The 1MC crackled, and the familiar tune of *Taps* played throughout the ship. Tonight, the haunting notes had special meaning, and Fisher felt an electric charge run up his back. *Men, whom I know, are missing.* Maybe dead. He had seen death, like that time *Hornet* passed the floating body of a dead Jap sailor before the Army bombers had taken off. The Army guys themselves were missing, but this was different. Men like him, closer than brothers, were suddenly gone. Alone on the dark sea, in peril, or worse. They didn't know.

After the song ended, the Bosun picked up the microphone. *Taps, taps. Lights out, maintain silence about the decks. Now taps.*

"All right, Clay. We best save the rest of this stuff for tomorrow night. Prob'ly go in the morning again."

The men undressed and draped their khakis on hangers that they hung on pegs. Their stateroom was a comfortable temperature, despite its location amidships, aft of the forecastle.

White climbed into his bunk as Fisher brushed his teeth at the sink. He felt it now, the exhaustion. A condition he had heard of.

Both lay on their backs in their bunks, eyes still open, and sensing the other still awake. Remembering. How could they forget? Dewey at Manila Bay. *You may fire when ready, Gridley.*

"I missed, Clay."

Fisher listened to his friend above him, berating himself, not yet able to forgive himself – yet asking for forgiveness. From another scared ensign.

"At least you dropped. I didn't even do that."

"Your bomb was hung up; that was mechanical. My foul-up was mental. I pickled too high. Short."

"Hell, KB, I pickled high, too. All that stuff comin' at us…I was damn scared."

"A heavy cruiser, a capital ship. And I missed it. All those drills, all that practice, and when it really counted, I failed."

Fisher didn't know what to say, and surprised himself when he spoke.

"We're so hard on ourselves. We've never dove on a cruiser before. Cert'ly not one firin' at us."

Silence returned.

"Wonder if the VT guys found them. Did they drop? Guess we'll find out one day," White said, more to himself than Fisher.

Hornet's gentle roll was all but imperceptible, but Fisher felt it, in his spinal cord, in his mind. He was on a U.S. Navy warship in battle, but it seemed like a routine night at sea off Norfolk last fall. Nice time of year. Clear skies.

Annie. *What is she doing now? Where is she? Norfolk? Iowa? My wife.* Fisher didn't know where she was any more than she knew where he was. She knew he was in the Pacific. He knew she was in the states. *My wife. I have a wife.*

"G'night, Clay."

"Goodnight, KB. We'll both get another crack at them."

"Ain't gonna miss next time."

"Next time I'll pickle mine. Follow'n your lead, KB."

Above him White chuckled. They became quiet, and soon drifted off.

CHAPTER 32

HIJMS *Hiryū*, 0230 JUNE 5, 1942

Hundreds of men assembled abeam the island, not in ranks but huddled together on the only patch of flight deck not actively smoking. Climbing the eastern sky, a gibbous moon shone its light on them. The moon was waning. Maruyama considered that thought and kept it to himself.

The light smoke mixed by the gentle breeze smelled of fuel oil, burned paint, and charred flesh. The hideous stench in their nostrils was an odor Maruyama knew he could never escape – no matter how long he lived.

Hiryū had run to the west as fast as she could before fire consumed everything in the hangar bays. Once the flames penetrated the engineering spaces, the ship was doomed. Around midnight, as the moon broke the horizon, yet another induced explosion knocked everyone off their feet, and the flames returned. With the fire mains out, destroyers alongside poured water into any opening they could, and the carrier developed a list.

Maruyama and his mates sought refuge on the boat deck aft until Hashimoto-san summoned everyone back up onto the smoldering flight deck. The pilots grumbled – the ship was clearly done for, and the Americans could appear at any moment. Dutifully, they climbed the ladders and shuffled down the smoke-filled passageways – lit by dim battle lanterns – until they found clear paths to the flight deck. Once outside, the moon provided enough light for them to be sure of their steps.

As the burned-out hulk wallowed in the sea, the captain addressed the crew from the base of the signal bridge.

"Men of *Hiryū*. You have fought well, and delivered *two* enemy carriers into our hand. No more could be asked of you, who landed crippling blows and fought to save our gallant flagship. You must now return to our beloved Nippon and man newer and more powerful ships in the service of His Majesty. With your contribution, His Majesty's Navy will reconstitute itself and sweep our enemies from the seas. It is my duty to remain, but know that my spirit, and the spirits of your fallen mates, will help guide you and exhort you to victory."

Here and there men shouted their encouragement and respect for the captain. One raised his burned hand from a stretcher. Most of the men were bareheaded, bowed-down human forms silhouetted by smoke and the flickering light of a fire forward. The admiral then stepped to the rail to address the assembly. Maruyama's mind went back to the last time he had seen him as he sped by in his *kankō*...only twelve hours ago. The twisted black mass of the forward elevator towered over the scene, backlit by the moon.

"Honorable *Hiryū* crew... As the commander of Carrier Division Two, responsibility for the loss of gallant *Hiryū* and our sister ship *Sōryū* is mine and mine alone. To atone for my failures, I intend to stay aboard *Hiryū* alongside your beloved Captain Kaku. As a captain shares the fate of his ship, so shall I share the fate of this carrier division. Today, before our brave Tomonaga-san flew off to sink the Americans in his damaged plane, I told him I would follow him. I now follow him and our valiant shipmates who fought to save this ship. Now I give my final command: you are to abandon *Hiryū*...and continue your service to His Majesty and total victory."

Although they expected to hear these words at some point, hundreds of men could be heard catching their breaths at the thought of abandoning ship – this ship, *Hiryū*, the *Flying Dragon*. Imperious *Akagi* and *Kaga* had lorded it over the ships of CarDiv 2, but all aboard knew that *Hiryū* was the best carrier in the Mobile Force. His Majesty would miss her the most.

Yamaguchi was not done.

"Honorable *Hiryū* crew... Face west to our homeland!"

While some shuffled, those who could did an about-face. Maruyama looked with them to the empty horizon.

"*Hiryū banzai!*"

"*BANZAI!*" the men thundered in unison.

"*Hiryū banzai!*"

"*BANZAI!*"

"*Hiryū banzai!*"

"*BANZAI!*"

As their hope for the emperor to live 10,000 years echoed across the water, the men turned back to face Yamaguchi. From abaft the island bugles sounded, and, at the first notes of *Kimigayo,* the crew joined in, singing in solemn love of country. Tears flowed, the men unable to comprehend the loss, the *humiliation*. Defeat. It was unthinkable, and only because of the admiral's command did the crew not stay to join him.

The moon had risen another ten degrees, and Maruyama was mindful of the time. He wished Nakao and Hamada were next to him and turned to find them among the throng of dim faces. He recognized an engine mechanic. Their eyes met, and the man turned away.

The ensign was lowered from the truck, and Captain Kaku bellowed the command to abandon ship. Maruyama returned with the others to the route they had taken up. Some men continued aft to the ramp where they could lower themselves to waiting destroyers. He recognized Nakao and grabbed his shoulder.

"Nakao-kun. Where is Hamada?"

Nakao glanced at Maruyama, then shrugged as he continued to shuffle aft with the throng. "Someplace, I saw him up here earlier."

Maruyama searched the shadows around him, hoping to pick out his friend in the moonlight. Like the admiral and captain for their crew, he felt a responsibility for Hamada. They'd been through much.

The men, crowded against each other in the suffocating passageways and down the gallery ladders, choked and coughed, but did not curse or cry. When they finally got to the fantail, a rescue destroyer's high prow surprised them as lines and planks were secured across to port. Sailors lashed the wounded, oblivious to their danger, to their stretchers and carried them hand-over-hand to waiting crewmen on the destroyer. The ships screeched when their steel plates touched in the light swells.

Maruyama and Nakao got in a group by the jackstaff and waited their turn to board. The destroyer sailors stared at the *Hiryū* crew. Even in the darkness, Maruyama could see their pity – and, in some cases, their contempt.

"There's Hamada. He just went aboard," Nakao said, pointing.

Maruyama nodded. "Good. We will fight again one day." A mental load lifted, he could board in peace. Nakao scrambled over, and before he jumped, Maruyama stepped on the rail to assess the heaving steel hull plates. Men on the destroyer barked at him.

"Now! *Now!*"

Maruyama jumped and was grabbed by men who shoved him aft before they reached for the next survivor.

He learned the ship was *Makigumo*. A plane guard escort. An ordinary screening vessel. Expendable. He walked along the rail aft, past the huge torpedo tubes and the twin turrets. On the fantail were two rows of depth charges. A chief shooed away curious *Hiryū* sailors who got too close.

Maruyama looked up at the carrier, marveling at the great stanchions that supported the aft end of the flight deck. Besides the smoke emanating from the ship, he could not discern any signs of damage. On the starboard side, a cutter returned to take a load of men to another waiting destroyer. He checked his watch: 0340. To the east, the sky grayed as it had yesterday, when he sat in his *kankō* on the deck high above. Forever ago.

Without a signal, the destroyer cast off. Maruyama felt the screws underneath him vibrate as it backed clear. Hamada limped up to him.

"Maruyama-san!" They embraced amid dozens of their shipmates.

"I'm glad you are safe, Hamada-kun. Are you able-bodied?" Maruyama noted the bandaged hand of his gunner.

"Yes. Did you know Lieutenant Kadano is aboard?"

"No! Good. I hope his leg is healing from the morning."

"They took him over on a stretcher. One of my fellow gunners is badly burned, too. Hope they have a medical facility on this ship."

Maruyama suspected the destroyer did not. *Expendable.*

As *Makigumo* stood off, *Kazagumo* came in alongside to take on more men. Maruyama could now make out areas of blown-open hull plates from induced explosions. Thin smoke seeped out of every crevice and hatchway. *Hiryū* rolled in the swells but showed no sign of settling.

After another efficient transfer, *Kazagumo*, her decks full, backed away into a red dawn. "When will we leave?" Nakao asked to no one. No one answered.

Makigumo edged closer, and back came alongside *Hiryū*. *Now what?* An officer jumped over and disappeared inside. The men spoke among themselves about the reason. Was he going to relay a Combined Fleet order to the admiral to save himself? Rumors and murmuring increased, and, to the west, *Kazagumo* steamed away at full speed. *Are we staying here to die with* Hiryū?

The officer returned to the fantail and climbed aboard. Again *Makigumo* backed away, then ahead with a hard turn to port behind the carrier. The ship's loudspeaker blared:

"We are right now going to torpedo and sink Hiryū. *Battle stations torpedo, port side. Target* Hiryū, *bearing 90 degrees. Prepare to fire."*

Hiryū survivors groaned and cried out at this horrible news. Hamada was overcome. "No, Maruyama-san! They cannot sink our ship! There must be a way to save *Hiryū!"*

Maruyama said nothing as the destroyer crept into position. Around him, some men wailed as they would over the loss of a loved one, and tears flowed again. Others, like him, watched in stoic acceptance. Orders were shouted, and the tubes trained out to port as warning bells rang. *Hiryū*, waiting for the end, looked as if she could operate planes – except for the elevator against the bridge and smoke rising from the length of her.

With a sudden hiss, a huge torpedo shot out from a tube and slapped the water, raising a gasp from the men. Maruyama and the others crowded the rail to see, as some knelt by the lifelines to allow others a clearer view. *How do the destroyermen torpedoes work?*

Nothing. A miss, or a dud. The destroyer circled to starboard for another run.

"Look for enemy planes!" a lieutenant shouted. More rumors of American submarines and mirages of enemy cruiser columns on the horizon circulated among the men. *Makigumo* made a wide circle and set up for another run. More shouts, more bells, and another sudden hiss and lurch as another 9-meter monster shot from the tube and dove into the sea.

Maruyama counted the seconds till impact, but soon lost interest. Like the others, he had become too exhausted to care. Spent. He could only gaze upon the smoking flagship, the finest in the Imperial Japanese Navy, a dark silhouette against the dawn.

Without warning, *Hiryū's* bow seemed to jump out of the water, and the men gasped in amazement. It settled back as the ship rolled to port before a deep rumble met their ears. *Makigumo* accelerated and turned west. Looking back on their doomed ship, the men of *Hiryū* cried out for the spirits of their lost shipmates. They cried for their lost sense of security.

Maruyama and Nakao worked their way aft to watch *Hiryū* sink as others – not wanting to witness it – filtered forward. The carrier remained on an even keel, and showed no signs of settling.

"Look! On the flight deck!"

Men pointed toward *Hiryū*, and all searched the deck. With an awful realization, they murmured that there was indeed movement on her. *Survivors!* One sharp-eyed sailor saw a man waving a cloth over his head. The *Hiryū* men cried for the ship to turn back. Maruyama saw one of the destroyer lieutenants cast a cold gaze toward the carrier.

"Keep quiet! Enemy submarines and planes will be here soon! We did all we could."

"We cannot abandon our shipmates!" a man yelled back.

"What have they been doing all morning? Rolling dice for your belongings?"

Maruyama scowled as the heartless officer went about recording the names of the refugees. Some uttered epithets at him under their breath. They were hungry and thirsty, with many injured, but they were all Japanese. They deserved more than to be treated as contemptible prisoners.

As the deck plates thrummed with the ship at full power, the lieutenant worked his way through the crowd. Maruyama waited for him to approach.

"Name and rank," he barked.

Maruyama stood at attention. "Maruyama Taisuke, Petty Officer First Class. Pilot/Observer."

The lieutenant wrote in his ledger. "Pilot, eh? Where were *you* yesterday?"

CHAPTER 33

MIDWAY, EASTERN ISLAND, 0430 JUNE 5, 1942

"Danny, wake up."

Iverson jerked awake from his deep sleep. Faint light from the east filled the open tent. *Wha...?*

Fleming poked him again. "Get up. Brief in thirty minutes. The swabbies have some hot coffee and bacon over there. C'mon."

Iverson pulled himself up and sat on the cot. He was at Midway. Yes, Midway. Been asleep four hours. He flew last night. Dark'rn Hades. *Major Norris.*

"Hey, did Major Norris ever show up?"

Fleming frowned. "No. Whitten was the last of 'em back, about 0130. They said the major took 'em down lower and lower to get underneath the stuff. Couldn't see a thing, and he kept going, pretty steep. Prosser warned him on the radio, but he didn't acknowledge. They think he was disorientated or somethin' and flew into the water."

Iverson processed the news. Another major, another commanding officer. *Gone.*

"A Jap submarine shelled us last night and we fired back. You hear 'em?"

"No, didn't hear a thing," Iverson said, still groggy.

On the strip, one of the big bombers rumbled down the taxiway.

"You didn' hear that? Boy, you were out like a light. Anyway, we've gotta stand alert 30 and be ready if the PBYs find something out there. We'll be the ones to go get it, so c'mon. Let's get some food."

Having slept in his flight suit, Iverson laced his boots and stood, catching his balance as he opened his eyes wide to gain his bearings. *I'm at Midway.*

They stood in line for breakfast: hot biscuits, gravy, and bacon on paper plates. Coffee any way you want it so long as it's black. They put their plates on an empty fuel drum away from the makeshift chow line. An Army bomber took off, followed by three others. Fleming watched in admiration.

"Zach Tyler is our new CO," Fleming said, his mouth full of biscuit.

Iverson nodded. Three skippers in the past 24 hours. The fighter boys had lost Major Parks, too. *Leading a formation around here is deadly.*

"We've got twelve birds up, six and six. My SBD from yesterday is still shot up, so I'm gonna take one of them *Wind Indicators.*"

"Mine's shot up, too. I'll fly a *Vindicator,*" Iverson said.

"No, they need an experienced flight lead, and I don' mind flyin' the old sputterin' hen. Flew one last night... Was like puttin' on a familiar glove."

They wolfed down their meal and gulped the last of their coffee as the sun peeked through the clouds. The day was going to be another hot one.

"Let's go see if the Navy has anything for us," Fleming said.

At the Operations tent, Colonel Kimes was in conversation with Tyler. Fleming joined them, and Iverson hovered behind. Kimes acknowledged Fleming and motioned him to join them at the chart table, a plywood board on two sawhorses.

"Dick, glad you're here. Okay, we've loaded you boys with 500-pounders and topped you off. The Army bombers are out searching, as are the flying boats. Looks like four burning carriers still to the north and an indication of battleships west of us about a hun'erd. They're retreating, but we're not sure if all the Japs are. Once we get a solid report, you guys are going, so be ready at zero-six for tasking. And if you find that sub that shelled us last night, put it on the bottom."

"Yes, sir," Tyler said as he nodded. "What are the Navy guys doing out there?"

"Don't know. Keepin' their activities secret. I'm not all that sure what the Navy did yesterday. It was the Army guys that hit 'em."

"Must be nice," Fleming said wistfully.

Kimes left as the other pilots gathered, and Tyler held an impromptu briefing. Weather. Runway condition. SBDs push over from ten in steep dives. *Vindicators* glide bomb – all they could rightfully do. There would be no fighters; the Japs had savaged them yesterday, especially the old hand-me-down F2As. Maybe the Japs still had fighters from an unknown carrier, but probably not.

On the flight line, an SB2U started with a bang and the engine coughed to life.

Iverson studied the chart. A heading of west took them south of Kure, a useful landmark to lead them back. Beyond Kure was emptiness. Trackless water. Oblivion.

At 0635, a jeep rolled up and Kimes jumped out.

"Zach! Saddle up! We've got two battleships, one apparently damaged, west of us at one twenty-five. Headin' west at fifteen knots or so. No reports of carriers. Hit 'em hard. Take off ASAP!"

Kimes handed Tyler the sighting report as the pilots donned their parachutes and cinched down their helmets. Tyler marked the position on the chart as Fleming watched. Iverson and the others stood behind, plotting boards in hand, waiting. Tyler measured the distance, and, with a straight edge, the bearing. His pilots waited, taking nervous glances at their watches.

"Okay, two battleships, one damaged and trailing an oil slick, two-six-four magnetic and one twenty-five out. Heading west at fifteen knots. From the time of this sighting till when we can get out there they'll have moved another twenty or thirty west. So, Dick, let's you and I fly two-six-eight. If we don't see 'em after a transit of 180 miles, let's set up a square search. Stay together until we find them, then Dick, you accelerate ahead and push over first, and we'll be right behind. If you get lost fly east, find Kure, then come home. And don't forget your damn recognition turns; the gunners are jumpy from last night. Questions?"

There were none, and the pilots trotted out to their planes where their radiomen waited. Though still low, the reflected sunlight turned the crushed coral brilliant white, and Iverson squinted to see. Reid was on a wing, waiting, and waved as Iverson approached.

"Reid! Hop in. We've got confirmed targets."

"Yes, sir. What are they?"

"Two battleships," Iverson said as he hoisted himself up on the left wing and slid his plotting board into the instrument panel tray. "West of us for about one-fifty or so. We're going out at ten-thou."

"Yes, sir. Any word about Major Norris?"

Iverson turned to look at Reid. The gunner was really asking about Norris's gunner, his friend. Corporal Whittington.

"No. No word. Bad weather."

Reid nodded as he climbed in and lowered himself into the circular seat. Iverson couldn't tell him what the pilots sensed. Vertigo. He'd had it last night himself. The stated reason Norris hadn't shown up was bad weather. The unspoken reason was he got disoriented and flew into the water. Almost took the formation with him. It could have happened to any of them. All Iverson had to do was fly form. The major had to lead and search in pitch blackness. *Could've happened to me.*

Starting charges fired, pistons coughed, and props fluttered. SBDs around them roared to life. Iverson lowered his parachute and himself into the seat bucket, strapped down the lap belt, hooked up his earphone cord, and flicked on the battery.

"Ready, Reid?" he shouted.

"Ready, sir!" Reid replied as he slapped the side of the fuselage twice.

Iverson then looked at the linesman tending the fire bottle and nodded.

"Clear!" Iverson bellowed, and engaged the starter.

After an hour, they saw the slick. Tyler veered the formation left to line up south of the oily east-west trail. They would find their quarry at the end. Iverson got his bearings with one last look at Kure over his shoulder. The faint circular feature served as their step-off point as the marines again flew into an abyss of open water.

Minutes later they came into view: two big ships trailing faint wakes, some thirty miles ahead. In his cockpit, Tyler assessed them with binoculars while Iverson and the others maintained position. They seemed small for battleships, but they were still far away. To jarheads like Iverson, it didn't make much difference. Except for carriers, one warship looked like another.

Tyler positioned them to come out of the sun – over their left shoulders and about thirty degrees up – and called for the SBDs to accelerate ahead of the slower *Vindicators*. The *Dauntlesses* would dive today – steep – and Iverson glanced down at the outboard lever marked DIVE BRAKES.

Approaching from the enemy's port quarter, 24 men in 12 cockpits looked for additional ships and fighters. Iverson scanned to the south and above. If there was a carrier nearby with fighters airborne, they would attack out of the sun, like yesterday.

"Keep your eyes peeled, Reid. You never know."

"Yes, sir."

"We're divin' on 'em. Gonna be steep today. Back me up on altitude."

"Will do, sir."

The two ships drifted down the right side of Iverson's cowling. He whipped his head back to check the sun; Zach Tyler's geometry was going to work perfectly. Behind and underneath were Dick Fleming's *Wind Indicators*. At this rate, all the SBDs would be in and off before the old SB2Us got to their release points. *Perfect.*

The ships turned left. *We've been spotted,* Iverson thought, and warned Reid. Ahead, Tyler maintained his heading, and, using his hands, signaled for everyone to arm up. Out of habit, Iverson checked his fixed guns: charged and ready.

The ships were big, with turrets forward and aft. One looked queer, but Iverson couldn't peg the reason.[1] Regardless, they were enemy ships caught in the open. With one last scan, he checked the horizon for specks, glints of sun. No CAP anywhere in the cloudless sky. *Good. VMSB-241 was livin' right.* Fuel tanks transferring, low blower, low prop pitch. Armed up.

Black puffs appeared above the ships, steaming a mile apart. From the brief, Tyler would take them to the trailing ship, the queer one. Twisting in his seat, Iverson saw the SB2Us behind his left wing, slightly low, going for the lead ship. Dick Fleming was in his run, his wingmen tight.

Puffs exploded ahead of them co-altitude. The flak the ships put up was thick, and Iverson wondered if Tyler would fly into it before he pushed. Still fast, Tyler brought them to a slight climb to bleed off airspeed. Iverson tightened up on the others, and, with his throttle closed at idle, kicked the rudder to skid off some airspeed. Ahead, Tyler opened his dive-brakes and the others matched him. About to overtake Glidden, Iverson lifted his nose up and away for a count as he moved his dive-brake lever down.

Despite oily smears on the glass, he saw the target through his cockpit floor window. A big ship making a big wake. Along its decks, the steady flashing of AA served as a warning of their preparation.

Tyler pushed straight over, followed by his two wingmen. Delaying a count, Glidden glanced over at Iverson to check his position and gave him a thumbs-up. He then lifted his own *Dauntless* up for a moment and pushed over. Once Glidden's nose broke the horizon, Iverson followed.

The idling propeller spun and engine noise subsided as the roar of the slip-stream outside increased. Using the fixed gunsight, Iverson put the ship inside and peered through the bombsight to track it.

Maneuvering to place his telescopic crosshairs in front of the bow, he held his dive and adjusted trim with his left hand as he corrected for roll with his right. The ball was off left and he trimmed it out, bringing Elmer's wingtip into view as he did. Iverson scanned around the sight to assess distance.

Faint, wispy lights floated up – and then shot past. Like yesterday, Iverson was again in the middle of them. He dove into a funnel of light, the tracers unsettling evidence of only a portion of the barrage of hot lead coming up at him on all sides. No escape. Ahead, the SBDs held steady, red dive-brakes bright,

---

[1] The IJN cruisers *Mikuma* and *Mogami*, which had collided during the night. *Mogami* lost 40 feet of her bow, and over the remainder of the battle many American aviators misidentified *Mikuma* as a battleship.

and Iverson noticed the lead planes pull off. Satisfied that he was stabilized clear of Glidden, he came back inside. Bullets ripped the air outside, as did the sharp pops of detonating shells.

"Four thousand!" Reid called out.

Iverson concentrated as he reached down to the bomb release handle. A white circle formed next to the ship's port quarter. Captain Tyler's bomb. *Short.* Another white bloom, sudden and close to the bow. Tracers snapped louder...

"Three thousand!"

Iverson aimed for a patch of water just ahead of the turning bow and held it as two more white circles of exploding spray appeared next to the battleship. The huge ship broke free of the spray, and, swathed in gray gun smoke, moved into Iverson's crosshairs. The fiery funnel walls narrowed, and Glidden pulled off right. *Holy crap!*

"TWO, sir!"

With sudden realization, Iverson yanked up on the release handle, having pressed it as much as he dared. The plane jumped as the bomb fell away, and Iverson flicked the flap handle forward, opened up the throttle, and snatched the stick into his lap. As he did, the vise-like force of 9 g's squeezed them tight.

Iverson gritted his teeth and strained against the crushing pressure as his vision tunneled. The horizon came into view, and with it, yellow dots of tracers, which zipped past him. He leveled off on the waves, like yesterday – *déjà vu* – splashes jumping up off his right wing. Ahead were two SBDs. *Join on them.* Behind him, Reid opened up.

"Yellow sons o' bitches!"

Reid held a long burst, holding it in vain frustration as Iverson turned behind the ship's fantail. "Reid, enough! Yer gonna overheat!"

Reid stopped, and the tracers did, too. The last SBD pulled off as a geyser from a near miss lifted water high as the ship ran from under the onslaught. The superstructure and fantail continued to blink and spit yellow flame. Iverson snapped his head between the SBDs ahead and the target receding from view. Smoke? *A hit?* No, the smokestack. The curtain of mist fell back to the sea. *We missed,* Iverson thought at he put the plane in front of him next to his canopy frame to join up.

"Sir! They got one!"

Looking south, he saw it, a long trail of black smoke that led to the water, irregular at the end, with a puff of smoke short of the second ship. Other *Vindicators* followed it in their dives, and more geysers and white columns of seawater bloomed next to the Jap battlewagon.

Who? *Who was it?* Were any already off? "Reid, which one was it?"

"Can't tell for sure, sir. Think it was the lead."

Dick? *No, can't be.* Not Dick. Crackin' jokes and keepin' his cool only this morning. *Take another drink o' Dutch courage, Danny.*

Iverson searched south and counted. The last *Vindicator* pulled out and off as the ship defended itself with manic gunfire. Another white column alongside...another near miss.

With the two ships not letting up, the marines cleared to the east as the leads gathered up their respective formations. As he joined on Glidden, Iverson took quick glances south: five dots heading east. In desperation, he searched the sky around them to find a sixth. *Not Dick. Please, please, God, not Dick.*

Behind them, the two Japanese ships held their fire and resumed their course to the west.

CHAPTER 34

USS *ENTERPRISE*, 0815 JUNE 5, 1942

"They don't need us up there," Spruance said as he waved his hand in front of his face. "You and I had a busy day yesterday, and it won't hurt us to relax for a while."

Lieutenant Oliver did as Spruance suggested and took his seat in the flag mess. Not that he had any choice as Spruance's aide. In a good mood, the admiral had a slight smile on his lips.

Spruance motioned to the steward. "More coffee, please." He absentmindedly drummed his fingers on the linen tablecloth as the Filipino mess man poured for both officers.

Impatient to get back to the war, Browning and the others had inhaled their eggs – still fresh after some ten days at sea – and gulped their coffee before they extinguished their half-smoked cigarettes in the crystal ashtray. Each requested to be excused to return to the flag shelter and Spruance nodded his consent. He didn't object; they were Halsey's men. Aviators. *Impatient.*

"How are you adjusting to carrier life?" he asked Oliver.

"Fine, sir. Figured it out fast enough. Can never get used to the hangar bay – so much open space. She sure rides well. Right now it seems as if we're in the turning basin and not the high seas."

Spruance smiled and took a sip from his cup.

Taking advantage of the moment, Oliver probed him. "Sir, how did things go yesterday? Are you pleased?"

With his hand still on the cup and arm resting on the table, Spruance considered the question.

"Typical battle. You have an idea of enemy strength and objectives, how they will probably behave. Then it starts, and reports are incomplete, off a bit, or even wrong. Thick fog of war. It's the waiting that's most difficult. The fliers were gone for over four hours, and we had no idea what was happening."

"Yes, sir."

"Even the radio. Oftentimes unclear, disjointed. It is remarkable, though, that we can even get a glimpse of what's happening over one hundred miles away."

Oliver nodded, waiting for Spruance to continue.

"And that radio direction and ranging antenna spinning over us. We can see into the future, see their attack direction. Paid big dividends for the Brits when the Germans attacked by air across the Channel. Probably what saved them from defeat."

Oliver nodded again. "Yes, sir, and it appears Makalapa Hill was right."

The admiral nodded as he picked up his cup. "Yes, and another critical factor. Remarkable." Spruance let it hang in the air, not acknowledging how the intelligence was collected. He took another sip.

"You know, the coffee is different on this ship from others I've served on. Have you noticed it?"

Oliver took a sip and tasted it.

"Now that you mention it, sir, it is. Can't put my finger on it, though." He took another sip and savored it.

Spruance lifted the cup to his lips and thought for a moment. "Cinnamon. A dash of cinnamon. Do you concur?"

Oliver sipped again. "Come to think of it, sir, it does taste like cinnamon," he said, amused.

Spruance looked at his cup, satisfied at having solved the mystery. "Cinnamon. Something for the flyboy's sweet tooth. Most of them *are* boys – not even twenty-five."

The mood became pensive as both thought of the fliers, the boys. *So* many missing. Maybe they'd come across some today. Spruance hoped the flying boats from Midway could search for survivors as well as patrol for the enemy. The volume of missing – and presumed dead – weighed on him.

"We lost too many yesterday," he said.

"Yes, sir. One must admire their bravery," Oliver said. He finished his coffee with a gulp, hoping the admiral would, too, so they could join the others topside.

"What do you expect today, sir?"

Spruance pursed his lips before answering. "Don't expect they'll attack Midway now, with the heavy losses such they've experienced. That amphibious group to the southwest probably withdrew. We may come across some stragglers as the day unfolds. Much, of course, will depend on the weather."

Spruance also sensed it was time to go. He drank deep and returned the cup to its saucer, then took up his napkin and folded it.

"Do you regret not having the battle line, sir?"

The admiral shook his head. "No. Those ships would just tie us down. We do have some nice ones on the 'ways, though, with 16-inch rifles: three turrets of three. Fast too, thirty knots at flank, like a cruiser. Amazing. But no…the world is changing."

Oliver nodded. *And right before our eyes.*

Spruance pushed away from the table. "Thanks for sitting with me, Oliver. Let's go up and see what they have for us."

"Yes, sir."

Kroeger stepped into the ready room and found he was alone with one of the *Yorktown* pilots. He sat in the front row, poring over a list. A roster. It was Lieutenant Shumway who had led their bombers yesterday. Who had jammed the skipper in his dive. Which had caused Fred to pull up – and get shot. Kroeger quelled his feelings of resentment. *This is war. Bad stuff happens.*

Shumway looked over his shoulder and saw Kroeger. "Lookin' for someone?"

Kroeger had stepped into the ready room because it was his home, his office. Where he belonged. But the question unsettled him, and he blurted out an answer. "Skipper Best, sir."

Shumway shook his head. "He's in sick bay. Coughed up blood last night. Don't expect he'll be flying today."

Kroeger froze, unable to speak. *Was he shot?* Shumway stood and approached him, hand outstretched.

"I'm Dave Shumway, Bombing Three. Looks like I'm going to be your new CO."

Still reeling, Kroeger shook his hand. "Edwin Kroeger, sir. Everyone calls me Bud."

"Nice to meet you, Bud."

Shumway saw that a troubled Kroeger was still processing the news. "The doc says he's med down and will be for a while. Dick – Lieutenant Best – thinks he inhaled some bad oxygen yesterday. How high were you guys on the morning strike?"

Kroeger recalled sucking on the hated rubber mask that didn't fit. Fiddling with the damn straps. Running out of air. The cold.

"About twenty, sir. Toward the end, just before we found them, my gunner and I ran out, and the skipper took us all down to fifteen where he removed his mask. We did, too."

Shumway nodded his understanding. "Yeah, no one likes being on oxygen. If at all possible, I'll try to keep us off it."

Kroeger nodded, his mind elsewhere.

"Looks like we'll be going after lunch. There's a report that two Jap battleships got close to Midway, but they're moving away from it now. That carrier we hit yesterday afternoon may also be trying to escape. Once the weather clears, the scouts are going to find 'em, and we'll probably go as soon as they do. How did you fare yesterday?"

"Sir?"

"On that carrier yesterday afternoon. I remember you were part of the formation. You get a hit?"

Kroeger thought back. The afternoon strike. Fire, smoke... He just dropped his bomb into it. Who knew if he had scored. *Fred.* Fred didn't recover...

"Don't know, sir. Dropped into the conflagration you and the scouts made."

Shumway nodded his understanding. "Yep, team effort. Plenty of credit to go around. Hopefully, we can find it today and finish it off. Anyway, can you help me pass the word and get the rest of the guys up here?" Shumway looked at this watch. "Let's shoot to meet at 0900, Bombing Six and Bombing Three pilots."

"Yes, sir," Kroeger answered, then added, "With Commander McClusky wounded, is Commander Gallaher our new group commander?"

Shumway shook his head. "No, he's in sick bay, too. Wrenched his back on the pull off yesterday, on that last carrier. Regardless, he's down. Lieutenant Short has stepped in for him."

Kroeger absorbed yet another shock. His group commander and both SBD squadron COs were out of the fight. In their place he and the others were expected to follow two unfamiliar *Yorktowners.* Today. He turned to the door, his jaw slack. Stunned.

"Bud?"

Kroeger turned to face Shumway. "Yes, sir?"

Shumway looked down for a moment, then up at Kroeger. "I'm very sorry about your wingman yesterday. I'm told he was a good man."

Kroeger nodded. "Yes sir. Ensign Weber...Fred Weber. We've been together since before December 7th...*were* together..." Kroeger looked away with lips tight. *Fred's gone.*

Shumway nodded. "You'll get a chance to avenge his death. Probably today."

CHAPTER 35

SICK BAY, USS *ENTERPRISE*, 1030 JUNE 5, 1942

"What?" McClusky snapped. "When?"

"At 1400, sir," Lieutenant Short replied. He and Shumway stood in front of McClusky, who was clad in a bathrobe and slippers as he sat at a table in the middle of sick bay. Around them privacy curtains were drawn. One suddenly opened, and an incredulous Willie Gallaher grimaced as he propped himself on an elbow to listen.

After yesterday's debacle, McClusky had had enough from the admiral's staff. Yesterday, they had caused the loss of good men and valuable planes from fuel exhaustion when the ship was nowhere near Point Option. No coordination with *Hornet*, no fighter protection for the poor torpeckers who had been all but annihilated. During the night, he learned the task force had run *east* when the enemy was wounded and retreating *west*, and now the staff wanted his men to make up the difference by flying at an extreme range of over 240 miles – with 1000-pounders! The only way they wouldn't run out of fuel was if the Japs were exactly where predicted, *and* if the ship had an open deck for them inside of Point Option. McClusky and the two pilots before him were skeptical that any of this coordination could be halfway close to the razor-thin fuel margin that required *perfect*.

"When did you learn this?"

Keeping his voice low, Shumway answered, "Thirty minutes ago, sir. On the Teletype screen. Sir, we're new here and don't know how *Enterprise* does things...but this is too much, and we can't guarantee most of our guys – and yours – won't end up in the water. We'd have a better chance of making it back if we carried 500-pounders."

McClusky nodded. "What are the winds?"

"Southeast, sir, and light, like yesterday," Short said. McClusky frowned. *More range for launch.*

Gallaher spoke up. "Commander, we cannot allow this. All we'll have left is our fighters."

McClusky agreed. His bandaged arm didn't allow for him to get into a uniform. Hell, he'd go up there as-is in his pajamas.

"I'm going to the bridge to discuss this with the captain. You two come with me. Willie, can you make it up to the bridge?"

"Yes, sir!" Gallaher said, throwing off his covers and reaching for his trousers.

A Pharmacist's Mate – alarmed to see two of his patients preparing to leave Sick Bay – stepped forward. "Commander, the Medical Officer hasn't discharged you two sirs."

McClusky faced the young man, who was now fearful that he had over-stepped. "Are you going to stop me?"

The mate's lip trembled. "No, sir."

"Good. We're going up to the bridge for a bit. We'll be back."

Captain Murray turned, surprised to see McClusky on the bridge and out of uniform. Behind him were Gallaher and two of the *Yorktown* pilots. All looked troubled.

"Wade, what are *you* doing up here?"

"Captain, this is Lieutenant Shumway and Lieutenant Short of *Yorktown's* VB and VS squadrons, and I asked Willie Gallaher to join us. We've learned of the plan to launch our SBDs at 1400 on a sighting report over 240 miles away with 1000-pounders."

"Yes. Report of a burning carrier we can put on the bottom, and possibly another carrier with heavy escorts coming to help." Murray assessed the men and saw trouble. "That's a hike. Can your boys make it?"

McClusky shook his head.

"Sir, it's too far with that heavy weapon load. These guys will get there, but they won't have fuel to make it back. The tail-enders, the ensigns with the least experience, are most at risk. We're going to lose many more airplanes if we do this."

Murray considered the risk. "We can't wait much longer to close them. We've only got about nine hours of daylight to get out there and back. What if they have a carrier and attack here before we get to them?"

"Captain, at that range and with this loadout, we're not gonna make it back. It's too far, sir. Recommend we run hard at them for an extra hour and swap out the 1000-pound bombs for 500, and launch at 1500. And, Captain, we're going to have to demand an accurate Point Option. Sixty miles off doesn't cut it."

A chagrined Murray nodded his agreement. "We were tied to *Yorktown* yesterday and had to maintain a CAP, which kept us into the wind."

"Sir, we all know that things happen, but, even if the plan you have now goes perfectly, we will *still* lose ensigns from fuel exhaustion. We can't bank on perfect."

Murray noted the *Yorktown* pilots, waiting. All four of the aviators had fought yesterday, and these two were going back. They would be leading *his* aviators, most of whom had been shot at already.

"Captain, with your permission, sir, I'd like to make this case to the admiral's staff. I've flown the SBD-3; flew yesterday when so many of the VB ran out of gas carrying the heavy bombs. These pilots add credibility, and I'd like them to accompany me."

Murray nodded. "Yes, and I'll go with you. Let's go."

The five aviators crossed the navigation bridge to the starboard side and outside, then aft to a ladder. Murray led as McClusky and the others followed by seniority.

Entering the flag shelter, they were confronted by Browning, who looked up from the chart table. Spruance was not in sight. Murray spoke first.

"Miles, my pilots have some concerns about the strike tasking this afternoon. Wade, go ahead."

All felt the tension rise as Browning – well aware of his audience – walked around the table, not taking his eyes off McClusky, who held his ground.

"Captain Browning, I've learned that my SBD squadrons are tasked to launch at 1400 hours on a sighting report with a contact over 240 miles away carrying thousand-pound weapons."

"That's correct," Browning said. He now stood in front of and glared down at McClusky.

"Sir, we cannot carry that out as planned," McClusky said, unflinching.

Browning looked at Murray, then back at McClusky. "The group has their orders. I suggest you follow them."

"This plan is going to run all the bombers out of gas!" McClusky shot back. An impatient Browning shook his head.

"You're wrong, and it's because you don't have experience in dive-bombers! Follow orders! I've got work to do," Browning snarled. All in the shelter froze and waited for McClusky's response.

"Actually, sir, I've got 400 hours in dive-bombers, but how about you? Have you ever flown an SBD?"

"Yes, but that has nothing to do with it!" Browning growled back. He then turned to Murray. "Captain Murray, sir, the admiral has signed the orders. It is imperative we hit as hard as we can as fast as we can."

McClusky wasn't buying it. "Have you flown a heavy SBD-3 with armor plating and self-sealing tanks? Twin thirties? Carrying a 1000-pound weapon with topped-off fuel?"

Browning was furious. "No, *I haven't*, but again, that's immaterial. Your pilots can end the war today by putting a heavy weapon on anything they find out there. And they had better make every bomb count instead of spreading them all over the ocean like they did yesterday. Those 500-pounders lack the punch. This is *war*, McClusky! Fortune favors the bold!"

The men around them naturally inched closer to the heated argument. Shumway thought someone was going to throw a punch. Murray watched them closely. *This has been building for a while.*

Raising his voice, McClusky responded. "Don't tell me about fortune favoring the bold! I was out there yesterday, and so were they!" he said, pointing at Gallaher and the *Yorktowners*.

A devilish smile spread across Browning's lips, and he chuckled. "McClusky, I know *all about* yesterday! I've heard the scuttlebutt from Willie's own pilots that you took them out there at 180 knots with the tail-end-Charlies barely able to keep up. Then you flew well past the point of no return. Because *you* don't know how to fly modern dive-bombers, your people ran out of gas yesterday. That was due to *your* leadership! Not only that, it was *your* fighter squadron who didn't lift a finger to help anybody – allowing *your* torpedo squadron to get their asses shot off! And you come up here shouting and waving your arms! Clean your *own* house, mister!"

McClusky looked as if he would explode. "Let's talk about yesterday, then! Point Option was sixty miles off! *Sixty miles!* How can anybody lead thirty planes with confidence if they can't trust the ship to be where it's supposed to be today when it was barely within two degrees of longitude yesterday?"

Browning's eyes narrowed. He was through with McClusky and his cocksure arrogance, and would deliver the knockout punch right now.

"Fine then, *lieutenant commander*, throw that out. Ignore the launch and recovery of the combat air patrol that kept your ass dry when you got back here. Ignore the threat the Japs posed to us all afternoon, and still pose to us, that makes us launch at maximum range. Ignore our depleted squadrons due to your poor performance and the poor performance of your people. Just tell me, and all of us, what would you do, *right now, mister*, to neutralize the threat to us, the fleet, and Hawaii? Because if we get it wrong, hundreds will die and *he* pays."

As Browning pointed toward where Spruance was last seen in the shelter, he saw he was pointing *at* Spruance, a silent observer to the proceedings.

"What's the disagreement?" he asked, looking at Browning.

"Sir, the group commander thinks we can't hit the Japs at the reported position inside a range his planes are capable of, with a weapon his planes are capable of carrying, at the time you directed in writing. Admiral, there's risk, always is, but the reward of putting the carrier and any other capital ships we find on the bottom or out of action requires the heaviest weapons we can muster! We can close over fifty miles in the time they are out, maybe sixty in these light seas. If our two new shipmates here can manage their navigation and formations, and if the captain can get his planes off in a timely manner, we'll accomplish the tasking you've given us."

Expressionless, Spruance nodded his understanding. He then turned his head to McClusky, who wasted no time.

"Admiral, with a two-hours-old report at 240 miles, which will be way more, sir, as we steam into the wind for launch, we are beyond the edge of the SBD-3 range with a thousand-pound weapon – and no fuel cushion if things go south. The current plan risks most, and maybe all, of your dive-bombers. Recommend, sir, that we steam toward them another hour at best speed, and, during that time, swap out the heavies for the 500-pounders. We hit them with 500-pound weapons yesterday and put them out of action. Follow-on attacks from us and submarines can put them on the bottom. Sir, this plan lands a crippling blow in minimum time *and* allows our boys to recover aboard safely to continue the fight."

As soon as McClusky finished, Murray added, "Concur, sir."

Spruance considered the two options as Browning and McClusky, now facing their admiral, awaited his decision – like two prizefighters after the final round.

He stepped to McClusky.

"I will do what you pilots want."

Stunned as if he had been hit in the face, Browning's jaw fell. He stared at Spruance, who turned to walk away.

"Thank you, Admiral," McClusky said. He and his aviators exited the shelter without making eye contact.

Embarrassed by the awkward scene, Oliver picked up the message board, and others quickly found things to occupy their attention. In the middle of the shelter, Browning stood and gazed out to sea, at the horizon – at what he had lost.

With a sudden lunge, he bolted to the ladder and flew down the rails.

CHAPTER 36

BOMBING EIGHT, NORTHWEST OF USS *HORNET*, 1630 JUNE 5, 1942

Clay Fisher couldn't believe his bad luck.

Here he was again, flying on Sea Hag's wing over an empty ocean, this time with the sun lowering off his left. Earlier, in the ready room, his heart had fallen when he'd seen the schedule:

Commander Ring

2) Fisher

3) Tappan

What had he done to deserve this? Griping wouldn't change anything; Skipper Johnson approved it, and now, he was also flying wing as he led his Bombing Eight division off their right.

They'd been airborne an hour, up high in the cold, on oxygen, with nothing but water and clouds below. Like yesterday. Where were the Japs? Radioman Ferguson came up on the interphone.

"Mister Fisher, I see a sheen on the water, ahead of our right wing."

Fisher studied it as he held position. Ring also saw it, and veered them right.

An oil slick, several miles wide. Nothing else around it.

Fisher guessed this was from the burning carrier they'd seen yesterday afternoon. Same general area. No escorts anywhere to be seen. Must have gone down. *We sank a carrier!* he thought, before remembering that it was *Enterprise* who had done so. He pulled his plotting board out and marked the position and time.

Ring continued ahead, also like yesterday, into the open expanse. The sun was setting, and, with the ship some 200 miles behind them, it would be close to sundown when they got back. Fisher took glances at his mates behind, wishing he could be in their formations instead of up in the lead with Sea Hag.

After twenty minutes had passed, he spied a wake, a single wake. Narrow…probably a small boy. Maybe trailing a carrier. They'd be on it in another five or ten minutes, and Fisher scanned the horizon for fighters.

"What's that one, sir?" Ferguson asked.

Fisher assessed the ship before it passed under his wing.[1] "Light cruiser. Maybe a destroyer. Looks like it's makin' better'n 20 knots." Fisher again plotted the position and time.

As they passed the lone combatant, Ring studied it but made no move to attack. He did make a contact report on the radio as his *Dauntlesses* continued to the northwest. Fisher did the math in his head. If they went back now, they'd make it aboard before sundown. *C'mon, Sea Hag! There's nothin' out here!*

Approaching 300 miles from *Hornet*, Fisher's alarm increased. Ahead was a clear surface, and the sun seemed to accelerate its steady fall to the horizon. He checked over his shoulder, hoping Johnson would come up to take the lead and get them back home. Fisher would leave Ring and join his CO; no more indecision like yesterday. Another minute passed.

"What are we doing, sir?" Ferguson asked. An honest question, and Fisher wouldn't berate him for asking it. He wished *he* could ask it. He checked his fuel – *never enough!* – and tried to formulate an answer for his gunner. He deserved one.

Ring nodded to the right and turned into Fisher. *We're going back!* Fisher thought. *Another wild goose chase.* Regardless, he was happy they'd soon be closing *Hornet* rather than opening on her. Two hours of transit; the sun would be down, but still dusk. Plenty of light for landing.

"Looks like we're goin' home, Ferguson. We tried."

"Yes, sir."

Ring steadied out and entered a shallow descent. *Now what?* They were way too far away to let down for landing. Maybe Sea Hag was tired of freezing at altitude. Fisher felt confident they had the fuel, and, passing fifteen thousand, removed his mask and let it dangle off his right elbow. He then heard Ring transmit.

"Ruff, we're gonna hit this guy. You've got the lead on the left."

Fisher's eyes opened wide. They were going to attack the light cruiser! Getting rid of the bomb was good, but the fuel they'd consume in the attack left no margin for navigation error on the long flight home.

The lonely ship came into view, charging toward them. Johnson took his division to a point ahead and right as Ring S-turned his little formation to fall

---

[1] HIJMS *Tanikaze*, a destroyer that had been sent to scuttle *Hiryū* when it was learned from a float plane that she remained afloat. Finding the sea empty (*Hiryū* had gone down in the interim), *Tanikaze* rushed to catch up with the rest of the Mobile Force.

in behind. Fisher would follow Sea Hag, with Ben Tappan last off. The sun was too low to be of any help, and suddenly the ship opened fire. *They see us.*

Johnson opened his dive-brakes and sliced down on his prey, now turning hard into him. Fisher felt rushed. *What am I forgetting?* He then remembered to roll back the canopy, and the increased roar of the engine and slipstream filled the cockpit.

"Ferguson, get ready to attack!"

"Should I defend or back you up, sir!"

"Back me up!"

Low blower, low pitch, carb heat. Charge guns. Fisher double-checked that the bomb was armed and, with his eyes on Ring, reached down to feel for the emergency release. Ring's wing turned red as his flaps opened, and Fisher slapped the dive-brake handle back to stay with him. Without a warning, Tappan overshot, then slipped back into position.

Johnson pulled off as the ship twisted under the column of SBDs that fell on it. The destroyer had a twin turret forward and two aft, with dozens of automatics the length of it. All the ship's guns fired at the deadly gray airplanes. White circles from near misses formed next to the ship as it reversed its turn at full speed. Fisher saw a hit. No – stack gas.

The radio chattered: *Enterprise* planes had the ship in sight, in from the north. Fisher's eyes remained locked on Ring, who then pulled hard away from him and dropped his nose.

A blast from behind shook Fisher, then another. *Go!*

He pulled down and stepped on bottom rudder as his nose fell in behind Ring, who was established in his dive into a confused nest of yellow fireflies on a background of white spray. Outside, the airspeed built as the prop windmilled lazily in front of the bombsight. Fisher assessed the target speed – much faster than the cruiser yesterday – and aimed at a spot well ahead, more than a ship's length. He tensed his body as tracers sliced past him, snapping at the air. The yellow balls floated in front of him then ripped past with no warning. He lost sight of Ring – *Forget it!* – and watched the ship reverse as he peered around the bombsight. The altimeter needle unwound, and his airspeed held at 240. Ferguson!

"*You okay?!*"

"Three thousand! Yes!"

The splashes around it stopped, and the ship heeled into him. With no time to reposition, Fisher did what he could, bunting as much as he dared in a vertical dive.

254 KEVIN P. MILLER

"Two!"

Fisher mashed the pickle button and yanked the emergency release to be sure. He felt the familiar jolt as 500 pounds fell away before he pulled hard, the g-force falling on him in crushing waves, his hand retracting the flaps while his vision narrowed to a soda straw.

Fisher leveled and jinked away left then back to the right. Ben was clear – *Good!* – but Sea Hag was nowhere to be seen. A sudden geyser lifted seawater hundreds of feet into the air off the ship's stern. Fisher continued right to the southeast and home, the ship ignoring him as it fired at threats above. More geysers as more plump SBDs pulled off. *Enterprise* birds. With a spark, one flamed up, pulsing bright, trailing fire that turned to a black line pointing to the water. Pull up! *Pull up, dammit!*

Holding a steady dive, the flaming *Dauntless* plunged into the sea, white spray mixing with flame, the rising cloud shaped like a black mushroom.

Alarmed chatter on the radio. Open the throttle and get away from the water. Get out of this desolate wasteland of blue. *Who was it?*

Fisher and the others steadied up for the 250-mile trek home. In the cockpit by his right knee were two low-fuel tank indications. The sun was setting behind his right shoulder. It would be down in an hour, earlier on the surface, and it was now a race against fuel and fading light.

Over his right tail, he watched the *Enterprise* planes plaster the enemy ship. Revenge for their mate. He heard someone say Adams. Yes, another pilot confirmed it. *They got Sammy Adams!* Fisher didn't know the man, but he knew him. He was one of them, he belonged here, and furious *Enterprise* pilots mourned his loss even as they pounded the Jap who had killed him.

Fisher leveled off and steadied up on a heading of 130. He leaned the mixture and noted both the airspeed and fuel flow. Next to him, small silhouettes of SBDs, backlit by the reddening sky, paralleled his course for home. *Sea Hag is probably one of them.* One plane was behind him... Must be Ben Tappan. Nobody joined on anybody else in their own solitary races against fuel and time. He closed the canopy to save fuel and to keep the cockpit warmer for Ferguson.

"How you doin' back there, Ferguson? See a hit?"

Ferguson answered. "Hard to say, sir. Maybe."

"Did we get hit before the roll-in? Felt something close."

"Don't see any damage from where I sit, but yes, sir, close as I ever want to get."

Fisher could only nod. After a moment he added. "Another hour and a half for home."

Ferguson didn't answer as they flew on in silence.

Climbing away from the lone Jap ship, an amazed Bud Kroeger judged it un-harmed after more than three squadrons had pummeled it. "Halterman, did *anyone* hit it?" Kroeger asked his gunner.

"No, sir," he answered.

Kroeger joined up on Lieutenant Smith as they headed home. Behind them the VS were off. They had lost one. Sammy Adams...one of the *Yorktown* boys. Nice fellow. And his gunner. After what they had been through yesterday, to lose their friend to a worthless tin can would be excruciating to the *Yorktowners*.

Kroeger's dive had been good. As he tracked the Jap, he marveled that the ship had emerged time after time from a blizzard of explosions and spray, bracketed by near misses. He recognized the ship as a destroyer, one of their big ones. The AA reminded him of a summertime picnic sparkler. That ship put up one hell of a fight.[1]

He suspected he was long as soon as the bomb came off. The second geyser was his – yes, long. More brackets followed, but no hits. *Amazing*

He moved away from Smith enough to check his own navigation on the plotting board tray. Over 250 miles. *The sun will be down almost an hour before we get there,* he thought. He had enough fuel for recovery if the ship was at Point Option and into the wind. He closed the canopy and secured carb ice. He and the others would need every drop of fuel.

Halterman yelled out, then came up on the interphone. "Whoa, sir. Flashes behind us near that Jap. Someone else is hittin' it."

Must be more from *Hornet*, Kroeger thought. Be an even darker recovery for those guys.

Minutes passed, and Halterman came up again. "Sir, I'm gettin' a strong signal from the ship."

"Good. Is this a good heading?"

"Yes, sir."

Kroeger breathed easier riding a strong homing signal. Heading solved. However, there wouldn't be a moon up when they got there, and the thin overcast above wouldn't help matters. It would be dark.

---

[1] *Tanikaze* was attacked by 12 SBDs from *Hornet* and 32 SBDs from *Enterprise* – plus 10 B-17's from Midway. None scored a hit on her.

"Cap'n's on the bridge!" a lieutenant sang out. "Belay your reports," a calm Mitscher said as grabbed his binoculars before stepping out to the starboard wing. The light cruiser *Atlanta* steamed 4,000 yards off his beam in escort. A new one, and for a moment Mitscher admired her lines. Her plates shone pink in the twilight.

The western sky blazed red. Not the most dramatic sunset he'd ever seen, but most sunsets out here in the tropics were breathtaking. Red sky at night – *sailor's delight* – but Mitscher had more on his mind. Twelve planes carrying 24 of his men were still out there. Had been for over three hours.

He asked for a radar update. Clear. He asked for the status of *Enterprise*. None of her bombers had returned.

Again he thought of Waldron, hoped he was out there. Owed him an apology. Waldron had all but begged for help yesterday. Mitscher allowed himself a smile. Maybe Johnny was in a rubber boat, using his trousers as a sail. He'd sail a thousand miles to Hawaii in his skivvies, cussin' a blue streak!

The officer of the deck approached him. "Cap'n, request permission to darken ship."

"Approved," Mitscher answered.

His mind went back to Ring and his dive-bombers. They had found something and bombed it. A single light cruiser. No carrier. At least it was something. Walt Rodee's scouts had come back with their bombs still attached. Empty-handed. *Again!* Mitscher knew he'd have to explain his performance on Makalapa Hill. *Snake bit* was not listed in *Rocks and Shoals.*

On the horizon, *Enterprise* formed a dark silhouette, as did the screen ships. Dusk now. Mitscher scanned the sky in search of information. Twenty minutes. Twenty more minutes till the last glimmer of sun, the dull glow of twilight. Then dark. Tough for submarines to attack him...much tougher for pilots to find him. The OOD stuck his head out of the pilothouse.

"Cap'n, radar shack reports a line of contacts bearing three-one-zero, forty miles inbound."

"Very well," Mitscher answered. Soucek appeared and stepped outside.

"Captain, I believe that's Ring."

"Concur. Better have their lights on during their recognition turns."

"Yes, sir."

"Gettin' dark, Apollo."

"Yes, sir. What are you thinking?"

Mitscher pulled at his chin. "Submarines are always a threat, but these boys are gonna need help. Turn on the deck edge lights. What do you think?"

Soucek looked across the water at *Enterprise*. "What's *he* doing? Don't see any lights."

Spruance found Murray in the chart room with the navigator. "George, a moment please."

Murray followed him out to the port gallery. To the east, *Hornet* was barely visible.

"Yes, sir, Admiral."

"Can your pilots land at night, and under these conditions?"

"Admiral, it's always riskier at night, but I recommend we illuminate our deck and masthead lights." Pointing at *Hornet*, he continued. "Not sure about him, but most of my guys are not proficient at night landings, and some have never done one. Imagine it's the same for him."

Spruance nodded. "I tend to agree that we need our lights on to help them. If they go in the water we're out of business, not to mention the human cost."

"Yes, sir."

"Lights on. Bring 'em home. Screen ships comb the waters for subs like their lives depend on it. And ours."

"Aye, aye, Admiral."

While Mitscher and Soucek discussed it, *Enterprise* illuminated her flight deck lights and island floodlights. "Answers our question, Apollo. Turn 'em on. Point a searchlight straight up. Help our guys."

"Aye, aye, sir."

Mitscher crossed the bridge to the port side gallery, his favorite spot to watch his boys return. Like a father, he took care of them. An SBD, wingtip lights illuminated, approached the ramp. The pilot took his cut and plopped down.

As it rumbled forward Mitscher peered into the cockpit. Stanhope? Ruff? Hard to tell in the low light. No, it was a younger man, a nameless ensign. The plane was from Bombing Eight. One of Stanhope's formation. The bomb yoke was empty. *Good! We've drawn blood.*

"Apollo, who's the pilot of this one?" he shouted.

Soucek checked the roster in Pri Fly.

"Ensign Fisher, sir, Bombing Eight," he shouted back.

Mitscher nodded. "Very well. Send him my congratulations on his landing."

"Captain, he's Sea Hag's assigned wingman."

Now troubled, Mitscher nodded again. *Did they get Stanhope?*

Despite the dangers from submarines, a relieved Kroeger saw light up ahead. Two clusters… Must be the carriers. He'd never seen *Enterprise* lit up at sea like this, and one of the ships had a column of light that bounced off the clouds high above. Between him and the light clusters were SBD wingtip position lights. He checked his wingtips to ensure they were on.

"There's home, Halterman. They're waitin' for us."

Halterman's receiver pointed them at *Enterprise*, and, as they got closer, Kroeger was able to discern that home was on the right, some twenty miles away. He adjusted the cockpit lighting and flicked the Grimes light down to check fuel. Fifteen gallons in each tank. They'd make it.

Ahead, the SBDs made their recognition turns, and Kroeger followed as he rolled the canopy hatch back. Only when he looked down and saw wake phosphorescence from a darkened escort ship did he know he was inside the screen. *Enterprise* was oriented southeast, into the wind, horizon barely discernable. He had trailed Smith the entire time and took interval on him as he completed his landing checklist.

"Prepare for landing, Halterman."

The night was dark – no moon – but the ship gave off plenty of light to determine lineup. Easing to 100 feet, Kroeger slid toward the wake. Ahead, lighted paddles of the LSO gave a cut signal to Smith. Kroeger concentrated on airspeed and altitude. *Don't get slow.*

From the LSO platform, Lieutenant Robin Lindsey showed him a "roger" pass before he suddenly lowered his arms. *I'm low!* Kroeger thought and gunned the throttle. He eased toward the ramp, eyes on Lindsey.

Lindsey then dropped his right arm, and, by reflex, Kroeger closed his throttle to correct. His SBD approached the ramp, and all Kroeger could see was

Lindsey, arms outstretched, eyes on Kroeger. The LSO then flicked the right paddle across his neck.

Kroeger chopped the throttle and eased back on the stick as the *Dauntless* slammed down on deck. The hook snagged a wire and wrestled the SBD to a stop. Kroeger and Halterman bounced in their seats and leaned forward from the sudden deceleration.

"Nice landing, sir!" Halterman said as Kroeger found the director and waited for the signal to taxi forward. Once free of the cable, he was directed ahead – *hurry!* – and Kroeger taxied out fast, knowing another low-fuel SBD was right behind. He heard orders on the flight deck loudspeaker but could not understand them. Past the barrier, the director then had him slow – *easy, easy* – as his spinning prop neared the planes in the pack up forward. They chocked him behind Smith's SBD, and the director reminded Kroeger to secure his position lights. *Dummy!*

He switched the engine off on signal, and after four hours in the seat pulled himself up and out of the cockpit. Once on the wing, he stretched his back. Another spinning prop that eased next to him seemed close in the darkness.

With his plotting board under his arm, Kroeger jumped off the wing and looked to get off the deck amid the silhouettes of SBDs and noise of running engines. Starboard side toward the island looked clear. With careful steps and an SBD elevator as guide, Kroeger made his way to the island under the bridge, Halterman following. At the island, he looked for the hatchway to the ready room.

Another SBD took a cut and the engine quit as the plane trapped aboard. Out of fuel. The sound of the cable pulled out of its housing echoed on the suddenly quiet flight deck.

Cheers rose from the deck crew aft. "Wow, Mister Kroeger, those guys must be livin' right!" Halterman said.

Kroeger could only nod as he undogged the hatch. His legs shook, and once inside the island he took deep breaths to collect himself.

CHAPTER 37

HIJMS *NAGARA*, 2100 JUNE 5, 1942

Genda knew he should not be outside, should not let the men see him – a senior staff officer – idle like this. The sun had been down for some time, and most of the survivors were below. If *Nagara's* chiefs caught them about the weather decks after darken ship they would be punished. Genda could be punished, too, but he doubted they would take on a staff commander. However, if they put him on report, he would gladly accept any punishment the captain wished to mete out. He deserved it.

From the boat deck under the catapult he had watched the sunset as the cruiser steamed into it. Around *Nagara*, the remnants of the Mobile Force held station on the Main Body with giant *Yamato* in the middle. The commander in chief was aboard. Genda had to face him, to atone. He dreaded it. Having Yamamoto merely *look* at him now would be akin to being run through by a sword.

His pen. His pen had indeed swayed the destiny of the empire. Just as he had feared. Genda thought of nothing else as the tension built in his midsection. More than a failure, more than a defeat. No, it was over now. Japan could not recover from this calamity.

The search. Perfunctory and routine, like any morning at sea. The Americans had spotted the invasion force the day before. Yet he and the rest of the staff had dismissed it – even clumsy Americans can use their flying boats to search. Hell, that night an American plane had attacked and torpedoed a fat *maru*. They knew we were coming! And we sniffed our disdain.

Four carriers attacked Midway…when two could have done the job, holding two in reserve! Tomonaga could have led all the planes from CarDiv 2, leaving *Akagi* and *Kaga* ready with antiship weapons – as Combined Fleet directed! Genda's insides had churned with acid since yesterday morning. It had been *his* directive to apportion the strike force from among four decks after *his* determination that battleship and cruiser float planes were sufficient to search thirty-degree sectors at dawn. How could he make amends for such unforgiveable blunders?

He thought of the invasion plan. Must adhere to the scheduled timetable! Tides, logistics, the Southern Operations campaign needs next month. Operation MI was no express train to Osaka, but the First Fleet Staff – *his staff!* – treated it as such! A *timetable!* Bitter bile rose to his throat as Genda held himself and the others in contempt. Had they not learned anything from Clausewitz? They were there to offer battle to the American Navy. Who among them thought the Americans would offer first?

He glanced up at the shadow of the Type Zero float plane on the catapult above him. An incomplete report from one such as this: tentative, confused, garbled, incorrect, the crew unable to spot an enemy *aircraft carrier* amid a defensive screen worthy of such a ship. Then a definitive sighting – *a carrier on our flank!* – and we dithered. *I* dithered when we should have recovered Tomonaga and run...or launched what we had at once and hoped... But not *close the enemy* as we loaded planes and warmed up engines in our cocksure preparation for launch. How much time did we think we had? An hour, *bah!* The force wouldn't have even sent the first *kanbaku* aloft in two. Remembering, he gripped the rail and peered into the darkness while wind lashed his face.

Deep down, Genda knew that he, too, suffered from Victory Disease. It was all so easy! The American Navy! The vaunted Royal Navy! The Dutch and Australians. It was almost comical, the way the westerners attacked with obsolete land-based planes, their befuddled pilots outclassed, leaving their mighty big-gun battleships and cruisers to their fate. What had they been doing the past decade while Japan prepared? Watching Hollywood movies and arguing about the World Series?

The image of the admiral taking his place in the boat as *Akagi's* burning and explosion-wracked hull bobbed above them was one he would never forget. Expressionless, Nagumo sat in the stern sheets as if on a throne, ignoring the chaos about him. Uncomprehending. Unflinching – despite the anguished shouts of the burned and dying from the anchor deck and deafening explosions aft. He hadn't seen Nagumo all day...Kusaka relayed his orders. But it was all an act. Only hours ago Genda had learned Nagumo had been relieved by Combined Fleet. Admiral Kondō now commanded the Mobile Force. *The force commander – relieved for cause!*

Nagara steamed on behind *Yamato*, its massive hulk visible in the starlight, trailing a wide wake. From the boat deck Minoru Genda contemplated the future of the Imperial Japanese Navy.

If only we had run.

Restless, Bob Laub walked down the passageway past the Officer's Country staterooms. He couldn't sleep, and headed to the wardroom. He didn't want to sleep and dream about that torpedo hovering in mid-air under a burning TBD before both dove into the gunfire-churned sea. He didn't want to visit the ready room either. Normally full of acey-deucy and bridge players before taps, the thought of seeing it empty repelled him. The wardroom was neutral ground. He heard soft phonograph music from inside a stateroom, a catchy tune from his boyhood. *Life can be so sweet, on the sunny side of the street...*

Still in shock, Torpedo Six hadn't flown since yesterday morning. Laub sensed his shipmates ignoring them...easier than dealing with the reality of what happened. Recovered... Would any of them ever recover? With Commander McClusky in sick bay, he wasn't sure who to report to anyway. The *Yorktown* SBD pilots seemed to be senior. They said that some of the VT-3 planes escaped but had to ditch when *Yorktown* was attacked. Nothing from *Hornet*. Fifteen planes. *All of them lost.*

The table normally used by VT-6 was empty, but two Scouting Six pilots sat across from one another at their squadron table. Dusty Kleiss and Rodey Rodenburg. Laub poured himself a glass of bug juice and walked toward them.

"Mind if I join you guys?" he said.

"Hey, Bob, sure. Please do," Kleiss answered. Laub placed his glass on the linen tablecloth.

He noted the matted-down hair and bloodshot eyes of the SBD pilots.

"Just get back? How was it?"

Kleiss shook his head. "Wasted flight. We were searching for a carrier, found nothing, and just before sundown came over to a little tin can that the *Hornet* guys were bombing. They missed it, pretty bad, and I thought, you know, they're just rookies and we'll sink this guy in no time, but all of us missed, too. That Jap was twisting and turning like I've never seen."

"And he got one of the *Yorktown* guys," Rodenburg added. "Nice fella. He's the one who found the carrier yesterday afternoon."

"Yeah. Sam Adams. He sure was a nice guy. Saw him go in," Kleiss said. As his words hung in the air he took a drink of water and changed the subject.

"Bob, I'm really sorry about what happened to you guys yesterday. Don't know what to say other than that. They shouldn't have sent you."

Laub nodded. He didn't know what to say either. Still *recovering*.

"Thanks, Dusty. We all lost friends yesterday, and hey, they may still be out there."

"Tom Eversole was my best friend. I mean, is..." Kleiss added, embarrassed.

Laub nodded. *That TBD is burning!*

"Did you see him?" Kleiss asked.

Laub didn't answer and stared at his glass. Kleiss and Rodenburg said nothing in the uncomfortable silence.

"Yes," Laub said softly. "Just before we turned in for our runs. The CO was hit about the same time. Didn't have a chance."

No one said a word, each man remembering yesterday.

"Tom was indeed a good man," Laub said, again breaking the silence. "And you scout bombers lost good men too. Just hope it was worth it."

"Today sure wasn't," Rodenburg offered.

After another lull, Laub spoke up.

"What about tomorrow? Heard there's a crippled battleship or cruiser out there."

"Don't know," Kleiss said. "Still heading west. I'll bet we go."

Rodenburg searched Laub's face. "What about you guys? Will you go again?"

"Rodey, knock it off. Don't ask him that."

Laub waved his hand. "No, it's okay. Two of our junior guys didn't go yesterday and they want to take a crack at the Japs real bad. Won't be able to face anyone if they don't."

"Be careful what you wish for," Kleiss muttered.

"That's what I said. We'll see. We've got three flyable birds."

Kleiss leaned in and locked his eyes on Laub.

"Bob, I hope you don't have to fly those crates into battle again. But in a way I do, so you can pay them back for Tom and the CO and the others and tell their families you did. Hope we can work 'em over first so you can put them on the bottom."

Laub reacted with a faint smile. "Thanks, shipmate."

"I look up to you, Bob. We all do."

Laub could only nod his appreciation. He felt unworthy. He felt guilty.

Still keyed up from his night landing, Ken White approached his roommate. "Clay, we took a vote, and you hafta tell Sea Hag how to drop his bomb."

Fisher looked up from his ready room chair. Around White were two other ensigns who had had it with their group commander. Ring had returned twice with his bombs still attached.

"Why do I have to tell Sea Hag anything? And what vote? I didn't vote," Fisher snapped back at him as he eyeballed the others. After three unsatisfying combat flights, he had had it, too. But White wasn't joking.

"After he landed, Sea Hag yelled at the troops on deck and said the release mechanism didn't work. But Clay, he tried to drop it with the transmitter switch on the throttle! He doesn't even know how to drop a bomb, and somebody's gotta tell him how."

"Fine, but why me?"

"Because you are his *personal teacher's pet wingman!*" White answered, drawing laughs from the others.

Not moving, Fisher made a face. "I ain't doin' it," he muttered, and looked away.

Listening from the front row, Skipper Johnson got up and stepped toward him. "Fisher, go and knock on Sea Hag's stateroom door, and when he invites you in, instruct him on how to drop a damn bomb. Now."

A displeased Fisher exhaled his disappointment and slumped his shoulders in acceptance. He rose to his feet. "Yes, sir."

White and the others suppressed grins as Fisher stepped to the door.

"Don't forget an apple, Clay. There's a bowl of fresh ones in the wardroom!"

Fisher heard his squadron mates laugh as he shut the door behind him.

He stepped to the ladder and went below one deck. Sea Hag's stateroom was just forward of the island, outboard. *Why me?*

Fisher stopped next to his door, and noticed the group commander's calling card affixed to the bulkhead:

Stanhope Cotton Ring

Fisher ensured his shirt was tucked in before he knocked twice. He heard Ring say, "Enter."

Fisher opened the door, and Ring looked up from his desk. "Yes, Fisher, what is it?"

"Sir, um. I thought if you'd like to discuss the new bomb release system on the SBD-3 model, I'd be happy to review it, sir."

"Come in."

Fisher entered and closed the door behind him. Ring motioned to a chair. "Please be seated."

Uneasy, Fisher took his chair.

"Well, then," Ring began. "Where shall we start?"

Fisher swallowed. "Sir, the dash three's we got have a new electrical arming and release capability the older model SBDs don't have. It makes it nice, too, because with the manual system you hafta reach down to pull the release handle, and that can move your crosshairs off target."

"Yes, I sure remember that from the SB2U a few years ago."

"Yes, sir," Fisher said, offering a smile of understanding.

"Well, this evening I did try the electrical system but the circuit seemed not to have closed. Perhaps it came loose during the run."

"Perhaps, sir. My technique, well, the way Skipper Johnson taught us, is to have my right thumb on the pickle button on the stick, just resting on it as I'm in the dive tracking. At release altitude, I try to hold the stick as steady as I can while I mash down on the button, hard, so the connection is made. I try to hold it for half a count so the bomb can come off steady and not throw it long."

Ring nodded in silent understanding.

"And, sir, the emergency release is my backup. If I don't feel it come off, I can reach down by my left ankle and salvo everything off – the main weapon and two wing stations if we're carryin' incendiaries."

Ring nodded again but seemed unsure. Fisher thought fast.

"It's right below the throttle, sir. Skipper Johnson says he has his left hand there the whole way down. It's tough to lean down like that, but I tried it tonight and was able to track the target okay."

In his chair, Ring went through the motions, imagining himself controlling an imaginary stick while reaching for the emergency release by his ankle.

"Yes, sir, gotta be a contortionist sometimes. Maybe if I had done it yesterday, I might have got my bomb off on the target."

"You missed yesterday?"

"Sir, the bomb was hung, and I had to pull out with it. Most airspeed I ever saw. Got it to come off before coming back here, using emergency release."

Ring nodded his understanding and smiled to himself at the modern cockpit gadgetry. "Okay. Electric push-button release from the control stick... What *will* they think of next?"

Fisher smiled back. "Yes, sir!"

"Thanks for coming by, Fisher."

"Yes, sir," Fisher said, taking that as his cue.

"Get some sleep, we're probably going to go again tomorrow."

"Yes, sir. Good night, sir," Fisher said as he exited. As he walked down the passageway, he hoped he could fly tomorrow with Skipper Johnson and his buddies.

CHAPTER 38

USS *ENTERPRISE*, 0740 JUNE 6, 1942

Spruance grew impatient as he read yet another incomplete sighting report from his own scouting planes.

Two enemy groups to the southwest moving slowly away, one with a battleship and cruiser, and one with a possible carrier and escorts. Almost an hour prior a pilot had reported a *carrier*. And inside 150 miles! Then, just ten minutes ago, another SBD pilot had overflown the flight deck and tossed out a bean bag. He reported a cruiser and battleship southwest of *Enterprise* with escorts moving west, slow, and also inside 150. *Why hadn't* he *radioed?* After the previous two days' mistakes and mix-ups, Spruance demanded more.

"Miles, we need to be sure of what's out there. Send float planes from the cruisers and have them maintain contact. I'm tired of guesswork."

"Aye, aye, Admiral. Will ensure relief on station," Browning replied. Spruance had put aside the theatrics from yesterday. He needed Browning. But he wouldn't forget – and would no longer blindly follow.

"Thank you. When will the *Hornet* planes be up?"

"Twenty more minutes, sir. Twenty-six bombers and eight escort fighters."

Once more, Spruance could only wait. Drained and irritable, he was tired of *waiting*. Was he in contact with the enemy or not? What units? What strength?

There *was* good news. During the night, Nimitz had sent a message that yesterday a Midway flying boat had rescued one of the *Hornet* torpedo plane pilots, an ensign, who had spent the night in his raft...after he had watched the dive-bomber attack from it.[1]

"Miles, on the basis of CINCPAC's message, he's skeptical there's a carrier out there, and so am I. Concur there are stragglers and cripples. Want to hit them hard today."

"Concur, sir, and we've got a bomb load to put anything we find out of action and enough fighters to defend if there is a carrier with a CAP up. After we recover the scouts we'll be able to get a strike off around 1030."

---

[1] ENS G.H. Gay, Torpedo Eight

Spruance nodded. Out of habit he went to the chart table. He measured from the 0700 fix: Midway was 300 miles east of them. Wake was to the southwest; the Japs were obviously heading for it and its air cover. His scout bombers had found nothing to the northwest. How far to pursue? Another hundred miles? Two hundred? He couldn't steam too far from Midway's air umbrella, and especially from the oilers. No, whatever was to his southwest would be it.

Laub sat in the ready room with an ensign when Group Commander McClusky stepped inside.

"*Attention on deck!*"

His left arm in a sling, McClusky waved his right hand. "As you were."

He walked up to Laub. "Lieutenant Laub, I need to speak with you. Let's go out here."

Laub followed him into the passageway, and McClusky led them to a vestibule under a ladder.

"Bob, how're your people doin'?"

"We're okay, sir…considering. Two of the guys who didn't go Thursday want to. They feel guilty and ashamed. Everyone else on board is flying and they aren't." Laub motioned toward the ready room. "One of them is that ensign inside."

"How're *you* doin'?"

"Okay, sir."

McClusky nodded his understanding. "How many planes do you have flyable?"

"Three, sir. We have four, but three are flyable."

McClusky nodded again. Laub knew what was coming.

"We're launching a strike in a few hours on contacts about 150 miles away. The report is a battleship and cruiser, maybe two cruisers, and some escorts. *Hornet* is attacking in an hour, then us. Can you go with us? About thirty SBDs and twelve VF. Plenty of cover."

Laub had given this thought, but McClusky continued before he could answer.

"The VB knocks them out with 1000-pounders, and the fighters strafe 'em. Your fish will put them on the bottom, but nobody wants to risk another TBD. I'm going to have fighters padlocked on you. Nobody in forty airplanes is going to let any harm come to you guys."

"Sir, we can go. We want to."

"Can you lead your division?"

"Yes, sir."

"Okay. I'm going up to tell the captain that Torpedo Six can fight. I'll let you know, but, for now, muster your people and get with the scouts for the plan. Lieutenant Short from *Yorktown* will lead."

"Aye, aye, sir."

McClusky clasped Laub on the arm. "Proud of you, Laub."

"Stanhope from Robert. Enemy below on port bow."

Fisher's eyes scanned in front of his left wing. Skipper Johnson saw something ahead, but Fisher hadn't yet. He checked his position in the scouting line and scanned again. He saw them then – through the clouds. Four ships.

"Ferguson, we've got ships up ahead, fifteen miles. Get ready."

"Yes, sir."

Sea Hag continued on, and Fisher realized they weren't going at them. Just like yesterday, Ring bypassed the first sighting to look for more. As the Japanese ships drew closer on his left side, Fisher spotted a battleship, cruiser, and two destroyers in escort. Not moving fast. He then noticed a floatplane circling below at a safe distance. *Must be one of ours.*

On they went. Though they scouted ahead, pilots like Fisher took peeks at the Japanese behind them. Armed up. Engine good. Fuel: plenty. Visibility excellent. From fourteen thousand, the visibility topped forty miles easy, but Sea Hag had to search around the scattered cotton balls below.

Before the Jap ships disappeared from view, Ring entered a left turn. Fisher smiled as the geometry built. Out of the turn they would be south of the enemy track. A left roll in out of the sun.

The formation tightened up, and XO Tucker moved up to lead. Fisher was in the pack – where he wanted to be. He'd be sixth down on a target the XO chose. The Japanese continued west, the capital ships line abreast, seemingly unaware.

Unlike the little devil yesterday, they were big, and not running hard. Fisher's division slid to Tucker's right side. They eased into the ships and Fisher noted the sun. *Another thirty degrees*, he figured, and watched for the dive-brake signal to pass it down the line.

Muzzle flashes from the southern ship, big ones. Seconds later, black puffs appeared – above them. Fisher checked his fuel tank balance, engine blower, prop pitch. Hatch – open. Had been the whole time. He'd get this one – drop it right down the stack. He was due. Three tries and nothing! The whole squadron was due, and Fisher was eager now, no longer fearful of the antiaircraft. Tucker eased them closer and opened his flaps. Fisher and the others matched him and worked to maintain position. Suddenly, the XO dove, dropping his nose as his two wingmen knifed down behind him.

"Here we *go!*"

All the ships fired a barrage, and, from amid the cordite smoke of the automatics on the superstructure, more yellow balls floated up toward them. Oblivious, Fisher concentrated on the forward turrets. Lieutenant Lynch was in, and the gaping red maw of Cason's dive-brakes hung in front of him. In a violent motion he pushed over, and Fisher counted.

One potato... Two potato...

Fisher pulled across the horizon and then pushed, knuckling his nose under with rudder as he pulled the throttle aft. The airspeed built at once, and he stabilized vertically. *Good dive, a little off the seat. Ship in the gunsight...now switch to the bombsight.* Without conscious thought, he rolled to keep the ship aligned, the controls acting as extensions of his being. Dazzling tracers crossed his bombsight view as the ships fired at the descending column of American planes.

"Six-thousand!"

The target turned, but not like the tin can yesterday. The red lines of SBD dive-brakes ahead of him moved out of the sight as explosions and concentric rings of white from their near misses bloomed alongside the ship, her rudder hard over.

"Four thousand!"

Fisher was committed now, and tracers above and below locked him in his dive. A shock wave of condensation from one of the near misses whipped past his sight. *C'mon...c'mon.*

"Three!"

He tracked the second turret, easing and rolling by reflex to keep his aim-point on it. Another white ring of churned-up water floated into his view as the ship sped past it.

"Two!"

Fisher mashed down on the pickle and, with relief, felt the bomb swing away. Straining hard, he pulled the stick into his lap with both hands as the g-force crushed them. As with his previous dives, he heard the gunfire chatter and the deep *booms* of the secondary guns. In rapid motions he slapped up the brakes and shoved the throttle to the firewall as the engine roared to life. Ahead was another ship, and he jinked right to follow Cason and Lynch before reversing left to avoid their flight paths. He bunted to the wave tops, not thinking but reacting: running, panting hard, less from physical exertion than from fear.

Clear of tracer fire, he looked back. The scouts were in on the other ship, bigger. The first one pulled off.

"Whoa, sir! Look at that!"

Fisher craned his head back to see. True to his word in the ready room, Gus Widhelm got a hit amidships, and black smoke bloomed above a sheet of flame behind the stack.

Then, a flash from above, and a black trail behind an SBD in line with the others toward the ship.

"Pull up!" Fisher shouted. "Pull up!"

The *Dauntless* went straight in behind the cruiser, revealing a curtain of white as the ship moved away.[1]

More geysers erupted next to the target, and another hit registered aft. Fisher could only wonder about who got hit and rode it in. Then another flash, this one above, at tip-over altitude. Another horrible and fiery plunge, the SBD breaking up as a burning wing fluttered free. *No!*[2]

Fisher joined on his wingmen to the south as the enemy ships, one burning hard, continued on. Two planes down. No chutes, no chance.

Planes from Thursday hadn't returned. Men he knew...they just hadn't shown up. Yesterday he saw an *Enterprise* bird get it. But here, Fisher was witness to the death of a friend – two friends and their helpless gunners – friends whose names he did not yet know. It felt different. He wished he knew, *now*, so he could mourn on the way back. He steeled himself as he went about his cockpit tasks for the return flight, trying to make sense of the loss. Anonymous loss.

---

[1] ENS D. Griswold, ARM1c K.C. Bunch, Scouting Eight
[2] ENS C.E. Vammen, AMM1c M.W. Clark, Scouting Six

Chapter 39

Flag Shelter, USS *Enterprise*, 0930 June 6, 1942

In his flying clothes and helmet, Laub followed Captain Murray, Group Commander McClusky, and Lieutenant Short up the ladder to the flag shelter. He'd been summoned to see the admiral himself…but why?

Outside on the flight deck, the plane handlers spotted his three loaded TBDs aft. They would be the last off. Aboard *Enterprise* word spread throughout the ship: *They're sendin' the torpeckers.*

Once at the shelter, Murray took Laub's arm and had him stand next to him. Browning approached, his eyes on Laub, who held his gaze.

Murray introduced them.

"Captain Browning, this is Lieutenant Junior Grade Laub, acting commanding officer of Torpedo Six."

Browning extended his hand, and Laub took it. "How do you do, Laub. Sorry we have to meet under these circumstances. Are your planes and men up to this task?"

Laub nodded. "Yes, sir."

"Who's flying? Anyone from Thursday morning?"

Laub nodded again. "Just me and my gunner, sir. The others, an ensign and warrant machinist, didn't fly Thursday."

Browning probed deeper. "Do you have confidence in them? We need your best men today." Browning glanced at Murray, who let Laub answer.

Laub opened his mouth to answer as he considered the question. *Our best men are dead, sir.*

"Yes, sir. Ensign Morris was too junior but he's a good pilot, quick on the uptake. Same with Warrant Officer Mueller. I have confidence in their abilities. They really want to go."

"And you?"

Laub thought of Skipper Lindsey. He practically had to be helped into his plane. Wasn't going to miss the big one. Laub wasn't going to miss it, either.

"Yes, sir. I'm senior. I'm ready."

Spruance walked out from behind the chart table curtain. The men stopped talking and opened a path so he could meet Laub. Laub had never met an admiral before.

"Admiral, this is Lieutenant Jay Gee Laub, reporting as ordered," Browning said, motioning to the young pilot.

Spruance offered his hand and a smile. "Mister Laub, nice to meet you."

"You too, sir," Laub replied. The admiral invited him to stand at ease. "What do you go by?"

"Sir?"

Spruance smiled. "Your *name*."

"Oh, I'm sorry. Robert, sir."

"Is that what everyone calls you?"

"Um…Bob, sir."

Spruance nodded. "Very well…*Bob*. Bob, do you know why I've called you here?"

Laub felt the butterflies return. Was he supposed to know this answer? Spruance waited.

"Um, no sir," Laub stammered, then blurted out a lame response. "I'll find out, sir."

Spruance smiled. "Annapolis?"

"No, sir," Laub answered, his face reddening. *Idiot! How're you gonna 'find out' what the admiral is thinking?*

Spruance nodded his understanding. "Well, I want to impress upon you that we do not take sending you and your men into combat lightly. You were hit hard Thursday, and you may not know this, but it was worse for *Yorktown* and *Hornet* – much worse. However, we need your ship-killing torpedoes to sink a crippled battleship and cruiser."

"Yes, sir."

"*Hornet* planes just hit them, and there are no carriers reported."

"Yes, sir."

"Captain Murray and Commander McClusky have assured me that the safety of your planes is paramount, and I've asked them to bring the strike leader here to hear this from me." Next to McClusky, Short nodded his understanding. Laub remained riveted on Spruance.

"Now, listen carefully. After the bombers and fighters finish with these two capital ships and silence their guns, I want you to deliver your torpedoes, but if, and *only* if, there are no antiaircraft guns firing."

"Yes, sir."

Spruance stepped closer to Laub as he brought the palms of his hands together and touched them to his lips. Laub was taken aback by the length of the gray stubble on Spruance's unshaven face. When the admiral lifted his eyes to Laub, a charge of electricity shot through his body.

"Bob, if even *one single gun* is firing, I do not want you and your planes to expose yourself to that fire. If any guns are firing, I want you to turn around and come home." The admiral's blue eyes bored into Laub. They grabbed him and would not let go.

"Yes, sir," Laub said, his head nodding in fear more than understanding.

"I am not going to lose another torpedo plane if I can help it. Do you understand, Lieutenant? *Not one gun.*"

"Yes, sir, Admiral. Not one gun."

"The decision is removed from your shoulders," Spruance added before he turned to Short. "Lieutenant, do *you* have questions about this guidance?"

"No, sir. Not one gun, and if we see any, we'll direct Bob – Lieutenant Laub – away. We won't lose any more torpedo planes, sir. We'll watch out for 'em."

Spruance nodded. "Very well then. Thanks for coming, and good hunting out there. Dismissed."

With another gentle smile, Spruance again extended his hand to Laub and Short. Laub reminded him of his own son Edward, out there on the submarine *Tambor*. How Spruance wished he knew of his whereabouts and safety.

The pilots left the shelter. As McClusky and Murray followed, Spruance stopped them.

"Commander, Captain Murray, a moment please."

McClusky and Murray stepped back to him as Browning stood nearby, listening.

"Was that clear enough?"

"Yes, sir," Murray answered. "You left no doubt, and if they don't go in, no one will accuse them of cowardice."

McClusky nodded his concurrence. "Admiral, after what happened Thursday, these boys are displaying courage by simply going back out there." Next to Spruance, Browning nodded his agreement.

"What if the Japanese launch a float plane at them?" Spruance asked.

A slight grin crossed McClusky's face. "Sir, that would be more of a fair fight, but we'll have fighters on top of them. No float plane is going to get anywhere close."

Spruance nodded. He'd done all he could.

"Thank you, gentlemen. Dismissed."

The first *Wildcat* jumped into the air, Laub's signal that the launch had started.

The mechanics had checked the TBD engines yesterday and this morning. As they listened from the catwalk, all three purred their readiness to go. The canvas-covered empennages and aluminum wings had their bullet holes patched with cloth and glue and rivets.

Another fighter lifted off, then another.

Next to Laub, Jamie Morris sat in his cockpit, watching the launch progress. In the ready room before takeoff, he had asked to take one of the gunners who was left out Thursday as an observer in his middle seat. The new guy, barely eighteen, was embarrassed he had been left behind. *C'mon Bob, he really wants to go.* Laub had shaken his head no. Not going to risk anyone for no reason. When Morris pressed him to reconsider, Laub snarled his answer. *No!* No time for hurt feelings. From what Laub could see, there'd be plenty of war left for the kid. Besides, he was the CO now, and COs made these decisions.

The SBDs rolled down the deck and disappeared off the end before they lifted back into view and cleared right. The *Dauntlesses* spotted in front of him belched oily smoke as it idled in wait. Another SBD gunned its engine and taxied into position. Between the jammed-together planes, Laub discerned the launch officer's flag in wild motion as the bomber revved his engine. When the flag disappeared, the bomber rolled forward, the guttural sound of its pistons at full power building and then fading as it rolled to the end of *Enterprise* and into the clear Pacific air.

Laub and Radioman Humphrey waited for their turn. "Humphrey, ready to go?"

"Yes, sir, Skipper."

Laub wasn't used to that. Commander Lindsey was the CO. But he was dead – Laub had seen him die. Allowing himself to be called *Skipper* didn't seem right.

The pack forward of them opened up as more SBDs lifted off while others taxied into position. Overhead the VF was joined. On the horizon, *Hornet* recovered her planes, just returned from where Laub was going.

The director motioned him up as plane pushers scurried clear with the wheel chocks. Taxiing ahead, he noticed them – the gunners in the catwalks and the deck crew along the edge. They watched Laub in somber awareness as he inched his big TBD forward. They all stopped to watch, to give their silent support and hopes and prayers that the old planes and the men in them would return. All were at risk. Every time a plane took off and went over the horizon was a risk. Some didn't come back. Loss happened…pretty much every time underway. However, with the silent stares of the men, Laub sensed a difference.

As the last dive-bomber cleared the bow, the director stopped Laub just forward of the aft elevator. What Laub saw on the island amazed him.

Every gallery was jammed with men, all of them looking aft – at him. Some were witnessing history. Others, human courage. Others, a suicide. Some were just compelled to watch, to see it for themselves. No *vulture's row* audience was ever this big, and, after Thursday, the whole ship knew what the torpedo men were risking. *Enterprise* pitched gently in the swells as her bow lifted above the western horizon for a moment then settled back down to reveal the blue sea in a steady rhythm. Signal flags fluttered stiff from the halyards. Laub contemplated the blue, rubber stained deck ahead of him, the lighter blue sky above, the hundreds of men on the island and in the catwalks, all of their faces focused on him. He'd never forget this moment. Humbling. No, *exhilarating*.

When the Launch Officer pointed at him and waved his flag, Laub held the brakes as he pushed the throttle forward, his plane straining and bucking, waiting to be set free. Oil, RPM, manifold pressure – holding in limits.

Laub focused on the launch officer, who continued to listen to the engine. He glanced up at Laub and nodded.

As the officer lunged and pointed forward, Laub released the brakes.

His TBD jumped ahead as it – and the torpedo it carried – rolled across the timbers to gain flying speed. Above and to his right Laub felt the eyes on him, hundreds of them – still – watching and contemplating the two men in the antique bomber going to do battle. For them and every man on the ship, and every man and woman at home.

Passing by the bridge, Laub fought the urge to look up, but sensed the captain and the Air Officer. They were up there looking down on them as they rolled past, he knew it. Maybe even the kindly admiral. *If there is even one gun…*

His tail came off as the bow lifted above the horizon, the deck edge under his cowl. With his left arm locked, Laub held forward pressure in anticipation of his transition to airborne flight. As he approached the end, the last sailor on the port catwalk offered Laub and Humphrey a little wave, the only man who did. His hands full, Laub cocked his head and smiled before he returned his attention to flying.

He bunted toward the waves as he got the gear up, and his heavy *Devastator* accelerated slowly. Gaining precious airspeed, he stopped his descent and began a climb to the right.

Laub reversed left to initiate the rendezvous turn, climbing as he did. Over his shoulder, he found Morris already airborne ahead of the ship and watched Mueller roll along the deck and into the air. Laub went about his post takeoff checks as he held an easy turn abeam *Enterprise*. *The Big E*, radiant in the late morning sunlight, dominated the deep blue water that stretched to the horizon in all directions as it rode majestically west toward the enemy. Above her, the fighters and dive-bombers circled overhead, waiting for the torpeckers. They watched and waited for the six bravest men on the ship to join them.

With his two wingmen aboard, Laub lined up his formation on the ship's port side so all who watched them off could see the three TBDs of Torpedo Six head out with the others in the group to attack the enemy.

Hundreds of men in the galleries and on the flight deck paid silent homage as they did.

Chapter 40

USS *Hornet*, 1100 June 6, 1942

Mitscher paced the bridge wing as the *Enterprise* planes circled over their ship while his own planes circled over *Hornet*, waiting to land. He clenched his teeth; George Murray had his TBDs up. Mitscher had none left, and that stark truth grated on him. That the *Enterprise* torpedo bombers could still fly out toward the enemy was a personal failure.

Yesterday, a flying boat had picked up one of Johnny's pilots, a wounded ensign who had spent a night on the open ocean in his raft. Maybe more were out there and would be rescued in the coming days. He hoped Waldron was among them. He was told the pilot's name: Ensign Gay. Soucek said he was a tall fellow, from Texas. Mitscher still couldn't place the man. Another personal failure. Soucek approached him.

"Cap'n, we're ready to bring 'em down now. All the VF are back, but we're missin' two bombers."

Mitscher shook his head. Another four men dead or missing. "Anything from Stanhope? Why hasn't he reported? Or is he one of the two?"

"Sir, we'll know in a few more minutes."

Mitscher nodded. "Yes. Signal Charlie."

"Aye, aye, sir," Soucek said and turned to return to Pri Fly. In the bridge behind him, Mitscher heard the Officer of the Deck give orders to the helm, which were repeated and then executed at once. *I give orders and must wait three damned hours,* Mitscher thought.

Stanhope. If he was in one of the planes overhead, he had some explaining to do, and for more than the two missing SBDs. No updated position course and speed, no amplifying report of ship types. He had a damned radio transmitter, and so did his wingmen. Mitscher had been unable to offer Spruance anything in the past hour. The *Enterprise* planes went out like his did hours ago, into the unknown.

Mitscher took his position on the port wing as his planes circled in order, fighters first. The pilots seemed subdued as they taxied over the barrier toward the bow. No clenched fists of victory, no broad smiles. Just another routine patrol.

The *Dauntlesses* let down into the circle, and Mitscher watched the first one turn off the abeam and slide toward the LSO, a little slow and wrapped up. *C'mon now, easy with the rudder there.* The LSO gave the cut signal, and the SBD settled to the deck with a bounce. The hook snagged the cable as the hook runner ran toward it. Free, the pilot gunned the engine as the next plane approached the ramp.

Taxiing past him, the pilot lifted his head to the bridge and gave a thumbs-up. It was Ring. Mitscher waved his hand to acknowledge him, but why the thumbs-up? What had happened? Two planes missing. Did they sink the two ships? He looked across the bridge toward *Enterprise.* Their planes were already headed to the southwest, and he *still* had nothing to relay.

One after another, the SBDs trapped aboard. Once free of the cable, they quickly taxied ahead to make room for the next. They were clean. *Thank goodness.* Must have attacked something. Mitscher kept his eye on Ring as he deplaned behind the fighters. *Get up here, Stan.*

Ring met with his pilots as they deplaned, discussing the flight as they talked with their hands, discussions Mitscher wanted to hear. Ring went from one to the other, shouting to be heard over the loud idling of the radial engines around them. Mitscher exhaled through his nose.

"Apollo, get Ring up here on the double," Mitscher growled.

"Aye, aye, sir!"

Ring stepped onto the bridge wing. "Commander Ring reporting as ordered, sir."

Mitscher turned from watching the flight deck activity.

"Stan, how'd it go? I haven't heard from you."

Ring expressed surprise. "Sir? I radioed a report, several of them. We found a cruiser and battleship and attacked both. Got a few hits and lots of paint-scrapers."

"And lost two bombers."

"Yes, sir. Their ack-ack was good, quite heavy."

"Who were they?"

"Two ensigns, sir – one was from *Enterprise.*"

"Names," Mitscher asked with an edge.

Ring realized the conversation had taken a turn. "Ensign Griswold sir, from Scouting Eight. The name of the *Enterprise* pilot escapes me for the moment, but I'll get it and send it up at once."

"I want to get that information over to *Enterprise* immediately."

"Aye, aye, sir."

Mitscher looked away toward the horizon, eyes narrowed, jaw set. Ring sensed trouble.

"Captain, I called the ship with reports. I never got a reply, but I figured you were in radio silence."

"I received no word from you, and our radios have worked fine all morning."

Ring had no answer. "No excuse, sir, except that maybe my plane's radio is malfunctioning. I'll have the men look at it."

"Yes. Now go below and get that man's name, and the gunner's name. Get it to the Comm Officer ASAP. We're probably going again this afternoon."

"Yes, sir. We'll put 'em on the bottom this time."

Mitscher faced Ring.

"Stan, sit this one out. Your plane is broken, and you've been going hard at it the past three days. Give one of your squadron COs a crack at leading."

"Cap'n, I'll get another plane. We can…"

"Stan, no. I said no. Give it to Walt Rodee. All the VB and VS we can muster."

Stung, a tight-lipped Ring nodded. "Aye, aye, sir."

"Get that name."

"Aye, aye, sir. By your leave, sir," Ring said. He popped a salute.

"Dismissed," Mitscher said as he returned it. Ring departed through the bridge to the ladder. As he did, Mitscher thought of Waldron's face at this very spot two days ago.

He practically begged me, and I told him no.

Laub picked up the smoke trailing from a capital ship off to the left, and the low silhouettes of her attending escorts on the horizon. The dive-bombers had ramped down to begin their dives, and a flight of *Wildcats* made lazy S-turns above to keep Laub's three TBDs in sight. With unlimited visibility, he scanned the horizon to the west and north. Clear.

Oddly, the SBDs pressed ahead to the west.

Maintaining a healthy distance from the ships, Laub could only follow Short and the other *Dauntlesses* high above. They appeared as little more than dots in a ragged echelon of vee formations. He scanned the horizon. With good visibility, the ships stood out on it like a man on a ridgeline. No other Jap ships, but Short continued on. Laub kept a wary eye on the little Japanese flotilla, four of them, one wounded, and, if Short returned, helpless.

After ten minutes had passed, the SBDs entered an wide turn to the left. Laub couldn't catch up to them and stay safe. He reversed back to the right. They would all converge on the enemy ships, still in view, and now coming at them.

Animated radio chatter from the leads directed traffic as the VB set up for their dives. No fighter threat, and only four ships – two of them big but damaged and moving at a moderate speed. At 1,500 feet, Laub rolled out on a heading to keep him a safe distance north.

Guns flashed from the enemy vessels, and black puffs appeared over them. The bombers spotted, Laub noted with pride that his friends didn't flinch or drift away from one another.

Confusion on the radio. *"Wally, this is Dave. I'll take the cruiser to the northeast."* The bomber pilots bickered over who was supposed to follow who. Laub recognized Short's voice: *"Step on it, dammit! Are we gonna attack or not? C'mon up here...the rear ship."* Behind Laub, Humphrey slapped the side of the TBD with his hand.

"There they go!"

From three miles away, Laub and the others watched the VS and VB dive on the Japanese ships. *How do they do it, straight down their throats,* Laub wondered. One after another they slid down an imaginary string toward the target. The heavy AA burst behind them. Wrong altitude set. Laub watched in horror as Short continued down. *Is he going to make it? Pull up!*

When Short began his pull off, a fearful Laub sensed it was too late. As the SBD was about to hit the water, it climbed away from it. A bright mushroom of fire blossomed amidships as it did.

"Whoa-ho!" Humphrey cried.

Another hit. More flame and smoke, and the ship's giant smokestack lifted off and fell into the water with a huge splash. A massive cloud of black and gray smoke boiled up from the superstructure.[1]

The radio was alive. *"Did you see that fuckin' thing explode? Choke on it, Tojo, you bastard! Look at that son of a bitch burn!"*

More bombers dove on the lead ship, more hits. *"That battlewagon is finished! Go for the cruiser and the cans!"*

---

[1] HIJMS *Mikuma*

Laub could only watch, could only assess the defensive fire. The trailing ship had stopped as flames poured from the superstructure. More bombers dove, and great waterspouts of seawater erupted alongside the lead cruiser. One bomb hit square on the stern. Above, the *Wildcats* peeled off to strafe what they could. An excited SBD pilot mistakenly transmitted for all to hear. *"That scared the hell out of me! I thought we weren't gonna pull out!"*

The six torpedomen waited for the SBDs and F4Fs to finish. Of the two targets, Laub liked their chances with the trailing ship, a battleship by the size of it, with a high prow and three turrets forward. From the bridge aft it was a flaming wreck, dead in the water. The escorting destroyers laid off on the other side, firing in a vain effort to defend it. Laub looped his finger in the air to signal Morris and Mueller. *We're gonna extend, reverse right 180, and look.*

The bombers were done, still whooping it up on the radio, pilots wishing they had another bomb and sounding like kids at a carnival. Some of the formations were already joined as they headed east for home. Laub rolled easy right to put the trailing ship on his nose.

"Bob from Wally. How does it look?"

Laub pressed his throat microphone. "Taking us in… You have us in sight?"

"Yep, gotcha. Jim, you have 'em?"

"Got 'em," the Fighting Six CO answered. "We're comin' back and will escort from overhead."

"Great. Anyone skosh on fuel?" Short asked. No one answered.

The burning battleship crossed over Laub's cowling as he turned, descending his little formation as he did. Laub held the target on his left canopy bow.

A muzzle flash forward, a small automatic. Seconds later, a stitch of spray off Laub's left wing, spray that walked toward the TBDs as Laub veered right to avoid it. The destroyers to the south were no factor, and the cruiser was now on his nose. The ship burned hard, the fantail a smoking mess. Now inside two miles, Laub approached it, but the angle off was too shallow. As he veered away to increase range, an automatic gun fired from somewhere inside the cloud of smoke on the fantail. As he continued ahead, more guns sent tracers in Laub's direction.

He reversed to take another look at the trailing ship, this time trying the starboard quarter. The setup took time. Took fuel. Laub had enough for one more look. He signalled to the others and turned away.

"Whaddaya think, Bob?" Short asked on the radio.

"Lemme try one more. Gonna take us a few minutes." Laub answered. To the east, the SBDs and *Wildcats* headed back to the ship. Short's division stayed with the TBDs. Torpedo Six would not be abandoned.

After five minutes, Laub rolled them back to the trailing ship – wallowing and smoking – and again approached it from starboard. It had a list, and Laub noted several turret gun barrels pointed askew in the air. Amidships was a charred hulk, an open pit from which thick smoke trailed above sheets of roiling flame. The smoke was thickest aft, and Laub chose the starboard quarter as an aimpoint. Three fish would finish her for sure. He signaled the others to take trail.

The men sensed this was the last gasp of the TBD as a front-line combat plane. Five years ago, it was what all the cadets wanted to fly. Now it was old and obsolete, unsuitable for this new way of war that emphasized *speed*. More than for the plane, Laub wanted to release his fish into the side of this Jap for Tom, and XO Ely, and the Skipper.

His heart sank when two automatic guns fired from the spot he had targeted. *How could anyone breathe in that inferno, much less fire a gun?*

He eased away from the smoking derelict and transmitted. "Wally from Bob. Unable today."

"Concur, Bob, you guys did yer best. Let's steer zero-seven-zero. We'll stay with you. Right now I'm at yer four o-clock high. Jus' keep yer turn in."

Laub acknowledged him and set a course for home. They had failed. Their last chance. Gone. Forever.

Once established on course, Laub signalled Mueller to cross under to his left. With a TBD on each wing, he signalled them to prepare to jettison their Mk-13s. Over his shoulder, the Japanese smoked and flashed. It couldn't be helped. *If there is even one gun...*

"Humphrey, I'm gonna jettison our fish."

"Yes, sir, Mister Laub. Too bad."

Laub clenched his fist and made a motion aft, then yanked up on the jettison lever. His plane lurched up as one ton of weight fell free. He glanced at both wingmen in time to see their torpedoes fall away into the waiting Pacific.

In the landing circle, Laub took interval on an SBD. He wondered if it would be his last carrier landing in the *Devastator*.

Gear down, flaps down, hook down. Level at sixty feet, he held it just above stall and slid toward the wake. The LSO showed him a roger pass.

Crossing the ramp, he took his cut and trapped. "Nice one, Skipper," Humphrey said.

And there they were, hundreds of men on vulture's row and the flight deck catwalks. Smiles and cheers. Applause. They pointed at the empty torpedo stations thinking Laub and his wingmen had scored hits against the Jap ships. Had the spectators even left?

They parked and chocked him abeam the bridge as Morris and Mueller chugged up behind. Busy with post-landing checks, Laub was surprised when the maintenance chief jumped up on the wing and slapped his back.

"Mister Laub, you got 'em, didn't you!"

Laub wished he could give the chief what he wanted. Validation. Revenge. An answer full of bravado. *Hell, yeah, we sent the yellow bastards to the bottom!* But he couldn't.

"We tried, Chief, but the ack-ack was too hot. Had to jettison the fish. We tried."

The chief's face fell, but only a little.

"That's okay, Skipper! We're just glad you fellas are back safe."

The chief stepped down the wing and clapped Humphrey on the back. Looking up to his right, Laub caught sight of the admiral on the port gallery.

The admiral smiled at him.

CHAPTER 41

BOMBING EIGHT, 1430 JUNE 6, 1942

Fisher marveled at the visibility. From 13,000 feet, he could see smoke from the Japanese ahead and his own Task Force Sixteen ships behind him. They were now less than 100 miles apart.

In the lead formation, Skipper Rodee led thirteen of his Scouting Eight SBDs. Trailing them, Fisher and Ferguson were in the first division of XO Tucker's Bombing Eight.

Holding his place in echelon, Fisher took peeks at the enemy ships. One, attended by destroyers, wallowed dead in the water, smoke trailing for miles. Another large ship was off by itself, giving off some smoke and moving slowly. Fisher took in all of it with confidence. The Americans owned the skies. There was nothing to fear until he and the others opened their dive-brakes and pushed over into that ring of fire.

He very much wanted to score a hit, even if on a helpless sitting duck that smoked from bow to stern. Skipper Rodee came up on the radio.

"Gus, we've got the smoker. You take the other big one to the northwest."

"Wilco, Walt."

"Abbie, split up your divisions at your discretion."

"Got it," Tucker answered. "We'll follow you on the battleship. Fred, you've got the one to the northwest."

Rodee transmitted again. "And get the tin cans if able."

Fisher was confused. *Who* was going to get the destroyers? He put it out of his mind and flew wing. He wanted a big target, especially after yesterday's futility.

Rodee led his planes to the smoking battleship, while Tucker circled his squadron around to the west to come out of the sun. *They see us,* Fisher thought, as water churned behind the destroyers, desperate to escape the coming onslaught near the battleship. He focused on the burning ship. Rafts. Rafts near the stern. *They're abandoning.*

The scout undersides turned red as they opened their dive-brakes. Moments later, the first one, Rodee, pushed over.

The burning ship resembled a barge of twisted and blackened junk metal. On its bow and stern, automatics opened up – *amazing* – and an escaping destroyer also fired. Black puffs of antiaircraft exploded across the circle from Fisher. The first division boys were in their dives on the helpless derelict while Fisher waited.

A hit lifted a massive piece of debris over 1,000 feet into the air. Shouts and whoops on the radio. Nearing the ship, Fisher saw men in the water next to it. Dozens of them. *Did they jump when they saw us?*

Another half ton of explosive tore into the flaming and smoking pit, and another black and gray mushroom cloud climbed high, accompanied by more excited cries. Fisher tried to keep his eyes on Lieutenant Lynch next to him and not the drama two miles below. He couldn't help it though, the scene held him, and his mind harked back to late summer bonfires in the field. Another explosion wracked the ship and pelted men in the water with steel debris.

The smaller cruiser was getting it from Mister Widhelm's division. They dove into another funnel of tracers and popping flashbulbs of shells along their flight paths.

The scouts were off west, some making strafing runs on the cans and having a real day of it. Fisher assessed the inferno below. The bow and stern were all that resembled a warship. On Tucker's signal, they opened their dive-brakes. Holding on to Lynch, Fisher looked under his tail at the dying ship – and the struggling men, hundreds of them, next to it.

I can't do it.

The XO was in, followed a count later by Don, then Joe. Fisher was armed up, low blower, pitch set. He was ready. In seconds he and Ferguson would be in again on a Jap ship, this one prostrate before them, with Jap sailors jumping from it to take their chances in the sea. *What if I'm short?*

Lynch pushed over as a geyser erupted along the port side, where the Japs struggled for their lives. The ship's weak tracer fire swept underneath the diving SBDs, way off the mark. Crossfire from the retreating destroyer arced through their flight paths, over the XO and Don, over the terrified men treading water beneath them. Fisher held his dive for a count, a long count. *I have to do this!*

Impatient and frustrated, Fisher warned Ferguson as he pushed down, scooping his nose to aim at the ship's pointed prow. As he did, an explosion covered it; yellow and red flame blossomed from an area forward of the Number 1 turret before it turned to black and brown smoke. More whoops on the radio.

I can't!

"Ferguson, this one's done, we're going for the can!"

"Yes, sir!"

Fisher repositioned his nose on a destroyer that fired at Lynch, who pulled off from his delivery. He had *saved* Fisher from committing murder, had spoiled his aim point. It was easier now. Fisher wanted to hit a ship – not kill helpless men.

Not yet aware Fisher had selected it, the destroyer increased speed.[1] The angle was shallow – glide bombing run. He felt slow and closed his dive-brakes. As the brakes retracted, his *Dauntless* lunged forward at the tin can, and the ship saw him coming.

Tracers from the stern and port side amidships rose toward Fisher in familiar slow motion. Their streams oscillated, fired by frantic gunners – scared kids like those in the water. *Like me!* In fear, they watched Fisher's dark shape grow larger. It was a duel to the death now, with hundreds of tiny projectiles floating toward a single plane with two men carrying one giant projectile that could kill dozens. That could kill a ship.

Fisher *would* kill them, *the Japs,* their fire ineffective, his dive angle steady. He was sure of it. *Cold blood.*

The destroyer turned toward him – not yet fast enough to escape. They didn't have a chance, but more of a chance than those poor bastards behind him next to a sinking and exploding hulk.

The ship's bridge wing filled his bombsight. Men stood on it, their faces facing him. *Jap officers!* Outside, tracers snapped the air among excited words on the radio. Riveted on his target, he ignored them. As if in a trance, he tracked the ship through the water. Oh yes, he would kill.

With a flick of his thumb, 1,000 pounds fell away as he yanked the plane up and overbanked right. Looking down the wing line, he noted the white rooster tail of the destroyer as it sprinted away from danger, its deck crammed with men who huddled close. Too late.

An explosion aft covered the stern with smoke and flame and white spray. *A hit!* He rolled out and pushed down to the waves, gaining airspeed as he did, his senses sharp and in total control of everything around him. A string of tracers floated off and dove into the sea in ordered sequence. The tracers missed. Again they missed.

"We got a hit, sir!"

---

[1] HIJMS *Arashio*

"Open fire!"

No sooner had the words left Fisher's lips than Ferguson opened up on the enemy ship. He sprayed it with a long burst, a release of pent-up tension and repressed fear. His way of contributing. Clear of the ship's light guns and out of range, Ferguson's machine gun shells would only bounce off the thin hull plates – if they could even reach the destroyer. Fisher heard Ferguson shriek with laughter, and the firing stopped.

The formations rendezvoused: all accounted for. The triumphant kids in each windswept cockpit smiled at each other and passed their thumbs-up signals in exultation and relief. Sensing there would be no more attacks today, they flew back to *Hornet* without a care. Within minutes, they saw her in the distance as fate smiled upon them this hour. They would take their good fortune and make the most of it. Tomorrow would come quickly.

Clay Fisher reveled in his hit. Retribution for those lost. Payback in his own small way. He could go home now as an equal to the graying doughboys of the Great War, having seen the elephant as they had.

Fisher held position on Lynch without thinking, his mind on the men he had just seen. Japanese ships had been shooting at him for three days, but today he had seen them as men. Orientals, but men. Like him. Up close, through his bombsight, and with his own eyes, he had seen them as they thrashed about in the water. Afraid. Dying. His bomb hitting a vital area or springing the hull plates of that burning battleship may have finished her. He pulled up, almost by reflex. Rash impulse or right decision? Lynch would surely ask him why when they got back. *I couldn't bring myself...*

He looked back over his shoulder. Smoke from the battle rose high above the enemy ships, and Fisher knew he would never forget the image.

Spruance *still* lacked a clear understanding of what his planes had done.

Was it a cruiser or a battleship? Or two cruisers? More? His returning fliers said there were two *groups* of ships, and *Hornet's* reports offered little clarification. The two *Yorktown* lieutenants now leading his planes differed on what they had both seen just an hour ago, and a camera in one plane had fogged up, making the film useless. Even the reports of his cruiser floatplanes that had bird-dogged the Japanese since midmorning were unclear. At least his three TBDs were back safe, but they hadn't dropped, as the Japanese still had means to resist. He needed detailed answers, now.

Browning suggested a plan. "Admiral, we can send a photo recon mission and have photos in your hands by sunset."

"Please see to it," Spruance replied.

Soon after, word came down to the Bombing Six ready room that a plane was needed to escort a Scouting Six SBD to photograph the burning Japanese ships. The duty officer turned to Kroeger, sitting in his high-back chair.

"Bud, they need a plane to escort the scouts on a photo recon of the Jap ships. Want it?"

"Sure," Kroeger said. "I'll get word to Halterman next door."

"Ah…no. You're gonna take a civilian. That guy from Movietown News, older fellow."

"*What!*" Kroeger exclaimed. "This is still combat. I'm not takin' any civilian on a sightseeing tour!"

"Bud, it's from above, and we're tapped out of pilots. But maybe I can scrounge one if you can't."

Kroeger hadn't flown yet and was the de facto squadron Executive Officer. This mission called for a veteran pilot, not a newbie ensign with a civilian newsreel operator.

Kroeger frowned as he got up to check with the *Sails* next door. "I'll take it, for cryin' out loud."

He entered the Scouting Six ready room. Many of the pilots who had flown on the last strike were still there. They had red lines on their foreheads, evidence of hours under their cloth helmets. Dusty Kleiss gulped down a paper cup of water as Kroeger entered.

"Hello, Bud. What can we do for Bombing Six?"

"Dusty, who's flying this add-on photo hop?"

"I think Cleo Dobson. *Hey, Dobby!*"

From the chart next to the chalkboard, the tall pilot walked down the aisle. "Yeah? Hey, Bud."

"Cleo, you goin' on this photo add-on?" Kroeger asked him.

"Yep. You goin' too?"

Kroeger nodded. "Yeah, just got word I'm going with you, and I'll have that Movietown guy with me."

"Okay, good. I've got a Chief Photo Mate. The bridge wants to know what's out there, so we'll get some brownies of them."

"Dusty, were you just there?" Kroeger asked.

"Yeah, two big boys, but cruisers, one heavy and one light. Your guys think one is a battleship, but the beam is too narrow. And two small boys in escort."

"You nail 'em?"

"Sure did. You guys put a bunch of bombs on the heavy cruiser, and we followed. It was a flaming wreck when we left."

"Flak?"

"Oh yeah, and heavy when we got there. *Hornet* had just left when we showed up, so they were ready for us. But we all made it."

"Easy to find?" Dobson asked.

"Easy. About two-six-zero and no more than a hun'erd miles. You'll see the oil slick as soon as you get to altitude. It's huge."

Kroeger and Dobson thanked Kleiss. Around them, excited aviators angled to go back. Seeking quiet, Kroeger led Dobson out into the passageway to talk.

"All right, Cleo, you're the scout pilot. I'll fly on your wing with my movie guy."

Dobson nodded. "Okay. We'll join overhead and go out there at about ten or so. We'll see what kind of reception they have for us and work our way in." He then lowered his voice.

"My fixed guns are ready, and I'm tellin' ya right now, I'm gonna strafe the bastards. Even if they're in the water. They shoot us in rafts and behead our guys... So, I'm gonna give 'em a taste. Same treatment they gave to the poor guys on *Langley* in the Java Sea."

Kroeger leaned in and looked up at Dobson. "Cleo, you better not. I've got a civilian."

"That old codger ain't gonna say a thing, an' he can barely see as it is. After we get the pictures, you can come back here if you want to, but I'm stayin'."

Time was short, and they had to man up for launch. And Kroeger had to meet his passenger. With luck he'd flown in an SBD before. Anything.

"Cleo, be smart."

"They told me to!"

"Who told you?"

"People senior to *you*. Anyway, you're warned, Bud. Go back alone when we're done. I'll be along shortly."

Disgusted, Kroeger turned for his own ready room.

You're gonna be sorry, Cleo.

Chapter 42

Over HIJMS *Mikuma*, 1730 June 6, 1942

As the wrecked warship listed to port, smoke seeped out from the length of it to form a thin gray curtain. To Kroeger, it reminded him of a veil a lady would use to cover her head at church.

The ship was more of a burned-out hulk, abandoned by the others, still visible as they steamed off to the west. Kroeger assessed them at twenty miles, a larger ship between two small boys, all trailing smoke.

With Dobson in the lead, they circled the doomed vessel, easing closer as they watched for gunfire.

"Are you gettin' this, sir?" Kroeger asked on the interphone.

The newsreel man, Mr. Brick, didn't answer. Kroeger twisted in his seat to check on him. Brick waved back as he continued to film the scene. The gentleman must be the oldest man aboard; two gunners had to help him up the wing, over the gunwale, and into the seat. The rear seat was a tight fit even for a young radioman. Kroeger returned his scan to the smoldering ship. *At least the old coot can hear me.* In Dobson's plane, the chief snapped photo after photo from his bulky camera.

Dobson circled away and descended below 500 feet. Approaching the ship from the port side, Kroeger slid to the outside to keep Dobson and the ship in view.

"Can you get closer?" Brick shouted.

He doesn't know where the switch is. Kroeger answered him on the interphone.

"Sorry, sir. We hafta stay here in formation."

"Okay, just asking!" he shouted back.

Dobson flew them down the port side, the chief clicking away. Dozens of men clustered on the fantail, some waving, and in the water near the stern, more men waved. *Do they think we're Japanese?* Kroeger thought. The men who bobbed in the water were covered with a thick sheen of oil, their heads black. No lifeboats were in sight, and the superstructure was a maze of blackened scrap metal. Kroeger guessed this ship would soon sink, and, with their mates retreating west and night approaching, he imagined the Japs were goners.

Dobson veered away from Kroeger as he entered a shallow climb – then turned back.

Don't do it, Cleo.

Dobson accelerated toward the ship. An hour ago, he had said he was going to strafe the Japs in the water like the Japanese had the Americans – *murder* them – the same helpless men who now waved at their American enemy in human kinship. *We're abandoned and dying. Please help us!* A spark on the water would light off the dark slick the ship stewed in, immolating the men and reigniting fires on the aft end of the ship. Maybe these men had killed the *Hornet* guys lost in the morning. But it was different now that they had no means to fight back, no way to escape. An ordinary wave served as their white flag of surrender.

Dobson pushed his nose down toward them. Kroeger's heartrate increased. *Cleo, don't.*

Was he really going to do it, now, with a civilian in the back seat recording it? Good grief! The men were going to die, but did it have to be Cleo – *and with me as an accomplice* – who'd slaughter them in a hellish and fiery death?

Kroeger had his thumb on the radio transmitter. It was just the four of them. Who would ever know? Would the geezer in back say anything? *They're all but dead anyway. Why not* put 'em out of their misery now and get a sense of satisfaction doing it? Maybe one of them would survive and tell the tale of American ruthlessness. A warning to the rest. You want a fight? You've got one! Maybe just one would live to tell it.

Thou shalt not kill.

Dobson veered left and leveled off as he flew along the port side again, the chief snapping away as before, with the sunlight to his back. The only hull paint that wasn't blackened was up on the prow, a dark gray. Most of the ship was charred molten slag: twisted steel frozen in grotesque shapes, revealing little of its original construction or purpose.

Dobson signaled for throttle and a climb. Kroeger stayed with him and gave Mr. Brick as update.

"That's it, sir. We're headin' back."

"Okay! Got some great footage!"

"Good, sir," Kroeger replied, glad they were done.

He took another look behind his wing at the smoking ship. *Cleo didn't shoot the poor devils.* Relieved, Kroeger settled in for the short flight back. He sensed this battle was over.

"Sir, got some bad news. The Japs got a sub in the screen and torpedoed *Yorktown*."

Spruance absorbed the words from his trusted lieutenant. Oliver stood before him in sorrow as he held the message. *I'm very sorry, Admiral.* Standing next to Spruance at the chart table, Browning shook his head in disgust.

"Very well. Thanks, Oliver," Spruance said.

"A destroyer too, sir. *Hammann.* It was alongside providing power. One fish cut her in half, and the other hit the carrier on the starboard side."

"Both sunk?"

"Nothing about *Yorktown*, but *Hammann*, yes sir."

A deflated Spruance nodded his understanding and studied the chart. A submarine got in the screen. How far were they from the salvage effort? On the chart he measured with his fingers…about 400 miles. A submarine between him and Fletcher, and there could be others. *Sara* was torpedoed east of Hawaii. *Just let your guard down for a moment…*

"Miles, when do we expect our reconnaissance flight back?"

Browning looked at his watch. "Should be twenty minutes, sir."

"Good. Get this word to the task force: sub attack northeast of Midway. Gotta keep our lookouts alert."

"Yes, sir. Do you want to continue pursuit, sir?"

Spruance looked at the chart again as he formed his answer.

"I'm inclined to recover everything and retire east unless TF-16 or CINC-PAC directs otherwise. We need to refuel, and everybody is exhausted. I can see it in their eyes."

And yours, sir, Oliver thought.

Browning pointed to the chart. "And Wake's up ahead. We're pressin' it, yes, sir."

"Concur. For now, let's recover them and turn northeast to the tanker rendezvous. Antisubmarine posture… Fifteen-knot advance should be sufficient."

"Aye, aye, Admiral." Browning said. Since yesterday's shouting match with the pilots, their relationship had been professional and cordial. Regardless, Spruance wasn't going to have Browning on his staff again. Wouldn't stand for it.

"And I want those pilots up here as soon as they land."

"Aye, aye, Admiral, I'll see to it."

Off the flight deck and inside the island, Dobson and Kroeger searched for the ladder to take them to the flag shelter.

The flight deck officer had met them when they stepped off their wings. The chief and Mr. Brick took their cameras below so the Photo Mates could develop the film.

"Ever been up here before, Bud?"

"No, but I think this is the ladder."

Kroeger led them up. Yes, the right one.

Once at the flag shelter, the two pilots waited. Oliver walked over to them.

"Recon pilots?"

"Yes, sir," Kroeger answered.

"Great. Did you get photos?"

"We had cameramen," Dobson said.

"Good. Wait here."

As Oliver notified Spruance, the two pilots continued to wait. When Browning stepped out from the windbreak, he leveled his eyes on Kroeger. He had seen Browning from a distance, but his imposing height and icy glare froze Kroeger in place. Spruance appeared and walked up to Dobson.

"Gentlemen, what did you see?"

Dobson answered. "Admiral, we saw a ship dead in the water and burning. There were survivors in the water next to it and a bunch of men on the fantail. To the west, about twenty miles I'd say, were three more ships: two small boys and a larger ship. They were all smokin' and moving west."

"Did it fire at you?"

"No, sir, we didn't see any fire. It's pretty much junk, sir."

"What type of ship was it?"

Dobson smiled. "I don' know sir, but it sure was a big one!"

Spruance's face tightened into a scowl. Kroeger sensed at once they were on dangerous ground.

"I asked what type of ship. Battleship? Heavy cruiser? Light cruiser? Can you tell ship types?"

"Yes, sir."

"Well, what type and class?"

Dobson was sinking fast.

"Sir...I...I don't know. It was pretty tore up. It had turrets forward, I remember that."

Unimpressed at the pilot's answer, Spruance clasped his arms around his chest.

"Do you have recognition cards to help you identify ships?"

"Sir, I, ah, I din't look at 'em."

"Why not?" Spruance shot back, exasperated. "This is important."

"Sir...no excuse, sir."

Spruance struggled to contain himself. He turned to Kroeger.

"And you? Did you reference the cards?"

Kroeger wanted to die.

"No, sir. I forgot them, sir."

Spruance recoiled in disgust. As he stepped back, a volcano built inside his slight frame.

"What squadron are you two in?" an irritated Browning demanded.

"Lieutenant Junior Grade Kroeger, sir. Bombing Six."

"Lieutenant Junior Grade Dobson, sir. Scouting Six."

Spruance pounced on him.

"A *scout* pilot, you say? And you don't recognize ship types?"

Dobson shook with fright. His mouth open, he finally stammered out an answer.

"Sir, I know ours pretty good, just not the enemy all that well."

Stunned at the answer, Spruance's face transformed into a sarcastic sneer. The ensign needed to know this was serious business.

"Not the enemy? Young man, that's why we just sent you! I expect more from my pilots, especially my scout pilots who have been trained to recognize and report ship types accurately. Have you received such training?"

"Yes, sir." Dobson said. He and Kroeger both stood at attention, trembling.

"Then no excuse! Captain Browning, get Captain Murray up here."

"Aye, aye, sir!"

Spruance then turned to Kroeger. The anxious pilot didn't dare lock eyes with him.

"And you, lieutenant? Are you senior here? What's your excuse?"

"No excuse, sir," a raspy-voiced Kroeger replied. He would have preferred diving into Jap antiaircraft to being braced up on the flag shelter.

Spruance grunted and paced a few steps toward the chart table before turning back to the petrified pilots. He'd end their misery.

"I'm disappointed in both of you. *Dismissed!"*

Kroeger turned for the ladder while a panicked Dobson snapped a salute as if jolted by an electric current.

"You men are dismissed. *Go!*" Spruance barked, pointing at the ladder.

Barely able to breathe, Kroeger led them down. He didn't turn back to Dobson or say a word until they reached flight deck level.

Clear of danger, the pilots panted their relief in the passageway. Dobson was white with fear.

"Bud, we're dead. No, I'm dead, and Skipper Gallaher's dead. Oh, my gosh! I'd rather get shot at than go back up there again."

"Yeah, that's what I thought. We best tell Mister Shumway and Short."

"Yeah. Just hope those guys got some photos to save our bacon."

"Yeah. Hey, Cleo, I wanna know... You had your chance out there. Why didn' you strafe those guys like you said you would?"

Dobson fought back tears of frustration. "You know, when I saw them poor bastards in the water – and then wavin' at us – I got chicken-hearted. I couldn' open up on 'em, Bud. I jus' couldn' do it!"

Kroeger put his hand on Dobson's shoulder. The past three days had been rough, and he'd never forget this flight. He hoped that he and Cleo would be friends into old age.

"You did right, Cleo. Ya did right."

CHAPTER 43

USS MONAGHAN, 0455 JUNE 7, 1942

"Childers, wanna see your ship sink?"

Childers propped himself up on his elbows. The crew of *Monaghan* had treated him and Harry well since the rescue; he was in an officer's country stateroom. They'd told him he was lucky they had a surgeon aboard. That he had lost so much blood he'd have died without one. *Monaghan* and the other cans had torn after the Jap sub that torpedoed *Yorktown* the day before. Depth-charged it for hours, but missed. When they got back, they learned that the destroyer alongside *Yorktown* had been cut in half and sank in minutes. *Hammann*, someone said. No warning. Gone in minutes. *You know not the day nor the hour...*

"Yeah, I wanna see," Childers answered. The sailors complied, one man on either side as they hoisted him to his feet and over to the porthole.

Outside, the dawn broke on a glorious Sunday morning. A mile off, *Yorktown's* flight deck caressed the water.

"Holy cow," Childers murmured, spellbound at the sight of his ship on its side.

"Wow, look at that, would ya! She's going," one of them said. *Yorktown's* brown deck timbers formed a wall, like a giant drive-in movie screen in an open field. Rattles and muffled thuds of machinery crashing from inside the ship reached their ears.

"Whoa!" the men exclaimed as the giant tripod mast was torn from its footings. It bounced off the near vertical flight deck before it crashed into the sea and disappeared. Around *Yorktown*, destroyers who had spent the night with her lowered their ensigns to half-staff, paying respects.

The ship settled lower on her port side, not quite capsized, graceful and majestic. Her battle ensign, still at the truck, dipped toward the surface and touched it. *Monaghan* and the other escorts stood off, their crews fascinated yet reverent. *Yorktown's* massive island superstructure now rested on the surface, and the men watched in amazement. Torrents of seawater roared into her uptakes as spray billowed out.

Childers noticed men outside on *Monaghan's* weather decks, each awe-struck at the scene. The carrier floated on its side for a long time in an apron of gurgling froth. When *Monaghan* moved to her starboard, they saw it.

"Look at that! There's where that sub torpedo hit her yesterday!"

None could speak at the sight of *Yorktown's* exposed hull plates and the mortal wound she received when the torpedo caught her at the turn of the bilge. *Yorktown* lay resting as the destroyer men stared in silent wonder.

"How did she last this long?" one muttered. No one answered.

After a moment, she lifted her nose and the men marveled again at her red keel plates and bulbous bow. She settled back for her final plunge. This was it.

USS *Yorktown*, the ship that had held off the Japanese twice in 30 days, fell back on her stern. Her forward flight deck rotated up and cut through the water to create the gallant carrier's last wake.

Childers had a lump in his throat. He *hoped* Wayne was safe someplace, but the near vertical hull signified the end of his home, the home from which he had turned twenty-one. The final resting place of unknown shipmates. *Please, not Wayne.*

With dignity, the great carrier gracefully sank from view. The .50 cal barrels on the bow pointed toward heaven as *Yorktown* slipped into a calm sea that finally covered the starboard forward corner of the flight deck. With barely a wave, she was gone.

A destroyer sounded a long blast, followed by blasts from all three. The deep, vibrating thrum of *Monaghan's* horn filled every space aboard. Men ignored the deafening blare as the small boys paid tribute. Then, silence.

"Wow. We'll never forget *that*," a Pharmacist Mate said.

Speechless at what he had witnessed, Childers didn't move. *Darce. Brazier. Hope they made it.*

One crewman noticed his moist eyes.

"Childers, I'm real sorry. Good ship."

Childers nodded as his chin quivered. "Yes, she was a good ship. Hope my brother made it." The tin can sailors didn't know what to say.

Foam marked the spot where she sank. A destroyer entered and slowly crossed through.

"What's *Balch* doing?" the pharmacist asked. "Like grave robbing, if you ask me."

Childers was grateful for the change in subject and felt *Monaghan's* steam engines speed up and the deck plates vibrate underneath his feet. The Yeoman next to him spoke.

"Looks like we're headin' someplace. Sure hope it's Pearl."

For the first time since they had helped him to the porthole, Childers looked away, knowing that whenever he wanted, he'd be able to replay this memory.

"Thanks, fellas. You can take me back, now."

Spence Lewis knocked twice on *Astoria's* flag cabin door. He heard Fletcher say, *"Enter."*

The admiral stood at his sink in a t-shirt, shaving. He saw Lewis in the mirror.

"Good morning, Spence."

"Good morning, Admiral. I'm here...with bad news," Lewis said, closing the door behind him.

Fletcher ran water over his razor and set it down. He dabbed his face with a towel to remove the shaving cream.

"Okay. Whatcha got?"

"Sir, *Yorktown* sank."

Fletcher frowned as he absorbed the news. "Figured she couldn't last. When?"

"Thirty minutes ago. Got a message from Elliott in *Balch*."

Fletcher picked up his khaki shirt and pulled it across his shoulders.

"Are COMINCH, CINCPAC, and TF-16 info addees?"

"Not COMINCH, sir, but Nimitz and Spruance, yes."

Fletcher buttoned his starched shirt, wrinkled from wear.

"COMINCH knows.[1] Expect I'll be answering for it at Main Navy."

"Admiral, it was bad luck they found us twice and not TF-16."

"Was it bad luck a Jap sub got inside the screen?"

Lewis didn't know how to answer. The kids on the small boys had let their guard down. Their commander was responsible for it.

"Sir, she was damaged from last month. We had to abandon her or risk more losses."

Fletcher opened his trousers to tuck in his shirt.

"I know, I know. We made the best decision we could with the info we had. In hindsight, we should have stayed with the whole force to bolster the screen." He buckled his web belt, making sure that the gold tip showed. Straight gig line. Decades of habit.

---

[1] ADM E.J. King

"Admiral, you're still in command. Spruance is refueling, and *Saratoga* is coming up with replacement airplanes for him tomorrow. Yamamoto is still out there, and his carriers are threatening Dutch Harbor."

In front of the medicine cabinet mirror, Fletcher carefully parted his hair. "I want to transfer to *Saratoga* tomorrow."

"Yes, sir."

"And after breakfast I want to review the message traffic. Any update from Ray since last night?"

"Not yet, sir. He's probably rendezvoused with the tanker and should be alongside for most of the day."

"Said his boys damaged a cruiser. Is that confirmed?"

"Now reported sunk, sir. Nothing else reported east of the International Date Line."

"Good, good," Fletcher replied. Yorktown's *gone. They'll blame me for that one, too.*

"Spence, I think this battle is over."

Lewis smiled and puffed up his chest. "Congratulations, sir! Four carriers. Makes our life a whole lot easier now."

Fletcher shrugged. "You know, we did well. We *won.* Midway's secure. But we lost *Yorktown,* and we lost a lot of men. We can't sustain these losses."

"Heroes all, sir. We'll never forget them. Admiral, we didn't see but a handful of their planes, but, like in the Coral Sea, this was fought in the air. This one, sir, is a modern-day Jutland. They'll be talking about it for years. Actually, sir, it's like Trafalgar – a rout. They won't come back here."

Fletcher appreciated his friend's words, but he was also a realist. *No way is Ernie King going to allow comparisons of me to Nelson.*

"You're kind, Spence. Let's get some breakfast. Another long day of report writing ahead."

"Aye, aye, sir."

Seated at the desk in his in-port cabin, Mitscher stared at the blank paper in front of him. Where to start? When they left Norfolk three months ago and transited high-speed to the canal? When they picked up the Army planes in San Francisco after another high-speed transit with little to no flying? When they launched Doolittle after steaming six thousand miles, then rushing back to Pearl, rushing to help in the Coral Sea and missing it, rushing to return to

Pearl, and, two days later, rushing for Point Luck? Mitscher's pilots were *green* and it showed, and his squadron commanders were little better. *Stanhope.* He trusted him, trusted his ability. But he had missed the Japs Thursday, and all – *all* – of his men had left him with nothing to show for it. Only Johnny had found the Japs like he said he would, his brave men following. He deserved a medal – *all the torpeckers did* – for facing the enemy in those beat-up TBDs. Was all this BuAer's fault for not getting the big Grumman torpedo bombers off the production line in time? He lit another cigarette.

Mitscher could not get over the fact that *Enterprise* and *Yorktown* had found the enemy and hit them and he hadn't. Those ships had won the battle. Only yesterday his pilots had scored hits on a half-dead cruiser. And the whole task force knew it. Soon the whole fleet would, as would Washington. What could he write that wasn't putting lipstick on a pig? Almost fifty dead, most of them from Torpedo Eight. And Admiral Ingersoll's son...

Johnny practically begged you, and you wouldn't give him one measly fighter.

Hornet was not a happy ship. His responsibility. He'd take her back to Pearl Harbor and turn over command to Charlie Mason. Maybe Charlie would do better. He rubbed his bald head in frustration. *We've been in commission less than nine months!*

Mitscher held his pen over the blank pad, waiting and hoping for the words to come. Whatever he managed to write, a come-around awaited him on Makalapa Hill.

On the mess deck, Kroeger referenced the frame numbers as he strode aft on the port-side passageway of *Enterprise.* He found the oversize door stenciled in block letters: MEDICAL DEPT.

Entering, he spoke to the first Pharmacist Mate he saw.

"I'm looking for Lieutenant Best?"

The man eyed Kroeger. "Not really a good time for visitors, sir."

"Please. He's my CO. We flew together Thursday morning."

The Mate was impressed. "Wow! Did you hit the Japs, sir?"

"He hit 'em twice," Kroeger said, pointing to the patient ward.

The man hesitated, and Kroeger pressed him.

"It will do him good. Please. I'll be quiet."

"Well, the chief said no visitors. You'll have to wear a mask, sir."

"No problem," Kroeger said with an appreciative smile.

Handing Kroeger a mask, the Pharmacist Mate led him to the ward. Peeking in first, he opened the curtain for Kroeger.

Best lay in bed, his face ashen. He also wore a mask. He studied Kroeger, not sure.

"It's me, sir. Bud."

"Oh, Kroeger. How ya doin'?" Best wheezed. A shocked Kroeger had never seen Best like *this*. Human and vulnerable.

"Is this okay, sir?" the Mate asked Best.

"Yeah, sure. He's fine," Best rasped, waving the sailor away.

The curtain closed behind him, and Kroeger stood alone with Best.

"What do you have, Skipper?"

Best propped himself up. "Latent tuberculosis, the doc says. Think I breathed some bad oxygen Thursday morning. Remember when we flew south after hitting that second carrier?"

"Yes, sir."

"Well, I wasn't feeling good. Even kept it from Chief Murray. To tell the truth, I'm not sure how I got us back. Anyway, I forced myself to land, but couldn't get out of the plane."

"Sir, I heard that, but thought you were just exhausted or wrenched your back on the pull, like Mister Gallaher."

"Shhh," Best admonished as he pointed. "He's right over there."

Kroeger lowered his voice.

"When do you come back?"

Best looked away.

"Well, they tell me after wasting a few years in the sanatorium, but the doc doesn't hold out for flying." Best lowered his voice to a whisper. "They're all quacks. I'll get back to Pearl and see a specialist who'll give me some damn pills. I'll be fine."

Kroeger wasn't so sure. Tuberculosis. *TB. Serious.*

"Hell, Kroeger, we dodged everything the Nips threw at us, and it's the damned *oxygen* that lays me flat." Best then coughed in a fit that lasted several seconds. A spot of red formed on Best's mask.

Kroeger didn't know what to say.

Recovered, Best wanted more scuttlebutt. "Just heard they rescued Joe Penland."

"Yes, sir. Lieutenant Shumway is still our acting CO till you get back on your feet. We're not scheduled to fly much today. Maybe some patrols later. We're headin' east to gas up with a tanker and transfer Mister Penland and those rescued."

Best nodded, his mind elsewhere.

"I was too hard on Weber. Dave's a good man, but he jammed us in the dive. Should have allowed us in first. That was Willie's brief. Weber did the best he could. Bad luck a Nip was there to pick him off."

"Yes, sir," Kroeger said. *There but for the grace of God.*

"Good man. Hard to believe he and the others are gone. Maybe the flying boats and small boys can comb the…"

With no warning, Best was wracked by another coughing fit. A helpless Kroeger could only watch.

"Do you want water, sir?" he asked. Must do *something.*

"No," Best gagged, waving him off. "They won't let me." He then pointed to the IV drip tube in his arm. Kroeger again waited.

"Do you think about dying out here, Kroeger?"

The unexpected question caught him off guard. *Sure,* he thought. *Doesn't everyone?*

"Sir, I try not to. I've been scared plenty of times, even before Pearl Harbor. Don't even need combat flying to scare myself. Yes, sir, I get scared…but I'm more scared not to go."

The skin around Best's eyes crinkled. Kroeger perceived he was smiling.

"Yes. I've scared myself, too. I get scared of prangin' the airplane, scared of letting you guys down. But I've never, *ever,* thought I was going to die. Never have. Can't even imagine it, even now with TB – if that's what I really have."

Kroeger nodded, again lost for words.

"Kroeger, if you can think that way – that it's going to be the other guy – you'll go far in this business. Don't be stupid, of course, and there's lots of things that can bite you, like contaminated O2 for heaven's sake, but –"

Best coughed again, hard, almost doubling him over and causing him to wince in pain.

"Kroeger, we're all gonna die…but you don't have to die now, even in this war. Maybe I'm the only nut who thinks that way, but it works for me."

"You'll outlive us all, sir."

Best smiled under his mask. "Take care of the boys, Kroeger, and Dave Shumway. He needs the support of you guys. Everything else going okay?"

Kroeger knew he should leave now. The dressing down from the admiral yesterday could wait.

"Everything's okay. Get well soon, sir. We'll make you proud."

As Kroeger opened the curtain to leave, Best rasped again.

"Bud, thanks for comin'."

Kroeger turned to see him nod in appreciation, his eyes full of meaning. Kroeger had never heard the CO call him "Bud" before.

"You're welcome, Skipper. By your leave, sir."

From his hospital bed, Best saluted, and Kroeger returned it.

Clay Fisher was spent.

Last night he had had his best sleep in weeks, but the physical stresses and constant tension of the past five days had left him drained.

They had won the battle. Licked the Japs. Scuttlebutt was that, after the refueling, they would get some of the new Grumman torpedo planes and go off to hunt more wounded Jap ships crawling west. *Fine. But first, I need a day.*

He thought of Annie. If only she knew what had happened out here. Then he thought of what he should write her. The completely botched first morning of battle? How close he had come to "buying it" that afternoon? The loss of so many, including the entire torpedo squadron? He'd gone to flight school with Grant Teats. *What caused me to go VB and him to get VT?* No, there was nothing he could tell her about this week except that he was there, and, for the moment, still alive.

KB entered the stateroom.

"Clay, I was just in the ready room. We've got an assignment."

Fisher shook his head. On a Sunday morning. *"Now* what?"

"We've gotta inventory the personal items of those lost in Torpedo Eight. We've each been assigned a pilot."

Fisher nodded. This was no red-ass. It was a solemn duty. In a dispatch, they had learned that Tex Gay had been rescued and said his squadron mates were *all* shot down in front of him. Tex had been able to ditch and spent the night in the water, the open ocean. Wounded, with sharks around. He was lucky.

"Okay. Who am I assigned to?"

"Bill Evans."

"Squire," Fisher said.

"Yeah. I've got his roommate, Hal Ellison. The XO gave me this key to their stateroom."

Fisher glanced at the key KB held. "Wanta go now?"

"Yeah. Let's get it over with."

They walked aft until they reached an athwart ship passageway and turned right. Then forward. Evans and Ellison had a stateroom on the port side inboard.

They found the room as the men had left it that morning. Robes hung from hooks. One rack was made and the other unmade. One of the pilots had hung his pressed wash khakis from an overhead pipe. On their desks were family pictures, stationery and envelopes. Fisher was moved by the silent evidence of life. One day they were young men just like him, resplendent in their choker whites, more radiant than Solomon. The next day, cut down and thrown into the furnace. Fisher had not been. Yet. When would that day come?

"Hal's girl...or wife," KB said, looking at the photo on his desk. Fisher thought of Annie's photo on his desk. Beautiful American girls, afraid for their men, and with no knowledge of what had just happened here. Or had they already experienced the terse horror of Western Union?

Fisher sat at Evans's desk. Letters to him with a return address of Indianapolis. From his folks.

"I didn't know Squire was from the Midwest," Fisher said. "Pegged him for an Ivy League type from New England."

KB said nothing as both sifted through the artifacts of their lost shipmates.

As KB rifled through Hal's sock drawer, Fisher came across Evans's journal and opened it.

Inside were paragraphs in Bill's longhand, passages of days at sea, a type of diary. Here and there were lines of poetry. Evans wrote of flying and of the sea and sky around the ship. In one passage he wrote of the Army bombers and Jimmy Doolittle. Fisher's eyebrows went up. Classified information. A censor would cut it out. Should he, now that Bill was gone?

He opened a folded typewritten page on onionskin paper wedged between the pages:

Four destroyers, two heavy cruisers, and an aircraft carrier flew their ensigns at half-mast in tribute to one reserve apprentice seaman, symbolizing as effectively as anything I have yet seen, the tangible evidence that this nation holds the life of even its lowliest as worthy of tribute as the mighty. Where else in this world can such be so? Words speak poorly in trying to catch the mood of that last far journey across the horizon; even in our thoughts we cannot bridge the chasm which separates the mystery of life from the mystery to which we go. It is fitting that men and officers stand quietly in the sun, stand quietly while taps are sounded, stand quietly as the smallest of boxes returns the unexplainable to the unexplainable. How fitting that man and his creations take cognizance of these things in which they are so little. Tomorrow or the next day it will be done again and then again as from the

*beginning of time, as we return mystery to mystery, and the wisdom of the
sea accepts them all.*

Fisher folded the paper closed and placed it back where he had found it. He
remembered that March day – had forgotten it actually – but now that Bill had
memorialized it in writing he'd never forget it. Fisher thought about Squire, how
he was, not knowing then that he had such a way with words. It was common
knowledge that Bill Evans was the youngest pilot aboard. Only twenty-three…a
year younger than Fisher. Decades wiser. Like Fisher a lowly ensign. *What a
loss.*

Three bells sounded, followed by a 1MC announcement.

"Divine services will be held on the hangar bay at ten hundred."

The men continued sifting, exploring their shipmates' lives with their hearts,
their minds not yet ready to record and catalog the last worldly possessions of
two lost aviators. Fisher and KB would box them up for shipment – in Evans's
case, to Indianapolis. How would Bill's family react? Fisher again thought of
Annie and his own family. Imagining.

"Clay, what say we go to services? We can come back for this later."

Fisher put the journal back. "Yeah. I'm goin.' Expect the whole ship will go."

"Yeah. I'm going to put on a necktie. Just seems right for Sunday, 'specially
this Sunday."

The two ensigns stood, leaving the stateroom as they had found it. After
switching off the light, Fisher closed the door. They walked aft in silence.

Alive.

CHAPTER 44

HIJMS *NAGARA*, 0850 JUNE 10, 1942

The sharp report of the shot-line gun signaled to Genda that the time had come. Stepping to the porthole, the sight of *Yamato's* secondary armament and upper works filled him with awe as it always did – until the dread of what it meant returned.

The other men in the confined cabin – Kusaka, Oishi, Ono, and the flag secretary, Nishibayashi – also waited with Nagumo for word to disembark. Nagumo and Ono would remain aboard – not invited – as four of the First Air Fleet staff transferred over to the flagship. There, they would explain their actions to the commander in chief.

Nagumo was crushed by his guilt. *I should be the one answering for my staff.* Not facing Yamamoto now was a most stinging punishment, a public cruelty Nagumo would not have thought the admiral was capable of. Next to him, Kusaka laced up the logbook for which he took personal responsibility. In the silent cabin, they awaited word from the bridge, condemned men waiting for the executioner in their gut-churning humiliations. Kusaka broke the silence.

"Nagumo-sama…I shall explain to the commander in chief in frank terms our understandings of the battle situations and rationale. I will ask that once we return to Kure, we may be allowed to rejoin you in a reinvigorated First Air Fleet." Each man in the room nodded.

A tight-lipped Nagumo could only nod back. In a just world, he would be arrested when they arrived, never to go to sea again. With Yamaguchi gone, who would command? Ozawa, probably. It mattered little. *I should have listened to him…*

Two knocks on the door, and Ono opened it for a lieutenant, who bowed. "Staff officers, the highline is rigged and ready!"

In order of seniority, the staff shuffled out into the passageway. Kusaka, who needed a cane to walk, would be the last to leave. Genda heard Nagumo express his thanks to him.

Warm sunlight greeted the officers on the main deck as each marveled at the massive bulk of *Yamato* towering above them. Only 25 meters separated *Nagara* from the behemoth, and even an air-minded officer like Genda could not help but stare at the giant symbol of Japan's naval strength. *Nagara* rode the swells in gentle motion next to the flagship that remained rock steady as the two ships steamed west.

Nishibayashi was first to the deck chair as boatswain's mates strapped him in tight. The life jacket he wore over his winter uniform looked out of place. Genda decided he would forgo it for his trip. To him, drowning in the turbulent vortex between the ships was no worse than having to face Yamamoto.

Flagship sailors in immaculate dress uniforms pulled on the line and Nishibayashi lurched across the steel chasm. Once he was aboard *Yamato,* the chair was quickly retrieved and readied for Genda. When an officer offered him a life jacket, a stoic Genda refused with a sharp shake of his head.

He strapped in, and, with his cover clutched in his arms, remained expressionless as he was hauled up and then pulled across, swinging and bobbing on the tensioned highline from the muscled pulses of the line handlers. Below him the sea raged and swished against the hulls of capital ships, and spray flecked at his trouser legs. Genda's eyes remained aft, to the east.

Once his request to come aboard was granted, he stood aside and remained silent as Oishi and Kusaka were carried across in the same manner. On *Nagara* he heard the bells and loudspeaker sound: *Admiral, departing.* The flagship did not respond in kind at Kusaka's arrival seconds later. All knew he was aboard. *He* knew the minute Kusaka, his ankles sprained and burned, stepped onto *Yamato's* huge cypress deck.

The agony prolonged by Kusaka's slow pace, an escort officer led them up and forward to the flag conference room, a room familiar to Genda from when he had delivered briefings from charts and diagrams that he knew better than anyone in His Majesty's Navy. Today, he would listen in humiliation as Kusaka explained why Genda's plan had failed his nation. *A stroke of my pen...*

Struggling with his cane, Kusaka led the First Air Fleet staff as they followed the officer inside the ship and up a labyrinth of passageways. Arriving at the door, the officer peeked inside, then opened it for Kusaka to pass.

Genda closed his eyes for a moment before he followed Kusaka and Oishi to the gallows. *This cannot be happening.*

Yamamoto and the assembled Combined Fleet Staff lowered their gaze as Kusaka led his humiliated staff into the room. The flag lieutenant indicated where they should stand. Kusaka was offered a chair but refused it. Genda glanced up enough to see an unmoved Admiral Ugaki scowl at Kusaka. *Big gun son of a concubine...*

No one spoke as the four guests in their disheveled uniforms, covers in hand, stood before Yamamoto and the others. The admiral refused to make eye contact and let the uncomfortable silence linger.

Ugaki began, his face full of disdain.

"First Air Fleet staff: On behalf of the commander, welcome aboard His Majesty's Combined Fleet flagship."

His cane quaking from the exertion, Kusaka bowed as best he could. Returning to his full height, he spoke as a shaken Yamamoto studied his friend's flash-burned face.

"Commander in Chief, admittedly we are not in a position to come back alive after having made such a blunder, but we have come back only to pay off the scores some day. I and the First Air Fleet staff with me are prepared to discuss our findings from the battle and how events transpired. We are confident that these findings may benefit future Combined Fleet carrier operations. We humbly ask, Admiral, that we may be given a second chance to employ these combat lessons against our enemy."

Yamamoto considered his words. Kusaka and the others waited, and Genda held his breath.

"You have my word that I will, Kusaka."

Genda exhaled, taking care that no one noticed.

"Please proceed, and be seated. I insist," Yamamoto requested.

Kusaka, now relaxed, took the seat offered and began. From across the room Ugaki and Kuroshima held their icy gazes on Genda. *They've already made up their minds.*

"Admiral, our first finding is that our search posture was inadequate. Due to the requirements of the Midway strike and holding our contingency force in reserve, we used seven aircraft, six of them float planes, and searched east and south. Had we pared our carrier strike and reserve forces by only six planes, we could have doubled our search coverage and at greater speed. And we should have launched them earlier, to be outbound at the first indications of twilight."

Yamamoto nodded as the others returned their focus to Genda, who felt their accusing eyes on him. *He* was the Air Officer who had devised the search plan, which *they* had approved with a casual nod. He'd done what he could with what he had amid conflicting requirements. Now, all were wise after the fact. Genda kept his eyes on the bulkhead. He recalled when Kusaka and Nagumo had shrugged and approved it. Combined Fleet big-gun admirals who judged him now would have done no different.

"Another finding is that we should have attacked Midway with one carrier division and held the other in reserve. When all four decks were needed to recover the Midway strike, we could not launch our reserves and even had trouble maintaining our combat air patrols from near constant enemy attacks. We did not foresee the level of resistance."

Yamamoto stopped him. "Did you know the invasion force had been spotted the day before?"

"Yes, Admiral, and their flying boats spotted us that morning. Routine patrols that we frankly discounted. What we did not anticipate was the fighting spirit the Americans showed, their courage flying obsolescent models into the teeth of our defenses. We mowed them down all morning – except at the end."

Yamamoto nodded and waited for more.

"We did have an option to attack…hours before *Hiryū* finally did. CarDiv 2 *kanbakus* were loaded and ready all morning. When we discovered and verified a carrier on our flank, we could have sent them and the Type 97s of CarDiv 1 – regardless of their weapon loads. This would have been a desperate attack with little to no escort and probable heavy losses, but we would have delivered a blow."

"And removed planes from your hangar bays," Yamamoto added, citing the American raid and the fires that spread from his loaded planes, ripping his ships open from the inside. Genda recalled the sickening image of *Akagi's* upper hangar bay: two figures – men – moving inside a sea of flame.

Genda remembered, too, the burning American torpedo planes falling to the sea, the pitiful glide bombing runs of their outdated bombers. It was clear on *Akagi's* bridge that the Mobile Force could mount a crushing blow and had time to do it, and clear now that there was no time, and anything was better than nothing. While they strove for perfect, the Americans had made the decision for them.

Kusaka finished, and Yamamoto spoke for the staff. His officers showed the stress from the past week. None of them could fathom all they had lost. That they *had* lost.

"Kusaka, your observations and lessons will be studied, and I am confident be incorporated into our new carrier concept of operations. We must not lose a single teaching point. Have you a written report?"

"It is still being written, Admiral. I have my staff here to assist."

Yamamoto nodded. "Please complete it and deliver it to Ugaki-san as soon as you can. My staff will show yours to working spaces and provide stenographers and typists."

From his chair Kusaka bowed slightly. *"Hai!"*

The meeting over, Genda stood at erect attention with the rest of the First Air Fleet staff, their humiliation complete.

Until they moored at Kure, and the brow went over. There, it would begin anew.

The sun-bleached coral burned Iverson's eyes as he walked down Eastern's airplane parking ramp. Since the action of last week there had not been much to do: a few patrols to the west but mostly lounging around in the tent and waiting for the horn that never blew.

Elmer Glidden walked next to him as they killed time. Iverson spoke.

"So, how much longer, Elmer? Think the Army guys sank the Jap carriers and scared off the rest?"

"Hell if I know. Besides, we did our part."

"Well, you're the captain."

The Japanese were gone, the danger gone. After a deadly 27 hours, boredom had returned to the isolated and windswept outpost.

Iverson looked out to sea. "Ya know, I wanted to fight, wanted to hit the Japs... Pay 'em back an' all."

Glidden nodded and waited for Iverson to continue.

"In a way, though, I wanted to prove myself. Maybe prove it *to* myself."

"Prove what?"

Iverson squinted into the sun and wind. "That I belonged here. That I measured up to those who stormed the 'Halls of Montezuma.'"

"To the shores of Tripoli..." Glidden sang in response. In the silence that followed he reached down and picked up a coral rock. As he threw it into the dense brush, a childhood memory flooded back.

"Yeah, Danny Boy, I know what you mean. Guess you never know until it happens – that first time you get shot at – if you'll turn yellow, or go to pieces...freeze up."

Iverson kept his eyes on the horizon. "Were you scared Thursday?"

"Hell, yes, but I was more scared that *night*. Hate flyin' at night in the goo."

Iverson nodded. "Yeah, me too, but we faced it. Took and returned fire…
We passed the test."

"Yep."

"An' before long we'll hafta pass it again."

"Yep. If not here, someplace else."

"Think there's gonna be a lot more war b'fore this is over."

"Yep," Glidden replied as he kicked at a rock.

Each pilot stood with hands on hips and contemplated the infinite Pacific –
and their futures.

"You know, Danny, we have some experience now. Steeper is better, speed is
life, keep the airplane moving off target, head on a swivel. All that motherhood
we gotta pass down to the newbies comin' out here."

"Yeah."

"Each of us can save a life."

"As we take 'em from the Japs."

"You got that right," Glidden said, kicking another rock. "An' the faster we
do that, the faster we go home."

Iverson glanced at a *Vindicator* parked on the coral. "Sure am gonna miss
Dick Fleming."

"I know… He was the funniest, wasn't he?"

"He didn't have to fly that old thing, but he did. I would've flown it, but he
insisted."

"I know. You hear stories from the Great War of guys falling on grenades to
save their fellows. Same thing, I guess. You just react."

Iverson nodded. "Yeah, but Dick had time to think about it. He insisted."

Glidden grimaced as the sun beat on them. The sound of surf crashing in
the distance carried on the wind, and frigate birds cried as they darted about.

"He took care of you, of us. *If not me,* and all that. We'll never forget him.
Hafta tell our kids about him one day."

"An' the majors."

"Yeah, good men those… You measured up, Danny. You *'kep' yer honor clean'*
an' all that. You went back. We're all gonna go back."

Squinting at the horizon, Iverson considered their uncertain future. Whatever it held, he hoped he could fly with Elmer again. He changed the subject.

"What do you want to do when all this is over? Back home?" Iverson asked.
"Door-to-door sales? Charm the housewives and sell Fuller brushes to 'em? I
can see you doin' that."

Glidden chuckled, then thought for a long time. "To tell you the truth, I can't think of anyplace I'd rather be than here right now. I love this." His words hung as they again listened to the surf.

Iverson lifted his hand to shield his eyes. "Lifer, then, aren't you?"

"Yeah, guess I am. Heaven help me."

Chapter 45

Naval Hospital Pearl Harbor, 1910 June 14, 1942

"Ma'am, may I please visit Lloyd F. Childers, Aviation Radioman Third?"

Wayne Childers twisted his blue Dixie cup hat in his hands and waited for the answer from the nurse, a full lieutenant by the braid on her cap.

From her desk she studied him with disdain: With that chevron on his shoulder he should know better. His wrinkled chambray shirt was unsat, and filthy dungarees were never appropriate for visitors. Besides, weekend visiting hours were over. Lights-out for the patients was in an hour.

"Sailor, you are not in the proper uniform of the day. Vistors must be, even on the weekends."

"Ma'am, I'm sorry, but my uniforms are…"

Wayne caught himself. The fact that his uniforms rested on the bottom of the ocean could be classified. What he wore when he abandoned *Yorktown* was all he had until he could draw a set of crackerjacks from Base Supply. They had told him to come back Monday morning…payday. Hundreds of his shipmates would storm the place along with everyone else on the island, and he hoped the chief would allow him to be in line when the doors opened.

The lieutenant eyed him. She looked older, like she was somebody's mother. No, what husband would have her?

"Ma'am, I arrived here a few days ago…these dungarees are all I have."

"Where's your sea bag?" she snapped.

Wayne swallowed. *It's never easy with officers.*

"Ma'am, I don't have it, but my brother Lloyd was – *is* – my shipmate. I learned he was here two days ago, and this is my first chance to get a ride over here."

"Where are you now?"

"Ewa Beach, ma'am."

The lieutenant seemed to soften.

"You are the brother *and* shipmate of Radioman Childers?"

"Yes, ma'am. Our mother is Marie Childers, from Norman, Oklahoma. Is Lloyd, I mean, Radioman Childers, okay?"

Now realizing why Wayne was in his unkempt dungarees, she looked at her watch.

"Okay, just this once I'm going to allow this. You have fifty minutes to visit. You are to keep your voice low, and if you don't, I'll remove you. And do not touch him."

"Is he okay?"

"Your hands and uniform are dirty, and I will *not* allow infection."

Concerned that she'd change her mind, Wayne nodded his understanding. "Yes, ma'am. I won't, ma'am. I promise. Don't want him sick."

"Or anybody else."

"No, ma'am. Nobody else."

She rose and motioned for him to follow her down the hallway. Ahead of them, a nurse in her white uniform wrote on a chart that hung from a door. Wayne's eyes were drawn to her white stockings, and, when he noticed her noticing him admire her, he turned red. A pretty one, she smiled and looked away. Wayne guessed she had plenty of suitors on the island; a lowly Aviation Machinist Third like him had no chance. Besides, nurses were considered equal to officers. Off limits.

The lieutenant turned down another hallway. Through open doors Wayne saw men – like him – with darkened faces and bandaged limbs. Some had lost hands or feet. Others were burned and disfigured. For life. Was this Lloyd's fate?

As fear built inside, Wayne lagged behind. The lieutenant noticed and, under her breath, she snapped, *"Keep up!"* Wayne matched her pace and kept his eyes forward as the echo of her thick heels thundered off the passageway bulkhead. When they got to a wide opening, she stopped and turned to him.

"Sailor, if you gawk at your shipmates again, I will take you out of here by your ear."

Wayne was as scared now as when *Yorktown* was attacked the first time, as scared as when he was sent to the principal's office for a paddling in fourth grade. His eyes bulged wide in fear.

"No. More. Chances!" she hissed.

"I'm sorry, ma'am. I won't... I'm sorry," Wayne answered, his heart pounding loud enough for her to hear it.

Leading him into an open bay ward, she strode among the beds as nurses administered to the patients. Some of the beds had curtains drawn around them. Now terrified of the lead nurse, Wayne refused to look at anything besides the back of her head.

The lieutenant stopped in front of a drawn curtain and peeked inside. She closed it and turned back to Wayne.

"Forty-five minutes," she said in a whisper. "Absolutely *no* touching of any kind. If you are done sooner, ask a nurse to escort you out."

"Yes, sir, I mean *ma'am*, ma'am, thank you. Thank you, ma'am."

The nurse sneered dismissively at Wayne as he shuddered. She then opened the curtain and said, "You have a visitor."

After another long moment, she opened the curtain wider and motioned for Wayne to enter.

Lloyd Childers smiled at his brother as he lay propped up in bed with a paperback novel.

"Hi, Wayne. How are you?"

"Hey, Lloyd," Wayne whispered. He stood at the foot of the bed as the nurse pulled the curtain closed behind him.

They looked at each other, each of them who had feared the worst about the other days ago. Wayne was careful not to touch anything, but as he gazed upon his brother, he realized the man in the bed wasn't an apparition. It was really Lloyd.

"When did you get here?" they asked each other at the same time.

Lloyd chuckled. "You go first."

Wayne nodded. "I got here last Monday, the eighth. Over a thousand of us were on the tender USS *Fulton*. I was on the *Portland* first; they fished me out of the water."

"You were in the water?"

"Yeah, most all of us were, including the captain! They had to lower the admiral to a whale boat, but after the second attack everyone thought she was gonna capsize..."

"Second attack?" Lloyd was puzzled.

"Yeah, the first attack was dive-bombers. One of them blew out the uptakes and snuffed out our boilers. We were dead in the water – and that's when you came by! I saw ya when Mister Corl flew past on our port side. I ran the whole length of the flight deck wavin' at you and you didn' wave back. I like to died thinkin' I'd have to tell mother."

"And then you were attacked after that?"

"Yeah, about two hours later, after we got the boilers re-lit. We could only get about fifteen knots, though, and SOBs got us with torpedoes."

Lloyd thought back to that morning as he and Harry flew with the CO into a tornado of swirling Japanese lead. Toward a carrier. He didn't even know if they had hit it.

"Torpedo planes got through?"

"Yeah, and we launched the VF as the Japs were in their runs. Lloyd, I'm tellin' ya, it was so loud… You ain't never heard thunder on the plains like that, and it was *constant*. I mean every gun in the task force was firing at the Nips until their barrels glowed red, and they still got through."

Lloyd nodded, processing it.

"Two fish hit us port side amidships, one after another. The first one knocked me down, the ship shook so bad. It was like a hound dog shakin' a bone, and we were the bone. The next one slammed me into the bulkhead just as I got to my feet. Within a minute, the deck starts to slant, and then the chief told everyone to get into the hangar bay."

Lloyd listened as his brother related the action. *They hit us...because we didn't hit them.*

"An' not long after that the word came down to abandon. Now, I don' know what I was thinkin' but I was near our berthing, and I wanted to fetch my wallet cuz I had a lot of cash. So, with the deck at a pretty sharp angle, I went down there and got it. The whole time I was thinking, *Please don't roll on me. Please don't roll.*"

Lloyd shook his head. "All for a few dollars?"

"*It was a hun'nerd and eighty-five bucks!* I won it playing cards two nights before with the VF mechs! I had to get it!"

"So you got your wallet?"

"Yes, and I scrambled out of there as fast as I could. Another fella in Bombing Three was doin' the same thing, and we went over the side by the aft elevator. She was listing steep, an' we had to kind of scamper and cross the deck on all fours. Down the nets, and we swam to a whaleboat from *Portland* that stood off a piece. You know, the water was warmer than I had expected – like Hawaii water."

"Didja get mine?"

Wayne looked at his brother. "Yer what?"

Lloyd sensed he knew the answer. "*My* wallet in the locker next to yours. Did you think to get mine?"

"Ah, sorry. No time. There was no time to…"

Lloyd shook his head. "Well, at least I know where it is."

Wayne laughed and caught himself. He nodded to the curtain and lowered his voice. "Lieutenant Broom Hilda said no laughing."

Imagining the nurse admonishing him, Lloyd chuckled. As he did, he grimaced in pain.

Wayne reached toward him before catching himself. "Lloyd, you hurt bad? You…still have everything?"

"Yeah. They shot up my legs pretty good, and I lost a lot of blood. Took one round on my right ankle that hurt like the blazes."

Wayne felt embarrassed that he had talked so much. He had abandoned a sinking carrier, but suspected his brother had a better sea story to tell. "Lloyd, what happened out there?" Wayne waited for his brother to answer. With a faraway look in his eyes, Lloyd tried to put it into words.

"We found them north of us on the way out and turned toward them. The *Zeros* attacked as soon as we did. The VF couldn't keep up with them, and there must've been twenty at least. We were constantly shooting, shooting guys shooting at us, shooting guys off each other's tails..." Lloyd thought of Darce. *You owe me, Okie.*

Patient, Wayne waited for him to continue.

"We crossed their screen, and it was gunfire everywhere. We lost some guys... One exploded off our right wing."

"Did you see the CO get it?"

Lloyd nodded. "He was right next to us. I think he was dead cuz the plane went down easy, on fire from the engine underside. We flew right by the splash." *The chief. He knew...*

Wayne nodded, imagining the terrible scene. He was afraid to hear more, yet wanted to.

"Harry said we weren't gonna make it, and when he said that, I got real scared. I mean, I had just turned twenty-one an' all...and it's over? In the back of a TBD, out in the middle of nowhere?"

"Did you drop?"

Lloyd shook his head. "I honestly don't know, and if we did, I don't remember. We may have. Wayne, they were everywhere. At one point, I stood up in my seat with my damn leg over the side so I could fire *down* at a guy that was just waiting to execute us. That's when a bullet clipped me and I swear I almost jumped out of the airplane. Hurt like a sonofabitch."

"*Holy cow...*"

"And then I ran out of ammo – and they were still comin'."

Riveted, Wayne probed further. "Holy Toledo. Wha'd you do?"

Lloyd hesitated as he gathered his thoughts. The fire, the fear, men struggling to jump clear of their burning planes. No hope of survival. *We're not gonna make it!*

"I took out my .45 and placed it on my gun so I could use the sight. When a Jap got in range, I squeezed off some rounds."

"*With your pistol!* Did you hit one?" Wayne asked.

"You know, I think I did! But I don't think anyone saw me. The damn fighter pilots get confirmations cuz they have cameras in their planes to prove it. All I have is my word, the word of a shot-up Radioman."

"Wow, Lloyd. Where did you land? What ship?"

"*What ship* is right! We didn't land on anything, we ditched next to a tin can. Good thing they had a doctor aboard. A surgeon, and not just a Pharmacist Mate. He did surgery on my legs to stop the bleedin'."

Wayne was speechless.

"I saw her go down, too."

"Yorktown?"

Lloyd brought his finger to his mouth. *"Shhhh.* Yes. A Jap sub torpedoed her, and we ran off to give chase. Those depth charges rumble and shake the ship like a rogue wave when they go off. They said the sub got away, and we went back to attend *Yorktown*. She floated through the night even after taking another fish. They took me to a porthole to watch her as she rolled over at dawn."

Lloyd paused and looked into his brother's eyes. "Best not repeat that."

"Did she capsize?"

"Kind of. Rested on her port side and sank. You could see the torpedo hole. The stern went and the bow lifted up a bit. Then she was gone."

"Wow!"

"With my wallet, you jerk!"

"Sorry! I'll get you a new one!" Wayne said with a smile, the break in the tension a welcome relief.

"Don't want no rawhide billfold either. I want tanned leather like from home!"

"Okay, okay. I owe ya."

At that, Lloyd thought again of Darce. *You owe me...*

He then turned serious. "Wayne, who else made it? Any word on that?"

"Who else?"

"Yeah, the gunners. Brazier was with Chief Esders, I saw him on the way back. But how about the other guys. Darce said I owe him. Did he make it?"

Wayne could only look down. "I'm sorry, Lloyd. He didn't."

Lloyd nodded. It was too much to ask. The tough Cajun had saved him, but when? How? He'd have to wait till they met in heaven to ask.

"Darn. He was a tough cuss. Sure wish we could have talked about that attack. How about the others?"

Wayne looked at his brother and said nothing. Lloyd waited for an answer, now uncomfortable at Wayne's silence.

Finally, Wayne spoke. "None of them, Lloyd."

Lloyd lay there, unable to comprehend. "None? No, Brazier was with us on the way home."

"He didn't make it."

Lloyd blinked hard as he faced the ceiling, still trying to grasp it. *"No one else? Am I the only gunner who made it?"*

"Yes, no one else. You are the only surviving gunner. Mister Corl and Chief Esders also made it. You three are the only ones."

Lloyd Childers opened his mouth to protest. To question, to cry.

"The *only one? Me?"* His eyes welled up.

"Yes, brother, and as much as I miss the others, I'm so glad God spared you." Wayne's chin quaked as his eyes watered.

Repressed emotions rose to the surface, emotions that had built since that terrible morning, his birthday. Lloyd had sensed this truth, but hearing it now with finality – *No others!* – unleashed a volcano of sorrow he could no longer control. Without warning, he burst into tears, his body wracked by waves of grief at the memories of each of his mates. And questions.

Why *me?* Why did *I* live and they didn't? Why did you spare *me*, God? And guilt. *Did I miss the Jap that got Darce? Am I to blame?*

Standing next to him, Wayne broke down, too. "I'm so sorry, Lloyd. They were good fellows…"

Through his sobs, Lloyd choked out his words. "Barkley…Barkley was a good Christian fella. He hoped to live to see…*to see…"*

Their boyhoods left out there, both men wept as one struggled with the news while the other watched him struggle. All of them dead, boys who would never know, with no markers for family to visit or signify they ever lived, each with stories of bravery and service in that dogged formation that flew into that hellish fire in those rickety planes that would never be told. Until they met in heaven, and only if any of their saved souls cared to hear of it. Would any of it matter then? *Eye has not seen, and ear has not heard…*

Outside, swaying palm fronds caressed the window screens. The scent of sweet plumeria – mixed with the pungent odor of fuel oil floating on the harbor waters – wafted into the open bay. Tears streaked the faces of two brothers, their bodies heaving as they held each other against the rules, not knowing why God took the others and not them, not knowing how to give thanks or for what.

Far from their home and the red soil of Oklahoma, but home.

Epilogue

After Midway, the Imperial Japanese Navy remained superior to the United States Navy in every ship class, but it never recovered from the loss of four frontline carriers and the men who operated what was arguably the most powerful and lethal military weapons system at the time.

For the remainder of 1942, the two bloodied navies escalated their deadly war of attrition in the South Pacific, with Japan offering battle with her carriers two months later – as if Midway was little more than a setback. Tenacious and then suicidal, Japan resisted for three more years in the face of overwhelming and finally mind-boggling firepower until Emperor Hirohito commanded the Japanese military and society to surrender and cooperate with the Allies. His sole condition of surrender was that he remain on the Chrysanthemum Throne.

In Europe, in large part because Japan was neutralized at Midway, Americans landed and engaged Rommel in North Africa, and the Soviets held in the east against a German Luftwaffe stretched to the limit. First up through Italy and then from across the Channel, the Allies repatriated Germany's occupied territories and eventually met the Soviets on German soil, victorious.

Though far from ignored, the Battle of Midway did not receive due reverence by the U.S. Navy until 1999, when Chief of Naval Operations Admiral Jay Johnson decreed that the battle be celebrated annually on June 4th, as the Navy also celebrates its birthday each October 13th.

Today, Midway Atoll is administered by the U.S. Fish and Wildlife Service. Closed to the public, a modest memorial to the battle exists on Sand Island. Even more inaccessible, the desolate waters to the north and west of Midway – above the dark resting places of seven ships – roll eternal. Only lines on a chart and accounts passed down through the generations commemorate what happened there.

AFTERWORD

John Paul Adams

Awarded the Navy Cross for his actions at Midway, to go with his other Navy Cross from the Coral Sea battle. After instructor duty, fights again in the Pacific with VF-88 aboard the new *Yorktown* (CV-10), earning a Silver Star during combat off Honshu.

Commands VF-41 and the University of South Carolina NROTC Unit. After 32 years of service he retires as a captain, and, from 1976-1988, serves as Vice President of the Naval Aviation Museum Foundation, organizing and managing the bookstore.

After a struggle with dementia, Johnny Adams passed away in 2011 at the age of 92 and is interred in Committal Shelter Number 3 of the Barrancas National Cemetery aboard NAS Pensacola. The author attended the internment.

The bookstore at the National Naval Aviation Museum that he managed with loving care became a souvenir shop, and at this writing no books about the battles Adams fought in are available there for purchase.

Clayton Fisher

Shot down and rescued four months later at Santa Cruz, where *Hornet* met her end after only one year in commission. Instructs carrier landing procedures to student pilots at NAS Glenview from the converted side-wheelers *Sable* and *Wolverine* on Lake Michigan. He flies the F4U *Corsair* as XO of VF-53 aboard *Essex* during Korea, commands a Utility Squadron, and retires in 1961 as XO of NAS Miramar. Settling in Coronado, he becomes a successful real estate developer and buys a home down the street from his flight lead Stanhope Ring, with whom he has no relationship.

Clay Fisher wrote and published *Hooked*, a superb memoir of his flying days, and passed away in 2012 at the age of 93.

Daniel Iverson

Flies in combat again that August with the "Cactus Air Force" at Guadalcanal's Henderson Field, where he is awarded the Silver Star to go with the Navy Cross from his Midway actions. Promoted to major, he becomes an instructor pilot at Naval Air Station Vero Beach where, in January 1944, he loses his life in a midair collision with a student. His friend and fellow instructor Clay Fisher was there when it happened.

The SBD-2 Dan Iverson and PFC Wallace Reid flew on 4 June 1942, Bureau Number 2106, is on display at the National Naval Aviation Museum. How it got there is another story.

LLOYD CHILDERS

Recovered from his wounds, he enters flight school and receives his wings. Transferring to the Marine Corps as the war ended, he remains on active duty and fights as a fighter pilot in Korea. Retrained as a helicopter pilot, he commands HMM-361 in combat in Da Nang, RVN. After 28 years in uniform, he retires as a lieutenant colonel, earns a PhD, and serves as Associate Dean of Chapman College.

Lloyd Childers died in Moraga, California, in 2015, at the age of 94.

HARRY CORL

Awarded the Navy Cross for his action at Midway and is promoted to ensign. Flying the new TBF *Avenger* from *Enterprise*, he is killed in action 24 August 1942 during the Battle of the Eastern Solomons.

The destroyer escort USS *Harry L. Corl* (DE-598) was named in his honor.

EDWIN KROEGER

Awarded the Navy Cross and DFC, Kroeger returns to combat in 1944 aboard the carriers *Hancock* and the new *Hornet*, participating in the Battle of Leyte Gulf as the commanding officer of VB-11. He serves as air group commander aboard the carrier *Midway* and commands the NROTC Unit at Columbia University. After serving as naval attaché to Yugoslavia, he retires as a captain in 1963.

Never to receive proper credit while alive for his decisive hit on *Akagi*, Kroeger eschewed attention for his role at Midway, and did volunteer and charity work at the Glenview, Illinois United Methodist Church, where he spent his golden years. After a brief illness, Bud Kroeger passed away in 2002 at the age of 89.

Genevieve, his wife of 62 years said, "He just lived a life of service."

ROBERT LAUB

Awarded the Navy Cross, Air Medal (with Gold Star), and Purple Heart for his 1942 combats, Laub transfers to the Aviation Engineering Duty Officer community, specializing in radio and radar. He remains on active duty after the war, with billets in flight test and materiel acquisition, and receives a "tombstone promotion" to rear admiral upon his retirement in 1957. He settles in Blue Jay, California, and is an active member of the "Battle of Midway Roundtable" Internet discussion group.

Bob Laub passed away in Northridge on November 10, 1988.

FRANK JACK FLETCHER

Despite the skepticism of Ernest King regarding the loss of *Yorktown*, Nimitz keeps Fletcher in command, awards him the Distinguished Service Medal for his victory at Midway, and promotes him to three stars. Two months later at Guadalcanal, enemy strength and logistic realities force Fletcher to withdraw for a time the carriers supporting the Marine amphibious landings, a decision for which he is vilified to this day. He meets and thwarts Nagumo again at the Battle of the Eastern Solomons, but the torpedoing of his flagship *Saratoga* and loss of *Wasp* to enemy submarines, not to mention the surface-gunfight debacle of Savo Island, prompt King to act. Banished to the "Elba" of the Northwest Sea Frontier, Fletcher never commands a task force again, and, notwithstanding the humble protests of Spruance, *The Quiet Warrior* is recognized by historians as the victor of Midway.

Fletcher retired without fanfare in 1947, and chose not to fight for his tarnished reputation. He passed away at La Plata, Maryland in 1973 at the age of 87.

In 1964, he responded to a friend producing a history of Midway: "I invite your attention to the remark which was supposed to have been made by Marshal Joffre, something like this: 'I cannot say who won the Battle of the Marne, but there is no doubt who would have lost it.' "

RAYMOND SPRUANCE

Having earned the confidence of Nimitz and King, Spruance later commands the Fifth Fleet. At the Battle of the Philippine Sea, the last great carrier duel, he, too, defeats Nagumo a second time, but decides to remain near the amphibious landing beaches of the Marianas, which he is ordered to support – and is again second-guessed by senior aviators for passing up an opportunity to pursue a wounded enemy. He commands off Okinawa, the final nail in the Japanese naval coffin, and is aboard his flagship USS *New Jersey* – where Nimitz held him hundreds of miles away as insurance – during the surrender ceremony in Tokyo Bay. Denied a fifth star, he serves as the president of his beloved Naval War College, is appointed as Ambassador to the Philippines, and settles in Carmel, California, where he dies in 1969 at the age of 83. With full military honors, he is buried last next to his friends Chester Nimitz, Kelly Turner, and Charles Lockwood at Golden Gate National Cemetery, overlooking the Pacific Ocean.

Well aware of his own shortcomings, Spruance was uncomfortable with the adulation he received at Fletcher's expense as his legend grew after Midway. Like Nimitz, he declined to write his memoirs. The lead ship of a class of U.S. Navy destroyers was named in his honor.

CHŪICHI NAGUMO

The catastrophe that befell Nagumo off Midway is swept away for Navy face-saving as much as anything else, and he is given command of the Third Fleet. Fights ably during the Guadalcanal carrier duels, damaging *Enterprise* and sinking *Hornet*, but at the sacrifice of most of Japan's remaining frontline carrier aviators. Brought home to command the Sasebo and Kure naval districts, he then receives command of the 14th Air Fleet at Saipan...with few airplanes. With his nemesis Spruance again on the horizon, his forces are powerless to repel the American amphibious onslaught. After a night of heavy drinking on 6 July 1944, as the Americans close in around his Saipan cave, he and fellow commanders commit *seppuku*.

Nagumo was posthumously promoted to full admiral two days later.

MINORU GENDA

In the months that followed Midway, Genda is again at sea, this time as Air Officer aboard the carrier *Zuikaku*, which deals severe damage to *Enterprise* at the Battle of the Eastern Solomons. Withdrawn to Imperial General Headquarters, in January 1945, he is given command of the 343rd Air Group. Tasked to open paths through the American combat air patrols from which the poorly trained *kamikaze* pilots could proceed, his pilots fight well until the end. Remaining in uniform, he rises to chief of staff of the Japanese Air Self Defense Force and is awarded the Legion of Merit by his old enemies upon his retirement in 1962.

He enters politics, and is elected to Japan's Upper House, where he serves for 20 years as a member of a right-wing faction of the Liberal Democratic Party. A hard-line hawk on defense matters, he fights against limits to Japan's military and is against Japan's ratification of the Nuclear Non-Proliferation Treaty on the grounds that Japan might one day need such weapons.

Genda died one day short of his 85th birthday in 1989.

TAISUKE MARUYAMA

Survives the war, and there is a credible account of him participating in the Battle of Santa Cruz attack on *Hornet*, as well as less credible accounts of him bombing

Saipan in December 1944 and attacking ships with torpedoes off Okinawa late in the conflict. Only 22 as the war ends, he embarks on a career in the lumber business.

In May 1998, he participates in a panel discussion about the Battle of Midway at the National Naval Aviation Museum, a panel that also features Richard Best and Lloyd Childers. As Maruyama recounts his actions through an interpreter, his dignified speech is serious and subdued. His only display of emotion is the pride he felt in landing a blow against the hull of *Yorktown*, which the interpreter relays to the audience. They break into long and heartfelt applause for the elderly warrior, a Japanese airman who had helped sink an American carrier 56 years earlier. The American panelists are not amused, and, at the reception, the hard feelings and suspicion among the aged antagonists are palpable.

Maruyama is invited to the 60th anniversary commemoration of the Pearl Harbor attack and participates as a guest of honor. Returning to Japan, he encounters the son of Rear Admiral Yamaguchi while awaiting departure at Honolulu International Airport. With tears in his eyes, Maruyama holds the hands of the son of his fallen admiral, relating later that it was as if he were back aboard *Hiryū* when Yamaguchi the elder held his hands before the afternoon attack.

Taisuke Maruyama passed away in 2010 at the age of 87.

WADE McCLUSKY

Recovers from his wounds to lead his air group off *Enterprise* when it returns to Pearl Harbor – only to learn that the island believes the Army Air Forces sank the Japanese Fleet at Midway. With a reputation as a "fixer," and after a stint of shore duty in Washington, he returns to the Pacific to command the troubled escort carrier *Corregidor* (CVE-58). By war's end, his marriage has failed due to the stress of repeated and extended absences.

During the Korean War, he serves on sea-going staffs and commands Glenview Naval Air Station. Remarried, he retires in 1956, receiving a tombstone promotion to rear admiral for his combat awards.

He settles in Ruxton, Maryland, works for the Martin Aircraft Company, teaches mathematics at Bryn Mawr, and works as a civil servant for the State of Maryland Civil Defense.

Wade McClusky died 27 June, 1976 at the age of 74.

The frigate USS *McClusky* (FFG-41) was named in his honor, and each year the McClusky Award goes to the top performing Air-to-Surface tactical squadron in the U.S. Navy. In the mid-2010's, a group of retired aviators, including flag officers, petitioned the Navy to upgrade McClusky's Navy Cross to the Medal of Honor. To date, the Navy has not done so.

MARC MITSCHER

After the dreadful performance of his ship at Midway, Mitscher feels certain his career is over. Given a second chance, he commands Task Force 58 under Spruance during another epic carrier duel, this one in the Philippine Sea in June of 1944. Always looking out for his men, from his flagship *Lexington,* he again says, "Turn on the lights" when his fuel-starved planes return in darkness after striking Ozawa's carrier fleet, endearing him to aviators everywhere.

He commands off Okinawa, and finishes the war as Deputy CNO for Air, ruffling feathers inside and outside the Navy for his vocal advocacy of carrier air power. Earning a fourth star, he is given fleet command, but poor health and the accumulated stress from years of sea-going combat take their toll.

"Pete" Mitscher died of coronary thrombosis while still on active duty on 3 February 1947, at the age of 60.

Said the New York Times: *He did not die in action. It is one measure of a sea-fighter's success not to die in action. But he died of wounds as surely as any hard-hit soldier ever did.*

STANHOPE COTTON RING

Awarded the Navy Cross for his leadership at Midway. After shore duty at Main Navy, he is the commissioning CO of the escort carrier *Siboney* (CVE-112), which arrives at Pearl Harbor the day after hostilities end. After the war, he commands USS *Saratoga* long enough to deliver her to Bikini Atoll, where she serves as an atomic bomb test article. He then commands the carrier *Boxer*. As a flag officer, he serves on various sea and shore staffs, including command of Carrier Division 1.

Medically retired as a vice admiral, he settles in Coronado, California, where he dies in 1963 at the age of 60.

Two sons followed in his Navy footsteps. His son William was a graduate of the illustrious Naval Academy Class of 1958 but was struck down by leukemia in 1965 at only 30.

Midway haunted Ring. In 1946, he wrote a 22-page essay on his recollection of Midway, which remained hidden until his daughter found it in 1999 and forwarded it to the Naval Institute for publication. Ring's "lost letter" leaves many questions unanswered.

USS *HORNET*

Three months after Midway she is the only operational carrier in the Pacific, and during the Battle of Santa Cruz – the fourth carrier duel of the Pacific War

– she launches a strike that causes severe damage to HIJMS *Shōkaku* while at the same time absorbing a strike from *Shōkaku* planes that *Hornet* pilots saw en route. Torpedoed and burning, she is towed at five knots toward safety when planes from the carrier HIJMS *Jun'yō* attack and deliver a torpedo into *Hornet's* starboard side. With the Japanese closing in salvage efforts are abandoned, but she withstands American gunfire and torpedoes to scuttle her. As a defiant *Hornet* awaits her end, the Japanese destroyer *Makigumo*, the destroyer that rescued Maruyama and other *Hiryū* survivors, delivers a final torpedo into the "Desecrator of Nippon," sending her to the bottom.

Hornet was in commission for one year.

Four months later, *Makigumo* struck a mine off Savo Island and was scuttled.

RICHARD BEST

Stunned, angry, and then heartbroken at the sudden illness that prevents him from flying or even serving, Best is medically retired in 1944 with 100% disability, a Navy Cross, and a DFC. Works for the Douglas Aircraft Company and Rand Corporation while still fighting the effects of tuberculosis. Outspoken and cantankerous, he willingly gives interviews and serves as a sharp-tongued panelist on numerous Battle of Midway commemorations well into his 80s.

The hard-nosed dive-bomber pilot who couldn't even imagine death passed away in October of 2001 at the age of 91. He is buried in Arlington.

Dick Best was immortalized in Roland Emmerich's 2019 film, *Midway*.

MILES BROWNING

The volatile officer goes to sea again with Halsey, his protector, who recommends him for the Distinguished Service Medal; not Spruance. He underperforms in the Solomons Campaign, though Halsey, amid whispers of scandal, strongly defends him professionally and personally. To get Browning away from Halsey, who King thought was ill-served by him, Browning receives command of the new-construction USS *Hornet* (CV-12). He is relieved for cause when found negligent in the deaths of two sailors who had fallen overboard while the ship was at anchor in 1944. King sends him as far away from water as he can: instructor duty at the Army War College at Fort Leavenworth, Kansas.

Retires in 1947 with a tombstone promotion to rear admiral. Appointed New Hampshire's civil defense director in 1950, he contracts lupus and dies in September 1954 at the age of 57.

Browning's grandson Cornelius became an Emmy Award-winning comic actor: Chevy Chase.

MAXWELL LESLIE

Awarded the Navy Cross, Leslie assumes command of the *Enterprise* Air Group and sees combat months later off Guadalcanal. He returns to combat at the end of the war as a staff officer supporting the Peleliu, Iwo Jima, and Okinawa invasions. Commands the escort carrier USS *Windham Bay* (CVE-92) and Naval Air Station Barbers Point, Hawaii. Retiring in 1956 as a captain, he is administratively promoted to rear admiral, and settles in Arlington, VA. He serves as an advisor for the 1976 film *Midway*, the first film about the battle that recognized the merits and success of the carrier dive-bombers.

Max Leslie died at age 82 of cardiac arrest in his Coronado home in September 1985. His ashes were scattered at sea from the carrier *Ranger* off San Diego.

USS *ENTERPRISE*

Participates in every major action of the Pacific War save Coral Sea, collecting 20 battle stars as her planes and guns destroy 911 enemy planes and sink 71 enemy ships. Undergoing repair at Puget Sound Naval Shipyard as the war ends, she transfers to the Atlantic Fleet where she makes four voyages to Europe to return home some 10,000 GIs. Decommissioned on 17 February 1947, the efforts to save her as a museum ship fail. "The Big E," the most highly decorated U.S. Navy warship of World War II, is sold for scrap on 1 July 1958 and then broken up in Kearny, New Jersey. Her wheel and engine order telegraph are on display at the National Naval Aviation Museum.

Her name is given to the Navy's first nuclear-powered aircraft carrier, designated CVAN-65, a ship from which the author flew. At this writing, the ninth U.S. Navy ship to bear the name *Enterprise*, another carrier, is under construction in Newport News, Virginia.

MITSUO FUCHIDA

After months of convalescence, which to him resembled prison as the Japanese took great pains to keep the truth about Midway from the public, Fuchida spends the rest of the war in Tokyo and is tasked to write the after-action report of the battle. Discharged in November 1945, he is later able to transform his report into a book he co-writes called *Midway: The Battle That Doomed Japan*. Published to great acclaim in 1951, the book is released in the west in 1955.

Fuchida is stunned to learn that returning Japanese prisoners were treated with kindness by their captors, even by the daughter of missionaries who were killed by the Japanese. He then learns of Jacob DeShazer, a captured Doolittle Raider, whose life was opened to God during his torture and imprisonment in Japan. Curious about this Christian faith, he reads the Bible and becomes a Christian in 1949. Two years later, he creates the Captain Fuchida Evangelical Association, based in Seattle.

His subsequent writings include *From Pearl Harbor to Calvary* and his memoir *For That One Day,* translated and published in 2011. Fuchida died from complications of diabetes near Osaka, Japan, in September 1976 at the age of 73.

For 50 years Fuchida's "eyewitness testimony" that the Japanese had carrier decks full of warmed-up strike aircraft as the ships turned to launch heading – when the Americans suddenly appeared in their lethal dives – was accepted by most historians. His self-serving account of these "Five Fateful Minutes" was discredited by historians Parshall and Tully in their 2005 masterpiece, *Shattered Sword.*

JOHN "JIMMIE" THACH

Word of the "Thach Weave" spreads throughout the fleet, and Thach returns ashore to teach his beam defense maneuver at NAS Jacksonville. Is McCain's Task Force 38 Operations Officer and is with him aboard *Missouri* for the surrender ceremony. Commands the escort carrier *Sicily* (CVE-118) during early combat in Korea and rises quickly, commanding the attack carrier *Franklin D. Roosevelt* (CVA-42), Carrier Division 16, and Anti-Submarine Warfare Force, Pacific Fleet. Against fierce opposition from Secretary of Defense Robert McNamara, Thach fights for the development of the A-7 *Corsair II*, and, after receiving his fourth star, becomes commander in chief of US Naval Forces Europe, retiring in 1967.

Jimmie Thach passed away in his Coronado, California, home in 1981, days short of his 76th birthday. The frigate USS *Thach* (FFG-47) was named in his honor.

DeWITT WOOD SHUMWAY

Two months after Midway, as CO of VB-3, Shumway leads his squadron into battle from USS *Saratoga* off Guadalcanal and receives two Distinguished Flying Crosses to go with his Navy Cross from Midway. Promoted to commander by war's end, he remains on active duty. In April 1946, he and eight other officers and men are killed when bombs delivered by planes from the carrier *Tarawa* mistakenly hit a practice target observation post at the island of Culebra near Puerto Rico. Dave Shumway is buried in Arlington.

ELMER GLIDDEN

Awarded the Navy Cross for his Midway actions, in August, Glidden goes ashore and flies with VMSB-231 at Guadalcanal's Henderson Field, where he earns a second award for his bold combat performance during months of brutal fighting along the Solomons chain. During the next two years of the Pacific War, he commands VMSB-231 twice and compiles a record-setting 104 combat dives, earning him the nickname "Iron Man" and acclaim throughout the Marine Corps.

He stays in the Marines for a career, with combat tours in Korea and Vietnam, and retires as a colonel while serving as chief of staff of Marine Corps Air Bases, Western Area, at MCAS El Toro.

He found work in South Florida and died at the age of 81 in 1997. Elmer Glidden is buried near his childhood home in Canton, Massachusetts.

HIJMS *MOGAMI*

Leaving her mauled and dying sister *Mikuma* behind, *Mogami* limps back to Sasebo – her engines in reverse the whole way – for a 10-month refit that removes her damaged stern turrets and replaces them with a flight deck to carry eleven float planes. Sees combat in the Battle of the Philippine Sea. After refit at Okinawa, returns to the Philippines where on 24 October 1944 her float planes discover a colossal American force of 12 carriers and numerous battleships and cruisers. That night during the Battle of Surigao Strait she is hit in the bridge by two shells from the cruiser USS *Portland*, once part of Fletcher's Task Force 17, killing her commanders. Battered by more enemy shells and taking a torpedo from a TBM *Avenger*, she is abandoned the morning of 25 October and sinks after a scuttling torpedo hit from the escorting destroyer HIJMS *Akebono*.

CLEO DOBSON

Awarded the Distinguished Flying Cross, and two months later fights from *Enterprise* off Guadalcanal. Transferring to fighters, he commands VF-86 aboard USS *Wasp*. On 15 August 1945, the day Japan surrenders, he shoots down a Japanese airplane attempting to attack the Third Fleet.

Medically retired due to a heart ailment, he settles in San Diego and coaches Pony and Colt League baseball, leading one team to a national championship.

A two-time California state champion shuffleboard player, Cleo Dobson suffered a fatal heart attack while playing in Balboa Park on April 18, 1967. He was 53.

Acknowledgements

The National Naval Aviation Museum staff – and the volunteers of the Emil Buehler Library in particular – were instrumental in helping me research the events and narrative accounts of this battle, one that I had thought I was quite familiar with until I began my research in earnest. Deputy Director Buddy Macon, Historian Hill Goodspeed, and library volunteer Bob Thomas cheerfully provided access to numerous primary source documents and offered invaluable suggestions. Thank you, gentlemen, and all the helpful staff at NNAM for your kind support and encouragement.

Thanks also to the Naval History and Heritage Command, who provided answers to specific questions regarding personnel and documents, and to the Battle of Midway Roundtable Internet discussion group which was always quick to lend a hand.

The body of narrative non-fiction related to Midway is enormous – and daunting. The author and all students of the battle are indebted to the historians and authors who have captured it over seven decades, in particular Barde, Buell, Carlson, Chambers, Cressman, Fisher, Fuchida and Okumiya, Gay, Holmes, Horan, Isom, Kernan, Kleiss, Layton, Lundstrom, Moore, Mracek, Parshall and Tully, Prange with Goldstein and Dillon, Rigby, Rose, Russell, Smith, Stafford, Symonds, Taylor, Tillman, Walsh, and Weisheit. Thank you, gentlemen and lady, for your service.

I am indebted to those with deep knowledge of the battle – friends and mentors all – who read the unedited manuscript to offer suggestions and question my interpretations. CAPT Will Dossel, CAPT J.R. Stevenson, CAPT T. Lad Webb, LCDR Ed Beakley of *Remembered Sky*, the late LCDR George Walsh, and Mark Horan. Ronald Russell, author of the essential *No Right To Win*, was particularly helpful with historic details and readability. My trusted shipmate and flight leader RADM "Bad Fred" Lewis – who once led an effort to memorialize Midway each June of which I was privileged to be a part – honors this work with his stirring Foreword, and graciously offered invaluable suggestions to improve the manuscript. Many thanks to each of you.

Special thanks to noted aviation artist Wade Meyers, who painted the original cover art after collaborating with me, before conducting his own exacting research on the SBD and the conditions at a specific moment in time over a specific latitude and longitude on June 4, 1942.

My loyal friend and devoted lover of the English language Linda Wasserman delivered another superb performance as copy and content editor. This work is her best ever. Many thanks once again to my Braveship Publisher Jeff Edwards whose suggestions and publishing insights are of immeasurable value to me and all in the Braveship stable.

Terry's love and support sustains me as always, as she did during my long absences at sea and today in lonely toil as a teller of sea-going tales. She is indeed the wind beneath my wings.

About the Author

Captain Kevin Miller, a 24-year veteran of the U.S. Navy, is a former tactical naval aviator and has flown the A-7E *Corsair II* and FA-18C *Hornet* operationally. He is the author of the *Raven One* trilogy of contemporary carrier aviation fiction, and lectures on the Battle of Midway.

Contact the author at kevin@kevinmillerauthor.com

I hope you enjoyed reading *The Silver Waterfall* as much as I enjoyed writing it. Whether you found it good or "other," I'd sincerely appreciate your feedback. Please take a moment to leave a review on Amazon or Goodreads.

Thanks and V/R,
Kevin

SUPERSONIC CARRIER AVIATION FICTION
FROM
KEVIN MILLER

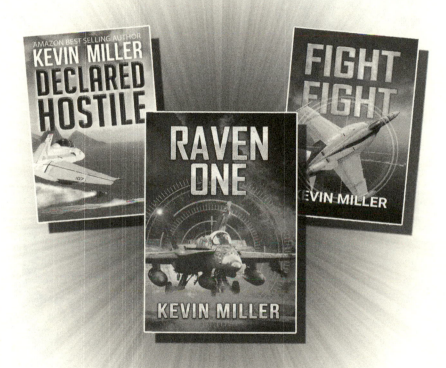

The Unforgettable Raven One Trilogy

www.braveshipbooks.com

CUTTING-EDGE NAVAL THRILLERS
BY
JEFF EDWARDS

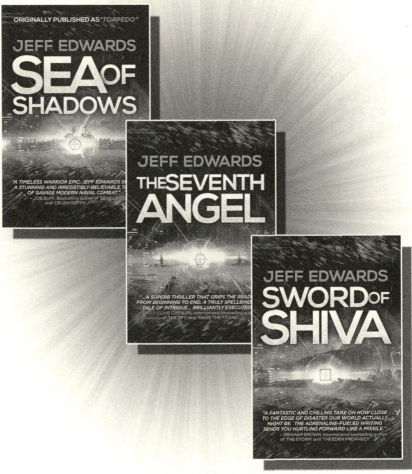

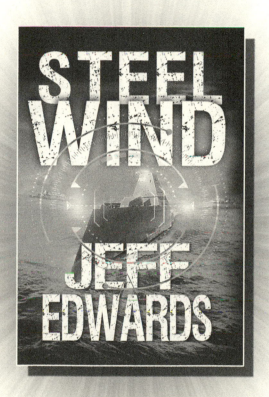

THE WAR AMERICA CAN'T AFFORD TO LOSE

GEORGE GALDORISI

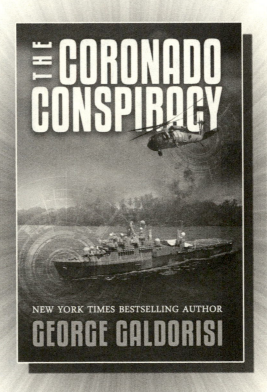

Everything was going according to plan...

WHITE-HOT SUBMARINE WARFARE
BY
JOHN R. MONTEITH

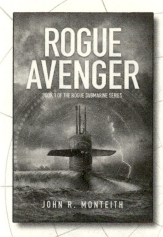
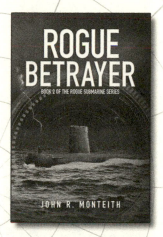
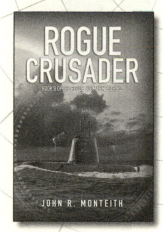
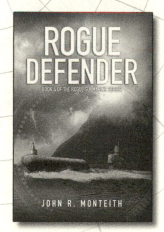

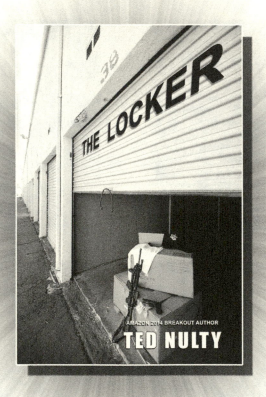

Made in the USA
Las Vegas, NV
14 June 2022